To

Thank you and enjoy the stories.

Jefferson
2015

TOUCHED BY EVIL

E. L. Jefferson

Touched by Evil

Cover design by Tovaun McNeil

An E. L. Book
Published by E.L. Books

ISBN: 978-1-4834-0024-2 (sc)
ISBN: 978-1-4834-0022-8 (e)

Printed in the United States of America

Second Printing

Publishing Services rev. date: 07/19/2019

ACKNOWLEDGEMENT

Thank you to my friends and family for all your support.

Evil exists in all of us.

How do you determine who is evil and who is not? By what standard do you judge what is evil and what is not?

Confronting evil face to face is the only way to destroy it.

When desire turns deadly, and you conquer your fear, confronting evil comes down to a battle of wills.

CARESSED BY EVIL

Karen did not feel like having lunch with the girls today. The office gossip had gotten old, and she did not feel like fast food. She wanted to go home and have lunch with her best friend. She liked training days because of the extended lunch breaks, as they allowed her and her roommate CJ to spend more time together.

Karen pulled up to her home, a warm feeling building inside her—the kind of sensation that came with knowing her home was safe and comforting. She thought to herself that, at twenty-four, she had done pretty well for herself so far. *I'm buying my own home; I have a good government job, a relatively new car, and the best friend and roommate anyone could possibly ask for. CJ means the world to me.*

CJ would do anything for Karen, and Karen felt the same way about CJ. At this point, the only thing missing in her life was a steady man. Sure, she could get dick anytime she wanted it, and she knew how attractive she was, but having a boyfriend also meant putting up with a lot unnecessary bullshit. CJ was always trying to fix her up, but Karen would always pass, for now, she thought, it was not that big of a deal. Her life was fine for now.

Karen pulled up to her driveway, parked, and went to the side door. Over the past two years, they'd found it easier to come into the house using the side door off the carport. In the warm months, this offered shade and quick access to the house. Karen opened the door, noticing that the door chime did not go off.

Oh, well. CJ must have forgotten to turn it back on. CJ was always complaining about the chimes and didn't see the need for them. *I'll remind*

CJ that my father installed them so that we'd know when doors or windows were opened.

Karen closed the door and headed for the kitchen. She figured she had about ninety minutes left before she had to return to work. She looked in the refrigerator and saw that their lunch had been prepared, but CJ was not home.

Ok. I can wait. CJ probably had to step out for a minute.

She closed the door. Looking down the hall, she saw the bathroom door open.

Immediately she called out to her roommate. "Hey, CJ. I thought you were—"

She stopped in mid-sentence when a man emerged from her bathroom. Her heart almost leaped from her chest and she turned to run.

She wasn't fast enough.

He grabbed her by the hair, yanked her head back, and threw her to the ground. He raised his foot and brought it down hard on her stomach. The pain shot through her body like a wave. She fought to breathe, unable to scream or cry out. The pain overwhelmed all other sensations.

"Try to run again, you black bitch, and you're fuckin' dead!" her attacker said. He reached down and snatched her up by the hair. "Come here, bitch!" He got behind her and put his arm around her throat. He started to choke her.

She grabbed hold of his forearm, crying and gasping to speak. "Please don't hurt me! I'll give you money, and I promise I won't tell anyone." She repeated her plea again, tears now flowing down her face. "Please don't hurt me."

Her begging only enraged him. "Bitch, I don't need your fuckin' money." He punched her in the back with all his might.

Oh God, Karen thought, as another wave of pain shot through her body. She fell to her knees, but he snatched her up again.

He shoved her up the steps and down the hall to the first bedroom on the right. "I'm gonna take what I want out of your sweet little pussy," he said, as he pushed her down the hall, "and that tight asshole."

Karen could only cry as he pushed her through the door, and against the bed.

"Yeah, bitch! Now it's time for me to have some fun." He moved his arm from her throat to her breasts. He put his hand under her skirt and ripped her panties off, bringing them to his face and inhaling deeply. "I'm gonna enjoy fuckin' you."

Through her pain and terror, Karen noticed he spoke with a Hispanic accent.

"Let me soften up the pussy, baby," he said. He kneed her in the groin.

She cried out and fell to the bed, the pain numbing her whole body. *I'm going to die*, she thought.

He forcefully ripped the clothes from her body and removed his own. He turned her toward him, to make her watch him stroke his dick until it got hard. He grabbed her by both legs and pulled her toward him.

Karen lay crying and praying that she would survived this nightmare.

He straddled her waist with his knees, holding his dick between her breasts, and asked her if this was what she wanted. When she only cried and turned away, he slapped her and shouted, "Bitch, tell me you want this dick!"

"Yes," she replied, her response weak.

"Say it like you mean it, whore!"

"Yes, baby," she said, raising her voice. "I want it."

He glared into her eyes as she said the words he wanted to hear, and positioned himself between her legs. "I like fucking you pretty bitches." Without warning, he brutally forced his dick into her pussy.

Karen cried out in pain, and that excited her captor. He began to push in, harder and harder. He battered her pussy, and her tightness gave as her juices lubricated his dick. "Tell me you want me to cum in this tight pussy, bitch! Say it!" he demanded.

She choked out a response, which drove him wild. He pushed harder and faster in her pussy, watching her reaction to his motion and pushing harder. Her pain was unbearable as he exploded in her, his cum flowing into her. Fright and the pain froze her.

He pulled out of her and looked down on her captive form. He seemed still unsatisfied with his torture of her. "Now, come here, bitch," he ordered, "and suck my dick."

He pulled out a large knife.

"Bitch, if you bite me, I'll cut out your pussy and stuff it down your throat."

The thought of what she was being forced to do made her sick, but she could not take the beating anymore. *If I do this,* she thought in desperation, *maybe he will leave.* She moved toward him, took his dick in her hand, put it in her mouth, and began to suck his dick.

He stood over her watching with perverse pleasure. His expression changed suddenly, and he became angry. He pushed her off him. "Bitch, I don't want to cum now. I just want to get hard again, so I can put my dick somewhere else."

He smiled with such evil, looking at her naked ass, and she knew what he meant. She cried like a helpless child.

He looked down on her, forcing her to turn around. "Oh, bitch, I'm just getting started."

I was supposed to be home twenty minutes ago, CJ thought, *but the guy at the market was irresistible. Besides, lunch was almost ready. I just needed the dressing for the salad, so we'll still have plenty of time to spend together before Karen has to go back to work.* CJ steered the car into the driveway.

Entering through the side door, CJ noted that the chime did not go off when the door was opened. *Good! Karen's finally come around and turned those annoying chimes off.*

CJ walked into the kitchen and put the grocery bags on the counter, but was startled to hear voices upstairs. Walking toward the steps, CJ noticed the bedroom door was open.

"Now I want to fuck that ass. Turn over, bitch!" a male voice shouted.

CJ had not intended to eavesdrop, but the voice was not coming from Karen's room. They'd always respected each other's privacy, but it was damn strange and totally fucked up for her to take a guy into CJ's room to have sex. *We'll have to have a serious talk about this later,* CJ thought. *I will just leave them alone.*

Then Karen cried out. "Please, don't do this to me. Let me finish the other way. I can't take it there."

The sound of a slap echoed in the hall. The male voice, louder now, said, "Bitch, by the time I'm done fuckin' that asshole, you'll be begging for it!"

Her assailant forced Karen around and pulled her by the waist. He took his dick in one hand and began forcing it into her ass. He grinned as she cried out in pain.

"Please don't do this to me!" she begged, as her tears fell onto the bed. She screamed out as he penetrated her asshole and brutally pushed his dick into her ass. Suddenly, he was pulled off her. He heard her involuntarily cry out as his dick ripped out of her. Someone else was in the room.

He was grabbed from behind, and he felt a powerful hand at the back of his head. The next thing he knew, he was slammed into a wall and the bones of his face shattered into a dozen pieces under his skin. His whole head went numb, as blood poured from his nose. He was lifted into the air and body-slammed hard to the floor. A foot crashed into his side. The pain almost made him pass out.

He saw Karen stand up on very shaky legs. She was crying, bleeding, and clearly in agonizing pain. "CJ, he raped me," she sobbed. "He hurt me so bad."

He now saw the rage on CJ's face, as CJ stared down at him on the floor.

"Baby girl," CJ said to Karen, "call the police before I kill this muthafucka!"

An electric shock course through his body, as CJ's deep male voice spoke to Karen. He saw Karen clinging to CJ's arm for support.

Karen looked down on her assailant. He was now totally at their mercy. Something happened to her at that moment, something she could neither explain nor comprehend. She looked up at CJ, and they both came to an unspoken understanding. She left the room.

CJ looked down at the thing on the floor curled up in a fetal position crying, its nose bleeding. *In a minute, I am gonna give you a lot to cry about, you piece of shit.* He heard loud music coming from the living room. It was not loud enough to carry outside the house, but it would mask the sounds of someone screaming.

Karen returned to the room. She seemed unnaturally calm. "I called the job and told them I had an emergency and wouldn't be back today." She glanced at the thing on the floor and quickly left the room again.

CJ took off his sweat suit and raised his captive off the floor. He grabbed him from behind and around his throat and squeezed. "What is your name, bitch? I want to know who it is I'm about to fuck."

"Mi-Mi-Miguel," the man stuttered, as CJ eased the pressure on his throat.

Miguel sobbed like a baby as CJ released a little more pressure on his throat. CJ pressed his chest and stomach against Miguel's back so that Miguel would feel the large bulge.

"Miguel," CJ said, whispering in Miguel's ear in a mock female voice that terrified Miguel. "Do you have any idea what you did to my girl, motherfucker? Do you understand how you've fucked her life up? Do you, Miguel? I love her with all my heart, like my little sister. You hurt her, so now I'm going to fuck you up. You broke into the wrong house today, motherfucker." He laughed. "I might be gay, but I'm still a man. I'm twice your size and there isn't shit you can do about it!"

Feeling the powerful arm around his throat and hearing the fury in CJ's voice, Miguel sobbed out an apology, but in his terror, he spoke in Spanish. He could not comprehend this: the thought of another man fucking him. He tried to pull away, but CJ drove his elbow into the back of his neck, taking the fight out of him.

Miguel fell back to the floor. He knew he could not escape.

Karen entered the room wearing a blue robe and sat down in a chair facing both men, trying to ignore the pain in her ass from Miguel's earlier penetration. He was now crying like a baby, held down to the floor by CJ.

"How does it feel to be the victim, motherfucker?" she screamed at her assailant. "How does it feel to be helpless and terrified? How does it feel to know you're about to be raped?"

She stood up, walked over to Miguel, and kicked him in the stomach as hard as she could. Miguel coughed and tried to double over, but CJ would not let him.

"Play with your dick, bitch," Karen ordered. "I want to see if you can get it up now, motherfucker!"

Miguel sobbed like an infant and quivered uncontrollably.

CJ grabbed him around the throat with his forearm and squeezed harder. "You heard her, bitch," he said. "Jerk it off for her now, you piece of shit! Right now!"

Miguel took his soft dick in his hand and started to stroke it, but he was too scared. Getting it hard was clearly not on his mind.

"Oh, poor baby. Can't get it up for us?" Karen taunted. "Maybe we can help you find some motivation." She picked up the knife Miguel had pulled on her.

CJ smiled. "Maybe if you suck a real dick and swallow some cum, your little shit will get hard." He turned to Karen. "Get two belts from the drawer behind you, Karen, and tie his hands."

Karen tied one hand to the leg of the bed and one to the dresser.

CJ moved in front of Miguel, who was on his knees.

Karen positioned herself so that she had a side view, kneeling at Miguel's side and holding the knife. "Now, bitch," she said, "Suck his dick. You better swallow every drop, and if you bite him, I will shove this knife in your ass and watch you shit blood." She put the tip of the knife against his asshole, so he would know she meant what she said.

"Open your mouth, bitch," CJ ordered. Holding his huge dick in Miguel's face and wiping away Miguel's tears with it, CJ said again, "Open your fuckin' mouth, bitch!"

Miguel opened his mouth and took the head of CJ's dick in his mouth.

Karen's anger grew more intense. "Suck his dick like you mean it, motherfucker! Suck it like you like it, bitch! The way you wanted me to suck your little dick!"

Miguel took more of CJ's dick in his mouth and CJ helped him by pushing it in further. Miguel started to gag, and CJ pulled back a little, letting Miguel suck as much as he could take for about fifteen minutes. CJ pulled his dick from Miguel's mouth and wiped his dick across Miguel's face. "I'm not satisfied with the head, motherfucker," he said. "Maybe you'll get better after I fuck you."

Miguel cried and pleaded for CJ not to do that, but his pleas were ignored. CJ positioned himself behind Miguel and laid his dick on top of Miguel's naked ass cheeks.

"Baby girl," he said to Karen, "give me that KY on the dresser."

Karen smiled as she handed the lubricant to CJ, and watched as he lubricated his dick. She felt no sexual desire for his penis, but she thought, *That dick is going to split that guy's ass wide open*, and she smiled.

Miguel tried to struggle against his bonds, but Karen punched him in the face with everything she had.

"No bitch," she shouted, "you're not going anywhere. By the time we're done, you'll be begging to suck that dick. Remember telling me similar shit when you raped me?"

Miguel screamed and began speaking in Spanish, as CJ started to work the head of his dick in Miguel's asshole.

Karen watched with perverse pleasure as the veins and muscles in Miguel's neck strained and bulged as the dick went in slowly.

CJ strained and began to sweat as he pushed in and out, working his dick in Miguel's rectum. "I've never had ass this tight," he commented. He smacked Miguel's right cheek so hard Karen could see a hand print form.

Miguel made strange sounding noises as CJ pushed farther in. Tears streamed down his face in rivers as the skin of his asshole tore.

"Come on, CJ!" Karen urged. "I want all twelve inches in his ass!"

"Ok, baby girl!" He repositioned himself behind Miguel to put it all in. "Oh, shit, baby girl, this tight ass is good."

Karen watched as CJ fucked Miguel without mercy. "Enjoy it, baby," she cooed.

Miguel was as red as blood.

"Say you like that big dick in your ass, bitch," she said. "Say it, motherfucker!" She grabbed his face, but he could only scream and cry as CJ shredded his ass.

"Say you want his dick in your mouth," she ordered, "and we'll give your asshole a break."

CJ pushed his entire massive dick in Miguel's ass and came, just as Karen finished talking.

"Oh, shit, baby girl!" CJ said, and he closed his eyes as his cum pumped into Miguel's ass. CJ held Miguel tight against his dick, which was completely in Miguel's ass. CJ moaned loudly with pleasure as he came again, sweat dripping down his face and onto Miguel's back.

"Did you like that, bitch?" Karen asked, as Miguel collapsed to the floor, crying and bleeding. His pain prevented him from speaking. Blood and cum ran down his ass and legs.

CJ pulled his dick out very slowly. Breathing heavily, he took a towel and started to wipe himself.

Karen stopped him. "Let's see if this piece of shit is ready to suck it. He's gonna suck your dick clean."

Sobbing uncontrollably, Miguel lay on the floor, his legs bent close to his chest in a fetal position, his head resting on the floor. With his eyes closed, he managed to speak. "Please, God, no more. I'm sorry, I'm . . ."

He could not stop crying, but he managed to keep begging for his torture to end. He looked up at CJ. Karen was now stroking CJ's bloodstained dick, getting it hard again. They both looked down on him with the most evil smiles he had ever seen.

"I'm not even close to being done with you," Karen said. "You fucked up when you came in here and raped me. After you get more of this big-ass dick, I'm gonna fuck you next."

Karen reached behind her and pulled out what looked like a police nightstick. "Yeah, motherfucker. I'm gonna shove this stick in your ass and listen to you scream until I'm satisfied. Now, bitch, suck this dick and swallow every fuckin' drop. We're just getting started."

Upon hearing that, Miguel cried hysterically.

Fulfilling one's desires is only human.
There is nothing evil about that.

BOUNDED BY EVIL

"I am so sick of her fucking excuses! Every day and night, it's the same shit! I'm telling you, Tony, I honestly don't know what to do anymore."

"Do you love her, Frank?"

"I'm not sure any more, bro. At first, everything was fine. Jennifer is my princess, and Francis is my sunshine. I thought I had the best marriage and daughter in the world. But, like I told you before, as Fran got older, she started the change most young girls go through, and we grew apart. Sometimes, Fran would act as if I wasn't her father at all. Later, after Fran moved out, Jen started to become more and more distant. When Fran came to us and said she didn't want to go to college, I was upset about her decision. But, after high school, what could I do? She is old enough to make her own decisions.

"Then, two years later, she got a job and moved out on her own. Prior to that, they'd both became almost secretive about something they kept between them. Fran and her mother would bump heads sometimes on issues, and they both pretty much shut me out of the loop. Fran disappointed me—yes, about the college thing, because she was always a smart student. It took a while, but I got over it. What hurts is that she won't even let me visit her at home. Jen sees her often. Why not me? I'm her father, so what the fuck did I do wrong?

"Then, Jennifer started these goddamn mood swings. I always believed that when the kids moved out, it was party time for the parents. You get to walk around your house naked, with spontaneous sex all the time. Like before the kid came, we used to have a lot of fun. Now, we're just totally fucked up and I don't know why.

"I do know I haven't changed. I mean, we have problems like most couples, but we've always managed to work through them. It's almost like when we first had Francis, and Jen slowly pulled away from me sexually. I knew that was because of childbirth, and it didn't last long. Now our sex life is non-existent. We're pleasant with each other, but there is also a lot missing between us."

"Look, Frank. You're my brother, and I know you're feeling a bit fucked up now, but it's like I've said before: You and Jennifer need to talk with a counselor. You two have a good marriage. Things are a little fucked up now, but that will change."

"Don't you think I've suggested counseling? She shuts me out and won't even talk about it."

"Well, if that's the case, then there is always my temporary solution, little brother."

"What, cheat with a hooker?"

"Why the fuck not? You aren't getting it at home. You're sick of jerking off and going to bed with a hard dick and you're miserable. What's wrong with letting off a little steam? And besides, it's not like you've never done it before." Tony laughed.

"But that was when I was in the fucking military," Frank responded. "That was over twenty-five years ago. I'm forty-five years old now. My daughter is twenty-one and out of the house. I shouldn't have to resort to that kind of thing."

"I knew you would say that, Frank. You shouldn't have to buy pussy anymore, but things change and people change. You're not the first married guy to experience this shit. I'm just tired of seeing you so miserable. Look. Just hear me out. I care about you, and I hope you can work this thing out with Jen. What I've suggested to you can help in the short term, if you just give it a try. Every now and then, I visit this little place just outside of town. It's a health spa, but they provide extra services, if you know what I mean."

"Yeah, Tony, I know what you mean," Frank said, laughing.

"Listen, there's this one chick there that can suck the skin off your dick and fuck you blind. She'll give you the ride of your life."

Frank started laughing again.

"She'll blow your mind, she's so good," Tony insisted. "I don't want to give too much away. It'll spoil the fun, but it's the way they set you up that's mind blowing."

"What is there to give away? You pay, you fuck, and you go home."

"No, little brother. It's much more to it than that, and that's what I want you to find out for yourself. I'm telling you: once you've had some of that pussy, you'll feel better and this really will help you work through your problem. Before you say 'fuck off,' Frank, take this."

"What is this?"

"It's a VIP pass. I picked it up for you, just in case. And they don't come cheap, so don't trash it."

"Look, Tony. I'll take it, but I won't promise anything."

"You don't have to. Just use it if you need to. It's ok. Oh, by the way, the girl you want is Jade. I had her about a year ago. Actually, I got a twoforone deal. Jade gave me some awesome head. Then, I got some of the best pussy I've ever had in my life, after Jade sucked my dick. The point is: I'm still blown away thinking about it."

"What is Jade? Asian or something?"

"I don't know. All the girls have one-word names, and they all have extremely hot bodies."

"What do you mean, you don't know? Haven't you seen her face?"

"That's part of the fun! You are gonna have to go check it out for yourself."

"All right. I'm taking your word for it because," Frank held up the pass as he spoke, "if I decide to use this pass of yours—"

His brother cut him off. "No, not mine anymore, little brother. Yours." He rose. "All right, Frank. I have a date later, so let me take you home."

"Ok, Tony, and I'll try to talk with Jen this evening."

"You do that, little brother."

"And, thanks again, Tony, for listening."

"Hey, no problem, man. That's what big brothers are for."

"Princess, I'm home!" Frank called out as he walked into his house.

"Hey, honey," Jen replied. "I'm in the kitchen."

"Hey, something smells good," he commented. "What's for dinner?"

"We're having meatloaf, mashed potatoes, and broccoli."

He smiled. "What's the occasion? That's one of my favorite meals!"

"No occasion. I just wanted to fix you a nice dinner."

Frank got behind Jennifer and put his arms around her waist. He kissed her neck as he brought his body next to hers. He thought to himself, *Maybe this is the start of something.* He felt ashamed of himself for even considering his brother's suggestion. His dick started to get hard as he held his wife closer, the softness of her blond hair caressing against his face. *This is how it is supposed to be.*

Jennifer put her hands on top of his, pushed them straight down, and pushed him away. She told him she needed to concentrate on fixing dinner.

Frank's hard-on faded away. "Ok, babe. I'll go watch TV."

Rejected and feeling sorry for himself, he contemplated how his wife of twenty-two years could treat him as if she could not stand to be touched by him. He did not understand why. *Tonight, I'm gonna find out what the fuck is going on. Maybe she is seeing someone else. Fuck if I know.* Anger and rage filled him. The sensation of being angry about this situation was curious. He also realized his dick was rock hard.

During dinner, they sat across from each other, eating and not saying much. The food was good, but Frank could not take the silence anymore. "Jennifer," he said, "can we please talk about what's bothering you?"

"What do you mean?"

"Princess, you know what I'm talking about. Us, our sex life, hell, our whole relationship. Can you please tell me what's bothering you?"

She looked at him as if he were an alien. "How many times do we have to go into this? You want to talk about sex. Is that all our relationship is built on?" she asked, with frustration in her voice.

"No, baby, it's not, but we haven't had sex in over six months. Jennifer, I love you, and I've tried to be understanding about what's happening, but I honestly don't know what's going on."

"Like I've told you before, Frank, I have some things on my mind that I'm trying to work out—"

Frank cut her off in mid-sentence. "Baby, maybe we can work on this thing together."

"No, I'll be ok." She took her plate and went into the kitchen, leaving a very frustrated Frank at the table.

I give up, he thought. *What more can I do?* Frank took a shower and went to bed, leaving his wife to clean up.

The next day at his office, Frank called his brother. "Hello, Tony. Are you busy?"

"Hey, what's up, Frank? No, I'm not busy. What's on your mind?"

"I didn't get anywhere with Jennifer last night, and I've decided to visit that place we were talking about."

"Good, glad to hear it. Just go, relax, and have some fun. It'll make a world of difference. By the way, I tried a new girl the last time I was there. Man, was she hot. I fucked her until I was shootin' blanks."

"Tony: one question. How much does this shit cost?"

"The VIP pass will get you one hour with Jade for straight or nude massage action. Anything extra will start at about five hundred bucks. But, man, I'm telling you: it'll be worth every dime. You're not hurting for money, so enjoy. Frank, listen to me. I don't want you to feel guilty for doing this behind Jennifer's back. It's not like you didn't try to work this shit out. Hell, if she can't take care of you, someone else will. Besides, what she doesn't know can't hurt her."

"And it's not like I'm there all the time," Frank added.

"I agree. Gotta run, bro, but remember: ask for Jade and have fun."

Frank got off work at five o'clock and decided that he would pay the spa a visit. Months of frustration had built up in him. He was tired of jerking off and being rejected by his own wife. *Fuck that bitch.* He justified in his mind what he was about to do. He drove down the highway, thinking to himself how good it was going to feel to actually fuck a woman again and not have to think about it while he jerked off. *I have a lot of frustration and cum to release.*

Just thinking about it made his dick hard. He found himself excited about the prospect of doing this, knowing it was morally wrong and probably illegal. However, he had decided, before having come this far, that he did not care and that it was too late to turn back now.

Frank drove another ten miles down the road until he spotted the neon sign, Joan's Sauna & Spa. He thought the name of the place did not give any indication that prostitution went on there. He pulled his car into the parking lot and went inside.

The Spa was tastefully adorned in Asian décor. The woman who greeted Frank wore a very flattering Asian style dress that hugged tightly to her every curve. "Hello sir," she said, "My name is Vivian. How may I help you?"

"Hello," he replied. "I want a rubdown." He handed her the VIP pass.

She took it, turned it over, and told Frank to follow her.

They walked through a doorway that led past several steam rooms, saunas, and several smaller rooms. Frank noticed that the place seemed to be busy for a whorehouse. *Maybe only certain customers get the special treatment I'm looking for.* Vivian led Frank through another doorway and into a room with a large padded table, a bed, and other comfortable looking furnishings. She asked Frank to sit down, and asked how he'd heard about the spa.

"My brother comes here, and he bought me this pass."

"If you could wait here just one moment, I'll be right back."

Vivian returned a few minutes later. "All right, Frank. Let me explain how this works. These passes are for a select clientele. I checked the code, and it showed your brother is indeed a client of ours. He purchased this for you. You guys must be close, because these are not cheap. I had to verify that you got this from a member. This pass is good for a steam bath, massage, two drinks, and a shower."

Frank felt confused. *I don't care about any of that shit. I just want to fuck.*

"After you've had a steam bath, your masseuse will notify me and I'll arrange for your other activities. So, how does that sound, Frank?" Vivian asked.

"Sounds good to me, but there is one more question." In a low voice, he asked how much for the other activities.

Vivian replied, in a very sexy voice, "Five-hundred dollars to start, baby, and it'll be worth every penny. You'll leave here drained and very satisfied."

That thought pleased Frank. He did as instructed and undressed to take a hot shower. He was given a choice of drinks. He chose white wine.

Jennifer sat home brooding all day, and thinking about her family. In addition, what was happening to their relationships? Most of all, she thought about how she had been treating her husband for the last few months.

Frank is a good man and provider. He makes more than enough money to sustain the family. I haven't had to work the entire time we've been married, and he has always been a good father to his daughter. What Jennifer could not put her finger on was how things went so wrong so quickly. *Frank never asks me for much and he almost never complains about anything.*

Jennifer knew he was disappointed about their daughter's decision to skip college, but they had gotten over that years ago. The events of the last few months had had a profound effect on Jennifer and her state of mind. The things she'd done had been a terrible burden on her. The secrets she'd been forced to keep from her husband plagued her every day. She had become so indifferent to her husband's needs that she did not care how he felt about anything. She knew he was not going anywhere, so she became apathetic toward him and his desires.

Last night as they had eaten dinner, she had sensed something different about Frank. The look in his eyes told her that something was on his mind—that he was waging a war within himself and that it was all about her. She knew that withholding sex from him was wrong, but she had made up her mind that she did not give a damn about his needs and feelings.

What she thought she sensed was that maybe he no longer cared about her feelings either. That he'd had enough of her shit.

Even when they'd gone to bed, Jennifer had felt something was wrong. Even though her passion for him had temporarily gone away, he would still hold her at night from behind, as he'd always done. Jennifer would tolerate his hard dick against her body, but that was as far as she would let it go. When it went down, he was sleep. As she had done for months, she would pull away from him, and lie there until she fell asleep. Last night, he had never touched her.

Something about last night frightened Jennifer into realizing that she needed to wake up. To come to her senses before she lost the man she loved. All she could do was repeatedly apologize to Frank in her mind. She had finally concluded that what she had been doing was not only wrong but also destructive.

After all her soul-searching, Frank did not deserve to be treated the way she had been treating him. She knew this, and she knew that she needed to talk to someone. She could not keep what had been troubling her inside any longer. *This situation is destroying everything—my home, my marriage—and now my life is falling apart, and I allowed it to happen.*

All these thoughts and many others ran through Jennifer's mind. The secrets she had kept from her husband and the way she treated him the past few months had been awful. She realized this now, and she realized this could not continue. She felt she needed to speak with someone close to her before she talked to Frank that evening. She decided to call Tony before he left work for the day. They had always been close, and she knew she could talk to him about anything.

"Hi, Tony. It's Jennifer. Do you have a minute?"

"Sure, doll. What's on your mind?"

"Tony, I really need to speak to someone close to me about something that's been bothering me for a long time now."

"Sure, Jen. Whatever you need. Would you like to have a late lunch?"

"No, this is more private family stuff. Frank won't be home till late. Can you swing by the house about 5:00 p.m.? That will give me time to air this out with you before I talk with Frank later this evening."

"Sure, Jen. I'll be there at 5:00 p.m. sharp. See you then."

Jennifer thanked Tony and turned off the phone, now feeling very nervous about their pending conversation.

Frank finished his shower, put on the robe provided for him, and he noticed that the five hundred dollars on the dresser was gone. His clothes were neatly folded and hung up in the closet for him. *Now, that's kind of classy.*

He poured himself a glass of wine from the bottle that had been brought in for him and waited. A few minutes later, Vivian came into his room, wearing a red two-piece negligée and a sheer robe. Frank found himself instantly turned on. *She has a beautiful body, large full breasts, and curvy hips I would love to explore.*

Vivian explained that she would be his facilitator, and that she would guide him through his encounter. He had a choice of six women, and she would bring his choice to him. She explained that, for the next two hours, they were there to please him. There were no limits to the number of times he could cum, as long as he could manage it. Nor were there limits on the ways in which he could be satisfied. Oral, anal, straight, and two on one—anything he wanted. She told Frank he would be begging them to stop fucking him.

"First," she said, "you have to wear a facemask that completely covers your eyes and blocks your vision."

This made Frank nervous, but he said to himself, *What the hell!* and agreed he would play along.

"The woman you choose will also wear a feminine version of the mask you are wearing. This protects the woman's identity as well as yours. Once you have established yourself after a few visits, the masks will no longer be necessary, if that is what you want."

Frank put on the mask. The fact that he could not see was exciting. "Vivian," he asked, "if I already know what girl I want, can I just request her now?"

"Absolutely, you can, Frank. Who would you like?"

"Jade is the girl I want."

"Someone has been talking to their older brother." Vivian smiled. "Wait one moment while I get Jade."

Standing naked in the dark wearing a mask and a bathrobe seemed stupid to Frank. He was willing to play along with it, remembering that his brother had come here. He heard someone return to the room.

Vivian stood in front of Frank and removed her robe, panties, and bra. Facing Frank, she whispered softly in his ear, "Put your hands gently on my shoulders."

Frank complied.

"Now, Frank, explore my body using both sides of your hands. Don't squeeze. Gently touch my whole body." Vivian's voice was low and sexy.

Frank began moving his hands gently down Vivian's arms, feeling the softness of her skin. He put his hands on her shoulders, and came down to her breasts; they felt wonderful. He cupped her breasts in his hands, instantly getting a mental image of them. He felt himself getting hard.

Vivian then guided Frank's hands with hers over the rest of her body. Her ass was firm and her pussy soft and warm; this sensation excited Frank even more. Her scent drove him wild, as his dick made contact with her body.

"Yes, baby. Your big dick feels so good against my body and in my hand," she said passionately. With her breasts against his chest, she whispered in Frank's ear. "This is how we see, baby. We don't need our eyes, and from here on, we don't talk anymore. We use all our other senses."

Moving to Frank's back, Vivian pressed her body against his, while another woman took his hands and placed them on her hips. Vivian whispered in his ear again. "This is Jade. I'll leave you two alone now, unless you want me to stay. Explore her body with your hands, Frank. Let her guide you."

Frank heard the door close as Vivian left the room. As before, Frank used his hands to explore Jade's body. She felt so good. Touching her shoulders, he realized she was taller than Vivian was. Her breasts were warm and full as he touched her body.

Her hands found his dick; her touch was warm and gentle. She used both hands to massage him, stroking the full length of him and bringing his dick to full erection. She put the head of his dick in her mouth and slowly worked it. Jade used her tongue to lick the head and her lips to bring more of his dick in her mouth, using very slow deliberate motions.

She took more of him in her mouth, working slowly. The pleasure she gave was mind-blowing, and his moans of pleasure grew louder. She put a finger to his lips to silence him. He understood, and his moans of pleasure grew silent, but he could not control his breathing, which got heavier and heavier.

She had more than half his dick in her mouth now. She adjusted herself so that she could slowly take more of him down her throat. Like a snake swallowing its prey, she took the full length of his dick into her throat. This went on for what seemed to Frank like hours, but it had only been thirty minutes. The slow methodical sucking, the feeling of his dick in her wet mouth and in her throat was an awesome feeling. Frank was driven wild, as he felt his large dick swallowed and taken down her throat repeatedly.

He felt his dick start to throb uncontrollably. His cum started to surge to climax, like an exploding volcano. He felt as if he was going to explode any second. There was no way he wanted this to end. Jade must have felt the length of his dick start to throb in her throat, as she quickly but gently pulled back, sliding her mouth off his dick. As she did so, he started to cum. The first wad filled her mouth. She guided his dick to her breast as he unloaded.

Frank felt as if he'd climaxed for hours. His cum flowed out of him in what felt like rivers. Her left breast was completely covered with his cum. She slowly rubbed his hard dick over both her breasts, his cum flowing down her stomach. Frank could not control his moans of ecstasy as she used his dick to rub his cum over her now completely covered breasts.

Tony arrived at Frank and Jennifer's a little after five. Jen opened the door for him. He could tell she was bothered by something.

"Hi, Tony. Come in. Let's go to the living room and talk. Do you want something to drink?"

"No, I'm fine. How have you been, Jen?"

"All right, but there are a lot of issues I've been dealing with that I need to get off my chest, before they drive me crazy."

"You talk, I'll listen," Tony sat in the chair across from Jennifer, ready to listen as she told her story.

"Tony, I don't know how much Frank has told you about what's been going on between us lately, but whatever he's told you, it's ok. I'm going to tell him everything I'm about to tell you. I just need to talk to someone I trust."

"Sure, Jen. I'm here for both you guys. You know that."

Jennifer began. "This all started about two and a half years ago. Remember when we let Francis go on her high school seniors' cruise to the Caribbean? Well, when she came back home, she wasn't the same person we'd sent away. I began to notice how quiet she'd become and how her attitude changed, not only toward us, but toward her friends as well, and even you. In the space of six months, she'd pretty much cut off contact from everyone she knew, and she no longer cared about college. She made that clear to us, in no uncertain terms.

"Frank tried to talk to her every way he knew how, but nothing worked. Fran told me she wanted to work and that she'd found the perfect job. She wanted to save enough money to move out on her own. She didn't want our help, and she didn't care about our advice or how we felt. She was certain, at nineteen, that she could make it on her own. After a while, Frank gave up trying to talk to her, and she began treating him like a stranger. Over the next two years, she did exactly what she said she'd do.

"Now, you have to understand that Fran is my daughter and I love her. There was no way I was going to let her just up and leave without telling me something. I got tired of being treated like a stranger. The year before she moved out on her own, I followed Fran as she left to go to work. I'm her mother, and I had no clue where she worked or what she was doing to earn her money. She wouldn't talk about it. She'd only say it was a good job and she enjoyed her work. The place where she works is called Joan's Spa. It's a new place, just outside the city."

Tony's heart started to beat a little faster at the mention of the Spa.

"I figured at least now I know where she works," Jen continued. "I waited outside for an hour after she went in, trying to decide if I should go in or not. I decided not to. If that was where she wanted to work, that was fine with me. Then I became upset, the longer I sat in my car, thinking,

This is what she gave up college for, to work in a health club? I changed my mind and went inside. I asked to see Francis.

"About twenty minutes later, Fran came into the lobby and asked me what I was doing there. She wasn't glad to see me; there was an almost controlled fury about her when she saw me. I said 'Baby, I just wanted to see where you worked.' Then she accused me of meddling in her affairs. I tried to tell her otherwise, but she wouldn't listen. At that point, I just left.

"A week later, Francis called me at home, and asked me to meet her at the spa at five o'clock. She said she wanted to show me something. When I got there, Fran met me in the lobby. We went into a room and she told me she wanted to explain something to me, but first, she wanted me to see what she did at the spa. Then she left me sitting in the room.

"A woman named Vivian came and got me. She explained that what I was about to see might be shocking. If I couldn't handle it, we would leave, but either way we'd talk afterward. While in the room, she told me I was not to talk for any reason.

"She led me to a very dimly lit room. Two people came in, a man and woman, and both wore masks. The woman sat on the bed, with the man standing over her. I was shocked to my core. The only thing I could think was, *I hope I'm not about to see what I think I'm going to see.* The man was wearing only a robe, and the woman started to stroke his penis. I was totally shocked. I couldn't believe I was watching this shit live. Then it dawned on me: even with her hair pinned up and the mask, I knew the woman was Fran!

"She started to suck the man's dick. She had to know I was watching, as she had invited me there to watch her. I was disgusted watching her do this, and ashamed to admit, turned on too. I was speechless, but I kept watching. The other woman, Vivian, didn't say a word.

"I was so intent on watching Fran suck this man's dick and all the shit that was going through my mind that I didn't realize Vivian had her hand on my thigh. I was disgusted at first, and I was gonna bolt the hell out of there, but Vivian pushed down on my leg and whispered to me how pretty I was and started trying to kiss me. She whispered, 'This is what Fran does and she's good at it.' Her lips found mine in the dark, and it was like something took over me. She had her hand in my jeans before I knew what was happening.

"I'm so ashamed to admit this now. I'd never been with a woman before, but I couldn't control myself. I actually got so turned on I let her do what she wanted. Her hands where all over me. We watched, touching and kissing, as the man came in Fran's mouth and she drank it down. Vivian then asked if I wanted to join my daughter, 'Jade.' Before I knew what was happening, I was naked, wearing a mask, and on my hands and knees and letting that bastard take me from behind."

Tony sat there, staggered, as he listened to Jennifer's story. His heart was racing, as his mind went back to when he had told Frank about the time he'd gotten a two for one. There was no way Jen could have described what she just had and what he'd experienced unless she'd been there too. Only someone who was there could describe what he experienced. The realization hit him with such force he could barely catch his breath or stand to run out of the house.

Jade crawled to the middle of the bed on her hands and knees. Frank gently held on to her ankles, following her to the middle of the bed, his dick rock hard and ready to enter her. Closer to her now, he let his hands find her pussy. It was so wet, ready to receive him. He couldn't see her, but the warmth of her body guided him to her. With one hand on her left hip and his dick in the other, he positioned himself to enter her from behind. His dick found the lips of her pussy and he pushed forward. *This pussy feels so good.* Her pussy was wet and hot, as he went further and further inside her. She reacted to him as he went deep inside her, and the feeling drove Frank wild.

She accepted his entire dick inside her, and as he began to stroke her, thrusting harder and harder, he could hear her try to stifle her moans of pleasure and pain. Her breathing became short and fast with each thrust. She buried her head in a pillow to drown out her cries, as Frank punished her soft wet pussy. The wet sounds his dick made as he fucked her told Frank that she was extremely wet, and the feel of her walls against his dick let him know that he filled her and she loved it. Jade began to counter-thrust in rhythm with his stroke. Frank was in Heaven.

Tony was speechless and in shock, as he realized it was his niece who had sucked his dick and his sister-in-law whom he'd fucked. He desperately tried not to let his shock show. He could barely contain himself. Jen continued to speak, but he did not hear her. He needed to get out of the house. He felt himself getting sick to the point of vomiting.

He had violated his brother's family, and just as that thought hit him, he realized where his brother was and with whom.

He bolted straight up and ran for the door. He hastily apologized to Jen, telling her he had forgotten about an urgent matter and he had to leave. He ran to his car thinking, *How could this have happened?* The panic and shame he felt was almost too much to bear. He had to get to his brother.

Frank could no longer control himself; he became lost in his desires. It had been months since he had some pussy, and Jade felt so damn good to him. Even the smell of her sex turned him on, as he came inside her. Holding her tight against his dick to drain into her pussy, he whispered to her. "Oh, God, Princess. Where have you been? I miss you so much. Baby, I love you. You're my princess always, baby."

Jade froze and her heart almost stopped with shock at hearing those words. The tone of the voice, the way he said Princess. *What the fuck? This can't be!*

She pulled away from him, one word repeating in her mind, over and over. *No! NO! NO!*

She turned to face him in the near darkness of the room, backing as far away as she could. She took off her mask and turned on the light. Her father sat before her, kneeling on the bed. She put her hand to her mouth to block the scream that was to follow, but she was in such a state of shock that no sound emerged.

Frank removed his mask, and Jade grabbed the sheet to cover herself. Frank stared in shock into his daughter's tear-filled eyes. He began to tremble, as countless thoughts coursed through his mind. He got off the bed and backed away from her. His heart pounded in his chest. His body trembled so badly he could barely stand. His eyes started to water, and he screamed. His screams grew louder with every breath he took, as he looked at his naked daughter frozen in place on the bed. The daughter he had just violated! The daughter he had just fucked.

He was still screaming when the police took him away.

Normally, fear and stupidity are not evil traits, but when one becomes overwhelmed with terror, these seemingly innocent characteristics often bring with them lethal consequences.

DECEIVED BY EVIL

Imagine you are driving alone at night, and your car is the only one on the road. You check your rear view mirror, and there is no one behind you. You are cruising at sixty-five mph, and there is lightning in the distance. It had rained earlier in the evening.

As you are driving, another flash of lightning startles you out of your daydreaming. You suddenly remember you have always been afraid of lightning, ever since you were a kid. Now, you are an adult and the shit still scares you, even when you are at home with the family. Of course, you would never admit it to anyone.

You think to yourself that you have about twenty-five miles to go, so it is not a big deal. The road is a little wet, but it is supposed to be—it rained earlier.

You drive down the highway and notice the sky is black, and somehow that seems odd. You ask yourself, *Where are the stars?* That damned lightning is everywhere, it seems, but the sky does not feel right; it does not look right. Then you say to yourself, *What makes you an authority*? You almost never look up at the night sky. That thought brings you no comfort but it releases something in you.

You look at the clock on the dashboard. It shows10:00 p.m. The late hour gives you an uneasy feeling, as you speed down the highway toward home and safety. A flash of lightning directly in front of you scares the shit out of you, as you make your way toward home. You think to yourself how happy you will be when you reach the safety of your home.

You check your rear view mirror, and now you notice another vehicle behind you. You can barely make out the headlights, but another vehicle is there. You are certain of it. That gives you comfort, for some strange reason, so much so that you almost wish the other driver were closer to you.

You continue on, knowing that every minute brings you closer to home and safety. That thought has you feeling at ease now, more than ever. You have not seen any cars pass you in the opposite direction on the road and that bothers you. That goddamned lightning is flashing with more frequency now, but there is no thunder. Just those damned constant flashes that, for an instant, illuminate the sky and those horrible looking clouds.

The clouds are black, ominous, shapeless, hideous things in the sky—made even more terrifying because now you feel as though the lightning is chasing you while you drive. You feel as if it is trying to prevent you from reaching your destination. However, you know that is silly, and yet, still, you cannot help being a little frightened. You take comfort in the fact that at least you are not alone on the road.

The other car is still behind you, but you notice it neither gets closer nor farther away. Your speed is constant, so you assume the other driver's is too. Still, you would feel a little better if the other driver was closer. You find yourself almost wishing that the other driver would escort you home. You know you do not have that much further to go. Just a little while longer and you will be safe at home. You think to yourself, again, how much you hate lightning. You cannot wait to be out of this shit and off the road.

At that exact moment, just as you finish the thought, a long jagged bolt of bright blue lightning splits the sky directly in front of you. The thunder is so loud it feels as if it shook the ground. In that instant, you let out a startled cry and tense up. You grip the steering wheel tighter. You feel as if your heart is going to go into overdrive, but the feeling quickly passes. You still feel a little tense, but it is passing.

You look into your rear view mirror and notice the other driver is still behind you. You wonder to yourself if that person is scared of lightning too, or is it just you. You continue on your drive home: less than ten miles now and you will be safe. *Fuck the lightning,* you think. *I'm not going to be frightened by that shit!*

A double flash of lightning gets your attention and you lose focus of your thoughts. You are acutely aware of the fact that you are scared, and the lightning reinforces that fear. As you drive toward home and safety, it seems to you that the sky has gotten darker and more ominous. *That is not possible,* you think. *Fuck this! I just want to get the fuck home.*

You try to suppress childhood fears surrounding lightning and remember to think like the intelligent person that you claim to be. Nevertheless, all you can think about is home and safety. *Home and I will be sheltered from the lightning.*

At least you are not the only person on the road on this ugly night. You look in the rearview mirror and see the other driver is still behind you. The other driver is still at the same distance from your car, and that gives you a little comfort. Seconds later, you see another flash of blue lightning, this time to the right of your car in the distance. You think if you can just hold it together, you will be fine. *I don't have that much further to go,* you think. *I'll be ok. Just over three miles to go, and this damned lightning can kiss my ass.*

You approach your exit off the highway and the only thought that comes to mind is home. As the exit gets closer, other memories come to the surface. Unpleasant memories of your childhood. For some strange reason you do not understand, they all involve thunderstorms and lightning.

As a young child, you would run into the house when the skies turned black and you knew a storm was approaching. You remember hiding in closets and covering your ears to protect them from the house-rattling thunder. All these memories are still terrifying to you as an adult. You think those particular memories are thoughts you could have done without at this moment. Nevertheless, you are almost home. *To hell with the lightning and the thunder,* you tell yourself. One more overpass and you are home free. All you have to do is drive to the top of the hill, turn right, and you are home.

You look in the rear view mirror and your companion on the road is still behind you, no closer and no further away. The car's headlights give you the comfort of knowing that you are not alone. At least there is one other human being on the road on this miserable night. You return your attention from the rearview mirror to the road ahead. In that millisecond of time, as you face forward coming to the top of the ramp, your exit in sight, you relax knowing your journey is almost over. Then you get the shock of your life.

Lightning flashes in what appears to you to be an almost strobe-like flash pattern. The lightning locks your attention, fright seizes your muscles, and in the cloud pattern for the briefest of instants, you think you see something. You cannot make it out; it happens too quickly. You are scared out of your mind, and you have to get away.

You step on the gas pedal hard; you jerk the wheel to the right, with your attention still on the sky. The face you just perceived in the clouds is almost on you.

Your car hits the guardrail at eighty mph. The rail acts as a ramp, deflecting your car at an angle into the air and over the edge of the ramp. You scream on the way down. The fall seems to take forever.

As you continue to scream, your fright intensifies. You cannot feel your body anymore, and all your mind can process is blind terror. The road is getting closer, and you continue to scream. Your car comes down, with the front windshield facing oncoming traffic. The fall appears to you to be happening in slow motion.

You see a vehicle coming toward you, but you are suspended in your car, upside down. The approaching vehicle has two female passengers in the front seats. You see the terror in their eyes, and you hear their silent screams as they barrel toward you at highway speed. You cannot even cover your face. You are so horrified that the only thing you can do is scream before the two vehicles collide.

You have one last conscious thought before death takes you. *The lightning! That goddamned lightning did this to me!*

What a shame that some people stumble through life oblivious to what they really are. Is this a severe character flaw or something more sinister?

PROVOKED BY EVIL

Jay often thought he did not know how much longer he could continue on in his current job. He'd gone to work today with the same apprehension, trying to convince himself he could perform his duties.

The job has its advantages, he thought. *The money is damn good, no supervisors breathing down your neck, women everywhere, and no damn uniform to wear. I just don't feel comfortable when I sit on those damn airplanes. I hate being cooped up in that small space, like a sardine in a can. Surrounded by all those fucking people is nauseating. Ah, what the hell. Being a Flight Assault Mitigation Specialist isn't so bad. Many jobs out there are a lot worse. Hell, I just left one to come here.*

Traveling was a prerequisite for his particular career field. While there were indeed many rewards, no career in law enforcement was without its share of dangers. Jay, however, knew he did not have the heart for physical combat of any kind. It did not matter if it were another man, woman, or raghead terrorist. He knew, in his heart, that if shit hit the fan on his airplane, he would bitch out and let his partner and the other passengers handle the situation. He would talk his way out of his cowardice, as he had done in the past at his last department.

If I can handle being a street cop, I can do this too. Being a cop on the streets of Washington D.C. was no joke. The only problem there was I always thought there were too many niggers on the force. When you needed help, though, the brothers would break their dumbass necks backing up white cops. As a F.A.M, that kind of help doesn't exist.

Jay had worked as a street cop, and there were other officers there for backup when the need arose. The job Jay currently held had no such luxury. If an officer found himself in trouble, he was on his own. Jay laughed to himself, thinking about that stupid job title.

Jay figured he had gotten by this long, so what if he was a coward? He could admit that to himself. No one else had to know. He had convinced himself many times since being hired that he was in this for the money and for no other reason. *The shit that went down on 9-11 was fucked up, but I was not the cause of it, and if it opened opportunities for me, I'll take them.*

He would constantly remind himself that he did not give a fuck about serving anyone but himself. He often thought that if this agency was willing to pay him one hundred grand a year to fly around the country and fuck flight attendants, he was more than willing to take advantage of every opportunity the job had to offer.

Jay figured that he had a few advantages that would keep him safe and under the radar. *I am relatively young, good looking, and white. That is one other huge advantage with this agency. Ninety-five percent of our organization's management is white, and at least we know how to watch out for each other. I'm not putting my ass on the line for anybody.*

Jay arrived at Reagan National Airport at 8:00 a.m. He had an early flight to Dallas, Texas. He had worked with the person he was partnered up with today on several occasions. He was a big guy, ex-swat officer, and black. Jay thought about another aspect of his job he did not like; he never knew who his partner was going to be from day to day. He preferred working with the brothers; they all thought he was cool. This was because of the bullshit way he presented himself, something he'd perfected working for D.C.'s Metropolitan Police Department for five years.

As soon as he got to the ticket agent's desk, his cell phone rang. He looked at the display and saw it was his operations office calling. He was informed that his scheduled partner had called in sick, and he was given the contact information for his new partner. Jay hoped his partner would be black, but he knew he probably would not be. Most likely, it would be someone he did not know and didn't care to work with. That thought pissed Jay off. *That's the way this fuckin' place works.*

At 8:15 a.m., Jay made contact with Mitch Kramer. Jay was rather disappointed when they met; Mitch was a much older man who had been with the U.S. Secret Service for a number of years. In Jay's estimate, Mitch did not look to be in the best of shape. *That's another problem with this place. They hire a lot of fat, out-of-shape white guys.* Mitch also spoke with a slight southern accent, which Jay found irritating. *Oh well*, Jay thought, he would make the best of it. After all, they were going to turn around and come right back after they landed in Texas. He was off for the next three days when they got back home, so thankfully it was going to be a short day.

The plane boarded at 9:30 a.m. The partners had to pre-board in front of everybody at the gate. Jay absolutely hated doing that, but his partner insisted so that they could brief the flight crew. After talking to the pilot and the purser Barbara, who, by the way, did not care much for their being on the flight, Jay and Mitch took their seats.

"Boarding," the announcement came over the plane's intercom. A few seconds later, the passengers started to come on board the plane. This was the part Jay hated the most. All these people had seen him board first, and might have guessed who he was. Try as he might, he would not or could not make eye contact with any of the passengers. He kept wondering to himself if they had an idea who he was. *Will today be the day that I have to put my ass on the line for these fuckin' people? To stop another 9-11 or some other crime on board the airplane*?

He felt scared and alone. *What would I do if something happened?* Dozens of scenarios ran through his mind. His heart began to beat a little faster, and he felt himself tremble.

He glanced at his partner, who was casually reading a magazine as the passengers walked by him. Mitch seemed completely at ease, but all Jay felt was anxiety. Jay noticed Mitch would look up every few seconds, making eye contact with the passengers as they boarded. Jay faced forward and tried to calm himself down.

A man who appeared to be of Middle Eastern descent sat next to Jay and that made him even more uneasy. *Why the fuck did he have to sit his raghead ass next to me*?

The flight attendant made her announcements to the passengers, then the captain spoke. A few minutes later, the airplane headed for the taxiway and then to the runway for the takeoff.

Once in the air, Jay started to calm down. *We have almost three fucking hours to go. Maybe some music will help calm my nerves. One of the best perks of this job is sitting in first class and having to do absolutely nothing but sit back, relax, and enjoy the ride, food, and drinks. If I'm lucky, I'll get at least one good-looking flight attendant with a nice ass to watch.* He felt himself relaxing as the sky waitress, as he called them, took his drink order.

The passenger sitting next to Jay still made him uneasy, but he thought *Fuck it! As long as he sits down and does not cause any trouble, it will be ok.* Jay hated all those fucking people, especially after 9-11.

It's been an hour and a half since take off, we've eaten, and now we're watching a movie. As usual, nothing's happened. Therefore, chances are: nothing will. That thought made Jay relax a little more.

He watched the overhead video screen, but then he noticed Mitch look away from his magazine. Mitch started looking up at the front section, where the attendants sat. This was an Airbus 320, so there were always two attendants up front. Mitch put his magazine down and started to watch the attendants in the front galley with a concerned look on his face.

Jay now noticed that the lead attendant, Barbara, had a worried look on her face. She was talking to someone on the phone and looking toward the rear of the airplane.

Another attendant came walking up front very quickly. She too had a worried look on her face. She and the lead attendant went to the corner of the galley, out of sight of the passengers, and talked. The lead attendant made a hand motion, indicating that Mitch should join them in the galley.

Jay now became very nervous. He had no idea what was going on, but he really did not care. *Whatever it is, Mitch is gonna deal with it on his own.* Another attendant came toward the front and stopped at the entrance to the first class cabin. One of the younger attendants up front said, "I'm not going back there again."

Jay noticed an attendant looking at him with a very concerned look on her face. This made him tremble. *Some shit is going down.* He wanted no part of it.

Mitch returned to his seat. Before he sat down, and with no one seeing him do it, he slipped Jay a note. Jay did not want to read it, but he had no choice. The note read: *Get ready, partner. We may have a possible arrest in seat 22D.*

Jay heard shouting coming from the rear of the aircraft now but could not make out what was being said. The attendants continued to look nervous, and the lead attendant now got on the phone to the captain.

A man in the rear of the plane shouted something Jay could not believe, but he could only make out part of what was said. He heard: "Man, what the hell do you think you're doing?"

Mitch turned around to see what was going on and quickly looked at Jay, who was still watching the attendant on the phone with the captain. She hung the phone up and walked over to them.

"The captain wants you two to go to the back of the plane and handle the situation," she said.

Jay asked what was happening back there.

"The man in seat 22D has pulled out his penis and told the rear attendant to suck it," she said. "He grabbed her, threw her into the back galley, and now he has her trapped back there. We think he may be high on something."

Jay froze in his seat, now so nervous he was lightheaded. Sounds of a struggle emerged from the back of the aircraft.

Jay turned around and saw two men fighting. Apparently, another passenger was now up and confronting the man causing the problem. The back of the plane was not very full and quite a few of the passengers were elderly. The man exposing himself was much bigger than the passenger who was trying to help the attendant, and the passenger was being pummeled. Another man got up to help, but he too was beat down. Now, women were screaming and children were crying in the rear of the airplane.

Mitch looked at Jay and got out of his seat. "Come on, partner," he said, his voice grim. "Let's go deal with this crazy motherfucker."

Jay said nothing to his partner and looked away.

"Jay," Mitch insisted. "We need to deal with this! What the fuck is wrong with you?"

Jay refused to respond to his partner.

Mitch looked at him with disgust and went to go deal with the problem.

Jay was terrified. *Mitch, you're on your own. I'm not getting in a fight with that motherfucker.* He stayed planted in his seat, trembling like the coward he was. He heard Mitch identify himself as he approached the troublemaker.

Mitch walked down the aisle, noting the frightened looks on the faces of the passengers. They were terrified, the women and the men both. The one causing the problem was now walking toward him, had his dick still hanging out of his pants.

One of the men the assailant had already bludgeoned lay on the floor bleeding from the nose and mouth, his wife or girlfriend next to him crying for someone to help him. The other man had made it back to his seat, but he looked to be unconscious and was bleeding from a cut under his eye.

Mitch was frightened, but he had to do his job. He turned, hoping that Jay was following behind him, but all he could see were the flight attendants cowering in front of the flight deck door. He fumed that Jay was apparently not going to come to his aid, but the approaching crazed passenger now took all his attention.

Mitch now realized how huge the man was and how crazy or high he had to be to be acting this way. He called out again to identify himself to the lunatic passenger and moved forward. Fear gripped him as he saw the look in the man's eyes. Mitch drew closer, and the man's insanity became more and more apparent. The man's eyes confirmed that there was nothing Mitch could do to him and that he was going to kill Mitch or anyone else who got in his way. *This guy's a crazed lunatic*, Mitch realized. Fear now turned to terror, but Mitch tried not to show it as he continued to approach the man.

A woman stood up as the assailant passed her seat; she did not seem scared but angry when she shouted at him, "Why don't you sit your crazy ass down and put that ugly little thing back in your pants!"

The man backhanded her across the face, causing blood to flow from her mouth. He moved to attack her again, as the woman's companion shouted her name, "Brenda!"

The crazed man then swung on the woman's companion, catching him square on the jaw. The man's jaw broke with a sickening crack, and he was out cold even before he fell back into his seat.

Mitch made his move.

He pushed forward quickly to within a few feet of the man. Again identifying himself, he removed the handcuffs from his belt. Keeping his voice as tough and authoritative as he could manage, Mitch said, "You are under arrest. Turn around and place your hands on top of your head."

The man closed the short distance between them so fast that Mitch had no time to react. The lunatic hurled himself on top of Mitch and slammed his fist repeatedly into Mitch's face.

After the forth blow, blood covered Mitch's face and he fell to the deck, where he lay, unable to move. The crazed man continued pounding Mitch in the face several more times, his fist was now covered in Mitch's blood. Mitch vaguely heard the rear attendant shouting for someone to help, but by now all the passengers had closed their eyes or were glued to their seats, unable to face the carnage that was taking place.

Just before he was bludgeoned into unconsciousness, and then death, Mitch had one last thought. *I probably should have shot this motherfucker.*

Jay tried to avoid the terrified stares of the lead attendant and the two younger attendants standing behind her.

In a hysterical voice, Barbara shouted at him that Mitch needed help. "That guy is beating your partner in the face and he's not moving anymore!"

Jay looked at them and said nothing. He fully realized that she could see the fear in his eyes. He was too scared to respond to her next remark.

"You have a gun!" Barbara cried. "Shoot this motherfucker before he kills your partner!"

Jay managed to respond in a trembling voice, "It's in my bag." He pointed to the overhead bin.

"You're a sorry piece of shit," Barbara said, looking away from him in disgust.

Her voice and actions drew the attention of the crazed man, who now headed for the front of the airplane.

One of the attendants quickly got on the phone. "Captain, we've got an emergency here. One FAM and three passengers are down, but the remaining FAM up front refuses to do anything. You need to land the plane."

The assailant now passed Jay's seat. Jay sat there, frozen and trembling like a scared rabbit, at the sight of the crazy man's eyes. The assailant pushed forward to attack the remaining flight attendants. The women screamed and tried to fight the man off. Yells echoed inside the cockpit from the captain and copilot, powerless to help their crew.

One of the attendants ran past Jay, blood streaming from her mouth. The assailant threw another woman around the galley like a rag doll. She fell to the floor, unmoving.

The nine passengers in first class were now all staring at Jay, disgusted that he was not raising a finger to help the now battered women. Two older passengers tried to help the unconscious flight attendant, pulling her away from the galley and putting her in an empty seat.

Barbara, the last attendant in the galley, was now screaming and trying to fight off the attacker. He knocked her against the galley wall and forced her down to the floor.

Jay could only see her legs from where he was sitting. He could barely see the man's back, but he knew he was sitting on her chest. The man had straddled Barbara's shoulders with his knees and now appeared to be trying to force her to suck his dick.

She was violently turning her head and screaming "No!", while kicking her legs.

The man now grabbed her head and shoved it hard against the deck and she fell silent. Her legs stopped kicking and the man's back began making forward thrusting motions as if he were fucking her.

The flight attendants in the rear screamed for someone to help Barbara. Jay's mind went blank. He did not know what to do, and he felt like a scared, trapped animal. He was so frightened he pissed his pants, terrified that the lunatic was going to come after him next.

Barbara came to, gagging and unable to breathe, and with the taste of cum in her mouth. The man was holding her by the hair, and she realized his dick was being forced in her mouth and down her throat. *Fuck this!*

Barbara bit down with all the strength she had. Now she tasted blood, as it filled her mouth. Her assailant's scream resounded over the roar of the plane's engines. He tried to stand and run away from her teeth, which were now tearing into his dick.

Barbara got to her knees, grasping his dick with her hands and teeth. She was determined to bite it off. Even a blow to her face failed to dislodge her grip, and her attacker fell back screaming, slipping in his own blood. She opened her mouth and freed him, spitting out his blood.

He was now bleeding profusely; she saw that his dick was bitten almost in half but still connected to his body by the skin. His drug-induced high was no longer effective to kill the pain he was now feeling. His screams filled the cabin. Barbara stumbled forward into the middle of the galley.

Carol, one of the rear attendants, ran forward from the back of the plane, determined to help Barbara. She got to the unmoving body of Mitch and moved his coat. His gun was still in its holster. She took it out and held it with both hands, pointing it in front of her as she continued to move forward to Barbara.

Barbara looked like a vampire that had just feasted on its victim. Carol looked at the man on the galley floor; his blood was everywhere. The crazed attacker lay there, curled up in a fetal position and bleeding like a gutted pig, but still screaming. Barbara screamed with a rage that frightened Carol to her core.

Barbara snatched the gun from Carol, pointed it at the bleeding thing on the floor, and shot it until it stopped that damn screaming and it no longer moved. Carol registered neither shock nor sadness at what she had just witnessed, even though she had never seen someone shot before. She had no feelings for the maniac who had just hurt and killed people on her airplane. That piece of shit deserved every bullet. She just wished that she had been the one who had shot that piece of shit.

Barbara looked down the aisle, and her eye caught the body of the officer on the carpeted deck. She focused on his bloody face, the pool of blood under his head, and the fact that he himself was not moving. A new uncontrollable fury filled her. *Something else needs to be put out of its fucking misery.*

She walked to the seat where that other piece of shit sat, the motherfucker who reeked of cowardice and piss. She heard Carol calling the captain on the phone, but Barbara was not going to be deterred.

Barbara pointed the gun at Jay, who was still cowering in his seat. "You no good piece of shit," she said with a hiss. "Give me one reason why you need to live!" Turning to the passengers, she commanded, "No one move!"

The passengers obeyed, sitting frozen in their seats, too afraid now to even breathe.

"Motherfucker," she shouted at Jay, "You couldn't even move to help your own partner! At least he tried to do his job, and it cost him his life. Why the fuck should I let you live? What are you willing to pay to stay alive, motherfucker? Answer me, goddamnit!"

Jay did not move or look at her, and Barbara thought about what he had allowed to happen to her. *I was beat damn near to death, knocked out, sodomized, and that animal's filthy-ass dick forced in my mouth. And then having to bite that filthy thing off to save myself.* She recalled the taste of his blood and semen that had temporarily driven her insane.

Jay watched like a deer caught in headlights as she pointed his partner's gun to his face. Barbara slowly pulled the trigger back, and his eyes focused on the hammer as it moved backward further and further. He watched, paralyzed, as the hammer slowly rose. He saw this all in slow motion, as the barrel of his partner's weapon grew bigger before his eyes. He saw the disgust for him on Barbara's bloody face. She looked him right in the eye and continued her slow squeeze on the trigger.

The last three sensations Jay experienced were the sounds of the captain's voice as he shouted, "Barbara, No!"

Then Jay heard the sound and saw the flash of light that heralds that death has come.

BANG!

Childhood fears never really leave you, and until you face them, the evil they represent is always with you.

EMBRACED BY EVIL

I *hate this fucking job,* Walter Jackson thought to himself as he sat the same security post he had worked for the last year. He was miserable. Today was like every other day for him, and he couldn't wait to get away from his job and go home.

He hated working as a security officer. His assignments were always the same, and he saw absolutely no future for himself as a security guard. *Patrolling office buildings and sitting posts for a living was not why I went to college,* he constantly complained to himself.

He watched the clock, waiting for his shift to end and for the relief guard to show up. He did not like the government workers in his building. In his opinion, they were all arrogant assholes who all thought they were better than him. Every day he felt like saying, "*The hell with it!*" and walking off this fucked-up job.

Today, as Walter waited for his relief to show, he hoped that maybe he would get some news on one of the dozens of applications and resumes he had sent out to various agencies. He knew, however, that leaving his current job right now would not be a smart move. As much as he hated his job, it paid his bills.

The other thing Walter hated about the building he worked in was all the mirrors that decorated the halls and the lobby where he sat. He had always had a dislike for mirrors. As a child, he had cut himself badly on broken glass as he and some friends had stood in front of a mirror playing a stupid game. The mirror they were using had fallen off the wall and he had tried to catch it, in the process cutting his hands so badly that he had to be rushed to the emergency room. However, even more disturbing to

Walter than those childhood injuries were the stories his grandfather used to tell him and his friends as they were growing up in an attempt to scare them. Some were stories about how mirrors did more than just show your reflection: they were also gateways to a world of monsters and demons. To set the monsters free, you had to recite silly sounding spells while standing in the dark in front of a mirror. This was what he and his friends had been doing when he'd had his accident. He'd never really forgiven his grandfather for that incident. As far as he was concerned, it never would have happened if not for those stupid stories.

Walter realized he had not thought about those things in years. He quickly dismissed the whole mirror thing as he prepared to leave work. His relief reported for his shift, but Walter did not greet the other security officer. He simply grabbed his gear and left for the day.

Walter knew how the other officers on his team felt about him, but he did not care what they thought of him. He did not have many friends, and he spent a great deal of time alone. It had been that way for him since high school and throughout college. His circle of friends had always been small. What friends he did make did not stay around long, and he was fine with that, since he did not like being bothered with many people. Walter had not had a girlfriend in years, which he knew was sad for a twenty-eight-year-old man. He thought that was ok, too.

Walter got into his car and decided to go have a beer at his favorite bar, which happened to be a strip club. He could at least look at the dancers while he drank a beer and fantasize about being with one of them. He knew that sex with one of the dancers would never happen. He then told himself he should just head home—the same routine he had followed for months now.

Walter got to the bar at four-thirty, went inside, and ordered a beer. He sat alone in a corner that gave him a decent view of the stage. He was just far enough away that he wouldn't have to tip the dancers but could still watch them.

In all the time I've been coming to this nasty-ass bar, you'd think I'd be a more popular customer, he thought. The servers and the dancers avoided him when he came in. No one greeted him, and he did the same. *You'd think someone could at least say 'Hi' to me. That's why I don't tip any of these skanks. What the hell. I'm not fucking any of them and I don't owe them shit.* As long as he bought a drink, the show was free as far as he was concerned.

He finished his beer and ordered another, wishing he could just touch one of the dancers. *It's not my fault these bitches can't do anything else but shake their asses for money. They won't be getting rich off of me! Fuck them.*

He left after an hour, having satisfied his needs for the time being. He got home with no particular plans; he simply wanted to unwind and relax. His place was quiet and peaceful—just the way he liked it.

Walter settled in and had just started to change into something comfortable when he got an eerie feeling. It was nothing that he gave much thought to at first. He continued to undress out of his work clothes, and put on something more casual, but the feeling hit him again.

This time he took notice. He knew there was no one in the apartment with him. However, he could not shake the feeling he was not alone and that something was watching him. He figured a drink would calm his nerves. After a fucked up day at work, it was all he needed. A little TV to occupy his mind and he'd be fine.

He now noticed the room he was in seemed a little dimmer than usual. That made no sense to him, because the living room lights were all on the same single switch. There were three light fixtures on the ceiling, and nothing had changed. He chalked his impression up to fatigue.

He finished his drink and turned on the 6:00 p.m. evening news. The main story was a report on a neighborhood shooting in which three young men had been gunned down; the authorities believed it was gang related. *Fuck them,* Walter thought. *They probably deserved to die. All those fucking niggers are criminals anyway.*

With that thought, Walter wondered to himself why he suddenly felt alone, not just alone, but secluded, as if he were the only person alive. He did not know why he felt this way, but he did, and now his home seemed darker and menacing somehow. He knew that made no sense, but he could not shake the unnerving feelings he was experiencing. He felt like he should not be alone in his apartment now.

He wanted to call someone to come over to alleviate his fear but could think of no one who would come spend time with him. Walter poured himself another drink, slammed it back, and decided to go to bed. *It's early, but what the hell. I don't have shit else to do.*

He felt ridiculous because he knew what he was feeling was nonsensical. However, he now felt a slow tingling sensation run down his spine, and it frightened him. *What the fuck is wrong with me this evening? I am a college-educated adult. There is nothing to be afraid of in my own home.* The more he told himself that, the more like bullshit it sounded. He was indeed afraid—and these unnerving feelings were getting stronger.

He took off his clothes and lay on the bed. He reached for the light switch, but something stopped him from turning it off. It was a sensation he had barely perceived on a conscious level—an almost primordial fear of darkness. He swung his feet to the floor and sat up on the bed. *Fuck this shit.*

Feeling both ashamed and embarrassed, he decided to take a shower to try to calm his jittery nerves. Crossing the room, he was startled when he thought he saw something move out of the corner of his eye. He looked quickly in that direction but saw nothing.

Walter's eyes focused on the picture of a half-naked woman that hung on his wall. Her eyes seemed to be watching him. His heart began beating a little faster, and his hands started shaking. He tried to get ahold of himself and headed into the shower.

He looked at himself in the bathroom mirror and recalled the peculiar game he'd played as a kid. The game had required him to stand in front of a mirror and repeat some silly phrase. No, it had been more than just words; it had been a spell his grandfather taught him. Yes, he remembered now: he and his friends would recite the spell in the hope of conjuring up a spirit or demon. The wraith would only show itself at a certain hour and under certain conditions, according to his grandfather.

That frightened him now more than ever. He did not want to remember the words to the spell. He wanted to pull away from the mirror, but he couldn't. The words he tried desperately not to remember now broke through his jumbled thoughts with perfect clarity. As the words came to mind, he found himself speaking them aloud in front of the mirror. He did not want to, but something was compelling him to speak.

"I, Walter, summon the demon in the dark that hides in shadow and owns the night. I summon you now into the light. Join with me and give me your power, here and now this very hour. In return, I pledge my soul, when the light passes and the night is cold. From this day and for all tomorrows, I pledge to serve he who lurks in shadow."

Walter's knees went weak, because he did not want to be in front of the mirror. He did not want to see what was going to show itself in the mirror. He felt his body trembling but could not find the strength to turn away. He closed his eyes and remembered all the horrible stories his grandfather used to tell him, and he was scared.

He opened his eyes. The only thing staring back at him was his own pitiful reflection. He felt a little relieved. *Fuck this shit.* With that thought, he crossed over to the shower, got in and closed the curtain.

During his shower, he felt uneasy, but the water felt good and he relaxed just a little, attributing the strange feelings to his own stupidity. Returning to the bedroom, he still could not shake the feeling he was not alone, but he knew that made no sense. He lay on the bed, and looked at the clock. It showed 10:00 p.m. Now, he realized he was tired and wanted to sleep.

The sleep he needed eluded him for what seemed to him like hours. The more he thought about his feeling of unease, the more anxious he became. He was afraid and he knew he shouldn't be, but he was. He made up his mind not to turn out the lights. *Just lie in bed and go the fuck to sleep.*

He closed his eyes, but seconds later he thought he heard something. His eyes snapped open, but he saw nothing. He turned over onto his side, but he realized that turned him away from the door. That bothered him, so he shifted to face the door. He looked at his clock; it still showed 10:00 p.m. *That can't be right.* Now, he refused to sleep.

Another sensation hit him, a mortal terror that overpowered him with dread. A thought that terrified Walter.

Get out of this apartment. Go anywhere, but get out of here now. Get the fuck out of this place now! he heard his voice scream in his head. He tried to bolt up to get out of bed, but he was so frightened now he could not move. His heart beat so hard he could hear it.

A presence other than his own lurked in the room. He could feel it. He looked down the hall and remembered leaving all the lights on, but now the whole apartment was dark, with the exception of the lights in his bedroom.

A voice sounded, but from where he could not tell. It was soft at first, then it got louder. Walter looked toward the bathroom. The voice was definitely coming from the bathroom. It was a horrible sounding voice, and it froze Walter's soul.

The words came through in short phrases. "Demon in the dark who hides in shadow, and owns the night."

His mouth went dry when he realized what was being said.

"I summon you now into the light."

He heard the words and realized the voice was like nothing he had ever heard before.

"Join with me and give me your power."

He could not move off the bed. He was frozen in place.

The disembodied voice seemed to be getting closer. "Here and now this very hour, and in return, I pledge my soul, when the light passes and the night is cold."

"*Run!*" he shouted to himself. His fear was now overwhelming.

He looked to the door to run but it slammed shut on its own. Fear now completely paralyzed him. Still, those words would not stop repeating over and over.

The voice was harsh and malevolent. He sensed its evil, but he was so frightened he could not move. His heart was beating so hard his chest hurt, and the pain started to spread all through his body. Still, those fucking words taunted him.

The voice slowly got closer, and something touched his skin. From behind, Walter felt icy hands touch his shoulders. Now, something leaned close to his ear and a foul odor assaulted his senses.

An inhuman voice spoke. "Remember the pledge you made to serve, the pledge to serve he who lurks in shadow. The pledge your grandfather had you recite as a boy. That pledge released him from my service and bonded you the moment your blood was spilled. It is time for you to fulfill your oath."

At that moment, the lights went out.

Walter felt a warm liquid run down his legs and tears flowed down his cheeks. He was held in place by a force he couldn't explain. His body was bent forward and a warm foul breath spread across his neck. Something shifted behind him.

Walter could not move or hide. He needed to escape, but there was nowhere to go. He needed an explanation of why this was happening to him, but there was none. He could feel every pulse in his body beating so hard. The pain it caused was unbelievable. His heart was racing out of control, as if it was going to explode from his chest any second.

Something was forced into his ass in the darkness and he screamed with all his might, all his rage, all his fear. Walter wished for death, as the thing mutilated his body. He knew this was not a dream when he heard another voice in his head, even over his own screams.

He heard the sound of his Grandfather laughing.

We have always been told that crime doesn't pay to instill fear in us. The truly evil among us know that's bullshit, it can be quite lucrative, depending on who profits.

STIMULATED BY EVIL

"We've been watching this damn house for a fuckin' week now, and it's the same shit every day," Chuck said, pounding his fist on the dashboard. "Every morning, at 9:00 a.m. sharp, these same workers show up, do whatever the fuck it is they do, and leave at 6:00 p.m. Not a damn thing has changed since last Monday,"

"There is a reason, dumb ass," Tony said. "We watch this shit to learn what's happening and when, and to check out the 'hood. We know they've been installing shit for a while now. We don't know what it is, but when they're done, we're gonna steal everything in that motherfucker, whether it's nailed down or not. We know the owners are long gone and won't be back from their fuckin' vacation for another five days. I hate these rich motherfuckers. They come in here, flashing their fuckin' money, buying these big fucking houses. We're gonna rob this motherfucker blind."

Rob chimed in. "Yeah, well I hope that dumb ass ho you fuckin' at the bank is right about the shit she told you about the motherfuckers who live here."

"Carla's been right so far." Tony grinned. "She works for the motherfucker that owns the house. He's the bank manager or some shit. I seen him. He drives that Jag in the driveway to work in the mornings. We saw him drive away in the BMW to the airport with his fuckin' family. He's a short fat-ass gray boy, always wears a suit and fucked up ties."

I'd would love to lay dick to the banker's wife, Rob thought. *Maybe next time I'll come back by myself and fuck the shit out of her.*

"Carla says he's a fuckin' dick to all the workers at the bank, and that he's a weird motherfucker," Tony said. "He's into some shit called wicken or wicked or some shit like that. Whatever the fuck that is. She says he was bragging about taking his fuckin' family to some fuckin' place in Europe for two weeks. He was talkin' shit, like how he wanted to get away from everyone before he fired them all. He's gonna be surprised like shit when he brings his fat ass home." Tony slapped his knee and laughed.

"Hey, Tony," Rob asked, "how do you know this bitch ain't gonna rat us out when word gets out that his crib got broken into?"

"Look, Rob," Tony replied, "that's not gonna happen. All that dumb ho cares about is this dick up her ass. I got tired of her talking about how fucked up her boss is, and how she'd like to fuck him over. So, I asked the bitch about the dude. She filled in all the blanks, so don't worry, motherfucker. She don't know shit, least of all what we're up to. And even if she did, I'm tappin' that ass every night. She won't say shit, the dumbass ho."

"So, when are we gonna do this thing?" Rob asked. "We've cased this place long enough, and we got about five days before fat-ass comes home. Everybody knows the workers are gone at 6:00 p.m. Chuck already scoped them out, asking if their company is hiring any new employees because he's looking for work. Dude told him they'd be done here by noon today, and he gave him a card to call the company. So, this is the last day of the job."

"We'll hit that motherfucker today about 2:00 p.m.," Tony said. "People in the neighborhood won't suspect shit. All they'll see is the same three-coverall uniforms working in the house until 6:00 p.m., as normal. The van won't be a problem, because they've used different unmarked vehicles the whole job. By 6:00 p.m., we'll have handled our business and got the fuck out." He turned to Chuck. "Chuck, you got the same type uniforms as they have on, right?"

"Yeah, Tony. No problem. You can buy that shit anywhere cheap."

"We're ready then." Tony's mouth cracked into a vicious smirk. "Let's go get something to eat, come back, and go to work."

They returned at 2:00 p.m.

"All right, this is the plan," Tony announced. "We'll park our van in the front of the house, like normal. Chuck, you and Rob go around to the back of the house, under the deck, with the toolboxes. We know there's an alarmed key box under the deck. That's how the workers got in every day. Rob, you cut the power cord to the key box and smash it open with the sledgehammer. Go through the house and open the garage door. I'll back the van up into the garage, and then we go to work."

Tony backed the van onto the driveway, and Chuck and Rob proceeded to the back of the house. Like clockwork, all went as planned. The lock box was deactivated and broken open. Chuck and Rob entered the house under the deck and hurried to the garage entrance.

Rob laughed. "Man, this is too fuckin' easy."

"Yeah," Chuck agreed. "Like taking candy from a baby."

They opened the door for Tony, placed their toolboxes into the back of the van, and reentered the house.

Tony gathered his crew together. "All right, here's the plan. We have three hours, tops, to do our thing and get the fuck outta here. Rob, you take the upstairs. Check every room. We want cash, jewelry, electronics, and video systems. Chuck, you take the basement, and man, tie your fuckin' shoes before you bust your ass."

"Fuck you, Tony," Chuck replied. "This is a big fuckin' house."

"I know, motherfucker," Tony responded. "That's why we're here. Same thing for you, Chuck. All small electronics, computers, phones, game systems, all that type shit, and we take every flat screen in this bitch. I'll take the middle level. The van is in the garage, and the garage door is closed and locked, so go get busy, niggas."

Tony proceeded to explore the house. *Chuck's dumb ass is right. This is a big fuckin' house, and it is well furnished. Too damn bad we can't take all this shit. This is a one-time deal. What we can't take, we're gonna trash anyway, so fuck it.*

Some statuettes on the mantle caught Tony's eye, and he paused to take a closer look. *These are some ugly little motherfuckers. They can keep this shit.* Each figure was about six inches tall. He had never seen statues like this before and, for some reason, they frightened him just a little. *They look like little hairy shrunken people or some shit, and they smell awful. Ugly little fuckers. Oh, well. Fuck these rich, weird fuckers. They'll be buying all new shit when we're done.* Tony laughed as that thought came to mind.

He stopped for a second to admire the kitchen. He noticed several appliances that would be coming with them. *Man, this is some nice top-quality shit.* He went over to the refrigerator and opened the door. Seeing all the food inside reminded him of times growing up as a kid. His family's refrigerator was damn near always empty, and it had never had this much food in it.

That thought made him angry. "Some fuckin' people have it so fuckin' easy."

He and his had always had to struggle and always had barely enough to eat. A bowl of strawberries sitting on the center shelf caught his attention, but he was not sure why. *I have never liked those motherfuckers; the damn seeds always get caught in my teeth.*

Thoughts of his childhood struggles returned. He remembered times he'd asked his mother to buy certain items when she'd go grocery shopping. She would have to say no many times, because they could not afford certain items. That thought made him angrier as he peered into the very well stocked refrigerator. *I hate these rich, arrogant, motherfuckers. They always looked down on me as if I'm a piece of shit. Well, I'll show these motherfuckers.* He unzipped his pants and pulled his dick out. *I hope I have a gallon of piss in me so I can spray all this shit.*

He pissed all over the contents of the refrigerator, leaving no level of the refrigerator dry. Every corner of every shelf was now dripping with piss. He purposely saved a little just for the uncovered strawberries. He laughed as he watched his piss cover the fruit and settle into the bottom of the fruit bowl. Putting his dick back in his pants, he slammed the door as hard as he could. He laughed as he walked away, shouting as loud as he could, "Fellas, stay out of the fridge. It's full of piss."

Rob was quick about his work, knowing the family had two kids. He walked quickly through the rooms, noting that each child had their own huge fully furnished room with an adjoining bathroom. Rob also noticed many horrible looking statues everywhere in the rooms. He took a closer look at one. *Goddamn, these ugly pieces of shit stink. They can keep these fucked up little motherfuckers.*

He smiled when he saw the game systems, iPads, and computers in each room. He quickly but carefully unplugged the consoles and computers and moved them to the hallway. He took a pillowcase off a pillow and stuffed every game he could find inside the makeshift sack. He took all the computer software in each storage rack from each room. He took all the music CDs he could find and the piggy banks off each dresser. *Damn, these are some heavy-ass piggy banks for kids.*

Rob quickly found enough booty to fill eight pillowcases. He carried everything downstairs to the waiting van. He called out for Tony but got no answer. *This is a big damn house, but he still should have heard me call. I heard him say some dumb shit about the fridge. Oh well, fuck it.*

He put the pillowcases into the van and returned for the computers and game consoles he'd left in the hall and loaded them into the van. *Now, I'll go back, get those fifty-inch flat screens, and go through the master bedrooms. We've hit the fuckin' jackpot.* He laughed as he ran up the stairs.

Returning to the van with the TVs, Rob saw other goodies inside. *The fellas ain't bullshitin'. The van is half-full with shit and we've only been here about an hour. Well, let me go through the master bedrooms and see what else we got.*

Running up the stairs, Rob headed straight to the bedroom on the right, across the hall from the children's rooms. He opened the door. The sight stopped him at the threshold. "Goddamn," he said out loud to no one in particular, "this one room is bigger than my whole fuckin' shitty-ass apartment."

He also noticed more of those stinky little statues. He quickly pulled out every drawer on all eight dressers. *This must be the dude's room because all the clothes are men's.* He crossed the room and opened the closet's double doors. Looking around quickly, he found what he was looking for: a safe. It had an electronic lock. *No time to fuck with that,* he thought. *We'll just take the whole damn thing.* He ran into the hall and leaned over the banister to call for Tony. "Tony, I found a safe. Hey, man, where the fuck are you?"

He spotted Tony and Chuck returning from the van.

"What's up, Rob?" Tony replied, smiling

"I found a safe, man. In the first master bedroom. We can't open it now, so we'll have to take the whole thing."

"Cool! Chuck, go to the van and get the dolly. Bring the safe down and we'll load that last."

"You bet," Chuck responded and went to get the dolly.

Looking at his watch Tony yelled instructions to Rob. "We're almost full, man. It's 4:00 p.m. Check out the other bedroom so we can get the fuck outta here."

Running through the first master bedroom, Rob spotted what he figured was an adjoining bedroom door. He turned the knob, but found it locked. He laughed aloud. *These motherfuckers don't even sleep in the same damn bedroom. Why the fuck be married, if you don't even sleep with the bitch?*

He ran out of the first bedroom and down the hall. He opened the door to the second master bedroom, flipping the light switch on as he entered. The smell of the room hit him first. Unlike the other rooms that he'd been in so far, this had a pleasant odor. The scent was sweet, but not overpowering, and reminiscent of roses. This room was soft, feminine, and very well decorated. Rob could almost feel the personality of the room's occupant. He noticed what he took to be jewelry boxes on one of the dressers and headed right to them. He admired the wife's pictures on the dresser and a few on the edges of the mirror. He picked up one of the pictures and stared at the woman in the bathing suit.

This bitch is fine as hell. The only way a soft-assed faggot like her husband can get a bitch like this is if he's payin' for the pussy. Hell, the dude is payin' and still ain't hittin' it. Stupid motherfucker has to sleep in another bedroom. That thought made him laugh until his eyes watered.

Rob opened the boxes, and his eyes got wide. "Look at all this shit," he cried. "Gold necklaces, big ass diamond rings and shit. Fuck this! We takin' all this shit for ourselves."

For an instant, another thought came to mind, as he looked at all the jewelry. *If they have all this shit lying around, why didn't the real workers take any of this shit?* He shrugged. *Oh, well. Fuck it.* The thought quickly passed and he went back to work.

Opening the top drawers on all the dressers, he quickly tossed out the contents after finding nothing of interest. Getting to one of the middle drawers, he pulled it open and found it full of woman's underwear, all folded and neatly placed in the drawer. He started to scoop the undergarments out to toss them aside, but when he touched them, he noticed their softness. He also noticed a very pleasant smell that momentarily distracted him. He further noticed another of those weird statues, but he could have sworn it had not been there a moment ago.

A loud thumping sound came from the stairs, and he jerked his head in that direction. He realized it must be Chuck taking the safe down to the van. Returning his attention back to the dresser and its contents, Rob found himself holding many pairs of the underwear in his hands. He noticed that some were thong underwear, and that the colors seemed brighter now. He now noticed something else he hadn't noticed before. *Looking at this white bitch's pictures and holding her underwear is makin' my dick hard.* He looked at the woman's pictures again. *I would give anything to fuck the shit out of you right now. I'd give you all this shit back, just for a piece of that pussy.*

Rob became mesmerized as he stared at a picture of her in a bikini. He became even more aroused as he stared at her underwear in his hands. He felt his dick getting harder as he stared at her picture, and the smell of the room increased his arousal. *This is what this bitch must smell like.* He dropped her underwear into the drawer and put his hand on his growing dick. He rubbed it through his pants, as he stared intently at her picture on the mirror.

He unzipped his pants and pulled out his dick. The cool air felt good on his dick, as he began to stroke himself. His dick filled his hand as he began to pull harder, but gently, imagining that it was her hand on his dick. He put a pair of her underwear on his dick to heighten the experience. *I'm gonna come back by myself when she's here alone and give her all this dick,* he thought.

Looking at the picture of her in the bikini, he imagined her sucking his long, full dick. It filled her mouth, and she loved it. He began stroking his dick harder now, as he saw himself pushing his entire dick into her tight pussy and then up her ass. He imagined her going crazy with pleasure as he fucked her for all he was worth. He felt himself getting ready to explode. He felt his cum start to ooze from his dick.

Quickly, he put his dick in the drawer. He wanted to explode all over her underwear. He could not help noticing the damn statue as he stroked his dick, and the fucking thing pissed him off. *Ok, motherfucker. I got somethin' for your ugly ass too.* He pulled his dick harder and harder. It felt good to him. He felt himself ready to explode.

Looking at her picture and lusting for her body, he felt the contractions in his dick that signaled he was about to cum. The sensation was powerful, but he looked at the statue again. It was spoiling his moment. He aimed his dick so that the first wad of cum shot right on the head of the statue.

He then quickly put his dick over the top of her panties and finished ejaculating. The undergarments felt good on his dick. He closed his eyes, putting half his dick in the drawer and covering it with her panties. He then shot his whole load. The pleasure he felt was overwhelming.

Rob heard a loud slamming sound and his pleasure was replaced with a sharp numbing pain, unlike anything he had ever experienced. His mind went blank for a fraction of a second, followed by body-wide numbness. Then he screamed with frightening force. Tears flowed uncontrollably down his face. Impossibly, his screams grew louder with every breath, as he pleaded for someone to help him.

He looked down at his dick. The drawer was closed with his dick caught inside. He screamed again. The pain was beyond excruciating, but he could not move. He could not pull away, and he could not drop to his knees. He stood frozen in place. He could barely see through his tears as his dick swelled horribly, and his pain increased to a crescendo.

Tony was ready to leave. *It's time to get the fuck outta here. We have enough shit, especially now that we got the safe. Let me find those two stupid motherfuckers and drop them the fuck off at their home. As soon as I sell this shit, I'm gonna blow town with all the money. Fuck those two. That's what they get for letting me fence the shit by myself. Anyway, this was my score. I never liked their asses anyway. They were just dumb enough to do this shit with me.*

He called out to both Rob and Chuck. "Yo, fellas. Let's wrap this shit up and get the fuck outta here! The safe's loaded. Let's roll!"

From the basement, Tony heard Chuck's response. "All right. I'm coming; I got this 50 inch TV coming up right now."

"You need help, man?"

"No, I got it. This motherfucker is going in my house," Chuck replied.

"Ok, hurry up, nigga. We gotta get out of here."

Tony looked up toward the stairs and shouted more instructions. "Rob, let's roll, man! The van is full!"

Rob heard Tony calling for him, but he could barely talk through his pain and tears. He only mumbled, and since the doors were closed, Tony could not hear him begging weakly for someone to help him.

"Please, somebody help me, please."

Rob looked at the part of his dick that was exposed. It looked like a short fat balloon ready to explode. His legs were numb, and the pain in his lower body and head made him feel as if he was on fire. He also noticed his cum oozing down onto the dresser from the head and face of that ugly little statue.

Waiting for the others, Tony noticed a door he had not checked out. He figured that while he waited for the others, he might as well have a look. He opened the door, stepped inside, and turned on the light. He thought it looked like a large utility room. Two more doors faced him, but the room was empty otherwise. *Fuck this! There's nothing here.* The door he had come through suddenly closed behind him. He walked over to it and tried the knob, but it would not turn.

I shoulda got one of the guys to help with this, Chuck thought to himself as he struggled with the fifty-inch TV. *There's a lot of weird-looking shit down here, and I can't get the fuck outta here fast enough. Oh, well. Fuck it. I just need to get this damn TV up these damn stairs, and I'm home free.* He knew he could not lay the TV down because that might damage it. However, he did not want to drag it up the stairs and risk damaging it that way because it was going home with him. His short arms made carrying the TV awkward. He could not carry it with his arms stretched lengthwise, so he had to carry it to one side, with his arms stretched in a vertical position. Chuck had to be careful not to bump the TV against the walls as he walked up the spiral staircase. It was not heavy, but having to carry it the way he did was difficult. Carrying it by himself up all the stairs also tired him out.

He swore he should have been out of the basement by now. *I don't remember this many fucking steps,* he thought. *It seems like I've been climbing these fuckers forever.* He looked up and saw the door leading out of the basement. One more turn of stairs to negotiate and he was home free. *I can finally get the fuck out of this weird-ass basement, and take my new TV home. I'm claiming this one for myself, no matter what Tony says.*

Chuck continued up the stairwell, taking the stairs one at a time because he was tired and felt like he had been walking all day. He leaned against the wall for a quick second of rest, still holding the TV. He looked up the staircase and said aloud, "Let's do this." He continued up the stairs, accidentally brushing against a light switch and turning it off. He managed to turn the lights back on using his arm to hit the switch again.

As Chuck looked forward, he saw one of those statues from the basement on the next step. *That damn thing was not there before the lights went out!* The sight frightened him so badly his heart began to pound in his chest. He stepped back away from the statue, but lost his balance. He quickly tried to regain his footing, but he couldn't get his foot off the step for some reason. He then realized he was standing on his shoelaces. Frightened by the sight of the statue and unable to move his feet, he stumbled against the wall. His momentum carried him and the TV backward down the staircase. He tried to let go of the TV, but his hands just wouldn't release it. He plummeted down the stairs, holding on to the TV. His head smashed against the screen, and on impact with the stair railing sent his head completely through the glass screen, up to his shoulders.

His scream only lasted a second, as he and the TV came to rest between the first and second rail supports of the stairs. Chucks head had broken between the railings, and the TV now rested around his neck. Glass lay everywhere. It looked as though someone had broken a large picture frame over Chuck's head. Plastic and glass stuck out of both his eye sockets. His neck was broken and a silver liquid spread all over Chucks face, burning off his skin. He tried to shout for help, but he was unable to talk or move.

The pain screamed volumes in his now-paralyzed body. As he suffered his agonizing death, he heard Rob and Tony upstairs.

"The hell with Chuck," Tony was saying. "We can't wait around here all day for his ass to come outta there. He's down in that damn basement bullshitin'. We gonna leave his stupid ass here. Let the cops find him down there, and he can take the fall for this shit."

In his mind's eye, Chuck saw them both get in the van and drive away. His last thought before death took him was, *Why wouldn't they help me?*

Rob could not stand the pain any longer. His whole body was in unbearable pain. His legs were numb; the pain in his back and head was agonizing. Every time he tried to use his free hand to open the drawer to free his dick, electric jolts of pain shot through his body at the slightest movement. His tears would not stop flowing, and now he saw blood seeping from the bottom of the drawer. He no longer felt his legs, and they were losing the strength to support him. He felt himself falling sideways to the floor. As he fell backward, the pain of his dick ripping off his body was horrific. Blood shot everywhere, in huge quantities like it was coming from a garden hose. He landed on his side, hands between his legs, his lower body covered in his own blood. Rob looked up at the dresser and saw the statue. It appeared to be looking at him, its head slowly bobbing up and down. Whimpering now because he had no energy to scream for help, he lay there, helpless, slowly and painfully bleeding to death. He heard Chuck and Tony down stairs talking.

"Man, look," Tony was saying. "Fuck Rob's punk ass. We gotta roll outta this muthafucka now."

In his mind's eye, he saw the van pull away and wondered why he had to die this way.

Tony turned the doorknob, but it would not budge. He pounded on the door and shouted for help. "Hey! Rob! Chuck! Open this goddamn door! It's stuck and it won't open!"

Tony tried the other two doors, but they too were locked tight. He tried kicking on both, but all he accomplished was pain in his legs. He looked around. The room had no windows; only a drain in the floor. He saw nothing to help smash the doors open. He kept pounding and shouting for help. Since no one came to aid him, the thought crossed his mind that maybe they had left him down there trapped in this room to be caught. He started to panic, even though he was infuriated by that thought.

He shouted out his frustrations. "I know those muthafuckas didn't leave me! This was my gig!"

Tony was furious now at the thought of his boys leaving him behind. He hit the doors harder. He moved from one to the other, in a mad fury, pounding on each door and screaming for someone to get him the fuck out of that room. He banged on the doors for what seemed like hours, until both hands and feet were hurting and sore from his futile efforts to escape the room. He stopped, looked at his watch, and realized it was past 6:00 p.m. *We have to get the fuck out of here. How the fuck can I get out of here, if I'm trapped in this damn room?*

Tony screamed in rage. "Let me out of here! Somebody open this fuckin' door!"

He rested against the wall for a while, after his last useless attempt to break through the doors. Both his hands were now sore and swollen. He sat down on the floor, encased in the silence of the room.

He heard voices. They sounded far away, but he could just barely make out what they were saying.

"Fuck, Tony, bitch muthafucka. Let's leave his ass here."

"Yeah, we searched this muthafucka and he's not here. The hell with him. Come on. Let's get the fuck outta here. We gonna keep all this shit for ourselves."

His heart started to pound in his chest, as rage filled him with new strength. He stood and began to pound harder on the door he had come through.

Tony shouted, with all his remaining strength, "Open this fuckin' door! You two muthafuckas better not leave me here! I'll fuckin' kill you muthafuckas when I get out. Get me the fuck outta here!"

His cries went unanswered. He heard the van start and pull away. His crew had left him behind.

Tony now heard a hissing sound emerging from the drain in the floor. He turned to look, but saw nothing. However, he detected a foul, putrid odor coming from somewhere. He thought it smelled like a rotting corpse. He did not know why that thought had come to him, but another equally disturbing thought also came to mind. *This odor is strong enough to be the smell of dozens of rotting bodies.* The smell was now so strong it assaulted all his senses at once. Without conscious thought, he immediately covered his mouth and nose and tried to hold his breath. That did him no good; the smell of rotting death was overwhelming.

Tony gagged and vomited. He vomited uncontrollably for what seemed like hours. He knew his stomach contents were long gone, but still he gagged violently. All his muscles spasmed, contracting uncontrollably. He vomited blood; it shot out of his mouth forcefully. His eyes burned from the thick and powerful smell of death in the room. He squinted across the room. One of the statues he remembered seeing upstairs stood before him. *That thing wasn't here when I first came in this room.*

He looked away from the statue and touched his head. He felt a burning sensation. His eyes blurred with blood, and he soon realized they no longer worked. He screamed out in agony. Every breath was torture, as his now fluid-filled lungs desperately tried to find clean air.

He brought his hands up to his face, but touching his burning skin increased his agony. His skin was melting off his face. He fell to the floor in a pool of blood and vomit, jerking and twitching like a fish out of water.

Incredibly, through all his suffering, Tony thought about all the horrible things he had done in his useless life: all the crimes he'd committed, the people he'd hurt, all the women he'd abused and raped, all the children he'd fathered but never attempted to take care of. In the instant before his heart stopped, he realized what a fucking waste his life had truly been.

A white unmarked van returned to the house Saturday morning. It backed up to the garage and pulled inside. The garage door closed.

Two vans exited the property at precisely 6:00 p. m.

On Monday morning, the bank manager returned to work. All the employees acknowledged him as he passed by. He arrogantly nodded his head in the direction of those greeting him as he headed to his office. He carried his briefcase and a rather large gift bag.

Carla noticed that he almost looked happy today. He was not wearing his usual smirk that he usually used to greet everyone on a daily basis every morning. *Well, whatever. I don't have to deal with him, and as long as he leaves me the fuck alone, I'm good.*

Carla was about to go to lunch when she was summoned to the bank manager's office. "Goddamnit," she said, in a low, irritated voice. "I was having a good day. What the fuck does he want?"

Carla had only been in his office on a few occasions. She made it a habit to avoid him and his office whenever possible. She was hungry, so she figured, *What the hell! Get it over with, and go eat.* She went to the manager's office and knocked on the door.

"Please come in, Carla."

She did so, and he directed her to take a seat on the other side of his desk. Carla sat down. She noted the bowl of strawberries on the desk and the three unusual-looking little statuettes. *Ugly little motherfuckers,* she thought.

"Carla, would you care for some strawberries?" her boss asked. "Please, take as many as you like. I love strawberries, and these are very special. They were treated with a very special kind of care, just for me. So please enjoy them."

He lifted the bowl to her, and Carla reached out and took three of the strawberries. *I like strawberries,* she thought. *Maybe fat boy isn't all that bad.* She brought a large strawberry to her mouth, but she stopped just short of biting into it. Something peculiar caught her attention, and she really took notice of those ugly little statues on his desk. Something about one of them seemed familiar. She knew she had never seen those things before, but there was something hauntingly familiar about them.

"Oh, I see you've noticed my figurines," her boss said. "I got these three while I was on vacation. I call them The Three Blind Mice. Yes, these three cost me a bit to acquire, and they made quite a mess of my finances temporarily, but they were worth every penny. Notice the one in the middle." The manager pointed it out to Carla. He did not need to though.

Carla saw why it was familiar to her. She put the strawberry in her mouth and bit down, and her heart started to race just a little. The middle figure had on a little silver necklace with a ring attached to it—an exact match for the necklace and ring she had given Tony. It was her class ring from high school.

She chewed the strawberry and her eyes zeroed in closer, as if they were magnifying glasses. The figurine mesmerized her. Its twisted face seemed familiar somehow. The taste of the strawberry was also familiar, and then something hit her, with a clarity that seemed impossible. The thought came to her with such lucidity that it felt like someone had hit her with a baseball bat.

Her heart pounded in her chest. *This is bullshit! This is impossible! That fuckin' thing looks like Tony! Even with the face all fucked up.*

Sitting at his desk with his hands resting on top of Carla's personnel file and an almost evil smile on his face, the manager spoke. "Carla, let me tell you why I wanted to see you."

Carla began to tremble.

"We need to discuss your future at this bank, as some very disturbing information about you has come to my attention. Oh, by the way, did you enjoy your strawberry?"

Sometimes hate is a good thing—it will blind you to the evil that exists within you and convince you to do what you believe is right.

MOTIVATED BY EVIL

Perhaps you worry every day of your life that you will slip up. You know you are an illegal alien in the United States. The authorities will catch you eventually. Someone, perhaps a police officer, will challenge your citizenship status. It frightens you to your core, this knowing that you'll be caught one day and deported to your country of origin, never to see your new family again. You fear you will be sent back to that filthy land you escaped from, back to the living hell you would rather forget.

Remember this: anyone who has something to hide knows fear. If you are here illegally, you have something new to fear, and it is not the police. An interesting letter is circulating on the Internet and it's gaining momentum and thousands of new readers every day. The letter is titled "America for Americans."

My fellow Americans,

I have an urgent message that concerns all of you. What I have to tell you is frightening and disturbing, but this topic needs to be understood by all American citizens. I urge you to listen to what I have to say, and then you decide. America is being destroyed from within. Illegal immigrants from all over the world who swarm over our borders by the thousands like insects each day are ravaging our society. They burrow into our cities and towns, like maggots feeding on a corpse, and they infest our nation like cockroaches.

The worst of these groups, and the first we will deal with, is the Mexicans. We can no longer count on our government to protect us or defend our borders. Our politicians are too concerned with counting votes and being politically correct, while at the same time stealing our hard-earned money and giving it away to foreigners to deal with this crisis. We, as American citizens, have the right to protect our homes and communities. We must take a stand, or our society is doomed.

Illegal aliens come to this country and contribute absolutely nothing to our society. What they do bring is crime and poverty to our neighborhoods and overcrowding to our schools. They pack our jails and destroy our housing and economic markets. They do not pay taxes, and they put a strain on our economy. Go into any hospital in America and you will see dozens of illegal Mexican men and pregnant women with multiple babies in tow. They use our hospital emergency rooms as their own private clinics. They have absolutely no way to pay for the services they demand. They do not care about the cost to American taxpayers in lost jobs and higher taxes. Go into any fast-food restaurant or convenience store, and the cashiers barely speak English. You place your order multiple times to the same idiot, and they look at you as if you have lost your damned mind because you do not speak their fucking language. On top of that, these illegal fuckers act as if you are the inconvenience to them, as if it is an American's privilege to be served by ignorant illegal aliens.

We, as Americans, need to stand up and shout out loud that we speak English in this country. Spanish, French, Italian, German, and African are not our languages. You are now in America, legal or otherwise. The least you can fucking do is learn the language. This should not be tolerated in America.

Those illegal fucking Mexicans come here, over and under our borders, and act like they are doing us a favor. Mexicans have taken over our service industries, Africans control our airports and taxi services nationwide, Middle Eastern terrorists now infiltrate our society on every level, Europeans, Asians and Canadians bleed our economy to the point that we can barely compete with the rest of the world, and the US Dollar is almost worthless.

My brothers and sisters, you have to understand there are many threats that we must deal with and struggles from within that are destroying us all. It makes no difference the color of your skin, where you live, or your economic status. If your great grandparents, grandparents, and parents were born here, raised here, and pay taxes here, you are an American and this is your fight. We are being conquered from within, and we must develop contingency plans to deal with this threat on our own, the way our forefathers once had to.

The first group we must put down are those fucking lazy, uneducated Mexicans. They come here overtly, illegally, and proudly break our laws when they want to, all the while demanding rights they have not fought for or earned. They do not care that American vets who have fought in wars to protect this nation are living on the streets of every major city in this country.

My grandfather fought in WWII. I'm a Vietnam vet, and our own government and politicians have turned their backs on us. They don't care that American families who have fallen on hard times are living on the streets—families who cannot get help from their own government. Our senior citizens, who have lived and paid taxes here all their lives, have to struggle and beg for the benefits they've earned. Our young people can't even find work in the goddamn fast food industry anymore. In my day, teenagers were expected to work in fast food and other convenience type-industries. These were the first real jobs many of us had when we were in junior high and high school. Now, those places of employment are the domain of illegal Mexicans.

Our elected officials love being seen making sound bites on the evening news. Sure, they'll say our vets and young people, in general, are the future of our nation, and they'll brag about how proud they are when they're in front of the news cameras. However, ask any injured vet of any conflict how hard it is to get any politician's or government's help. Federal, state, or local, it makes no difference. We know the reality is very different after the cameras are turned off.

Our own President has failed our vets, his fighting men and women, all young people, and the country itself. Those same politicians who can't help their own people would freely open our borders to illegals and welcome them with open arms into our nation, all the while assisting them with financial aid, housing, and employment. Our country is being overrun by Mexicans, Europeans, Asians, Middle Eastern fucking terrorists, Indians,

Africans and those disgusting marijuana-smoking Caribbeans. These fucking leeches come here and put honest, hard-working Americans out of work because businesses can get away with paying these illegal fuckers pennies on the dollar.

I have witnessed firsthand American teenagers turned away from employment. This occurs in many fast food restaurants because they are filled with old Asian men, women, and Mexicans who can barely speak English, if at all. We, as Americans, need to witness firsthand the hurt on a young citizen's face when they go to seek out that first job. An illegal fucking alien turns them away. They have the audacity to tell our children "We no hire now, go way." They ridicule our children and call them horrible names in foreign languages, all because our children want to work in their own neighborhoods. You, as a parent, a citizen, an American, should be outraged by this.

Our young people are being supplanted by illegals and are being made to feel useless in their own society, and we are allowing it to happen. It is time for this bullshit to end. I am not advocating the overthrowing of our government or civil disturbances of any kind. Our plan is to take back our communities from within, one at a time. We will start with ridding our communities of the Mexican infestations. As you are all aware by now, many communities across the country have allowed illegal Mexicans to set up day labor sites where they can gather like packs of feral animals and wait for people to offer them work. It is at these sites where my plan is to be set in motion.

Read the story of how a small Virginia community took action to rid itself of unwanted illegals, and how our crusade to save America can work.

Every morning at 8:00 a.m., Jose and his friend Enoch would join other men at the neighborhood 7-11 on the corner, where they would wait for individual people or business owners who needed day laborers. It did not matter what the work was, from landscaping to painting to hauling trash, skilled or unskilled labor, as long as it paid in cash for that day's work.

Jose began to notice that each week there were fewer and fewer workers coming out to the corner. However, that was no big deal. *More work for the rest of us,* he thought. Jose did not really enjoy doing these kinds of jobs, but it was the only work he could find. He knew he did not speak English very well, and he was in the country illegally, just like Enoch.

Jose had known Enoch for over a year. Even though he liked Enoch, he did not completely trust him. Jose had hoped for a better life in America, which is why he had risked so much to come here. He needed to make money to support his girlfriend and their child the right way, he had told himself. *Day labor is better than committing crimes to pay the rent.*

Crime was how Jose paid his bills before he met Enoch. A life of crime was one Jose swore he would not start up again. He did not have many regrets for the crimes he'd committed in the past against whites. He did not like or trust any white people, but he had to work for them now to support himself, at least for the time being. He knew one day that would change.

Jose's routine was the same every day. Go to the 7-11 every morning and buy a cup of coffee for one dollar using the five bucks he carried each day. The remaining four dollars he would use to buy something for his lunch. Jose would drink his coffee and stand around for hours until someone came by, offering to put him to work. He would ignore the dirty looks people would give him and the ugly things they would say to all the men there who just wanted to work. He also watched out for the police, or the government men who would come to the location sometimes with the police to drive them away.

Today was Friday, so he thought he could deal with the routine for another day, since he took the weekends off. As he waited for a work offer to come his way, he saw his friend Enoch talking to a man in a pickup truck. The man was white, but the person in the driver's seat was black. *This might be a job,* Jose thought. *Enoch is good at hustling work for us.* Jose's heart rose and he smiled. *Usually white men in pickup trucks mean work. Sometimes a businessperson wants men for jobs that could pay up to one hundred dollars a day, and the work could last for several days.* That thought cheered him up, because if this was a good paying job, he could take his family to dinner tonight and maybe a movie.

Jose watched Enoch take something from the white man, and the truck pulled away. Jose sighed. *Maybe that was not for work. Maybe Enoch is up to something illegal again.* His momentary joy passed, and he reminded himself that he was done with committing crimes. He had promised his girlfriend: no more crimes. She had threatened to take their son and leave him if he went back to that life.

It did not matter, though, what Enoch was up to. If it was not real work, Jose was not going to get involved. He looked at his watch. It was only 9:00 a.m. Jose knew that, usually by noon, all the men here would be on jobs somewhere. *No big deal*, he thought. It was just a matter of time before he would be somewhere working.

Enoch approached Jose, all smiles. "Good news," he said.

"What news?" Jose asked.

"The guy I was just talking to, in the pickup truck, was looking for five men for some major landscaping work. The job pays two hundred dollars a day and would last for at least a week."

"Two hundred dollars a day is good money!" Jose was now excited. "When do we get started?"

"He wants us to be ready for pickup at 10:00 a.m." Enoch explained. "I have to pick up three more men to go with us and explain the kind of work we'll be doing. Then I have to call the man who hired us at the number he gave me." Enoch held up a phone to show Jose.

"That's what he gave you, a cell phone?"

"Yeah, I'm gonna be, like, the foreman for this crew."

They both laughed.

"Come on bro," Enoch told his friend. "Let's go find three more guys and get paid!"

They recruited three more workers, which was not very difficult considering the money they would be paid, and Enoch called the man they would be working for to pick up the crew he had gathered.

Jose had one very important question. "Will anyone be checking our legal status on this job?"

The other workers gathered around to hear the answer.

"No one cares where we are from," Enoch told them. "All they want is a few days of landscaping labor. Water and food will be provided each day, and we get paid in cash at the end of each workday."

That brought smiles to the faces of all the men, since they were all in the country illegally. Their legal status aside, they still needed to work to support themselves and their families.

Enoch made the call, and their new employer was at their 7-11 location promptly at 10:00 a.m. He arrived at the site in a white van, the five men got in the back, and they drove off for the work site.

Inside the van, the passenger, William, told the men that they would be performing various landscaping duties. He spoke to Enoch, who translated in Spanish for those who did not speak English very well. "Some of the work you guys will be doing," William explained, "will include planting, lawn work, hauling away debris, digging drainage trenches, and building a retaining wall."

Each man smiled, acknowledging that he understood.

William also told them that water and food would be provided at the work site, at no cost to them. After the work was explained to the men, William asked if anyone had any questions. The men, still smiling, all looked at each other and shook their heads.

All except Jose, who asked a question. "Mr. William, where is the site and when would we get off each day?"

"The work site is an hour away, off Interstate 15. Today's work will be completed by 4:30 p.m. Since it's Friday, we're gonna pay you after work, cut you guys loose a little early. On Monday morning, we'll start at the same time and work till 5:00 p.m."

William exchanged a knowing look with the driver as they continued to the work site. Thirty minutes into the drive, William offered each man a bottle of Gatorade from the cooler he had up front. Each man took a bottle, including William.

"Drink up, men," William said. "We're gonna need our strength. It's gonna be a hot one today."

Twenty minutes later, everyone in the back of the van was sound asleep. William looked into the back of the van and saw all the men knocked out. He then proceeded to check the men, shaking each one to ensure they were all asleep. "Scott," he said, "they're all knocked out."

"Good," Scott replied. "Now, William, tie their asses up good and tight with the flex cuffs and put the hoods over their heads."

William smiled. "I'm on it."

As he tied the men up, William removed all the contents of their pants and jacket pockets and placed the items in a canvas sack. He went through each man's wallet. He took any money he found and discarded everything else into the sack. Any jewelry the men were wearing was also removed and placed in a separate small metal box.

"William," Scott asked, "you find anything interesting?"

"No, Scott. Just the usual shit A few dollars on each guy and they all wore a crucifix of some kind. Scott, how much longer till we get to the site?"

"About another fifteen minutes."

"Good. I have other shit to do this evening, after I dump their crap." William's voice was tinged with anger.

"Don't worry, my friend," Scott assured him. "We'll both be done before rush hour."

They pulled off the highway and continued into the woods for another few miles, until they reached their destination. There was nothing around for miles in any direction. They had chosen the perfect location for the dumpsite. The van came to a stop in a heavily wooded area surrounded by tall trees and thick brush. Scott pulled the van alongside the three other vehicles that were waiting at the location. He and William greeted the other men who were waiting for them. They greeted each other, and Scott started giving orders.

"Let's get on with it," Scott shouted, "and then get the hell outta here. Is the perimeter secure?"

"Yeah, it's clear for two miles," a man named Harold responded. "John and Frank left a few minutes ago to post as look-outs."

Scott nodded. "All right then! Let's get our guests of honor outta the van."

William, Scott, and Harold went to the van, pulled the unconscious men out, and carried them a few yards down to a clearing. They lay the captive men in a straight line next to a large pit.

Scott and Harold each lit a cigarette. William went to another large truck and maneuvered it down to the clearing so that the trailer was positioned several feet away from the pit. William exited the vehicle and watched the two men smoking. "Those stinking things are gonna kill both your old asses one day."

"Hell," Scott replied, "we all gotta go someday. Might as well enjoy some things while you can."

All three men laughed.

Harold looked over to the bound and hooded men. "Hey, fellas, our boys are starting to wake up. William, start the motor."

"Ok," William said. "Scott, give me a hand with this damn thing."

Scott and William sat the captive men up and placed them back to back in a circle in front of the pit. The men started to curse and demanded that they be set free. They were quickly silenced at the sound of shotguns being racked and the feel of gun barrels against their heads.

"Now that we have your undivided attention," Harold announced, "I want you illegal fuckers to know something. We don't want you here. We don't need you here. We're tired of you motherfuckers destroying what it's taken us Americans years to build. Now it's time for the Mexican invasion of our country to come to an end. For you four anyway, the invasion comes to a dead stop. There will be thousands joining you in the months to come. Until you fuckers realize we don't want you here, this is the kind of shit we have to resort to. For years, your people have flooded our cities and taken our jobs. No damn more. A new day for America is coming." He pointed to Scott. "Scott, remove their hoods. It doesn't matter now if they see us."

Scott did as ordered, and each captive man looked around to see the faces of their captors.

"We tried to be civil with you fuckers," Harold said, "but you wouldn't listen and you wouldn't stay away. If I thought that letting you go with a promise to never come back to our town would work, then we wouldn't be here. But that's been tried, and it failed. Because you people always come back, like roaches, and the best way to get rid of roaches is to exterminate them."

Jose listened to Harold as he spoke, looking at him through tears of blind terror. Bound as they were, he knew what was coming for his group. They were going to die here. They all shouted protests and pleaded for their lives to be spared. The captive men spoke in both Spanish and English and tried desperately to free themselves. It would do them no good.

Harold told William to get things ready, as he continued to speak. Harold looked at the condemned men with disgust in his eyes. "You see, that's part of the problem. I can't understand a damn thing you're saying to me. You see, I don't speak Spanish. None of us do. And we sure as Hell ain't gonna learn that shit. I know you fuckers understand every word I'm sayin'.

"You see, every man here has been a victim of one crime or another committed against him by one of you. Maybe it was not your crime, but it was one of your people. It doesn't really matter now, but at the time, it was hard for us to understand what was happening. For years, the crime rates were low here, never anything major. Then, in the early eighties, when you people came swarming in, everything changed. Now we have to deal with gangs, home invasions, armed robberies, drug trafficking, and our children being afraid to go to school because of you fuckers.

"So, we got together and came up with a solution to our problem. Since you people won't go away, we've decided to get rid of you ourselves, permanently. You're too spread out to get you all at once. Once you people are entrenched in a community, it's hard to get you out. So, we decided that before you have the chance to send for all your relatives and friends to join you in our community, we'd make it easy for the men to gather in one place to get work. Since you stupid fuckers are afraid of the police, if any or all of you turned up missing, you wouldn't report it because you shouldn't be here in the first place.

"I'll let you in on a little secret. The police chief, members of the town council, and people in the mayor's office are with us too. So, you people have good reason to be afraid of the police and everyone else here in authority." Harold started to laugh, and the other men joined him as they looked down on the horrified captives. The men trembled and continued crying.

Scott spoke next. "The beauty of the whole plan, though, is that just as you destroy our communities from the inside, we solve our problem the same way. Come here, Enoch. We bring in one of your own to join us, our inside man."

Jose could not believe his eyes. His heart pounded in his chest, and tears of anger and betrayal poured down his face. It was as if someone had torn out his still beating heart, as he realized the person he had called his friend was a part of this horror. He begged Enoch to let him go. He pleaded for his life. Jose tried to remind his supposed friend of the son and girlfriend waiting for him at home.

Enoch knelt down in front of Jose and laughed in his face. "There ain't shit I can do. You all gotta die, bro. You see, this is how I make my money. Don't worry about Rosa. I will personally take care of her. Yeah, man. I plan to fuck her every night." Enoch tapped Jose's foot and walked away, still laughing.

"Enoch," Harold called out. "Come on. Let's get this shit going."

The four men walked over to the trailer and removed a large canvas tarp from the machine it covered. William and Harold tied gags around the men's mouths. Like the other captured men, Jose tried to resist, but he could do nothing. Horrified, he realized what was about to happen. His pleas joined those of the others, as they begged in muffled voices that could not be heard beyond the woods. Like them, he cried like a baby. His eyes bulged from their sockets and his terror intensified as Harold started the machine. The roar of the motor increased his horror tenfold.

"William, do you smell something?" Harold asked.

"Yeah, man. They're shitting themselves." William laughed out loud. "It happens every time."

Jose watched as Enoch and Scott positioned the chute of the large machine over a hole that was four feet wide and eight feet deep. The canvas tarp covering the hole was removed, and Jose knew he was staring at his grave.

Scott told the others to bring the first man to the machine. "Let's get started."

Enoch switched the big, heavy-duty grinder to full power, increasing the roar of the engine. Scott and William lifted a very large piece of wood and fed it into the large, spinning metal teeth of the machine. It was gone in seconds.

"Ok, we're ready," said Scott.

Jose watched in horror as the first man was selected. The bound man chosen for death first could do nothing. He tried to resist with all his strength, with all his will to survive. He was helpless, as two of his captors violently snatched him to his feet. They lifted him off the ground and carried him to the big grinding machine. He cried, kicking and screaming in a muffled voice as his head drew closer and closer to the giant spinning metal teeth of the machine. The terror on his face and in his eyes was unimaginable. He realized he was seconds away from meeting a horrible death.

Scott chided the victim. "Don't worry. You won't feel a thing." The man was thrown into the chipper headfirst. The machine made quick work of his flesh-and-bone body. Jose, despite his abject horror, could not pull his eyes away as the man's body was pulled into the grinding teeth of the machine. Tied and helpless like the other men, and forced to face the front of the machine, he watched as the body thrashing horribly, like a giant puppet whose strings had been cut. When the legs of the corpse stopped moving, the captors used long two-by-fours to push them into the hungry teeth of the machine. They were gone in seconds.

What came out of the chute at the other end of the machine was a thick red liquid soup of muscle, flesh, bone, and shredded clothes. The sound the crushed body made as it came out the other end of the machine was akin to water sputtering through a garden hose. What was once a human body was now pooled at the bottom of an eight-foot deep hole. The mass of flesh covered the bottom of the pit.

Jose watched again, as in went the next man, his screams of horror muffled by his gag as he pleaded for his life.

Harold spoke to the condemned man as he was carried to his impending death. "Look here boy, we're not cruel. That's why we put you in headfirst. If we wanted you to suffer, you'd go in feet first. Besides, you fuckers brought this on yourselves. Maybe your next life will be better—if you believe in that type of shit."

Jose shuddered, as again his captors threw the man forcefully into the machine headfirst. The captors laughed as the body was consumed in seconds and spat out of the chute into the grave. The unadulterated horror numbed Jose to the fact that he would soon be next.

William and Enoch came for the third man, who was so traumatized by what he had seen that he had passed out from shock.

"Passing out is not going to save your Mexican ass," Enoch shouted, as he snatched the man to his feet. They forced the man to stand, and shit and piss slid down both his pant legs.

"Damn" Enoch cursed, "this motherfucker shitted on himself." Enoch let the man's tied body fall to the ground, and the man did not move.

William looked at the condemned captive closely. He bent down to check the pulse at the neck. "Scott," he called out. "It appears we've lost our first one to a heart attack I guess." He laughed.

"Damn, that is a first," Scott said, joining in the laughter. He looked at the now-dead Mexican. "Ok, throw his stinkin' ass in. What the fuck, he's already dead."

Jose watched horrified as the third body was sucked into the machine. The sound of the body being destroyed left him trembling uncontrollably.

He was next.

Enoch and William approached him. "You're up next to go, bro," Enoch announced.

Jose again tried to beg for his life, all the while looking deeply into Enoch's eyes for some sign of compassion, but the gag stifled his words. He tried to struggle but his efforts proved futile. Tears streamed down his face and piss flowed down his legs as he realized what was about to happen. His muffled screams became louder as they brought him closer to the death machine.

Enoch further tormented Jose as they approached the machine. Speaking to him in Spanish, he told Jose how much he was going to enjoy fucking Rosa, making her suck his dick with their small child watching. He told Jose he was going to make Rosa his bitch, and she was going to love it. This drove Jose into a mad frenzy. He tried to shake loose of their grip by pulling and kicking, trying to break free, but it was no use.

All the while Enoch taunted him and laughed. "Scott, can we do him legs first?" he asked. "I want to hear him scream."

"Enoch, you are one sick dude," William responded. He turned toward Scott, after Enoch made that statement. "We are not evil men. We don't do this for the joy of killing or making people suffer. There is a purpose in what we do here, and I won't have you turn this into some kind of sick game for your enjoyment. Hell no! He's not going in feet first. Put him in head first like the others," Scott ordered.

Jose's cries became louder and louder. Just as he had heard from the other men, he now knew their terror, their horror, their sorrow. He was lifted off his feet and tilted toward the spinning metal teeth. He could hear Enoch laughing and the countdown as he was swung back and forth.

"One!" Jose thought of his baby son. He would never see him grow into a man and he was sorry for that. He asked for his son's forgiveness.

"Two!" He saw Rosa one last time in his mind's eye. How beautiful she was. He remembered her gentleness, and how her smile always comforted him and how warm her body felt. Now, he cried because he felt sorrow for the life she must live without him. Jose felt regret for bringing her to this country. It had been a chance to try to start a new life.

"Three!" In his mind, he said goodbye to everyone he had ever loved. He knew it was time to die. He faced death headfirst, and for a fraction of a second, he felt the indescribable pain of the top of his skull being crushed, the flesh being torn from his face, and then nothing.

Enoch used the two-by-four to feed Jose's lifeless body into the machine, forcefully thrusting the wood into the now lifeless corpse as it was consumed and spat out into the pit.

"Ok, boys that'll do it for today," Scott announced. "Let's get this shit cleaned up, and get the fuck outta here."

Enoch fed all the two-by-fours they had used into the machine, as well as several large branches. The dust from the wood mixed with the blood in the flesh-filled pit. The pit was now over half filled with the liquefied remains of the dead men. Enoch laughed as he continued to feed wood into the machine.

Scott backed up the big F-150 truck that was carrying a fifty-gallon drum of cleaning solution that Enoch would use to clean and wash the blood and pieces of flesh off the machine. William, Harold, and Scott talked and smoked cigarettes as they watched Enoch clean the equipment.

Scott brought out three shovels after they had packed up all the other tools and the cleaning equipment. He also radioed for John and Frank to come in. The last task to be performed for the day was to fill in the pit with dirt. The men started to shovel dirt into the pit, as John and Frank walked up.

Enoch asked Harold how long it would take to get back to town. "Rosa's pussy is waiting for me, and I can't wait to fuck that bitch." Laughing, Enoch continued to shovel dirt into the pit.

"Well, you know, Enoch," Harold replied. "I don't think you're gonna make it back to town." Harold looked at Frank.

Enoch heard the shotgun blast and then felt the excruciating pain. He fell to the ground screaming, holding what was left of his left leg and crying because it was blown off below the knee. Through his screams and gasps for air, he looked at the men standing over him. "I'm one of you! Why did you do this to me?"

"You see, Enoch," Harold replied, "you have to understand something. First off, you were never one of us. Second, fuckers like you are the reason we want all you illegal bastards out of our country. The sheriff gave us your name and the list of crimes you've committed. After a little persuasion on my part, I convinced him to let us deal with you. We've been watching you and your boy Jose for weeks now. All we had to do was offer you a few dollars, and the thought of you having his woman turned you into a fuckin' animal. Look what you did. You turned on him quicker than shit through a goose. How the fuck could you think you'd ever be one of us? You're not an American, you motherfucker. You're barely fuckin' human. We hate everything you're about, and soon all real Americans will join us in ridding our country of your kind."

Crying and holding his leg, Enoch knew it was his turn to die. He was terrified.

"Do we let his ass bleed to death first," William asked, "or do we finish him off now?"

"I'm tired of hearing him scream," Harold replied. "Gag his ass, and throw him in the pit with his friends."

John twirled a towel and stuffed it into Enoch's mouth, while William secured it with a flex cuff. Screaming and crying, Enoch tried to plead for them not to kill him. The thought of being buried alive in human remains and in agony almost drove him insane.

"Bye, Enoch," John said. "Your agony shouldn't last too long. Drowned in human blood and buried alive is a quick death."

They kicked him into the pit.

Enoch could not stand, and he found himself submerged and drowning in human remains. The gag did not stop the pit's contents from flowing into his mouth and nose. The pain of his lost leg was unbearable but soon forgotten, when the stench and the taste of the nearly liquefied bodies entered his nose and mouth. He tried to spit the ooze out, but the more he gagged, the more of the liquefied bodies he sucked in. Then the dirt started to rain down on him and darkness soon followed. He cried tears of blood, as the dirt mixed with the liquefied bodies of the dead. The mixture turned into a quicksand-like substance.

Enoch soon died and sank to the bottom of the pit. He died experiencing what no human should know in life: what it really meant to go to Hell.

When you're confronted by something so evil it literally rips your heart out, what do you have to lose? Do you fight back?

SANCTIONED BY EVIL

Donna was running late. It was 10 a.m. and she had a million things to do today. She did not want to get backed up. *I have to stop by the cleaners before I go to the mall. I need to pick up Michael's suits, before he has a fit.*

Michael constantly reminded her of the fact that she did not have to work. She only had the baby to take care of, so there was no excuse for her not getting more done during the day. Michael also never let her forget he had to work his ass off to support the family.

Donna got so tired of hearing how she did nothing except lie around the house all day getting fat while he had to bust his ass at work. *As if taking care of his fucking house is not work.* When Donna thought about these things, it made her so mad she could barely think straight. *It was his fucking idea for me to quit my job, and for us to move to Hicksville, North-fucking Carolina after the baby was born.*

Donna found herself getting angry and absorbed in her thoughts as she drove to the cleaners. She recalled a conversation she had with her mother a few months before the baby had been born.

Mom told me it might be a good idea for me to support his plans. Yeah, it sounded good at the time. 'You can spend quality time with Heather' she had said, and why? Michael got a new fucking job as a partner in a real estate development firm. The job pays really well, so for the first few years of the baby's life, Mommy can take care of her. Donna realized now that it had sounded better than it turned out. *The real reason Michael wanted to make this clean start was that he wouldn't hear of anyone else watching his kid. Not our kid, his kid. Not even my mother, who volunteered to babysit if I returned to work.*

These thoughts upset Donna and she knew she had to calm down. Her thoughts returned to driving and all she had to get done today. Coming up on the cleaners, she wondered how the hell Michael had ever found this place. *There are three or four dry cleaners in the immediate area where we live that are closer. This damn place is out in the goddamn boonies.*

She pulled into the parking lot, put the car in park, and looked at the dashboard clock. It showed 10:35 a.m. *I'll be ok time-wise.*

She turned to look at little Heather in the rear of the car. The baby was strapped into her car seat and she flashed that big toothless baby smile when her mother touched her little hand and called out her name.

"Mommy will be right back, sweetie."

Donna took the clothes that needed cleaning from the front and back seats and went inside, leaving the baby in the car. Ten minutes later, she was back in the car. She hung up Michael's suits on the front hook above the front passenger's seat and headed home.

As she drove, she could not help but think of all the shit she had been through in the last nine months since Heather had been born. *Michael has changed,* she thought. *He seems so distant, and it's almost as if he blames me for getting pregnant. I admit, at twenty-four, I hadn't planned on having a kid. During the pregnancy, though, he was so supportive, and I thought he was happy with the situation. Right out of college, we were both looking forward to starting our careers. I know a paralegal's salary isn't the best, but I could have alleviated some of the pressure on him. But, no. Mister-fucking-macho had decided he'd take care of us so I could stay home with the baby.*

Thinking about all this gave Donna a headache. She decided to concentrate on driving and finishing her errands for the day. She would drop Michael's suits home and then hit the mall. Afterward, she and the baby would go back home, they would rest for a while, and then they would go grocery shopping. *All the shit I do, and he says I don't get enough done.*

Donna pulled into her driveway at 11:15 a.m., grabbed Michael's suits, and went around to the rear passenger door to get the baby. She opened the door and a panic she had never experienced took hold of her entire body. Heather was gone.

Donna wanted to pass out, but she knew she could not. Her baby had been taken from her. She took out her cell phone and called the police.

Next, she called Michael to try to explain to him what had happened to their baby. She was frightened out of her mind and had no idea how to explain this to her husband. *How the hell do you tell a father that his baby girl has been taken when she was with her mother*? Donna's heart pounded in her chest as she waited for him to answer the phone.

"Hello, Michael speaking."

"Michael you need to come home now!" The panic in her voice was unmistakable.

"What's the problem, Donna? I'm busy as hell."

Crying and hysterical, Donna tried to explain what she thought happened to their baby.

"Someone took Heather out of the car while I was at the dry cleaners. I was only in the shop for a few minutes. I didn't notice Heather was gone until I got home. I assumed Heather was in her car seat sleeping. I didn't notice the baby was gone until I got home. Michael, I'm so sorry. Please hurry and come home."

Michael could not believe what he had just heard. He experienced both anger and fear, mixed with horror at the thought of his child being kidnapped. This had to be some twisted joke Donna was playing on him. He kept thinking this could not be happening.

"I'll be right home," he said into the phone. "Have you called the police?"

"Yes, as soon as I got out of the car."

Donna stood outside, crying and looking at the now empty car seat as if staring at it would bring her baby back home. She kept playing and replaying events in her mind. *I was only in the cleaners for a few minutes.* She thought she had kept a close eye on the car the whole time while in the cleaners. *I let someone take my baby. Oh, God! How could this have happened*?

Donna felt so bad she wanted to die. Only one thought crossed her mind now. *Where is my baby, my precious nine-month-old little girl*? Donna leaned against the car and cried uncontrollably.

The police pulled up fifteen minutes after her call. Two officers approached her; she was still outside crying when they arrived. The officers identified themselves and explained to Donna that they had received the call about a missing baby. Donna tried her best to explain through tears what had happened. One officer took notes while his partner relayed the information via radio. The officers then tried their best to calm her down.

Once inside the house, Donna tried to compose herself. She knew she needed to have a calm mind to explain this all again to Michael when he got home.

A short time later Michael pulled up to the house. He saw two police cruisers in his driveway. His heart was pounding in his chest; he did not know what to think. All he could do was think about his baby girl. He parked his car and ran for the house. Before he could get there, an officer who was doing something to his wife's car stopped him and asked that he identify himself. Michael explained that he was the father of the missing baby and was allowed to go in the house.

Todd called his buddy Kyle on his cellphone with some major news. "Kyle, dude, you won't believe what I just found."

"What are you talking about? You sound excited."

"I have something you won't believe."

"Come on, Todd. Don't be a dick. Tell me what it is."

"Look, dude. Just bring all your gear and meet me at our regular spot."

"Why now, Todd? I have shit to do before my ole man gets home. Can't whatever this is wait till later?"

"Fuck your ole man, dude. I'm telling you: we are going to have a blast when you see what I got. Meet me at the spot in thirty minutes, and you can see for yourself."

"All right, Todd. This better be worth it, and since we have to do this now, you better have some weed when I get there."

"Don't worry. I'll bring the smoke. Just remember to bring all your shit and extra cartridges."

"Ok, Todd, I'll see you in thirty minutes."

Thirty minutes later, Todd saw his friend Kyle walking through the woods carrying his gear.

"All right, Todd," Kyle said. "What's so goddamned important that you drug my ass up here for? Whatever it is, I have to be home before my ole man gets off of work."

"Dude, fuck him. I'll tell you what. When we're done, I'll help you with your goddamn chores. He'll never know you left the house."

"Ok, that's a deal. Now, what's so important?"

"Remember how we always say we wish we had something other than birds and dogs to shoot at? Something exciting? Something different that wouldn't die on us right away?" Todd's excitement was palpable.

"Yeah, and I still do," Kyle said. "The shit we use has gotten too fuckin' boring."

"Well, buddy, I got us a target that can't fly, run, or tell on us." Todd pointed to a box on a tree stump. "Look in there."

Kyle walked to the box and looked inside. He could not believe what he saw. "Man, you're a fuckin' genius! A baby girl! Where did you get it? This is the coolest idea you've ever had. This should last for hours, and you're right. No one will ever know."

The boys looked at each other and laughed. They unpacked their gear, smoked a joint, and loaded their weapons.

What happened for the next few hours was beyond anything any sane person could ever possibly imagine. The boys undressed the baby, put tape over her mouth, and sat the child in a plastic milk crate. They tied both of her small hands to opposite sides of the crate. That was done to ensure that the baby would stand and could not sit for long. When sitting down, the baby's head barely came over the edge of the crate.

The boys then hoisted the crate about twelve feet off the ground, securing it between two trees. They un-bagged their gas powered pellet rifles and took out hundreds of rounds of ammunition. They smoked another joint and then loaded their weapons.

To start the atrocity that would follow, Todd smiled as he spoke to Kyle. "Watch me take that stupid smile off her little fat face with my first shot."

They began shooting the baby from opposite angles with the stinging pellets. Todd enjoyed the look on the child's face—horrific and indescribable as the first of the stinging pellets hit her tender little body. She started to cry uncontrollably, but the tape around her mouth effectively silenced her cries. He laughed uncontrollably as the baby looked around as if she was trying to find her protectors, but she could not see them. Her little body jerked horribly from the pain inflicted upon it.

Welts and open wounds appeared all over her tender skin, as the stinging pellets made contact with her fragile body. Todd chuckled. The helpless baby could do nothing but shed tears and bleed. The baby's little body shook and contorted in a vain attempt to avoid the pain. Todd watched and laughed at her as the burning pain rained down on her. She tried to sit to avoid the pain, but every time more stinging and burning shots rained down on her.

Her little eyes soon filled with blood, as her skin was slowly ripped from her head and face by the multiple hits of pellets. Todd wanted to prolong the baby's torture for as long as they could. "Let's each take one shot at a time—one firing then the other," he suggested to Kyle.

They stopped every so often to smoke, re-load, piss, or do the drugs Todd had brought with him. After two hours of torture, Todd noticed, with disappointment, that the baby had stopped moving. Her blood now dripped to the ground between the openings in the bottom of the crate. After a few minutes, no more blood could be seen dripping to the ground.

"She must be dead," Todd announced. "We better make sure. Let's each take one shot at her eyes." They each fired, but the baby did not move.

The torture of the child, in combination with the drugs they had smoked, left Todd feeling euphoric. He high-fived Kyle and they both swore that from here on out, this was the only kind of target they would ever use. They began planning how they would find and kidnap another baby. Their drug-induced minds produced multiple horrors at the thought of torturing more innocent lives. Before leaving, they both pissed in the small puddle of the baby's blood that now covered the ground beneath her. The two boys bagged and slung their rifles and left the baby there hanging between the trees. They left the baby as a dead monument to cruelty beyond belief.

Shortly after Michael arrived at home, the sheriff and a detective arrived. Michael felt reassured by the sheriff's presence and the way in which the man coordinated the work of his men.

He found Donna, her eyes bloodshot from crying, barely able to contain herself, awash with tears and guilt for what she had allowed to happen. Michael, too, tried to contain himself as the officers questioned them both.

The sheriff dispatched men to return to the cleaners to see what could be learned at that location, and to canvas the immediate area. Fingerprints were taken from Donna's car, and the detective gathered all the information he would need to start his investigation. The sheriff spoke with his detective one last time, and then all the officers departed the home. The sheriff once again told Michael and Donna that the police would do everything in their power to locate baby Heather.

Michael sat on the couch holding his crying wife after the officers left his home. Anger simmered into rage as Michael considered what had happened and what might be happening to his daughter. He wanted to blame Donna. His daughter had been with Donna. Donna should have been more careful. However, just as quickly, it dawned on him that Donna would never knowingly allow anything to happen to their child. At that moment, feeling her trembling in his arms, he wanted—no he needed to comfort her, to let her know that everything would work out. He also realized how much he truly loved her. This abduction had devastated his wife. His only thoughts were to assure her that he did not blame her for what had happened.

He whispered softly in her ear, "Everything will be ok." He tried to hold back his own tears, but he could not.

Two days had passed since the child went missing, and Detective Sam Harrison had no new leads. The prints taken from the car had yielded no new clues. The police had visited the dry cleaners and talked to all the merchants in the area. No one had seen anything out of the ordinary on the day in question. Evidence collected at the scene and from Donna's car was still being processed, but so far, it had turned up nothing.

On the third day of the investigation, Harrison got his break. A call came into the police station about 1: 30 p.m. Saturday afternoon. A very frantic-sounding man, a Mr. Evans, stated that his son and his friends had found something in the woods that seemed suspicious. The son had led him to a location about half a mile from his home in a heavily wooded area. As soon as the man had arrived there, he knew something was wrong. He had rushed home to call the police.

Detective Harrison took a ride to the Evans address and met with the man. He asked Mr. Evans to take him to the location in the woods he had mentioned on the phone.

Arriving at the scene, the detective cautiously approached what appeared to be a crate of some kind tied between two small trees. Upon closer inspection of the area beneath the crate, he saw what appeared to be bloodstains. He immediately instructed Mr. Evans to return to his home exactly the way they had come. He also requested that Mr. Evans call Harrison's office immediately, and inform them that he was on scene at the location. Detective Harrison got on his cell and waited several seconds to pick up a signal. He called dispatch, and asked to speak to the sheriff and to request crime scene support.

"Sheriff White here. What have you got, Detective?"

"Sir, I think you need to see this for yourself. That call that came in a few hours ago about something found in the woods by kids? Well, I think I just found the missing Carrington baby. We're gonna need crime scene techs and homicide investigators out here."

"I'll make the notifications. You secure that scene."

"Yes, sir."

Less than thirty minutes later, the first uniformed officers arrived on scene, soon followed by the sheriff and several crime scene technicians. A one-hundred-foot cordon was established around the area where the crate was discovered.

The crime scene was methodically processed and photographed; dozens of evidence markers were placed throughout the cordoned off area and photographed. A short time later, Harrison greeted Homicide Detectives Graham and Lee, who arrived to take notes and direct the crime scene techs.

Four hours into the investigation, the homicide detectives were ready to lower the crate, having collected all the evidence they could on the ground. From the vantage point of the ground, all Harrison could see in the crate was a bloody pulp. It appeared only remotely human, except for the little arms tied to the sides of the crate. As the crate was lowered to the ground, what he saw broke his heart

The Carrington baby's body was naked and insects had clearly been dining on the child's flesh. The baby's body was swollen and encapsulated in dried blood. Much of the child's skin looked like it had been stripped away, bit by bit. There also appeared to be literally dozens of small metal objects imbedded in the baby's flesh. The investigators discovered dozens, possibly hundreds, of rounds of small metal pellets littering the area around the scene. Those same pellets were embedded in the plastic crate. It was not hard for the investigators to piece together what had happened here, but it was truly horrifying to believe someone could do this to a helpless baby. Every officer present shared the same look of horror on his or her face that Harrison knew was on his. He watched as every officer on the scene fought to hold back the tears that threatened to flow after witnessing the aftermath of the atrocity that was committed against this child. Harrison knew these people and their level of professionalism. He also knew that everyone had a breaking point, and this was especially hard because some of these officers had children. He walked a short distance away from the scene after viewing what remained of the child's body and lit a cigarette. Sheriff White joined him.

"Sheriff," Harrison said, "I've been a cop and a detective for twenty-five years. I've seen shit that would make most men blow their fucking brains out or send them over the edge, but I've never seen anything like this. The word monster doesn't begin to describe the kind of mind it would take to even conceive of doing shit like this to a helpless baby."

"I know exactly how you feel, Sam," the sheriff replied. "Like you, I've been in this business a lot of years and I thought I'd seen it all. Rapes, murders, gang violence, domestic assaults, but this level of evil has me fucked up too. So we can both imagine what the effect of seeing something like this is gonna do to the young officers here."

"Yeah, it'll make them question if this is really what they want to do with the rest of their lives." He looked at the sheriff. "Sheriff, how the fuck do we tell the Carrington's that we found their baby girl in this condition?"

The homicide investigators walked up. They had overheard Harrison's question. "This kind of shit is never easy, detective, especially when it's a young child, and more so when it's a baby," said Detective Lee.

"To answer your question, Sam," the sheriff replied, "we'll find out together. You'll be with me when I tell parents."

"Yes sir, sheriff."

"What's the preliminary, Lee?" Sheriff White asked.

"From what we can gather, sir, at least two people stood at distances of between seven and fifteen yards and fired pellets at the baby in the crate.

"We can tell, by what we found on the ground and the number of strikes on the crate, that a large number of pellets were fired. We've collected cigarette butts, discarded pellet cartridges, and several sets of footprints at the immediate scene. We also discovered marijuana roaches and residue on some of the CO_2 cartridges and on empty cigarette packs left at the scene. The thing is, sir, I think we have all we need to catch these animals if they haven't fled the area. It's almost as if they didn't care about covering their tracks. They left the baby in that crate and just walked away when they were done, as if they didn't care."

"They may have been too high on drugs to care," the sheriff commented. "If that's the case, then you may be right and that may give us what we need to capture these sick fucks." The sheriff's words were calm but Harrison could feel his anger.

"In my opinion, sheriff," Detective Lee said, "anybody who could do this needs to be slaughtered." The look in the sheriff's eyes told Harrison that the sheriff concurred with that assessment.

"Hopefully the evidence collected here will lead us right to these sick fuckers before they can hurt someone else," Harrison said.

"We're pretty much done here, sheriff," said Detective Graham.

"Ok, then let's wrap it up," the sheriff said. "Let's get the victim to the medical examiner's office. Detective Harrison, I want you to talk to Mr. Evan's son again. He may remember something that could help us. Boys like playing in the woods, so his son or his friends may have seen something helpful."

"Yes, sir, sheriff. I'll get right on it first thing Monday."

The investigators prepared to wrap things up on the scene. Two of the officers who were assisting volunteered to place little Heather's body in a small black body bag and carry her to the waiting medical examiner's vehicle. Harrison watched silently as the two young officers, being as gentle as they could, lifted the baby out of the crate and placed her lifeless body in the little black bag. Each officer knelt beside the body, heads bowed down, as tears flowed down their faces. They said a silent prayer for the child before they carried her away. Now, it was Harrison's turn to hold back tears.

Sheriff White and Detective Harrison pulled up to the Carrington's home at 8:00 p.m. Saturday evening. They both wore very somber expressions. The sheriff had worked out what he would say to the couple. He knew that there was absolutely no way to break this kind of news to anyone gently. Experience had shown him that the best way to tell someone their loved one had died or been killed was to come straight out and tell them the truth. There was no need to provide many unnecessary details that would just make an already bad situation worse. He wished he knew a better way in this case.

He knocked on the door. Mr. Carrington answered.

The sight of the sheriff and the detective sent Michael's heart to the pit of his stomach. In a daze, he invited the two officers in and offered them seats; He explained that Donna was asleep and that her mother was with her.

The sheriff looked Michael in the eyes. "What I have to tell you, Mr. Carrington, is not good news."

Michael put his face in his hands, dreading what the sheriff was about to say.

"Mr. Carrington," the sheriff said softly, "it breaks my heart to tell you that we found your daughter's body in the woods about five miles from the cleaners. We received a call from a man who lives about half a mile from where your daughter was found. His son and his friends found something that didn't look right and they called it in to us. Now, I know this is hard for you to hear, Mr. Carrington. I wanted to be the one to tell you what we found, and that we have good leads to follow and we're gonna catch those responsible."

Looking at the sheriff, all Michael could do was sit paralyzed and listen as the sheriff gave him news no parent ever wanted to hear—that his baby was dead. He tried to be strong as he absorbed the news, and he could tell that this was just as hard on the officers. He could see it in their eyes, and he could also tell that they were not telling him everything.

"Can I see my baby girl?" he asked, in tears.

The sheriff explained that her body was at the medical examiner's office and that his office would arrange for Michael to identify her body tomorrow if he was up to it. Michael insisted that he would be.

As the officers left, the sheriff said he would send a car to pick Michael up tomorrow. Michael closed the door and sank to his knees, sobbing. Now he had to tell Donna.

The sheriff told Harrison that he would have a talk with the medical examiner before the Carrington's got there. He was not sure just how much the doctor would tell them concerning the death of their baby, since it was so horrible. Nevertheless, they did have a right to know. He simply did not want the family traumatized any further. However, the sheriff was not sure if there was anything he could do to prevent it.

The next day, a police car arrived at the Carrington's home to escort Michael, Donna, and her mother to the medical examiner's office. The officer assigned to take them there was Officer Ryan Tucker. He had been on the force for two years, and he was one of the officers at the scene when the child's body was found. In fact, he and another officer had carried the child's body to the medical examiner's vehicle.

Tucker had been instructed by the sheriff to say absolutely nothing about the investigation to the family. "Escort them to the medical examiner's office, and return them home," had been his orders.

Officer Tucker had strong personal feelings about the case, and he was having nightmares after having witnessed what had been done to the baby. Officer Tucker did not want to arrest those who were responsible. He wanted to murder them. He knew that was wrong, but he could not help the way he felt.

After a silent ride, the cruiser pulled up to the county coroner's building. The Carringtons got out and went inside, where a receptionist guided them to the medical examiner's office. Dr. Wilson did not keep them waiting. He introduced himself, and he informed the Carringtons that it was not necessary for them to see the child. Due to the nature of her injuries, Dr. Wilson had already identified her body using her birth records. He'd had the records emailed to his office.

"Her injuries? What do you mean: her injuries?" Donna asked.

"Yes, Mrs. Carrington," Dr. Wilson replied. "I understand how upsetting this must be for all of you, which is why you need only verify your signatures on her original birth certificate."

The couple verified their signatures beneath the baby's footprints. Donna touched the card and began crying uncontrollably. Dr. Wilson told them to take their time and that someone would contact them regarding when they could pick up their daughter's body. The doctor left the room.

Michael left Donna in the office with her mother and went to catch up with Dr. Wilson. He explained that he had to see his daughter one last time, and that he could not live with himself if he did not. No matter what was done to her, he had to see his baby one last time.

The doctor agreed, but he warned Michael that it would be extremely hard on him and that he should seek counseling afterward. Michael agreed, and Dr. Wilson escorted him to where his daughter's body was kept. Michael followed the doctor into the room, trembling. The doctor opened a door on a refrigeration unit and pulled out the metal table on which his baby lay.

Michael convulsed as the sheet covering her little body was pulled back. "Oh, god! What happened to my baby?"

His legs were so weak he almost fell to the floor. The doctor had to help steady him. He stood there, barely able to control himself. The damaged remains of his baby girl sent images flashing across his mind of what she must have endured—the unbearable pain she must have suffered. Tears flowed freely down his face.

He leaned down to her body. "Baby girl, I am so sorry that I was not there to protect you," he sobbed. Over and over that thought repeated in his mind.

On the ride home, no one spoke. Michael rode in the front seat of the cruiser, while Donna's mother held her daughter in the back seat. All Michael could think about was his little baby girl, and that he would never see her alive again. He would not be able to watch her grow and experience all the things a father should with his daughter. All this because she had been stolen from them and brutally murdered. Michael was numb with grief and felt that there was nothing he could do. *Nothing except wait for the police to bring those fucking psychos to justice before they killed someone else's child.*

Officer Tucker pulled up to the Carrington's home and said goodbye to the three as they got out of his cruiser. Donna's mother led Donna to the house, while Michael thanked the officer for bringing them home.

As Michael walked away, Officer Tucker called him back. "Mr. Carrington, sir, I just want to let you know how sorry I am for your loss and if there is anything I can do to help you, I will. I want you to know, sir, that the whole force wants the animals that did this dead. I could lose my job for saying this, but I'd rather turn those fuckers over to you than arrest them."

Before he could comprehend his thoughts, Michael responded, "I'd love for that to happen."

He thanked the officer again and went inside his home.

Three days went by and there was no further word on the investigation. The Carringtons made plans to bury Heather on the last Saturday of the month, which was four days away. Michael and Donna were not speaking much—their loss was still too painful. Michael had long since stopped blaming Donna for what had happened to Heather, but Donna was still destroying herself over it. Michael honestly did not know how to help her. He was just thankful her mother was there to help him care for her.

Michael sat in his study brooding. *Why the hell would God allow something like this to happen to my baby—or to any child? She was only nine months old! What could she, an innocent baby, have possibly done to deserve such a horrible death?* Those thoughts gave Michael no comfort at all. He felt in his heart that there was no fucking God and what had happened to his daughter proved it. The more he thought about it, the angrier he became. *What kind of fucking God would allow a baby to be tortured to death?*

He could no longer cry. He had cried all the tears he would ever cry. The only thing left in him now was hate for the monsters who had killed his baby. Hate for the parents who would bring such abominations into the world. Hate for himself because he could not protect his daughter from them. Michael did not want to sleep, and he did not want to talk to anybody—not friends, not family. He only wanted to punish those who had killed his child, and he thought to himself that he could do that, if only he knew who they were. He could call the sheriff's office to see if there was any news, but he knew they would only go so far with what they would tell him. They damn sure would not give him any information that would lead him to his child's murderers.

Michael decided that he had to get out of the house, go for a walk; these thoughts were driving him mad. He had no outlet for his rage, and he felt helpless. He felt there was nothing he could do about the situation but wait. He let his mother-in-law know that he was going for a walk and that she could reach him on his cell phone. As he prepared to leave the house, he felt numb to everything and everyone.

He was on indefinite paid leave from work, but he no longer cared about his job. Michael was angry. His anger was so great that all he wanted was to lash out at someone. Anyone would do. The look in his eyes was one of defiance. He was a man not to be fucked with tonight.

His wife had not spoken in days; her doctor had prescribed powerful sedatives for her so she could sleep through the night without waking and crying. *Get out of the house and go for a walk before you explode,* he thought. He had no destination in mind; he just wanted to walk until he fell off the face of the planet. *If I can't avenge my daughter, then maybe I can join my baby in death.* Even that thought gave him no comfort. He wanted to crucify those responsible for her murder.

Twenty minutes into his walk, Michael's cell phone rang. It was Officer Tucker.

"Mr. Carrington," Officer Tucker said, "your mother-in-law told me I could reach you at this number. I hope I'm not disturbing you, sir."

"No, I'm just taking a walk. I need to clear my head. What can I do for you?"

"Mr. Carrington, can we meet someplace tonight that would be convenient for you? I need to speak with you."

"Sure, what's this about?"

"Sir, I have information that I think you'd find interesting. It's really important we meet."

"All right. I'll meet you at a bar on the corner of Seventh and Jay Street. The bar is named The Spot. I'll be there at 9:00 p.m."

"I'm familiar with the place. I'll be there at nine."

When Michael arrived at the bar, he saw the officer dressed in civilian clothes and sitting at the main bar. He walked over and sat next to him.

"Hello, Mr. Carrington. Can I buy you a beer?" Officer Tucker asked.

"Sure, and call me Michael."

"Ok, and I'm Ryan."

"So, Ryan, what is it you want to talk to me about?"

"Michael, let's take our drinks to a booth, and we can talk there in private."

In a very low voice, Ryan told Michael why he needed to see him. "Michael, have you talked to anyone at the sheriff's office lately?"

"No, not for a couple of days. Why, what's this all about?"

"Good. I want you to hear what I have to say before you do talk to the sheriff. I was at the scene when your daughter's body was found. I've been assigned to one of the detectives working the case. We have a solid lead on one of the people responsible for your daughter's death. One of the young kids that found your daughter's body told one of the detectives that they sometimes see older boys shooting guns not far from his home. Sometimes, these older boys would let them fire their guns as well. The younger boys we spoke with gave us the older boys' names.

"One of the boys responsible for your daughter's death is named Todd, and we found out that Todd and his buddy Kyle were seen coming out of the woods on the day your daughter was killed. We were also able to get a match on a right thumbprint taken from your wife's car that matches Todd's. That puts him at the scene when your daughter went missing. Once we got that hit, we had the fucker. I was able to read the case file, and I ran the fucker's name through the system. Todd Byrd, age sixteen.

"He's been in trouble with the law and at school from a very young age. He was kicked out of school last year for smoking, drugs, and bringing loaded weapons into the building. He's been charged with seventeen counts of cruelty to animals for shooting neighbors' pets with pellet guns and has two assault charges against female classmates. This kid is all-around bad news."

Michael was stunned to learn that a sixteen-year-old punk could be responsible for what had been done to his daughter. He relived the memory of seeing her little body riddled with scars, the flesh torn away from her body and her missing eyes. Even in his mind, he could not continue with the memory. Seeing his baby that way, on that metal table, and knowing what had been done to her took all the strength Michael could muster to contain the rage that was building inside him.

Now, the more the officer told him, the stronger his rage grew. Michael's mind became so focused that he knew, without any doubt whatsoever, that no matter what happened from here on, he had to be the one to kill the piece of shit that had killed his baby.

Ryan continued talking, but Michael barely heard a word he said. His thoughts were focused now on avenging his daughter. Ryan also told Michael that Todd had a best friend, according to their information, and that he too had been in a great deal of trouble. That focused Michael's attention back to what Ryan was saying. Ryan told Michael that the other boy, Kyle Long, was going to be picked up the next morning for questioning on his way to school. After he was questioned, the police were going to pick up Todd.

"We need Kyle to tell us everything he knows about what happened in those woods on the day your daughter was killed. The thing is: if he cooperates, who knows what the District Attorney may do. That little bastard may come away with a deal if he rats Todd out."

The thought of either of them getting off lightly for what they had done made Michael sick to his stomach. He wanted to throw up, but he kept his composure. Michael was not going to let that happen. *It was Todd's fingerprint on my wife's car. So it was that motherfucker who took my baby. He's the one I want. The police can have the other one, but Todd is going to die by my hand.*

"Ryan, why are you telling me this?" Michael asked. "You have to know what's going through my mind." He made no attempt to hide the intense hatred in his eyes.

Ryan looked him in the eyes and answered the question in a low, but very passionate, voice. "Because I saw your daughter after they killed her. I saw how she was killed. They murdered her, and my heart shattered. At that moment, I felt like she was mine. I wasn't just talking the other day when I told you that, if I could, I'd turn the animals responsible for this over to you. It's within my power, and I'm asking you: What do you want me to do?"

It did not take Michael long to decide. He told Ryan he wanted Todd—that he would make him pay for Heather's death.

Ryan gave Michael a computer printout of Todd's address, which also had a picture of the boy. Michael studied it, and his loathing grew stronger. Now he thought he could and would exact retribution for his baby daughter's death. In that instant, he knew exactly how he would do it.

"Won't it look odd to the police when this little fucker up and vanishes during the investigation?" Michael asked.

"It's not unusual for criminal suspects to disappear once they know they're under investigation," Ryan responded. "Especially when the charge is first degree murder. We can make sure he finds out he's a suspect. He'll be expected to run, or at the very least get with his buddy Kyle to compare stories. When he does, we'll be waiting for him."

During the next couple of hours, Michael and Ryan outlined a plan that included luring Todd into a trap they would set for him. The first step would be for Michael to take a letter to the Byrd home, addressed to Todd Byrd Jr. The letter would state that someone knew he and his friend had killed a baby a few days ago. If he wanted to save himself, he needed to meet the writer of the letter at a particular location at a specified time. There, they would discuss what needed to be done for Todd to save himself. The letter also would warn him not to call anyone, especially the police, nor attempt to leave town, because from the moment he got the letter, he was being watched.

The two conspirators continued their talk for another hour, each man assuring the other that what they discussed on this night would stay between them. They discussed how they would each take steps to insure that nothing they were going to do could be traced back to either of them.

Ryan offered Michael a ride home, but Michael told him he would be fine walking. He had a lot to thinking to do.

Ryan said he would call Michael the next day concerning their plans. The two men shook hands and parted.

As Michael walked home, he experienced a curious sensation. Knowing what he was planning to do to his daughter's murderer, he first thought he should feel some guilt. *The deliberate planning of another person's death is a sin.* However, just as that thought came to him, another thought occurred to him. It came to him with perfect clarity. *Isn't killing your child's murderer justified in the eyes of man? Fuck God.*

His every thought was focused; his body felt strong again. He was filled with a renewed sense of purpose, as if a veil had been lifted from his eyes. He promised his daughter he would mercilessly make her killer pay.

Michael returned home at midnight. Everyone was asleep as he made his way to his study. He sat at his desk and wrote a very simple letter that would set his plan in motion. He wrote:

I know what you did to that baby in the woods a few days ago. If you want me to keep quiet and save your ass, meet me at the old baseball field at the corner of Sixth & Elm today. Come alone.

Michael sealed the letter in an envelope, addressed it to Todd Byrd Jr., and put it in his jacket pocket. Shortly, he would drive to that animal's house and put it in his mailbox, but first he would check on his wife.

Michael went to their bedroom and noticed the lights were on. Donna was sleeping; he walked to her side and touched her face. *She looks so beautiful when she sleeps.* He sat on the bed next to her, and spoke softly. "Baby I can't change what happened. I wish I could, but I will make it right for Heather. Rest well, baby."

Michael got off the bed and turned out the lights. He left his house to deliver the letter. After the deed was done, he sent Ryan a text message.

The next morning Michael woke up next to his wife who was still asleep. He did not want to disturb her, so he quietly got out of bed, went into the bathroom, got dressed, and went downstairs. His mother-in-law was in the kitchen fixing breakfast.

"Mom, I'm gonna be gone most of the day and I probably won't be back until late. Mom, I appreciate all your help."

"Do what you need to, baby. I'll take care of things here. Don't you worry about a thing."

Good, she will take care of things here, and I'm gonna go take care of avenging my baby.

Michael left the house.

Officer Tucker was sitting in his personal vehicle on the street about twenty-five yards away, watching the mailbox in front of the Byrd residence. The house was at least fifty yards away from the mailbox at the end of the driveway, so keeping an eye on it discreetly was not a problem. He had called in sick today, so that he and Michael could carry out their plan. He knew that after he did this, he was resigning from the force and heading west. He wanted nothing more to do with being a police officer. Before he left the force, he wanted to do his part to make sure that at least this one monster would never walk the streets again.

He waited patiently for someone to come to the mailbox. He had been watching the house for hours and no one came out. The letter was there; he checked before he started watching the house. He knew the boy was inside asleep, because he called the house pretending to be a friend. *You sleep now you little fucker. After today, you'll be put to sleep permanently.*

Twenty minutes later, Ryan saw his target walking down the long dirt driveway. He started his car and waited for him to check the mailbox. The boy walked past the mailbox without looking inside. Ryan cursed to himself and called Michael, but he did not pick up. The boy rounded the corner, and Ryan pulled up to the mailbox and removed the letter from the box. Ryan stayed at a discreet distance from his target as he followed him down the street.

Michael returned his call. Ryan let Michael know that there would be a slight change of plan. "Michael, that little fucker left the house without checking the mailbox. I'll follow him until I come to a location where I can stop him on the street, and arrest his little ass. Michael, are you ready on your end?"

"I will be by the time you get that little fucker here."

Donna woke up to find that she had slept through the morning and that Michael had already left. Her mother told her that Michael would be back sometime tonight, but if they needed him to call his cell. Donna ate the meal her mother had prepared for her, but she found she could not enjoy the food or anything else. She also found that she was glad Michael was not home now. She did not want to face him, and she did not want to discuss the burial plans for Heather. Donna had asked that her mother and Michael deal with that. It was too much for her to deal with now.

Donna got out of the shower and found she had no energy to do much of anything. She did not want to be anywhere, except with her baby. She found herself staring at Heather's crib and wondering where her baby was. She honestly did not know where Heather was. For a split second, she started to panic, until the memory of her circumstances came rushing back to her—as if a great force had thrown her to the ground and rattled her whole body. *Heather is dead.* Donna remembered. *My baby is dead.* The thought repeated many times in her mind. Donna wanted to cry, but she couldn't. She found she could not feel anything, and she did not know why that was the case.

Looking at her baby's empty crib made her realize something that she hadn't before. Donna went over to the crib, picked up one of the blankets lying inside, and brought it to her face. She could detect the scent of her baby on the blanket, like only a mother could. She closed her eyes and enjoyed the sensation. When she opened her eyes, she was happy. *My baby is just asleep, not dead. That's all. And soon momma will be asleep too.*

Donna went downstairs to thank her mother for the meal and told her that she was going to lie back down because she did not feel too well. Her mother told Donna to get all the rest she needed.

"Momma will take care of everything, baby." She gave her daughter a hug.

Donna thanked her mother and went upstairs. She picked up the bottle of sleeping pills the doctor had prescribed for her. She read the warning label that stated death or coma could occur if more than one tablet was taken within a twelve-hour period. Donna poured the contents of the bottle into her hand and counted twenty-two of the small pills. She put them all into her mouth and swallowed them with water. She took her baby's blanket and held it up to her face as she lay down on her bed.

Mommy will take care of everything. That's right, baby. Mommy will be with you soon, baby. I love you, Heather.

Donna closed her eyes for the final time.

Ryan had followed the boy for almost a half mile, until he realized where that little bastard was headed. The cleaners where Michael's baby was abducted was less than a hundred yards away. That thought infuriated Ryan. He sped up the truck to get ahead of the boy and pulled over about ten yards ahead. Ryan got out of his vehicle with his badge in one hand and his service weapon in the other. He identified himself as a police officer.

The boy was so frightened he could not move. Ryan could almost see his heart pounding as he walked toward him with his weapon pointed at the boy's face. He ordered the boy to put his hands on top of his head and walk toward the vehicle. Ryan got behind him and pushed him forward.

"If you move or talk, I'll blow your fucking brains all over the street," he warned.

Frightened out of his mind, the boy did what he was told.

Ryan put his weapon in the front of his pants and ordered his captive to put both hands behind his back and not to say a word. Ryan cuffed him and patted him down for weapons. Moving quickly, Ryan pulled the boy to the rear passenger door of the SUV, shoved him inside, and climbed in behind him.

Before the boy could fully understand what was happening or ask a question, Ryan punched him in the face with everything he had. The blow knocked the boy out cold. Ryan quickly tied a gag around the boy's mouth and put a black hood over his head. He pulled the strings around the opening and tied them tight; he then used flex cuffs to bind his feet together.

Ryan looked at his bound captive and spoke aloud. "How's it feel, you sick little fuck? How's it feel to be trapped like an animal? Today, you die for what you did."

Ryan called Michael to let him know he had the boy and he would bring him to the agreed-upon location.

"Bring him to the old Miller Farm on Clay Street," Michael instructed. "It's an old abandoned property 30 miles outside of town. Pull up behind the main house, and you'll see my vehicle. I'll be ready by the time you arrive."

Michael sat in the barn waiting. *I'll never see my baby again; my wife may never be the same again. My family has been destroyed, all because some punk kidnapped and killed my child.*

Michael cared about nothing else, except making the person responsible for his baby's death to pay in blood. He knew it would not be quick. He would show Todd the same mercy Todd had shown Heather. He would make his daughter's killer feel every excruciating moment of the pain he was going to inflict upon him.

I'm going to enjoy every second of Todd's suffering. That thought gave him a great deal of pleasure.

Forty minutes later, Michael heard a car pulling up outside. He came out of the barn to meet Ryan.

Ryan stepped out of the SUV and went to the passenger side door as Michael walked up. "I got the little fucker, and he's all yours." Ryan also gave Michael the letter that he'd placed in the mailbox. Ryan pulled the boy's bound and gagged body out of his vehicle and let him fall to the ground. "Do you need any help moving him?" Ryan asked.

"No," Michael said. "This is as far as I want you to go. I'll take it from here."

Michael thanked Ryan, shook his hand, and dragged the boy into the barn. The gag muffled his screams of protest.

Ryan got into his vehicle and left the area.

Michael dragged his captive to the spot in the barn where the boy's punishment would take place. He was pleased that the boy was clearly in mortal terror. The kid clearly had no idea what was happening to him or why. He smiled at the skin burns that were emerging from the friction of being dragged across the ground.

Michael used a cable that he had prepared to bind the boy's legs together at the ankles. He then threw the loose end of the cable over one of the low-hanging support beams in the barn and pulled with some effort until the boy's body was lifted three feet off the ground. So that his body could not swing, Michael used bolt cutters to cut away the cuffs that bound his hands. He tied each of the hands to hooks in the floor using nylon straps.

Michael ripped off the boy's shirt and used scissors to cut away his jeans and underwear. Then Michael removed the hood that was covering his head; Michael saw that the boy was gagged and crying. The look of sheer panic on his face was priceless. He put a chair in front of the boy and sat down; he wanted to enjoy the look of horror on his face. He wanted to enjoy every tear that fell from his eyes, but he also wanted to see if he, Michael, would feel any sorrow or compassion for the person he was about to torture to death. His answer to himself was, *Hell, no.*

The boy was indeed crying, hung up by his feet with his arms stretched out and tied to hooks. He tried to plead for his life through the gag, his eyes wide with hysteria. He wanted to know what was going on, and why was this man doing this to him.

Sitting in his chair, Michael asked the boy a question he knew the kid could not answer. "How does it feel, you piece of shit? How does it feel to be tied up and helpless, as helpless as a baby, knowing that your useless life is about to end?"

The boy's head was pointing to the floor, hung over a deep hole in the ground. His only response to Michael's question was muffled words and tears of blind terror.

"I see you've noticed the hole below you," Michael said. "When I'm done, that's gonna be your grave. It's an abandoned well. You fuckers left my baby hanging in a goddamn tree. I guarantee you: no one will find your ass here."

Michael stood and moved behind the hanging boy. "How the hell do you torture an innocent, helpless baby, you sorry piece of shit?" he shouted. "My baby!"

He shouted again as he picked up a four-foot piece of steel rebar off a table and slammed the metal rod across the boy's back. The boy tried to scream with all his might but the gag stifled any sound he made. Michael hit him several more times across his back with the steel rod. After the fourth strike, the boy's back opened and blood splattered with every blow thereafter.

As Michael struck the boy with the rebar, he saw in his mind's eye his baby being shot with pellets and crying for her daddy, wondering where her daddy was. He saw the wounds inflicted on her, and it drove him wild, now that he had the monster responsible for her death in front of him.

The boy continued to scream. *The pain in his back must be impossibly worse,* Michael thought, with satisfaction. The boy lost control of his bladder and pissed himself as Michael continued hitting him with the metal rod. Michael hit him several times across his ass, with the same result. After the fifth strike, large welts across his ass began to swell, and his skin split open like an over ripe melon.

The boy tried to move, but he only succeeded in causing his muscles to cramp severely, causing more pain. Michael walked around to see the look in his eyes, to see the pain on his face. Even through the gag, Michael could tell he was crying to the top of his stifled voice. Michael wanted him to scream louder, and before he was done, he would make his captive do just that.

Breathing heavily, Michael sat in the chair to catch his breath. The boy's blood and other body fluids dripped into the well. The boy was in so much pain that all he could do was scream. His eyes focused on Michael when he spoke, but Michael could tell his words were beyond comprehension now. He felt no guilt or compassion for the thing hanging in front of him.

He was indifferent to the pain he was inflicting on the boy's body. He only thought about his Heather; the baby he would never see again. The thing in front of him had taken her away from him.

Michael lit a cigarette; he had recently started smoking again after having quit for three years. He just wanted to sit for a while as he smoked and look into the eyes of his baby's killer. Michael wanted the boy to know that death was coming. Before his captive left this world, he wanted him to know what real pain felt like.

Michael got up to get the baseball bat that was on his table of torture. From his inverted point of view, all the boy would see would be Michael's legs and waist through his tears. Michael waved the bat in front of the boy's head and smiled broadly when the boy's eyes grew larger still, as he realized a beating with the bat was next. The boy's cries grew louder.

Michael put the bat on the chair and walked over to pick up a two-gallon bucket filled with water and salt. The mixture was so thick with salt it had the consistency of syrup. Michael picked up the bucket and poured its contents onto the boy's bleeding and swollen ass and back.

The boy reacted as if a thousand volts of electricity had shot through his body. His whole body spasmed as the salt made contact with the open wounds on his back. The liquid slowly mixed with his blood and oozed down his back, filling every cut.

The boy twisted and pulled involuntarily against his restraints in a desperate attempt to flee his torturer, but he could go nowhere. Michael picked up the bat, stood in front of the boy, and swung the bat at his face. The bat hit the boy square in the mouth. Blood splattered everywhere. The sickening sound of his jaw shattering on impact was pleasing to Michael. Michael now used scissors to cut away the gag. The boy could not fully open his mouth due to his shattered jaw, but blood, teeth, and vomit now came pouring out of his mouth with every attempt to scream.

"I'm not gonna let you pass out on me," Michael said reassuringly. "Don't worry about that. You're gonna feel pain ten times worse than the pain you inflicted on my baby."

Michael lit another cigarette and watched as the boy bled into the well. The boy's face quickly swelled to monstrous proportions, his bodily fluids pouring from his body. With his cigarette in his mouth, Michael swung the bat and made contact with the boy's stomach. The impact was a loud slapping sound. The boy's stomach contents released, along with a great deal of blood, into the well below. After the third strike to his stomach, his skin started to redden horribly and split open. Michael next used the bat to break the boy's hips. To be sure the bones were shattered, he hit them three times on both sides, swinging the bat with all his might. The more the boy screamed, the more pleasure Michael got from beating him.

"I'm almost done using the bat," he informed the boy. "This part will be over shortly."

Michael swung the bat at the boy's exposed penis. His dick and balls swelled grotesquely. The boy by now had stopped screaming, the pain was so intense. Michael walked over to the table, picked up a pouch, and sat back in the chair to finish another cigarette.

He truly enjoyed watching his baby's killer hanging upside down and bleeding. The boy was barely breathing. *I wonder how much longer this piece of shit is gonna last? I don't give a fuck. I'm gonna carry this thing out exactly as I had planned.*

Ryan left the police headquarters, thinking about his new beginning. *Now I can start over. Being a cop really wasn't for me, even though, at times, it was rewarding in many ways to be of help to others. I did feel satisfaction when I helped to put criminals away for the crimes they'd committed against innocent people. Nevertheless, after having seen what was done to the Carrington baby, I know that I no longer want any part of being a cop.*

That experience had had a profound effect on Ryan. It had changed him and it had changed how he viewed people and the world. He had known—at the moment he had seen her dead body—that being a cop had lost all appeal for him.

Ryan knew that it was no longer a matter of protecting people. After seeing the dead baby, all he had wanted was to punish the criminals himself. That was no role for a police officer. Helping the father of that child take revenge for her murder gave him the satisfaction of knowing that even though he was no longer a cop, he could live a good life, knowing that—at least in this one case—the murderer had gotten exactly what he deserved.

Ryan felt he could resign from the force and head west to pursue a career that would make him happy. Maybe he would finally apply his Communications degree, something that did not require him having to confront the ugly things people did to each other on a daily basis.

I can live with the role I played in helping Michael, he thought, *because Todd deserves whatever Michael does to him.* He just hoped that this would bring some kind of closure to Michael's life and that afterward he and his wife could move forward.

Ryan had closed out his affairs at the station, turned in all his equipment, and signed all the required paperwork. He gave a forwarding address and was ready to leave this chapter of his life behind him. *I'll head out in the morning and I won't look back. I have a new life to start.*

Michael looked at his captive hanging above the well. His body was covered in blood; he was bleeding from every orifice of his body. It gave Michael extreme pleasure to know that his baby's killer was soon going to die, and that he was the one that was sending him to Hell. Michael unzipped the pouch he had gotten off the table and pulled out a pistol.

"Look at what I have!" he screamed at the hanging boy.

Michael wasn't sure what the boy could see through his swollen eyes while hanging upside down, or whether his pain would let him focus on anything. He didn't care.

He shouted at his semi-conscious captive again. "You know all about these pellet guns, don't you, you sick piece of shit. Isn't this what you and your friend used to kill my baby? You had fun shooting at her with a fucking pellet gun, just like this one. Well, before you die, motherfucker, you're gonna feel her pain."

Michael flicked the cigarette he was smoking at the boy's face. It made a hissing sound as the lit tobacco made contact with his blood and fell into the well. Michael did not need to take aim. He was only six feet away and he began shooting. He was surprised at the smacking sound the pellets made as they hit the body and splattered in the blood. Michael fired the first full cartridge at the boy's chest. The boy's body flinched involuntarily as each pellet made contact with his swollen flesh.

Michael shouted at him again. "How did that feel, for someone to do to you what you did to a helpless baby?"

Again, the bound boy said nothing. Michael reloaded the gun, and this time he fired the whole cartridge at the boy's swollen penis. Every hit made his penis jerk from the impact. The shooting went on for what seemed like hours, but Michael could see that the impact of each projectile still elicited agony. The moans of pain were loud and should have been terrifying to listen to, but they were like music to Michael. The pellets split the boy's penis and testicles open and blood ran down his body in torrents with every beat of his heart.

Michael knelt down in front of the boy, lit another cigarette, and tried to figure out if he was still alive or not. He watched the blood flow down his chest and into the well, but he had stopped moaning a few minutes ago. Michael thought back to his baby girl on that metal table; he remembered what her eyes looked like—as if someone had scooped them out. Now he knew why that was.

A rage grew in him he did not want to contain. He took two steps back from the boy, pointed, and fired the gun at the boy's left eye. The pellet made an almost splashing sound as it tore into his eye, and even through his shattered jaw, his screams filled the barn. Michael fired ten shots at each eye. The boy screamed and his body jerked, until he was physically unable to move any longer. He hung there dead, with blood and other fluids flowing out of his eye sockets into the well.

Michael sat down, lit another cigarette, and stared at his baby's murderer. He was satisfied with what he had done. To Michael, the scales of justice were balanced. Heather's murderer was killed, just as she had been killed—slowly and painfully. Her killer had suffered her same fate. Michael had made sure his victim felt every agony-filled second of it, just as his helpless child had. *This piece of shit would never harm anyone's child again.*

In his heart, he knew he'd done the right thing. He'd done what any father would have done, if given the opportunity. He was content now. *Rest in peace, Baby. Daddy made things right.*

Michael's cell phone rang. He did not answer it, even though it could be Donna or her mother calling. He did not want to be distracted, because he still had to dump the body and get the place cleaned up. He threw the gun, bat, and rebar down the well. Next, he threw down the drop cloths that he had placed around the opening below the body.

His cell rang again. He decided he better answer it.

It was Sheriff White calling.

Michael's heart almost leapt from his chest. He turned away from the dead body and froze while the sheriff spoke.

"Mr. Carrington," the sheriff said. "We have both your child's murderers in custody."

Michael turned to face the dead body in front of him and froze in place.

The sheriff continued. "We had planned to pick up one of our main suspects on his way to school this morning. His name is Kyle Long. We wanted to hear what he would tell us before we picked up his buddy. We got another huge break in the case early this morning, when we got a call from Tony Byrd, the brother of Todd Byrd. He called to let us know he was coming to the station this morning to tell us all he knows about his brother murdering your child."

Michael's heart began to pound in his chest.

"Tony Byrd called the station late last night to tell us that his brother came in high last night. He overheard a phone conversation: his brother was bragging to someone about having killed a baby girl in the woods a few days ago. Tony, it seems, is the exact opposite of his brother. We had no idea Todd had a twin brother, and he doesn't visit often. Tony doesn't live with Todd and their father. He knew his brother kept a diary of sorts and he knew where it was. When his brother went to sleep, he got it out, and everything he'd done was written in it. We were waiting for Tony to come into the station this morning, but he never showed."

Michael lost all sense of time and space. *What have I done?*

The sheriff continued. "We picked up Kyle as planned, and less than an hour later, he gave us everything we needed. Soon after we had his confession, it didn't take long before he turned on Todd. We picked up Todd at his house, passed out on drugs. We searched his house and found his guns and everything else we need to nail his ass. We owe thanks to his brother Tony. I have men out now trying to find him."

Michael lost all the strength in his body, as his phone fell to the ground and shattered. He dropped to his knees. He looked at the broken and mutilated body hanging in front of him. Trembling, he found the strength to utter only a few words. They came as whispers at first and then got progressively louder.

"Oh God, oh God, oh God, what have I done? DEAR GOD IN HEAVEN, WHAT HAVE I DONE?!"

Michael stayed where he fell, begging for forgiveness. There was no one there to grant it.

Some physicians practice to save their patients.
Others though, who have seen real evil
practice to save us from their patients.

CONSUMED BY EVIL

The doctor is in session with his first patient of the day: *Airline pilot Henry Kiernan 10:00 a.m.*

"Before we begin," the doctor said, "there's something you need to know about how I practice. I don't know who sent you to me, and frankly, I don't give a damn. My style of practice is about getting right to whatever's fucking with you. So, please don't come in my office bullshitin' and wasting my time. My calendar is full. I want the truth, and I need you to be brutally honest with me. I won't hold back on you or mince my words. My goal is to get to the heart of the matter as quickly as possible, because I don't have all day to sit here bullshitin' with you unbalanced motherfuckers.

"Many people can't handle my style of practice; so, if at any time you feel uncomfortable during the session, you can get your shit and leave. I was paid the minute you walked through my door.

"There are, however, a few rules we need to go over. One: I ask the questions, you give me straight answers. Two: I smoke during my sessions. Feel free to join me. If you're a non-smoker, I don't want to hear your complaints. Three: If, during the session, you need a drink, go for it. You're grown. The cabinet's over there, so knock yourself out. However, you are not allowed to get fucked up. Four: If you leave before our session is completed, that's on you. As I stated earlier, I get paid whether your problem is resolved or not. Five: If you feel like you're losing control and you think you might want to attack me, don't. I won't hesitate to fuck you up. Six: Don't come in here asking me to prescribe a damn thing for you.

I rarely write prescriptions. If, however, I deem you're in need of some shit, that's my call—not yours. Now, shall we get started, Mr. Kiernan?"

"Yes, doctor. I understand."

"What brings you to me today?"

"I've been having a lot of strange feelings lately. I can't seem to concentrate on anything at home or work. I find I don't enjoy many of the activities I once did. Even my family has noticed I'm not the same, but I don't know what's going on."

"When did this shit start?"

"Maybe six months ago."

"Now, didn't I tell you not to come in here trying to bullshit me? Everybody hollers that 'six months' shit. Whatever's got you all fucked up started before six months ago. Now, go back beyond six months and tell me what happened to bring about this change in you."

"I'm an airline pilot for a major carrier. As you probably know, we're away from home quite a lot. On one particular trip a year ago, I had a layover in New York and I met this woman at the hotel bar where I was staying."

"What airline?"

"I work for North American Airlines."

"Please go on."

"We ended up having sex, and she got pregnant. Everything started from there."

"First of all, see how easy it was to pinpoint the problem when you stop bullshitin'? Secondly, you didn't 'end up' doing anything. What are you not saying to me? You meet women all the time. How did you come to fuck this particular woman?"

"When I met her, I was instantly attracted to her. She's young and very pretty. She seemed interested in me, and when she asked me what I did for a living, I told her. We talked for quite a while. Afterward, we had dinner together. After we ate, she invited me to her room."

The doctor lit a cigarette after his patient finished speaking. "You know," he said, "you didn't have to carry your ass to her room. So, you knew you wanted to fuck this woman from the minute you saw her at the bar. She gave you the opportunity, and you went for it."

"I was attracted to her, and yes, I wanted to be with her."

"Is this the first time you've fucked around on your wife?"

"No. There have been other occasions."

"Is this the first time it's bitten you in the ass?"

"When you think of it that way, doctor, I'd have to say yes."

"There is no other way to think of it. To your knowledge, has your wife ever fucked around on you?"

"No, not to my knowledge."

"How's your relationship with your wife?"

"Until my problems started, we were fine. Now, things have changed."

"Are you still fucking your wife?"

"Now, you wait just one damn minute—"

The doctor cut him off mid-sentence. "No, motherfucker, you answer my goddamn question. Are you still fucking your wife? It's a legitimate question, and you will answer me or get the fuck outta my office."

"I've been unable to," the patient responded, his anger fading.

"Why the hell do you think that is?"

"These past few months have been hard on me. You have no idea."

"Bullshit. I have more than an idea of what's going on. You know exactly why shit has been fucked up. You just want to live in denial, and I told you that's not the way I do shit. If you continue on this course, you can get the fuck out of my office. Do you understand?"

"Yes, doctor. This is just difficult for me." The shame in the patient's voice was apparent.

"If the shit were easy, you wouldn't need me. Now, tell me, what else is going on that has you all fucked up?"

"I've been diagnosed with herpes." He lowered his head after he responded.

"I don't know why the hell that shocks you. How'd you find that out?"

"A friend of mine is a doctor, and when I explained to him what I'd done, he examined me and gave me the results. I got symptoms of herpes four months after the last time I slept with her."

"That information was not in the records I reviewed prior to your session. What's this doctor's name and where does he practice?"

"His name is Anthony Dukes. He works in Washington, D.C."

"Now we're getting somewhere. Does your New York girl know she's burning?"

"Yes. She told me, after I found out about my condition, that she is a carrier."

"Did you have relations with your wife before you knew you were burned?"

"Yes, I have, but my friend told me I might not pass the disease on to her."

"Have you told your wife you're burning?"

"No, but to my knowledge, she's never had an outbreak."

"We'll come back to that." The look on the doctor's face was one of disgust. "Continue with your story, Mr. Kiernan. We have a great deal to talk about."

"After our first encounter, I told her I wanted to see her again, so we exchanged numbers and said we'd keep in contact. This was before I knew anything about the pregnancy or the herpes."

"You said to yourself: 'What the hell. I found me some young New York pussy that I can hit whenever I'm there!' Is that right? How old are you?" The doctor smiled after he asked the question.

"I'm fifty-one."

"Did it ever occur to you that she was playing your dumb ass?"

"What do you mean? And I resent being referred to in that manner."

"I don't give a fuck what you resent. I call it the way I see it. You got yourself into this shit. As to whether or not you saw her game coming, we'll get to that later. Continue with your story. Getting laid usually doesn't depress most men, especially when the woman is young and fine, so please continue."

"I didn't hear from her again until about two months after our first encounter. She asked me when I was going to be back in New York. I explained that I could get back anytime, if she wanted to see me. So we made arrangements to stay at the same hotel. That's when she told me she was pregnant."

"Did you fuck her on that occasion?"

"Yes, we had sex."

"What crap did she run down on you?"

"I don't understand what you mean, doctor."

"What the fuck did you two talk about after you were done fucking her?"

"Doctor, I'm becoming uncomfortable with the way you're talking to me. I'm not some uneducated idiot off the streets."

"Well, that's too damn bad. Did you hear a word I said to you before we started this? You came to me. I didn't ask you to come here. Now, if you stop bullshitin' and talk to me straight, we can get to why you're all fucked up. Judging from what I just heard, you aren't the smartest motherfucker walking the streets either. If you can't handle the way I conduct therapy, you don't have to stay. There's the door, goddamnit. It's your call."

"I know you're right. It's just the shame of this situation is hard on me. I need a drink."

"Go for it. Get your drink on."

The patient poured himself a glass of bourbon and continued. The doctor lit a cigarette.

"When I suggested that she get an abortion," the patient continued, "she told me that she couldn't do that. She wanted to keep the baby. This was her first child. Doctor, I have two grown children and I sure as hell didn't want another baby. She said she wouldn't interfere in my life, that she just wanted me to help her financially."

"That is part of the game she was hittin' you with. How old is this woman?"

"She's twenty-five. At least, that's what she told me."

"Why are you so sure you're the father?"

"I paid for the DNA test after the baby was born. It confirmed I was the father."

"Did your doctor friend help you with that as well?"

"Yes, and I'm grateful for his help."

"Has any of this shit got back home to your wife yet?"

"No, but it's only a matter of time before it does."

"What makes you believe that?"

"Over the last few months, this bitch has called my company trying to find me, posing as my daughter. Every time she has called, I answered her. Sometimes I couldn't call back right away, but I always returned her calls. I send her money when she needs it, and now she's making even more demands since the child was born. She's sent letters to my home, addressed to me. I wish this had never happened. The thing is: I don't know how the hell she got my address. I never gave it to her."

"How the fuck do you think? At twenty-five, she's pretty savvy and scheming. She played your dumb ass to the hilt. The internet is a motherfucker." The doctor lit another cigarette and stared at his patient. "Wishing for a thing to never have happened when you had complete control of the circumstances in which the incident occurred speaks not only to your character, but to your judgment and level of impulse control."

"I understand that, doctor, but this thing has gotten to the point that I honestly don't know what I should do. This has made me a nervous wreck. I can't tell anyone, and if she threatens my job, I don't know what I'll do. If I tell my wife what I've done, I know she's going to leave me."

"What the fuck did you think could happen when you go out and have unprotected sex with women you don't know? Obviously, you weren't thinking at all."

"I wasn't thinking about the consequences of my actions, no. I looked at her and wanted her. I even feel like I could kill her for ruining my life."

"First of all, little Miss Hot-Ass didn't ruin your life. You were thinking with your dick, and it caught up to you big time. Secondly, how could you sit here and say you could kill the mother of your baby? That tells me a bit more about where your head is. You got yourself into this predicament, so you need to take responsibility for it. That's the first step in coping with the shit you've gotten yourself into."

"You have to understand, doctor. I have a great deal to lose because of this situation."

"What would that be?"

"Every goddamned thing I've worked hard for all my life: my job, my home, and my family."

"Tell me this: why wasn't all that shit on your mind when you fucked the woman you met in New York, and all the other times you've fucked around on your wife?" The doctor typed on his desktop computer while he waited for the patient to respond.

"I always told myself that what I did in the street didn't concern my wife. What I did away from home wasn't about her. I just wanted something extra."

"No, call it what it is. You wanted some strange pussy. With your job, you could play all you wanted as long as you didn't fuck up."

"I guess something like that, I suppose."

"You said earlier that her demands had started to increase. Please explain what you mean by that."

"I send her five hundred dollars a month, and now she wants more money. She's threatened to take me to court, and she wants me to put her baby on my health insurance policy."

"Shouldn't that have been 'our baby'? After all, you did fuck her, and it took two of you to make that baby."

"I don't want that damn baby. My wife handles all the bills, because I'm gone so much. If I were to put the baby on my health insurance policy, she'd find out."

"It's a little too damn late for that now, isn't it? You could have eliminated the possibility of her getting knocked up by wearing a goddamn condom. What would you say is your net worth? I'm trying to see, from your perspective, everything it is you have to lose because you fucked up, had a baby outside your marriage, and now can't do right by your new baby."

"My home is valued at six-hundred-and-fifty-thousand dollars, cars and possessions around one-hundred-and-fifty-thousand, savings, money market, and retirement accounts, I'd say around four-hundred-and-seventy-five-thousand. Those are my combined assets with my wife."

"So, just under a million three?"

"Yes, I suppose."

"That's not a bad piece of change you're sitting on. Now, how the hell could you not have realized that every time you fucked any woman other than your wife you were ejaculating all your hard earned money into their pussies?"

His patient looked down and said nothing.

"I need an answer to my goddamn question," the doctor insisted.

"I just never thought this kind of thing would happen to me, and now my head is all messed up. I really don't know whether I'm coming or going, and the stress is killing me."

"Let me do a quick recap before we move on."

"Sure, doctor. I'm not sure if I want to hear it though. This has been terribly hard on me."

"You're a fifty-one year old airline pilot for a major carrier who fucks around on your wife and can do it with impunity due to the nature of your job. Your last encounter with a woman you met in New York produced a baby. The bitch gave you herpes, and she knew she was burning. Since you had unprotected sex with her on another occasion, prior to finding out her health status, you may subsequently have passed a very nasty disease to the woman you've been married to for over twenty years. You haven't found the balls to tell her that she may have herpes. You've also jeopardized the medical practice of your doctor friend because he didn't report your infection status to any agency that needs to have that information, as is required by law, nor has that DNA result been filed. You also said that you've had thoughts about killing the mother of your baby. In addition, you have a great fear of losing your job and all the shit you've worked hard for all your life. Did I miss anything?"

"No, that about sums it up. You don't have to make me feel worse than I already do."

"What do you have to say about the choices you've made?"

"I never intended for any of this to happen."

"Who gives a fuck about what you intended? The fact remains that this shit has happened because you allowed it to. You got played by an attractive woman who set your ass up in a major way, twice."

"How do I fix this shit, doctor? Please help me to fix this."

"You tell me: how can you make this shit right?" He smiled.

"I don't know. I'm so filled with worry that I can barely function. I'm scared, doctor. I'm really scared."

"You should be. You have to understand one thing. You have gotten away with doing whatever the fuck it is you do for so long that it's all been a big game to you, until now. Do you understand where I'm going with this?"

"I don't know what to do, doc, and I need help to fix this. Can you help me to fix this situation?"

"I can't help you fix your past fuck-ups. I can help you to see how those fuck-ups are going to affect the lives of the people you've involved in your shit, though."

"What do you mean? I need your help here. I'm in serious trouble."

"I've given you every opportunity to take responsibility for the shit you've gotten yourself into and you refuse. So, here's how this shit plays out:

"You're a fifty-one year old pilot who flies large jets around the country carrying hundreds of passengers a day. One of those passengers could be me. At this moment, your personal life is so fucked up that you can't concentrate on anything. By your own admission, you currently don't have the focus necessary to perform the duties of an airline pilot. You shouldn't be flying anyone anywhere. Your airline and your chief pilot will be informed of your current unstable condition. We don't need another 9-11 incident, and people who are unstable have been known to take out everyone around them. Now, I'm not here to judge you or how you live your life. The fact remains, though: a man of your years should be smart enough to override the impulse to fuck a strange woman unprotected. Nowhere in our conversations did you speak of using protection. They're called condoms. While they may not be one-hundred-percent effective, they offer a lot of protection when compared to your dumb ass using nothing at all. Because you weren't concerned about damaging your health or your spouse's, this is the result. You can no longer control your impulses, which makes you a dangerous person right now.

"Your health care provider will be informed of your current health condition. You got some young skank you met in New York pregnant, and make no mistake about it: she's encroaching on your life and your wallet. That scares you to death. She gave you a goddamn baby you don't want, and herpes, and you may have subsequently given that shit to your wife. You spoke of killing the mother of your baby when compared to the cost of you losing everything you've worked for. People who have something to hide know fear, and fear can make you do really dumb shit. The New York City police and the local police departments in your area will be notified about the threats you've made against the mother of your baby.

"You allowed your wife to contract the herpes virus from you, her husband—the motherfucker she's lived with for over twenty years, the man she trusted. You're so fucking worried about a baby you've never seen and losing all your shit that you haven't even told this woman what you've done to her. That makes you the lowest piece of shit on this fucking planet. Since you can't find the balls to tell her, I will make sure she is made aware of your current health status.

"Your boy, Dr. Dukes, will be in hot water as well. He violated a number of regulations to help you hide the fact that you carry herpes and you infected your wife. The DNA test he helped you acquire should have been filed with the proper agencies. You see, the courts, ethics boards, and other entities need to know certain shit we doctors do for a reason. In helping you, he violated those regulations, and I'll inform the medical review board in DC."

The patient looked at the doctor, not believing what he'd just been told. He sat in his seat, stunned into momentary silence.

"Why would you do this to me? You're supposed to help me."

"It's still all about you, right? You did this shit to yourself. This is what happens when you act impulsively and recklessly. It's not just your life you've fucked up. How about you give some thought to the baby you helped to make? This isn't just about you anymore. You've involved everyone around you, and you can do a lot more damage to others. I'm not gonna let that happen."

"What about your obligation to me? What gives you the right to disclose to others what I tell you in confidence?" The patient's anger started to show.

"You are correct that I have an obligation to you as a patient. However, I have a larger obligation to public safety, which outweighs your right to privacy. I deem you to be a menace to public safety. Therefore, I can—and I will—disclose to the proper authorities what I know about you."

"Do you know that will ruin me?"

"Quite frankly, I don't give a fuck about how your life turns out. You set all this shit in motion, not me. Now you have to face the consequences of your actions."

"I don't know what to say. I came here thinking you would help me—help me find some solutions to my problem."

"What the fuck would you have me do?"

"What about me? I've bared my soul to you and I'm desperate for help. So, to help me with my problems, your solution is to tell the world?"

"I can't make this shit any clearer. There is nothing else we need to talk about. I can't fix what you've gotten yourself into. All I can do is try to make you see that all your problems are of your own making. You need to carry your ass home and talk to your wife. Now, if there's nothing more, I have other patients to see, so please get the fuck out of my office."

Mr. Henry Kiernan left the doctor's office even more hurt and confused than when he had entered it. He went for a drive and eventually parked his car at his favorite park. He sat in his car, in a spot overlooking the city from Haynes Point Park. He thought to himself how beautiful the city looked from so high up, how peaceful things seemed from this point of view. His cell phone had been ringing for hours. He set it to vibrate and threw it on the passenger seat of his car. From the park, he could see the airport, and he watched as the airplanes landed and took off.

He knew he would probably lose his job. This meant he would never fly again, and that thought saddened him. What he most regretted was not being able to face his wife to tell her what he had done. It had been hours now since he'd left that fucking doctor's office. True to his word, the doctor must have talked to her by now. She had been calling for hours.

He pondered what he was about to do, and he realized that there were a great many things he now regretted. There was no way humanly possible to fix them now. He couldn't face what he had done. He walked back to his car, took the gun out of the glove box, said a silent prayer, and voiced good-byes to his family and friends. Placing the barrel of the gun against the roof of his mouth, he pulled the trigger.

The doctor's office manager let him know his 1:00 p.m. patient was waiting. He told her to give him fifteen minutes to review the case file and then send the patient in.

Police Officer Joseph Felton entered the doctor's office and took a seat. Before the session began, the doctor went over the ground rules.

"Now, that's out of the way," the doctor said, "what the fuck can I do for you today?"

"Is that how you really talk to all your patients, doc?"

"Is there a problem with your hearing?"

"No. I just wasn't expecting that kind of language from a therapist. Actually, I like it. I hate phony fuckin' people. I prefer to keep shit real."

"All therapists are not alike. I don't believe in wasting my time or yours. I prefer to keep things simple, and I see no reason to complicate shit with twenty-dollar words that I'd have to explain to most anyway. I'm not here to treat you like a child or to insult your intelligence. So, give me the same courtesy. Now, once again, I ask: what the fuck can I do for you?"

The patient looked at the doctor and did not know whether to laugh or get angry. "It's cool. I'm a cop. I hear this type shit on the streets every day. I can take it. My supervisors told me that, in order for me to return to work, I needed to have a psychological evaluation."

"Evaluation? Did they bother telling you why? Surely you know more than that?"

"I have a few issues I'm having a hard time dealing with."

"What the fuck are these issues you're referring to? Obviously, you're aware of why your people sent you to me. I told you before we started this that I don't have time to waste bullshitin' with you. So, tell me what the fuck is going on."

"I have goddamn anger issues all right—and certain sexual fantasies and urges I'm having a hard time controlling."

"I'll state again as simply as I can, this time in language you can understand. Can you please tell me what the fuck you've done to have your superiors on the verge of firing your ass?"

The patient's irritation with the doctor's language started to show. He raised his voice when he spoke. "Hey doc, you need to tone down your language. I'm not gonna allow you to continue to curse at me."

The doctor was working on his desktop computer when the patient spoke. When the doctor finished with the computer, he returned his attention to the patient. "Fuck you," he said. "You are not in charge here. Furthermore, motherfucker, this is my house. Let me break it down for you. First, I don't owe you shit: not respect, courtesy, or any other social nicety. Your police conduct record tells me everything I need to know about you on the job. I don't give a fuck if they fire your sorry ass today or tomorrow. It's plainly obvious to me that if we don't get to what's got you fucked up by week's end, you can kiss your law enforcement career goodbye. Have I made myself clear?"

"Yeah, doc. Crystal."

"Now, why are your people ready to fire your ass?"

"I work in the southeast section of the city. Crime in those neighborhoods is rampant. Drugs, prostitution, murder, gang violence, you name it. I deal with this shit every day, so if I sometimes get a little over-zealous when I make an arrest, then fuck it. I get those pieces of shit who commit crimes off the street."

"How many times has doing your job as you see it gotten you jammed up?"

"I've had a few complaints filed against me by the street scum I've arrested. So what? Big fuckin' deal."

"Well it obviously is a big fuckin' deal if the department wants your ass gone. How many excessive force and misconduct complaints have been filed against you? Let's deal with the excessive force complaints first."

Both men lit cigarettes as they continued their conversation.

"I've had at least thirty excessive force complaints in a sixteen-year career," Officer Felton explained.

"Thirty complaints and you don't think you have a problem? Why so many? That's almost two a year. Aren't you trained to make an arrest without beating the shit out of people?"

"What we learn in the Academy and what happens in the street are fuckin' worlds apart. Sometimes the only way to get those fuckers to talk is to kick their asses around a little."

"But you got caught over thirty times kicking the asses of those who you perceive as the bad guys."

"I have a damn good arrest record, and my work on the street has put a lot of fucked up people in jail."

"I wasn't speaking about your arrest record, but all the assault charges filed against your ass."

"You learn when you work the streets. It goes with the territory."

"According to some of the information sent to me, you were involved in an incident that sent a black male suspect to the hospital last month. What happened there?"

"We had an all-points bulletin for this drug dealing scumbag who was wanted for questioning in a homicide case. I work the midnight shift. I recognized one of his crew on the streets. So, I asked the motherfucker hard where his boy was, and if he didn't tell me, I told him he'd end up in a box. I got what I needed, and I went to go find the motherfucker."

"What happened when you found him?"

"My partner and I caught that piece of shit selling drugs to kids not two blocks from an elementary school. He saw us coming and took off. We called it in and began a foot chase."

"What happened when you caught his ass?"

"We arrested the motherfucker. What do you think we did?"

"What the fuck did you do to your suspect when you caught him that was so fucked up charges of police brutality were filed against your ass again?"

"I had to tackle him to bring him down. His goddamn head was slammed to the pavement, and he got a minor skull fracture."

"So, you had nothing to do with the broken arm and ruptured spleen? And where was your partner?"

The officer was angry when he responded. "He may have been a little bruised up. So fucking what?" he shouted. "This motherfucker is a goddamn scumbag drug dealer." He continued, even angrier now. "I'm not the one selling that shit to kids on the streets. I'm not going to apologize for shit because he got a little banged up. I may have went to his ass in the heat of battle, but fuck him. I took a murder suspect down! Who gives a shit how I did it?"

"I don't give a shit how you talk in here, goddamnit," the doctor said, "but when you get excited, it's like you're ready to pounce. I suggest you calm the fuck down. The fact that you get emotional when you talk about your issues shows me exactly the kind of out-of-control cop you are. In the pursuit and apprehension of a suspect, your fucking emotions take over and you're likely to do anything. This makes you a serious liability to your department. Now tell me: where the fuck was your partner when you beat the shit out of your suspect?"

"He was right there. He only helped me when we cuffed the motherfucker."

"Did he try to stop you from beating the suspect?"

"Yeah, after I got him down."

"Is it your job to exact retribution?"

"That's not what I do."

"What do you call kicking the shit out of suspects?"

"Fighting is a fringe benefit of the job, doc."

"Is that supposed to be fucking funny?"

"Not funny. It's reality."

"Who the fuck appointed you judge and jury? So, it's your job to catch and punish suspects? The hell with the courts? Is that the way you see things?"

"You don't see the shit I have to deal with on a daily basis," the officer said, with disgust in his voice.

"You don't have a fucking clue about what I see," the doctor replied. "I see motherfuckers like you every day. I see the result of what people like you do when you go on rampages. I see the worst in human behavior every day, so don't tell me what the fuck I have or haven't seen. Let's concentrate on your shit. What did your partner do when you got back to the station?"

"He put in a request for another partner."

"How'd that make you feel?"

"I didn't give a shit."

"Why?"

"Because I've had other partners before: some good, some pussies. I prefer to work alone, anyway."

"Is that because when you are alone you can do what the fuck you want in the street and not have another officer around to report it?"

"That has nothing to do with it. My methods are a little unorthodox, and some rookie cops can't handle it."

"Unorthodox or illegal?"

"What's your point?"

"If you can't see where I'm going with this, it's because you don't want to see the point."

"I see you accusing me of shit, just like everybody else."

"I haven't accused you of shit. I'm trying to get you to talk to me about what's going on."

"I'm trying. This shit isn't easy."

"It should be, if you've done nothing wrong. Nor should you be defensive, if you have nothing to hide. But we both know that's bullshit, don't we?" The doctor smiled and looked directly at his patient.

"Hey, I do my fucking job. There are other pussy cops on the force who would shit themselves if they worked my beat. I don't run from problems. I deal with the shit."

"And you have no problem with your methods?"

"If the shit works, I don't."

"What is the racial makeup of the area you patrol?"

"It's predominately black."

"What percentage of the suspects you arrest would you say are black?"

"Eighty percent. What the fuck has that got to do with anything?" he responded angrily.

"Are you a racist?"

"I do my goddamn job. I don't give a fuck what color scumbags are."

"You didn't answer my question. Are you a racist?"

"No. I work in a predominately black area. Of course most of my collars are gonna be black."

"According to reports sent to me by your department, which includes the arrest record you're so proud of, you could have arrested dozens of whites, but you chose not to. Mostly young white women and young white males, whom you observed coming into high crime areas to buy drugs, were let go and you busted the dealers. Why?"

"I'm after the scum who sell that shit on the streets."

"What about the motherfuckers who buy that shit on the streets? Are they in any way less guilty of perpetuating the very thing you hope to eliminate?"

"I guess you have a point, but that's not my fuckin' focus."

"Please explain that asinine statement."

"I see the dealers as the problem. Take away the supply, and buyers go away."

"Please spare me your insights into the intricacies of supply and demand. No, motherfucker. You see a bunch of useless, no-good niggers on the street selling that shit to good upstanding white citizens, and you want to punish them for it. Isn't that the case? Based on your own department's internal affairs reports for the last four years, you requested to work drug unit details in parts of the city with the highest concentrations of open-air drug activity. Was that so you could target the dealers? You've never wanted to be part of the sting unit that arrests the buyers. In fact, your record shows you've flat out refused that detail."

"That's bullshit. That's not the way it is. I choose the tough assignment because I get the job done."

"Well then, tell me something. Tell me what happened to you, Officer Badass, that turned you into a motherfucker your department now wants to get rid of."

"I don't fuckin' know."

"I told you, I don't have time to waste bullshitin' with you. Either tell me what I need to know, or get the fuck out of my office and kiss your career goodbye. It's your choice. Either way, I don't give a fuck."

The officer looked at the doctor and the disdain for him and this line of questioning was obvious. "Look. I've always been aggressive on the streets as a cop. Like you, I don't have time to be bullshitin' or wasting time playing games with scum. About four years ago, my daughter was in the ninth grade. She experimented with crack at a friend's house and it damn near killed her. She can barely function now. Her mother blamed me because, in her eyes, my job was more important than our family. That was never the case. I was a good father. Yeah, I worked long hours, but I had a family to support. She told me that if I'd been home more, then maybe that wouldn't have happened to our daughter. She blamed everything on me. We didn't last much longer after that, and we divorced less than a year later. My daughter lives with my ex, and I only see her maybe once a month."

"When you do see your daughter in her current condition, what goes through your mind?"

"All the things she loved doing have been taken away from her—all the things she could have accomplished if it weren't for that shit that poisoned her."

"In your eyes, who do you hold responsible for what happened to your daughter?"

"Who the fuck do you think? The motherfuckers who sold that shit to her and her friend."

"Think before you answer my next question. Was your daughter in any way responsible for what happened to her? After all, teens think it's a rite of passage to experiment with drugs and other shit they know could hurt them."

The officer paused briefly to consider the question. "In a small way, maybe, but she is my baby girl. She was so young when that shit took away her life. If she couldn't have gotten any of that shit, she'd be fine."

"You said she and a friend tried the drug. Was the friend that gave her that shit not partly to blame for what happened to your daughter?"

"Yeah, she provided the shit, but she was just a kid too. Look, doc. The people who sell that shit are the people I blame. Not the kids who get caught up. If it wasn't available, they couldn't use."

"Come now, Officer Felton. Do you really believe that shit?"

"Yeah, I do, and I'm gonna do whatever I have to when it comes to taking down the fuckers who sell that shit. I don't give a fuck what their goddamn color or ethnic background is. If that means killing every fucking one of them, I'll do just that. And you can write that down and send it to whomever the fuck you want."

The doctor had a slight smile on his face when he looked at his patient. "I saw that the record showed you've had a few complaints filed against you by women who work as prostitutes. What is that about?"

"That's all a bunch of bullshit. I was cleared of all that crap."

"Why don't you tell me about one of those incidents that included a woman filing charges against you? What happened?"

"Like on many typical nights, I was on patrol on my beat, and I'd sometimes see a known prostitute get in a car or van with a trick. I'd follow them till they stopped and I'd bust both of them."

"Would they be doing anything or did you just assume the woman was a prostitute and the man a trick?"

"Every time I'd walk up to the car, she'd have his dick in her mouth. Does that answer your question?"

"If it went down like that, why would you ever get a complaint filed against you?"

"Look. All those skanks lie and will do whatever they have to, to avoid getting arrested or to get the arresting officer jammed up. I see that type of shit all the time."

"Have you ever fucked a prostitute in exchange for not arresting her?"

"What?" He reacted with shock, when he heard that question.

"You heard what the fuck I said. How many of those skanks have you fucked in exchange for not hauling their asses off to jail?"

He looked at the doctor intently before responding. "I only got involved with a few in the last couple of years."

"We both know better than that. This is a major part of the reason why you're here. You've been accused of doing more than just having sex with prostitutes. What else have you been into on the streets? Tell me about the sexual urges you find hard to control."

"Look, this is something that I'm not proud of. The shit just happened and I couldn't stop." He looked away as he spoke.

"You want to tell me what you're talking about?"

"There was this one hooker who I had a few times. One night, she was giving me head in my patrol car. After she finished, she told me she could turn me on to something that would blow my mind. I asked her what it was, and she told me to come by her place the next week."

"What was it she turned you on to?"

"Her own young daughter."

"How old was the daughter?"

"Ten, I think."

"What the fuck did you do with a ten-year-old little girl?" the doctor asked, trying to control his own anger.

"When I got to the hooker's place, she took me into a room and the girl was sitting on the edge of the bed. She looked a lot older than ten. I didn't fucking know she was that young until her mother told me. Her mother led me over to her and she sat in a chair across from us to watch. The next thing I know, the girl is in my pants and she's sucking my dick."

"How long did this bullshit go on?"

"With her daughter? About once a week, for about four months. Sometimes her mother would join us."

"How did it make your grown ass feel knowing a child was performing oral sex on you?"

"Like I said, this is some shit I'm not proud of. But the two of them was the best head I ever had in my life. Before I knew what was happening, I only wanted her daughter. I couldn't control myself. It was like I was on drugs or something."

"How the fuck long did you have that child sucking your dick?"

"With her, it was less than four months, but it didn't stop with those two."

The doctor found it difficult to maintain a neutral expression on his face as he talked with the patient. "What other shit did you do out there on the streets?"

"Hey, like I said, I'm not proud of what happened, but I found that I enjoyed it and couldn't control myself."

"Had you done anything to try to control these fucked up impulses?"

"Not at first. The shit felt too good and I needed it."

"You did not need that shit from a child. If you knew what you were doing was wrong, why didn't you just walk away? Better yet, why not find a real woman to take care of your needs?"

"Because the more I did it, the more I liked being with young girls. The bitch that turned me onto that shit would line up other neighborhood girls for me, about once a week. It was addictive."

"As a goddamn police officer, what you were doing didn't bother you?"

"No."

"Why do you think that was the case?"

"I don't fucking know, and I didn't give a shit."

"Don't hand me that bullshit. You know exactly why. You saw them as throwaway people. You saw them as less than human, as objects that you could use as you saw fit. Because you're a white cop and working rough areas of the city, who's gonna know and who gives a fuck? Who would believe a junky prostitute over a white cop? How many children have you been involved with?" The doctor's anger was palpable.

"Since this started? A lot. I didn't fucking keep count."

"When was the last time you were with a child?"

"I had one a few weeks ago."

"It's that simple? You had one a few weeks ago. That child was an innocent victim. That child was a helpless human being. That child was nothing more to you than an object to satisfy your craving for sex. How is it you were able to get away with this shit for so long, without any of the children talking?"

"Look, they were paid or threatened. I don't fucking know, and I didn't ask questions. All I know is I would be told when and where to be. If I agreed, I'd be there."

"Were you ever involved with young boys?"

"Fuck no!" He looked at the doctor with disgust on his face.

"Motherfucker, don't come off on me like you're above being with little boys. If it doesn't bother you to be with ten-year-old little girls, there's no telling what you'd do. You get off on little girls sucking your dick, so why not a little boy?"

"I'm not a fuckin' faggot."

"That's what ninety-nine percent of all pedophiles claim. I wish the fuck you would sit here looking me in my eyes and say you're not a pedophile, you rotten motherfucker!" The doctor's anger was obvious.

"I've never had a boy."

"Think about what you just said. 'I've never had a boy'. Not that you're not interested, not that the thought disgusts you. 'I've never had a boy'. You haven't been offered anyone's little boy yet. You'd jump all over that, because in your sick, twisted fuckin' mind, you've turned the 'hood you work in into your own private sexual playground. You're as much a predator as any other child molester."

"I'm no fuckin' child molester. Their parents make them do the shit. Every time I was with one, the mother was there watching."

"It's just another fringe benefit, is that it?"

"That's the way I saw it."

"What would you do if you couldn't get a little girl, once you found that's what you were interested in?"

"I'd get pissed and threaten to lock somebody's ass up. Then somebody's mother would do it."

"So, you lock up only the ones you couldn't extort for sexual favors, including their children. How many little girls do you think you turned out, girls whose innocence you've stolen, just as your daughter's life was stolen?"

"You leave my daughter out of this, doc. She has nothing to do with this."

"Oh, rest assured, we will come back to that subject. Now, answer my last question: How many children's lives do you think you've ruined?"

"I don't know. They're all fuckin' ani—"

The doctor's eyes slightly widened. "Was 'animals' the word you were looking for?"

"Hey, the way I see it, if I can get a little head for free, why the fuck not? Those skanks are on the streets trying to make a living. A lot of them do that shit to take care of their kids. Most of the time, I let the shit go unless it's obviously in my face. I'm helping them."

"So, it's fine for women to sell themselves on the streets to make a living, as long as you can get a free piece of pussy or some head from either them or their children, now and then. Is that it?"

"I call it a fringe benefit." A smile formed on the officer's face.

"I call it fucked up. How are prostitutes any less a menace to society than drug dealers? What they do can have just as many negative consequences to society and to the neighborhoods they work in. It's not like the shit they do is legal, but you take shit to another level. Your atrociously abusive behaviors include not only prostitutes but their children as well. And you call it a fucking fringe benefit?"

"Yeah, well, in our eyes, selling pussy ain't the same as selling drugs."

"Who are you referring to when you say 'our'?"

"Officers on the street who see what I see every night," he nonchalantly responded.

"Is your only sexual outlet the prostitutes you bust on the streets and their children? How is your personal life?"

"Fucked up."

"Can you explain that?"

"My personal life is in the toilet. My last girlfriend and I felt that it was best if we parted company."

"What were the issues there?"

"I fucked up. I would get angry about shit that would happen on the job, and I'd bring the shit home. We'd argue a lot, and one time I hit her. She said she had grown afraid of my mood swings."

"How long were you two together?"

"Less than a year. The bitch didn't give me a chance."

"So, all women are bitches now?"

"I didn't say that."

"You didn't have to. It's evident in the way you treat women. Especially the ones who, as you say, sell themselves on the streets to take care of their children. Not because they want to. For them, it's a necessity. You see an opportunity to exploit them and their children. You choose not to be the guardian of women that you should be. It's within your power to at least help some of them. Yet, you exploit their situation just so you can get a quick nut and go home. Having said that, why should your ex-girlfriend have stayed with a motherfucker that was beating on her?"

"I never said I beat her. I got angry and hit her one time."

"Why should she put up with you hitting her? You're a cop with a gun, which must have frightened her."

"She wasn't scared of me. She was a disloyal bitch." The officer's anger grew.

"How the hell can you be loyal to someone you don't trust and who beats you?"

"She wanted out of the relationship anyway."

"How was the sex between you two?"

"It was ok at first and, after a while, it went downhill."

"Why do you think that was the case?"

"No matter what I did, I couldn't please her. It wasn't enough. The bitch was a nympho. Fuck her, anyway, I don't need her."

"Bullshit. You got used to being with children and women you didn't have to give a fuck about."

"So fuckin' what?"

"So what? Now you know what the problem is, motherfucker. You want children sexually."

"I didn't ask for this shit to happen to me. It just did."

"No, the bitch that gave you, and then sold you, her ten year old daughter made you do it."

"That's the way it happened. What the fuck do you want from me, doc?"

"Let's get back to your last girlfriend."

"What about her? I don't wanna talk about her."

"I didn't ask you what the fuck you wanted to talk about. Were you able to satisfy her in bed?"

"She complained that I didn't care about her needs, that once I got my nut, I was done with her."

"So, you're saying you're a minute man. You'd cum quick, and she couldn't get hers."

"That was her major bullshit complaint."

"Don't feel too bad. I hear that a lot about white men. Was sex with your wife like that when you two were together?"

The look on the patients face was one of contempt. "No. We had a great sex life until my daughter's accident, and then it all went to shit."

"Let's talk about that. Were you fucking prostitutes when you lived with your wife?"

"Hell no."

"Why not? They were around then."

"That shit never occurred to me. I was happy with my wife."

"Did you fantasize about being with children at that time?"

"No. I never thought of anything like that."

"Had you ever thought about fucking any of your daughter's friends before her accident?"

"Of course not. Hell no."

"You ever fantasize about fucking your daughter?"

The patient quickly jumped out of his chair to attack the doctor, a look of rage on his face.

The doctor responded instantly and was ready for the attack. "You had better sit your punk ass back in that seat. I told you, motherfucker, I have no problem fuckin' you up. I'm not a small child you can intimidate or a crack head junkie who's afraid to go to jail. I hold the cards here, you twisted fuck. Now, sit your bitch ass back in that seat."

The officer looked into the doctor's eyes and saw something that gave him pause. He returned to his seat, his rage still building.

"Now that bullshit's out the way," the doctor continued, "I need you to do a small comparison for me. How is sex with the street women different than that with any other woman?"

"I don't have to waste time being nice or friendly with those bitches. I don't have to spend a dime or give a shit how they feel. I get my dick sucked or I fuck one of them, and it's done."

"Have you had any real women in your life since your last girlfriend?"

"No, goddamnit, not really. What the fuck does this have to do with anything?" He was ready to explode with anger.

"Why not? Afraid you can't handle a real woman?"

"Look, I don't want to answer any more of these fuckin' questions, and I'm tired of this psychobabble bullshit."

"Fine with me. There's the door. You're free to walk out that motherfucker any time you want. But know this: you'll be one unemployed piece of shit cop by the time you get your sorry ass home." The doctor smiled after he finished his statement.

"I don't give a shit!"

"Yes you do, but you have to live with the choices you make and the consequences that follow, not me."

"So how fuckin' long do I have to keep coming here until you decide that I can go back to work?"

The doctor lit a cigarette before he responded. "You don't understand how this shit works, do you? It's not a matter of you going back to work. Working as what is the question."

"What the fuck are you talking about?"

"You forget why you're here."

"Look, all you have to do is tell the department brass that all I need is some rest and I'll be fine."

"You must be out of your motherfuckin' mind if you think I'm going to tell anyone you're fit for duty as a cop. We both know that's bullshit."

"Well, how long will I have to keep coming here to see you and putting up with this shit?"

"Never again. Once the force releases your ass, you couldn't afford my fee."

"What? You're gonna recommend that I be terminated from my goddamn job?"

"No. My recommendation will be that you are psychologically and emotionally unstable and that under no circumstances should you be allowed to carry a weapon."

"What? You asshole! They'll terminate me if you give them that recommendation."

"That's not my problem, and I don't give a fuck. You see all those degrees on the wall over there? I didn't buy those motherfuckers on eBay. They say I am vastly qualified to determine the mental status of anyone I talk to, and you are indeed a time bomb waiting to explode."

"You'd ruin my life and career over this petty shit?"

"I'm not ruining your life. Maybe they'll assign you a desk job. I don't know. In any event, that's out of my control."

"I don't wanna sit on some fuckin' desk. I can't do that. I'm a street cop."

"Does wearing that gun on your hip make you feel manlier? So much so that you two can't bear to be without each other?"

"You know what, doc? Fuck you!"

"No, I'm afraid not. Now your session is over. Please get the fuck out of my office, and rest assured your department will have my report today by close of business."

Felton left the doctor's office in a rage and slammed the door on his way out. He got to his car and sat inside for a short while, trying to decide what he should do. *If that fucking doctor recommends that I not carry a weapon, I'm going to be fired from the force. I could also face charges for having sex with minors, if that motherfucker reports me.* He realized that there was a doctor-patient privilege between them. He knew the doctor could not reveal anything to the authorities that they discussed without jeopardizing his practice. *Fuck that black-ass arrogant prick. If he does tell anyone what I told him, I'll sue his ass off—and he'll lose his fuckin' practice and his license.*

He decided to go home and sleep his anger off, and later he would go see his favorite little dick sucker. He got home thirty minutes later to his dirty apartment, lay across his bed, and fell asleep.

A knock on his door woke him at 6:00 p.m. He looked through the peephole and saw a pizza deliveryman at the door. He opened the door and told the delivery guy he hadn't ordered a pizza. Before he could react, the deliveryman pulled out a canister of mace from inside his pizza bag and sprayed Felton in the face. The deliveryman quickly forced his way into the officer's apartment, followed by three other men. They rushed in and closed the door.

The officer now felt punches to his face by one of the intruders. His eyes were still burning from the mace. Each of his arms was now held by two of the other intruders, and one mercilessly punched him in the face. After the fifth blow to the right side of his face, he felt his jaw shatter. Blood poured out of his mouth. He wanted to fall down, but they held him up.

The fourth intruder took over the punishment to his face. All his blows made contact with the left side of the officer's face. Teeth and blood flew out of Felton's mouth with each blow.

The intruders sat him in a chair and tied his hands behind his back and his legs to the chair. Then, without mercy, each man took turns punching the officer in the face and kicking him in his stomach and chest.

Felton was in agony. He found it hard to breath, and he wished for death. The intruders did not grant his wish, as the beating to his body continued. He soon passed out from the pain.

The man posing as the deliveryman halted the beating and spoke to the others. "Hold up, fellas. It's not time for this piece of shit to die yet. He done passed out on us. Get some water to pour over this motherfucker's head."

One man grabbed the officer by his blond hair and held his head up, while the fake deliveryman poured water over his bloody face to try to wake him.

Felton came to, but just barely. His face was so swollen he couldn't talk. His eyes were almost swollen shut. He tried to think but his pain was too intense. He couldn't swallow, so blood and saliva poured from his mouth. One word did come to mind though: *Why*?

Just as that thought came to him, one of his attackers spoke. "Hey, muthafucka, can you hear me? You're probably wondering why this shit is happening to you. I'll tell you, bitch. We know who you are. You're a piece of shit cop who thinks he can do whatever the fuck he wants. We hear you like fuckin' little girls and making them suck on your dick—little girls from our 'hood, motherfucker! We hear you been doin' this shit for a while now. We have news for you, bitch. Your days of abusing our women is over. Motherfucker, how long did you think you could get away with this type shit? You see, bitch. The boys here wanted to just come over and smoke your bitch ass, but I wanted to make sure you felt a lot of pain first. Then, I got an even better idea. Check this out and tell me what you think. We know you have a daughter. We hear the bitch is crippled. I figured if you can make our little sisters suck your dick, we should make your daughter do the same shit to us."

Felton tried to react, but all he could do was moan in protest and try to shake loose. Being tied to a chair and helpless, he could do nothing.

"We have your wife's address, and when we get finished with you, we're gonna pay that bitch a visit too. I want you to die knowing that we had fun with your daughter and your wife. I want you to imagine my big dick in that crippled bitch's mouth, and me shootin' nut down her throat. And while I make her suck my dick, my boys are gonna be gang fuckin' your wife, and we're gonna make the shit last for hours. We'll make sure they have a real good time. We gonna fuck those bitches raw, muthafucka. You fucked around in the wrong hood." He laughed after tormenting the helpless officer with his words.

The beaten and helpless officer heard every word spoken, and he knew, in his heart, these vicious men meant every word. He also knew there was nothing he could do to prevent his family's fate. Tears of regret and pain poured from his eyes. Even though his pain was intense beyond belief, he imagined the scenario that was just laid before him. He prayed for God to help them all. He also realized, at that instant, that he thought of his ex-wife and child as his family. He told himself he really loved them both.

The phony deliveryman took out a semi-automatic pistol from under his jacket and attached a silencer to the barrel. He looked down at the bound and helpless officer and spoke. "Hey, you piece of shit. You ready to die? Look at me, bitch. I want you to see it comin'."

He pointed the gun at the officer's head. Felton looked down the barrel and could only cry as his killer pulled the trigger. The bullet soundlessly exited the gun and entered the officer's head.

At 3:00 p.m., the doctor's third patient of the day arrived at his office: Nurse Tamara Williams.

After she took a seat, the doctor explained the rules for the session.

She had a bewildered look on her face. She then looked away and laughed. "Are you serious?"

"What do you think?"

"You have got to be kidding me," she stated, still laughing.

"Do you see me laughing?"

"We do need to get a few things straight, doctor. You are not going to be cursing when you speak to me. I did not come here to be verbally abused by you. I don't smoke or drink, and I would appreciate it if you didn't do either while I'm here. You need to know that there is nothing unbalanced about me, and I don't care who you are. You will address me with the same respect that you yourself expect. You being a psychiatrist doesn't mean you're anything special to me, and your implied threat to harm me was totally unprofessional and uncalled for. Have I made myself clear?"

While Tamara spoke, the doctor worked on his computer.

She asked him," Did you hear what I just said?"

He looked directly at her when he replied, "I heard every word you said."

"Good. Now, can we get started? I have other business to attend to today."

"In the last year," the doctor began, "how many patients suddenly became ill when they were recovering or mysteriously died while in your care?"

"Please explain what are you talking about?"

"Let me try this one more time," the doctor said. "First, I'm not one of your helpless, crippled, or sick-ass patients. You are not in charge here. You don't dictate terms in my office. This is my practice. I will speak however the fuck I deem necessary. I will conduct my office affairs as I see fit. It is your license and possibly your freedom at stake, not mine. You are free to get the fuck out of my office whenever you wish. However, if you wish to continue to practice medicine, I suggest you come down off that fucking high horse you're on and cooperate with me. Have I made myself clear?"

She gave the doctor a nasty look, got up and headed for the door.

The doctor activated his intercom and asked his office manager to contact Doctor Wheeler at Mercy General Hospital.

Tamara stopped at the door and turned to face the doctor.

"I told you," he said, "you are free to carry your ass out that door whenever you wish. I will not sit here playing goddamn games with you."

She hesitantly returned to her seat.

The doctor lit a cigarette.

She had a look of revulsion on her face.

"Now, for the last time, are you ready to get started?" he asked.

"You know, Doctor Feelgood," Tamara said, "I was told you are one of the best practicing psychiatrists in the state. I guess I'll have to make that determination for myself, because so far, I am not impressed. In addition, please address me as Nurse Williams, Doctor Feelgood. That name certainly does not fit you at all, if this is how you deal with patients."

"I'm not going to address you by any title at all. Titles are meaningless on that side of the desk." He pointed to where Tamara sat.

"Then how shall I address you? Because, based on what I've seen so far, you don't live up to your name 'Doctor Feelgood.' Nothing you have said so far has made me feel good." A smile of contempt formed on her face.

"That's not what I'm here to do. I'm totally indifferent to how you feel. You may have major issues that need to be addressed. The first being what your mother was smoking when she named you Tamara."

"Excuse me!" She quickly became angry and defensive.

"If you want to sit here and play fucking games and throw insults back and forth, I'll indulge that shit until Doctor Wheeler calls back. I have other patients today, and I want you the fuck out of my office."

"Look, doctor. I don't want to be here anymore than you want me here, but we both know I was ordered to come here."

"You are wasting my goddamn time. My time is valuable not only to me but also to my patients. If you wish to continue these antagonistic, unproductive behaviors, please do it at your place of employment, not here."

"Can we get started doctor?" she said, with contempt.

"Yes, if you're ready to stop bullshitin'. Now, why the fuck are you here?"

She sighed heavily as she looked at the therapist.

"Don't come in here and act brand new on me," he warned. "Doctors, and especially nurses, are some of the most foul-mouthed motherfuckers you can talk to, on or off the job. I have an active practice at two area hospitals. I know how you motherfuckers speak about each other and your patients, so get over it and answer my question."

"You know full well I was ordered by my hospital administrator to come see you."

"Why?"

"As a condition of employment, doctor."

"Stop wasting my motherfuckin' time and talk to me straight. You know full well why. I need to hear it from you."

"The hospital suspects that patients in my ward are being harmed by one of the nurses."

"You are the charge nurse for your ward. You have access to every patient in the ward. Have you harmed any of your patients?"

"I supervise a staff of nurses, and I oversee the care of dozens of patients. When I do personally care for patients, I've always administered the care prescribed by the doctors."

"That was not my question."

"No, I am a nurse. I have no reason to hurt the people I'm supposed to be caring for, nor would I. Even if I did, I wouldn't be stupid enough to admit it to you or anyone else." Her dislike for that question was obvious.

"Then, if that's the case, why do your people suspect you of doing something so horrible?"

"There are many nurses who work in my ward. No one suspects me of anything. We've all been ordered to undergo these useless evaluations—that means every nurse who works on the ward."

"We will see how useless these evaluations are. What ward do you supervise, by the way?"

"Intensive care. I work the evening shift at my hospital. You mean you didn't know that before I came in here?"

"Of course I did. Now, answer my question. What has happened at your hospital to make your people think that patients are being mistreated or harmed?"

"Patients come in to intensive care suffering all kinds of injuries. Sometimes, if they are lucky, they get better. We do lose patients, but every hospital does. Unfortunately, not all patients get better."

"How many patients have died in the last couple months while being cared for in your specific ward?"

"Six patients that I'm aware of, doctor."

"What type of injuries did these patients present with?"

"I can't remember them all."

"Try. Give me the ones you do remember. You are the charge nurse for your ward. That's some shit you need to know."

"One was a motorcycle accident, another was a stabbing, and one a shooting—and one guy I remember fell from a ladder."

The doctor worked on his computer as the patient recalled what she could. "Do you remember the race of any of these individuals?" he asked.

"Their race? What difference does that make?"

"I just want to know what you recall about these patients."

"I can't remember, but I'm sure I can find the information for you."

"We'll come back to that. I've requested some information from your hospital."

"Fine." She shifted in her seat and appeared to be a little uncomfortable.

"How long have you been a practicing nurse?"

"Ten years."

The doctor consulted his notes. "According to my records, you're thirty-six."

"Correct."

"How is your life outside the walls of the hospital?"

"If you're trying to ask about my personal life, it's fine."

"Are you currently seeing anyone?"

"I don't see how that is any of your business."

"Everything that concerns you—your medical career, your past, present and future—is my business, as long as you sit your ass in that chair."

"Yes, I've been involved with the same guy for four years now. Is that helpful to you, doctor?"

"What does he do for a living?"

"He is a sportscaster for WJLA news Channel 13. Jimmy Hale. You have probably seen him on TV." She smiled with pride.

"No, I don't waste my time watching TV."

She rolled her eyes and looked away from the doctor.

He clasped his hands together and leaned forward on his desk. "What justifies that air of arrogance that you project?"

"Because I'm confident, I'm arrogant? Because I'm sure of myself, I'm arrogant? Because I'm educated, I'm arrogant? Is that the way you see me, doctor?"

"Actually, no. That is not how I see you. Normally, confidence, self-assuredness, and intelligence are all admirable qualities, so much so that those who possess them do not have to flaunt them to be noticed by others. You, however, need to feel as though you're superior to everyone around you. That's a problem."

"That's your opinion."

"No. That's a simple observation based solely on your responses to me. I would say that someone like you has a very small circle of friends and confidants. Many people would be turned off by your conceited attitude."

"I have all the friends I need."

"How many of your close friends are black?"

"I do have a few black female friends, not many."

"Why is that?"

"Why is what? Who I choose to be friends with is my business, and I don't see how this is relevant to why I'm here."

"You wouldn't. That's why I'm the psychiatrist, and you're a nurse." The doctor smiled as he lit a cigarette and made note of his patient's reaction on his computer.

"Have you always been attracted to white men?" he now asked.

"I can date whomever I choose. I prefer to be with white men."

"That wasn't my question. Please stay on point"

"No, I was not always attracted to white men. I started dating white guys in college. Can we move on now?"

"Why?"

"Why are you so concerned about my dating habits?"

"Who you're fucking doesn't concern me."

"Then why ask about my preference in men."

"Do you date black men?"

"No."

"Why?"

"I did date black guys in high school. However, I came to the conclusion, long ago, that the vast majority of black men are pieces of shit. As I said, I prefer white men."

"That is one hell of a condemnation of black men. Did you have a bad experience in your past that caused you to feel that way and avoid dating black men?"

"It has been my experience that black men bring too much baggage and drama to a relationship. I choose not to deal with that."

"Explain what you mean when you say baggage and drama."

"Most black men are intimidated by successful, educated black women. I don't have time for that. I don't need a man I have to financially support, and I don't need the emotional baggage that comes with them."

"What baggage would that be? Please go into detail." The doctor listened intently.

"Most black men are lazy and don't want any more out of life than to work menial jobs, stay drunk, and lay up with as many women as they can. They have babies everywhere that they can't afford and have no interest in taking care of. They believe that all a woman needs is his dick, and that's the extent of their contribution to a relationship. Black men have no concept of what loyalty is, and their only goal in life is to fuck as many women as they can. The vast majority of black men are incarcerated for all kinds of crimes, and the children they father often end up in jail like their daddies. I have worked hard to get where I am. I don't need a hustler in my life. I will not date a man who has been in jail for anything, has babies, no education, who doesn't work, and has no plan for the future. I don't associate with a lot of black women because I get so sick and tired of hearing them complain about the sorry-ass men in their lives. Most of the women I know who choose to be with black men are women who are educated and have good careers. Yet they choose to waste their lives on sorry-ass niggers who won't amount to a damn thing."

"This topic makes you angry."

"Yes."

"Why? If you don't deal with black men, what do you care?"

"Because I have had friends who found themselves in terrible relationships, always with black men, and it hurt to see them destroy their lives over a piece-of-shit man who wasn't worth a damn to begin with."

"Do you have white friends who date black men?"

"Yes."

"What do you think about those situations?"

"I avoid being with them when they are together. When it ends in a disaster, as a few have, I tell them I don't want to hear about it."

"So, are you telling me you have no contact with black men at all? Not even the men in your family?"

"On a personal level, no. I don't have much contact with my family. I prefer to have as little social contact with black men as possible. That's my choice, and it's not a problem for me."

"Does the way you feel about black men affect the way you perform your duties as a nurse?"

"No, not at all, doctor."

The look he gave her told her he didn't believe what she said. "We'll come back to that."

"Fine. Can you please tell me where this is going?" she asked angrily.

"We'll get there soon enough. I'm conducting this session. Can you describe for me a little of your experiences with the man you're currently dating."

The doctor's intercom beeped. He was told Doctor Wheeler was returning his call. He told his assistant to inform Doctor Wheeler he was with a patient and he'd call him back.

"What do you want to know?" she replied, sighing.

"How is your relationship?"

"I would describe it as fulfilling and wonderful."

"Describe your relationship for me."

"Jimmy is a great guy. He graduated college the same year I did. My profession does not intimidate him. He is supportive of my needs and goals in life. He has a great career and a bright future. He comes from a good family. He comes home to me every night, and I've never doubted his faithfulness to me. We just bought a home together last year, and we plan on having a baby and getting married this year. We truly love each other."

"Prior to meeting Jimmy, how would you describe your other relationships with white men?"

"About the same as what I have with Jimmy, except we were not talking marriage or anything. My experiences with white men have always been positive and drama-free. At least they were going somewhere and had more on their minds than drinking and partying."

"So, all black men, in your opinion, are pieces of shit who only want to get high, party, and fuck everything they see."

"The vast majority, yes. We both know that's what youth is about, but at some point that changes. When it comes to men, and especially black men, that part doesn't sink in, and I don't have time for that."

"Are you aware of how your use of language changes when you talk about black men compared to white men?"

"What are you talking about, doctor?" She appeared confused.

"Playing stupid on me again."

"I am far from stupid, and I resent being called that."

"Then stop acting like it. Whenever you described any experiences with black men, your language becomes laced with very colorful expletives. Nurse Talk 101. Let's move on. How was your relationship with your father?"

"I have always had a good relationship with my father. He is a strong and gentle man. My mother adores him still to this day, and so do I."

"How does he feel about your choice in men?"

"My parents accept the choices I make for myself and the direction my life is taking."

"You say they accept the choices you make. Accepting a choice and parental approvals are two totally different things. Your parents love and support you, but do you know what their opinions are on your choice to date white men?"

"My father told me long ago that he couldn't choose my partner for me. He told me just to make sure whomever I do choose is good to me. That's approval enough for me."

"Have you always introduced your men to your father?"

"Not always. Only the ones I was serious with, and they were few."

"Have your parents met Jimmy?"

"Of course they have."

"What did your father think of him?"

"As far as I know, he was fine with him. My father wanted me to marry a brother. I know that deep down, but that was never going to happen. My mother liked him, but she probably feels the same way as my father. As long as my parents love me, they will accept my choices in men. But even if they didn't, this is my life and I will live it to make myself happy, not my parents."

"That doesn't sound like the kind of approval you were looking for."

"I am an adult. My parent's opinions mean a lot to me, but I won't live my life based on their views of the men I choose to be with. As long as those men are good to me, that's all that matters."

"Do you have relationships with any of the men in your family besides your father?"

"I have no siblings, and I choose not to deal with many of my relatives."

"Why?"

"I've never really been close to any of my aunts or uncles, and growing up, I didn't spend a lot of time with my cousins."

"There must have been times when you were a young child at family functions, surrounded by children of other family members, all playing together."

"Yes, there was. Now, can we move on?"

"Is there some reason why you don't want to talk about your early family relationships?"

"I told you. I don't have any fucking relationships with any family members outside of my parents. I don't see them often either."

"You're a goddamn liar. Something extremely significant happened to you as a young child. Something within your family that altered who you were to a significant degree."

"What do you want from me?" Tamara's anger grew as she spoke.

"The truth. Something has you fucked up inside, something you've been holding in for years—probably since you were a very young child. We need to find out what the fuck is going on."

"You're a fucking bastard." The look in her eyes was one of hate.

"Are you ready to talk about what it is you've kept buried inside you all these years?"

"No."

"Fine with me. You can let whatever it is you're keeping bottled up inside you destroy your life. On the other hand, you can face it head on. Either way, it's your call. You need to decide quickly, because I don't have time to waste fuckin' around with you. As you said earlier, you're grown and quite capable of making your own decisions, fucked up or otherwise. Be prepared to live with the consequences of those decisions, when the anger inside you erupts and destroys everyone around you and all that you've worked for. No matter how it plays out, I don't give a fuck, so decide now."

Tamara stared at the doctor as he lit another cigarette. The anger she felt became more intense, as she let her thoughts go back to a time she had tried all her life to forget.

She told the doctor her story:

"I was twelve years old. I went to stay with my uncle and his wife on my father's side of the family for a weekend, while my parents went out of town. It was during the summer months, so I was out of school. I enjoyed spending time with my aunt and uncle, and they were always so good to me. They had two sons: Michael was my age and Reggie was eighteen. Reggie had taken Michael and me to the movies early one Saturday afternoon, while my aunt and uncle went shopping. I remember us having a good time that day. When we returned home from the movie, I remember Michael and I went bike riding for most of the afternoon.

"I got tired of riding and wanted to go home, so I left Michael with his friends and went home. My aunt and uncle hadn't returned home, but Reggie was there. We watched TV for a while, and I remember him asking me if I wanted to play a game with him. He said we had to play the game in his room. He sat me on his bed, told me how pretty I was, and touched my face. He sat next to me and said that when people like each other, they play the touching game. He put his arm around me and asked me to kiss him on his cheek. Being twelve years old, I didn't see a problem with kissing him on the cheek."

Tamara put her hands to her face and started to cry as she recalled the memory.

"Take your time, go slowly," the doctor said. "I want you to recall the entire memory, just as it happened." His words calmed her, but only slightly.

"This is hard for me doctor. He raped me, I was so young, so innocent and there was nothing I could do to stop him. Please, I can't go on with this. Tears began falling down her cheek as she briefly continued. I don't remember how long it lasted, but I was grateful his mother walked in to stop him."

"The look on her face showed she was appalled. I don't think she made a sound for the first few seconds. She just stood in the doorway, looking down on me."

"I remember her closing the door and telling Reggie to get his goddamned clothes on and get out of the room. She came to me and held me in her arms, crying and repeating over and over that she was sorry. She put me in the bathtub, cleaned me up, and then put me to bed.

"It took a while for the pain to stop. I remember her staying in the room with me the whole night. The next day, she begged me not to tell my parents what had happened. She told me that they would punish Reggie for what he'd done.

"The minute my parents came to get me, I ran to hug my mother. Without my saying a word, she knew something was wrong. When we got home, she asked me what was wrong and I told her what Reggie had done to me. I said that Auntie knew, because she walked in the room while he was on top of me. She held me and we both cried. Like my aunt, she said over and over how sorry she was that that happened to me. She also said to me that if we told my father, that he would probably kill Reggie.

"I remember telling my mother that I didn't want my daddy in jail. She said 'Me neither, baby,' as we both sat there crying. I remember my mother taking me to the doctor to be checked out the following day. I never knew what story she told the doctor about what happened to me, but I wasn't impregnated by that piece of shit, and, thankfully, I didn't contract any diseases.

"My mother made me promise never to tell my father what happened to me. One night, she promised that I would never have to see any of those people again, or anyone else in my family. She held me as I fell asleep in her arms. I remember her saying, 'Niggers aren't worth a fucking thing, to do this to my precious baby.'

"The next time I would see that piece of shit would be two years later, in the hospital. He'd been in a car wreck while coming home from work one day. He wasn't expected to survive, so the whole family was there. I remember not wanting to go near that bastard. My mother told me that, in this instance, it was ok, because he might die and that he deserved to die for what he did to me. If it happened that day, she'd like to be there to watch the motherfucker die.

"I remember, when we walked into the room, no one was there but his mother. She could barely look us in the eyes. He was hooked up to oxygen masks and IVs. I remember thinking, *I wish I could hurt him the way he hurt me*. My mother held my hand, as we looked down on his helpless body. His mother held his hand on the other side of the bed and cried.

"My mother looked at him and said something I would never forget. 'Maybe this is payback for what you did to my baby. I hope you die, you sorry piece of shit. I hope you die and rot in Hell for what you did to my baby.'

"His mother said nothing. She sat there, holding his hand and crying, not even looking up at us. I guess he heard my mother wish death on him because he opened his eyes and turned toward us. He looked at me, tears coming down his face. He looked like a monster, with all the tubes and bandages on his body.

"He looked at me and said, 'I'm sorry.' That was all he could say: those two words. As if saying that would somehow make up for what he'd done to me.

"My mother's response to that was 'Fuck you.' Then she spat at him and we walked away.

"I remember smiling when she said that. We left the room and went home. That bastard died a week later from his injuries. I think it was at that point I knew I wanted to be a nurse. My mother somehow got us out of attending that motherfucker's funeral. My father never knew what he'd done to me."

"Did your mother ever seek counseling for you?"

"No. We talked about what happened, and I knew it wasn't my fault that piece of shit raped me."

"Do you think it was a wise decision to keep what happened to you from your father?"

"At the time, yes. There is no telling what my father would have done to that motherfucker. And, like I said, I didn't want my father to go to prison for possibly killing him."

"He may have sought prison as punishment, after he went to that ass with a baseball bat."

"It doesn't fucking matter. That bastard died, and he died in pain, and I'm happy he's dead. My father never had to lay a hand on him, and he doesn't need to know what happened." Tamara's anger grew as she pondered the decision her mother had made.

"Do you think your uncle ever found out from his wife what his son had done to you?"

"I would say no, because he and my father are very close, and I don't think that would be the case if he knew."

"Do you think that what happened to you as a young child has anything to do with the way you feel about black men?"

"I'm sure it probably does. How the fuck could I not have been affected by being raped?"

"Do you see all black men as rapists?"

"I see all black men as pieces of shit. I think I said that earlier."

"Does that include your father?"

"Of course not. My father is a good man."

"Then all black men are not worthless pieces of shit."

"I have never felt that way about my father."

"Your father is not the only good black man in America, but if you can find one exception to your rule that all brothers are pieces of shit then it stands to reason that there are many more exceptions out there."

"I feel the way I feel. I don't give a damn about any of you niggers."

"Yet, you sit here and tell me that the way you feel about all black men in general does not affect the way you interact with your male patients, especially those that happen to be black."

"That's what I said."

"Tell me how that's possible, given how you feel about black men?"

"I don't let my personal feelings interfere with my professional duties. It's called detachment. You remember what that is, don't you? You went to medical school."

"Yes, I do, but I don't practice with the baggage you obviously carry and have been carrying for years."

"I have resolved my issues."

"Please tell me how the hell you accomplished that?"

"I worked it out."

"And what the fuck does that mean?"

"By not putting myself in situations where I have to deal with you people."

"When you say 'you people,' who the hell are you referring to?"

"Niggers. If you've listened to anything I've said, you know I don't deal with niggers period—black men, women, or children. You people."

"If that's the case, then why the fuck are you sitting your ass in here with me now?"

"Because I don't have a choice, and we both know that."

"Didn't you know I was a black man before you came to see me? You put me in the same category as every other black man. I am highly educated and very successful. That doesn't matter to you though. You've passed judgment on me before even meeting me."

"Of course I knew who and what you were. As I stated earlier, if given the choice, I would have gone to see someone else."

"Yet, knowing how you feel about black men in general, why didn't you request to see another doctor?"

"I wasn't given a choice. Otherwise, I wouldn't be here."

"Does the way you feel about black men extend to children as well?"

"To a certain degree, male children. Yes, it does."

"What fuckin' degree would that be?"

"Yes, to the degree that those little niggers grow up into mostly useless men."

"Please explain what the hell you mean by that."

"I don't have any malice toward children in general, but when I see a little black boy, I'm taken back to what happened to me as a child. I see that young child grow into a man who will be capable of doing what every other black man is capable of, and it frightens me."

"You hate your own people to the extent that you believe innocent children cannot grow into anything but rapists, thugs, and criminals? What happened to you was tragic. No child should ever experience the pain and horror you did. I can understand your feelings when your cousin died. But by keeping what happened to you between your aunt, your mother, and yourself, even with his death, you still haven't gotten closure. Because of the tragedy you experienced, you should have received professional help. Because you've carried this around with you for years, believe it or not, it has had an effect on you."

"I've moved on with my life and accomplished the goals I set for myself. My life is great, and I no longer have issues dealing with what happened."

"So, you believe that because you shun black people of all ages that you've solved your problem?"

"What I do and how I handle my problems works for me."

"What is your opinion on the issues that affect black Americans in this country?"

Tamara looked at the doctor and laughed.

The doctor lit a cigarette and observed her behavior. "What do you find amusing?" he asked.

"Your question."

"Why do you find that question humorous?"

"Do you really think, after all we've talked about here today, that I give a flying fuck about the state of black affairs in this country?"

"No. I wanted to hear what your response would be."

"Why?"

"Then it's fair to say that you wouldn't lift a finger to help another black person in any way, outside of your medical duties."

"Pretty much. I barely want to deal with those fuckers at . . ."

"Please finish your statement."

"Why do we have to keep going over this? What do you want from me? If I choose to avoid certain people, so what the Hell? It's not a crime, and I choose how I want to live!"

"I want you to finish your last statement. You barely want to deal with those fuckers where? Finish the fucking statement!"

"At work was what I was going to say. All right, are you satisfied now?" Her anger was surfacing again.

"So, why didn't you finish the statement originally? Is there something you need to tell me, or is there a great deal you aren't telling me?"

"Where the hell are you going with this?"

"I'll tell you where. Right to the heart of what's truly fucked up about people like you."

Tamara displayed anger at that statement by rolling her eyes.

The doctor lit a cigarette.

"People like me? What do mean, people like me?" she responded with hostility, by leaning forward with her arms folded.

"As I said earlier, what happened to you was tragic. Instead of truly dealing with that pain, you've allowed it to turn you into a truly selfish, self-centered, and possibly very evil, fucked-up individual."

"Oh, is that correct? Please explain, Doctor Feelgood. I can't wait to hear this." She faced the doctor with her arms folded and listened.

"You say you don't have anything to do with black people outside of your work environment. You avoid contact with blacks to the extent that you can, socially or otherwise, and to a certain extent, this includes your immediate family. Your hatred for your own kind runs so deep that it includes even small children—children who couldn't possibly harm you in the way that you, yourself, were harmed.

"By your own admission, you adore your father, who happens to be a black man, but he isn't placed into the same category of hate you feel for all other black men. You even keep your associations with black women to a minimum, even professional black women whom you barely acknowledge as peers. The fact that you adore your father but hate all other black men is a disturbing contradiction. You love your father, but all other black men are pieces of shit.

"What sets your father apart from the rest of the race? The fact that your father raised and protected you as a child? Protected you? No, that's not entirely true. You see, your father wasn't always there to protect you. He allowed his little girl to be brutally assaulted by a family member, and he did nothing about it. He wasn't given the opportunity to seek justice for his little girl, because your mother decided that it would be best if he never found out what happened to you. You've lived your whole life seeing your father as a man you love, but a man who couldn't protect his baby girl. That has always been with you, just under the surface of your thoughts. That is why you don't have a great deal of contact with your family. This is why you only brought certain men around your parents—white men that, in your opinion, could protect you and are better than your father. Trust me on this: your father is well aware of this fact. Unfortunately for him, he'll never know why his daughter chose to date outside her race. He sees that as an indictment on him, as a man and as a father."

"My father would have protected me if he'd known what was going to happen. He wouldn't have let that bastard harm me. You don't know a damn thing about my father, or how he feels! I can take care of myself now and I can make damn sure those bastards don't hurt anyone again!"

"But your father couldn't have known what was going to happen to you. You weren't in his direct care at the time of the incident. Now, what bastards are you referring to?" The doctor smiled as he asked that question.

"Fuck this. I don't need to hear any more of this shit!" She stood and turned toward the door.

"The minute you step your ass out that door, your medical career is over," the doctor warned.

Hesitantly, Tamara sat back down.

"Now," the doctor said, "answer my last question. What bastards were you referring to?"

She did not respond to his question.

He shook his head. "Not to worry. We'll come back to that last remark. You, Ms. Williams? I see black people like you every waking minute of every day. Motherfuckers like you enjoy looking down on others because it gives you a feeling of superiority—which, by the way, is very misleading. You feel a sense of accomplishment when you look at those who you deem as less accomplished, and you say to yourself, *I'm better than you.* You say to the world 'Look at what I've done. Admire me for my achievements.' Again, by your own admission, as educated as you are, you said you wouldn't lift a finger to help another black person. You know what is so surprising when you judge others at a glance? You don't have a fucking clue if the assumptions you've made are true or not. The truth is: more often than not, those assumptions turn out to be dead wrong. However, because you are who you are and think the way you do, this bullshit cycle continues. Being a black man, I know what that feels like to be looked at like you're less than nothing by your own people—not by the white community, but by your own kind. We judge our own people as being worthy or unworthy based on outward appearance alone. This shit starts in grade school and is nurtured at home. We are judged by the clothes we wear, the cars we drive, the type of work we do, and by where we live or don't live. To hell with a person's character.

"We, as blacks in America, judge each other on skin color, eye color, and hair texture. I've always found that to be the highest order of insult one black could express to another. Not only is it asinine, but it shows how very little we as a people have changed in our thinking from the days when we were forced to walk around in chains.

"You pride yourself on your education and your profession. That is understandable, and you should take a measure of pride in your accomplishments. History teaches us that education alone doesn't always raise one's awareness or heighten one's since of community. We, as blacks in this country, go out of our way to hurt each other in every way possible: professionally, economically, and socially. We generate billions of dollars in this economy, yet we control not one single institution. Hell, a well-educated and highly qualified black man runs for this nation's highest office and his own people support the white woman running against him. You know what's shocking about that scenario? Blacks say he's not ready. I say if we aren't ready to take the lead running this motherfuckin' country now, we never will be. People like you hold the rest of us back—motherfuckers who wouldn't give another black person the time of day or a kind word. And it's all because you see yourself as better than everyone else.

"When shit gets tight, what's the first thing motherfuckers like you say? 'The white man is out to fuck me,' or in your case 'the administrator.' You need to realize that we, as black people, treat each other like shit. White America doesn't have to do a damn thing to us except sit back and laugh at our asses. Many of us are incarcerated, and crime in our communities is rampant. However, maybe it wouldn't be so if more of us came together to reach out to our youth. But someone like you would never be a part of that process.

"We do more than enough harm to each other simply by failing to help each other. So much so that white America can pretty much ignore our dumb asses and let us continue to inflict the pain on ourselves that came at the hands of slave owners hundreds of years ago.

"We fight among ourselves over petty issues. We see a brother or a sister trying to improve themselves, and we ridicule them as trying in some way to be white or cross over into white America. We see one of our own make it through hard work, and they become the enemy. We hate them for leaving our lazy asses behind. Educated blacks see themselves as the saviors of our culture and heritage. Then, at the end of their academic training, they perpetuate our cultural stagnation by doing just what it is you're doing now: shutting your eyes to the plight of our young people and those that could benefit from what you've learned." The doctor finished talking, turned to his computer, and began typing notes.

His patient said nothing for a few minutes, then she spoke: "Doctor, in your own words, what the fuck has any of that got to do with me? Exactly what was that diatribe supposed to accomplish?"

"Exactly what I thought it would."

"And that would be what, exactly?"

"It gave me a chance to observe your reactions to a very provocative topic—a topic that hits close to home for many of us. Your reaction to what I was saying tells me that your hatred for blacks runs so deep that you justify the shit you've done based on what was done to you as a child."

"What have I done, doctor? Are you trying to accuse me of something?"

"Earlier, you said that you were able to see to it that those bastards never hurt anyone again. I'm gonna ask you again: Who the hell were you referring to? The six people you killed?"

"I haven't killed anyone. I don't know what the hell you're talking about."

"Then who the hell were you referring to when you made that statement?"

"I was referring to the fact that I'm old enough to take care of myself and that I wouldn't allow any man to hurt me ever again."

"You're lying to me."

"I don't have to lie to you about anything, Doctor Feelgood!" Her anger was palpable.

"You said that six patients have died while being cared for in your ward. Is that correct?"

"Yes."

"You said you could only remember four clearly."

"Yes, that's what I said."

"According to hospital records, the last three patients were children, all male, black, and under thirteen years old. One child presented with severe asthma, one with a broken leg, and the last with third degree burns over twenty percent of his lower body. Does this ring any bells?"

Tamara shifted in her seat as if she was suddenly uncomfortable when these particular cases were brought up. "Yes, I recall the cases now."

"I thought you might. Let's talk about the young man who was burned and survived. According to his chart, the emergency room physician ordered isolation in the intensive care ward and a 20 mg Demerol drip to control the pain until the patient could be admitted to the burn ward. Somehow, five times that amount found its way in his saline drip. In this particular case, you were the attending nurse for that patient. You want to explain how the fuck a lethal dosage of Demerol found its way into his IV?"

"I don't know!"

"What the fuck do you mean 'you don't know'? Was he or was he not your patient?"

"Yes, he was my fucking patient, but other nurses have access to the goddamn drug cart!"

"Did you administer the Demerol to the patient?"

"Yes, but I didn't give him that much Demerol."

"If you were his nurse, you and you alone were responsible for this patient's medica—"

She cut the doctor off. "I had two other patients on the ward I was responsible for when that patient was admitted. Someone else could have administered other injections."

"According to hospital records, only one patient was prescribed Demerol, and that was your burn patient. How did such a high dose get into his IV drip? And don't sit here and tell me you don't know, because the patient sure as Hell could not have done it himself."

Tamara said nothing. She sat in her seat, with her arms folded, staring at the floor.

"According to the pharmacy records, you signed out seven twenty mg bottles of Demerol at the beginning of your shift for the drug cart. Why did you need all that medication? It is highly unusual for that much Demerol to be signed out at once and in those doses."

"In Intensive Care, Demerol is used a lot to control pain. You'd know that, if you worked in that ward of the hospital."

The doctor smiled as he looked at his patient.

"Do you want to know how they caught on to what you were doing? It was actually quite brilliant—dangerous and stupid, but brilliant."

Tamara's face took on a worried look.

"According to my information," the doctor explained, "you did sign out one-hundred-and forty milligrams of Demerol. At least, that's what you thought you were signing out. What they gave you at the pharmacy at the beginning of your shift were seven vials filled with sterile water, which contained a harmless marker. You were recorded injecting the patient's IV with what you thought was a lethal dose of Demerol. You then left to get rid of the vials. Another doctor came in behind you, switched IV bags, and injected the 10 mg of Demerol into the patient's IV. Another intensive care nurse witnessed the injection and stayed in the patient's room until you returned.

"A concealed video device was taken from the patient's room after the second team left. Shortly afterward, you were called away to finish some paperwork. The IV bag they retrieved from the patient's room was sent to the lab. Now, smart-ass. What do you think the lab found in that one-liter bag of saline solution? One hundred fucking milligrams of sterile water and the marker."

Tamara sat in her chair and started to cry.

"What the fuck do you have to say now?" the doctor demanded. "Do you have any fucking idea of what that much Demerol would have done to someone that young and in that condition? Of course you do! You're a highly educated, well-trained, fucking professional killer, aren't you?"

She did not respond. She wiped the tears from her face and looked at the doctor.

"Want to talk about the other patients who weren't so lucky?" he asked.

"You can go straight to Hell, doctor."

"I won't be going to Hell anytime soon, but I can sure as fuck tell you where you're headed."

"Where would that be, Dr. Feelgood? I haven't told you anything, and if what you say is true, why am I not there now?"

"I'd have to conclude that your people are not ready to go public with this shit yet. You know: lawsuits and shit."

"I don't believe a thing you just said. I'm not going to allow myself to be trapped into confessing to something I didn't do. If I was recorded doing something like that, why haven't I seen this so-called video?"

"Would you like to see it now?" The doctor smiled. He typed commands onto his keyboard, and a video started to play. He turned the monitor toward his patient.

Tamara watched the video with a cold detached look in her eyes and said nothing until the recording stopped.

"Satisfied?" the doctor asked. "Now do you want to tell me about the others?"

"Sure, why the fuck not? They were all going to fucking die anyway. Could have been soon after they were brought in, or years later—who gives a fuck? I just helped them get there quicker."

"So, you *are* the nurse who's been killing patients."

"I killed no good rotten bastards that deserved to fucking die. I put those filthy niggers out of their misery to make sure they wouldn't get the chance to hurt anyone."

"How did you kill the others?"

"You really expect me to tell you that?"

"Why the hell not? Your ass is going to jail anyway. Your life is ruined. Don't you think their families deserve to know how and why their loved ones died?"

"Fuck them and their families. My family was almost destroyed by fuckers just like them. I don't owe them shit."

"What about the two children? They were just kids. Did they have to die? What possible harm had they done to you?"

"Did I ask to be raped at twelve years old?"

"No, you didn't, but those children didn't deserve to die because of what happened to you. They were only children, and you took their lives out of some sadistic need to avenge what was done to you."

"How do you know they wouldn't have grown up to be rapists, murderers, or something worse?"

"Who the fuck gave you a license to decide who lives and who dies? Who gave you the authority to be anyone's executioner? It's your responsibility to heal, not kill the sick and injured. Do no fucking harm—you remember that from the oath you took as a health care professional?"

"To answer your question, doctor: the State of Maryland."

"Was that supposed to be fucking funny?"

"I thought so."

"I am going to see to it that you never practice medicine anywhere and that your ass is put under the jail."

"You can't do a damn thing to me, Doctor Feelgood. You're a psychiatrist, and anything we discuss is covered by a little thing called doctor–patient privilege. You can't disclose a goddamn thing I've said to anyone. What you have shown me on your computer doesn't prove shit. If that video was all they needed, I'd be in jail now. If you tell anyone anything we discussed, your ass is going to be hauled before the state licensing board, sued for malpractice, and stripped of your license to practice in your field of psychobabble bullshit."

A smile formed on the doctor's face. "You have it all figured out don't you?"

"What do you think?"

"Why did you start to cry when I told you what was found in the saline bag?"

It took me a minute to realize that if they gave me saline and not the other medication, then I couldn't have killed anyone. They can't prove shit and what you know can't be used against me." Her response was calculated and cocky.

"You're absolutely right. You've covered all the bases. It's a damn shame I can't stop you. Your session is over. I'd like you to now get your psychopathic ass the fuck out of my office."

"With pleasure, doctor. Will we be seeing each other again?"

"Probably not, but I'd keep my eye on the news in the next few days. Breaking stories happen all the time."

She got up to leave, stopped at the door, turned, and faced the doctor. "Should I be worried about that breaking news comment you made?"

"I sure as fuck would be if I were in your shoes. It's amazing how news stations and reporters come by the stories they report. Sometimes, it happens by chance. Other times, they receive anonymous tips here and there. The beauty of that is: they don't have to reveal their sources. That's a protection they have. Freedom of the press can be a beautiful thing. It often holds up in court. Did you know that?" he stated, with intensity in his eyes and a broad smile on his face.

"Fuck you."

"Your session is over. Get the fuck out of my office. Please give my regards to Mr. Hale at—what station was that again? WJLA News."

"Motherfucker, are you threatening me? I'll have your black ass in front of a judge so fast it'll make your fucking head spin." Her rage was obvious as she spoke.

The doctor stood as he replied. "I'm only going to tell you to leave my office one more time."

She left, slamming the door behind her.

The doctor smiled, returned to his computer, and started writing his notes.

Tamara left the doctor's office and decided that she'd go shopping for the afternoon. She'd seen a few items she wanted to buy in a boutique, then she'd head home to prepare Jimmy a romantic dinner and they would spend the rest of the evening making love. Driving to the mall, she found herself going over her session with the doctor. She told herself not to worry about the session. *He can't do a damn thing about anything we talked about. My career is safe. They have nothing on me they can use. I'll just have to control my urges to seek my brand of justice until this shit cools down. If I have to transfer to another hospital, so be it. Once all this shit goes away, I'll make even more of those sorry bastards pay with their lives. Fuck all of them.*

Later that same evening, a certified letter arrived by courier at the home of Eric and Maria Williams, Tamara Williams's parents. The letter was addressed to Eric Williams. Mr. Williams signed for it and went into his study. He sat at his desk and opened the letter.

Dear Mr. Williams

My name is Doctor Feelgood. I'm a psychiatrist in private practice. The reason I'm writing to you is that I've been in therapy with your daughter, Tamara, at the request of her hospital administrator. The hospital's senior staff suspects your daughter may be responsible for killing numerous patients in the intensive care unit where she works. During our sessions, she admitted to me that she has, in fact, killed at least six patients. Two were only children. Your daughter has a deep-seated hatred toward black men. All her victims to date have been black males, ranging in ages from as young as six to late thirties. Mr. Williams, I have also learned that your brother's son Reggie raped your daughter when she was twelve years old. I know that Reggie passed away due to a car accident when your daughter was fourteen. However, this has had a profound effect on your daughter's psyche. During our session, your daughter informed me that you were never told of this incident. Your wife Maria and your sister-in-law decided that it would be best if you never knew what had occurred with your daughter. Your wife's fear was that you would have killed Reggie for what he'd done. Mr. Williams, I know that this is shocking news and it must be difficult for you to learn that your daughter was sexually abused as a child. Your daughter needs intense psychiatric help. She is a danger to everyone she is exposed to . .

Mr. Williams looked up and let the letter fell to his lap. Tears flowed down his face as he thought about what he just read. He tried to control his shaking hands but found it difficult.

Shortly afterward, his wife walked into the study and saw her husband holding the letter and that his hands were shaking. She knew something was terribly wrong. "Baby, are you ready to eat? Who was that at the door?" She noticed the tears on her husband face and that he appeared upset.

He held up the letter and spoke to his wife with a shaky voice. "Maria, why didn't you tell me what Reggie had done to my baby?"

She looked at her husband and she started to cry.

That same afternoon, a package arrived at the WJLA news office, addressed to anchor Virginia Summers. She took the package and sat it on top of her desk. She was due on air in fifteen minutes for the afternoon report, so she asked her staffer to open the package. Thirty minutes later, Virginia returned to her office.

Her excited staffer urged her to review the notes and the video tape that were in the package she had received. "Virginia, this is hot. If this information is true, we have a cover-up at Mercy General Hospital—a fucking nurse is killing patients and the hospital knows. And check this out. The nurse the hospital suspects is Jimmy Hale's girlfriend!"

Virginia perused the notes. "I know her, and I can't stand that conceited, arrogant bitch.

"Are we gonna do the story, Virginia?"

"I need to check some things out first and try to verify as much of this as possible. Hell, yes. We're gonna run this tonight on the late report if this checks out. This is huge."

During the course of the day, calls were made, faxes were exchanged, facts were verified, and anonymous information was confirmed or dismissed. What information the reporter could gather was quickly made ready to be presented to the public. The story of a cover-up at Mercy General was given the green light for broadcast on the late news report.

Jimmy Hale was headed home when he got a call on his cell phone. A friend at the station told him that a story concerning his fiancé, murders, and a cover-up at Mercy General Hospital was going to air on the evening broadcast. Jimmy couldn't believe what he had just heard: that his woman was involved with deliberate patient deaths at the hospital where she worked. He told himself he wouldn't believe it. They must have the wrong person.

Shortly after the phone call, he pulled into his drive way and parked his car. Tamara was home; her car was in the driveway. He opened the door and was overwhelmed by the aroma of the meal she had prepared. He went into the kitchen and saw the love of his life waiting to greet him.

"Hey, baby," she greeted him. "How was your day? I missed your afternoon sports report, so tell me all about it."

"Everything went well, Babe. No big surprises in the sports world today. Babe, I have to ask you something. Is everything ok at the hospital? The station is gonna run a story about some kind of cover-up happening there, something about a nurse killing patients. Have you heard anything at the hospital?"

Tamara's heart started to beat a little faster when he asked that question. She tried her hardest to control the panic that wanted to overwhelm her. *No that motherfucker didn't! I'll kill that no good black bastard*!

"Well, Babe," she said, keeping her voice casual and steady. "There's always something going on at the hospital. But I don't know anything about a cover-up or nurses killing patients."

"Baby, from what I'm told the story involves you somehow."

Tamara froze for an instant, but then, just as quickly, recovered. "I don't have a clue, Babe," she lied. "I don't know anything about that. In the last few days, I've had to write up two nurses, but believe me, it wasn't that serious."

Jimmy kissed her on the forehead and let her finish preparing their meal. He went into the living room, turned on the TV, and set the station at channel thirteen. After a few minutes, the couple sat together in the living room to enjoy the meal Tamara had prepared.

She put in a movie for them to watch while they ate dinner.

Jimmy forgot about their earlier conversation as he ate and enjoyed her company. Shortly before they finished dinner, Jimmy got a call; he was told to turn on channel thirteen news.

Tamara watched as he picked up the remote, still holding his phone, turned off the movie, and changed the channel to his station. Tamara looked on in silent disbelief as reporter Virginia Summers came on and gave a preview of tonight's breaking news story. *I can't stand that white, know-it-all bitch. I know she's jealous of Jimmy and me.*

"This is Virginia Summers. Tonight, at 10:00 p.m., we will bring you an exclusive breaking news story involving patient murders and cover-up at Mercy General Hospital. We will also show you video of a highly shocking nature. Therefore, parents are cautioned that this may not be suitable for younger viewers. Please join us at 10:00 p.m. for this very shocking and disturbing story."

Jimmy looked at Tamara, but no words passed between them.

She got the dishes and took them into the kitchen. Her house phone rang and she quickly picked up the receiver and looked at the display. She saw it was her parent's number. She pressed the ignore button and returned the handset to the cradle.

The doctor's last patient of the day was at 5:00 p.m.

"Doctor, your next patient is waiting in the lobby," his office manager informed him. "Charles Kirkland Jr., and doctor, this guy seems really disturbed."

"Understood. Give me ten minutes, and then send him in."

After his patient took a seat, the doctor explained the rules for the session. "Do you understand the guidelines for your session, Charles?"

"I understand, doctor."

"Good. Now what the fuck is going on with you?"

"Doctor, can I have a drink?"

"Yes, you can. Just remember what I said about not getting fucked up."

The patient poured himself a double Grey Goose on the rocks, and the doctor lit a cigarette.

"No problem, doctor," Charles said. "Can I ask you a question?"

"Yes, you may."

"Do your patients respond well to you when you talk to them the way you do?"

"I get the information I need to help them solve their fucking problems. I don't believe in candy coating shit. My methods work well for me. Now, are you going to tell me what the fuck your problem is or are you gonna sit there and drink all my damn vodka?"

"I don't know where to start," he stated, looking into his glass.

"Try at the beginning. That usually works well."

"Is it crazy to want to die, doc?"

"Motherfuckers who come in here talking about wanting to die are usually full of shit. Usually they want drugs. If that's your angle, you can get the fuck out of here now."

"No, sir. That's not where I'm going. It was just a question."

"Do you really want to die, Charles?"

"I don't know anymore. Sometimes I feel that way."

"Why? What the fuck is going on in your life that makes you feel that way?"

"I feel lonely and sad all the time. I'm up one minute, down the next, and I don't know why. I feel like my life is going nowhere."

"Are you currently on any medication or are you fucking with illegal drugs?"

"I'm not on any meds, but I have experimented with drugs in high school and college."

"What drugs have you experimented with?"

"Weed, mostly, and I have used coke."

"Exactly how long have you been smoking that shit?"

"On and off for about seven years."

The doctor turned to his computer and pulled up the patient's file. "You're twenty-five and you've been smoking that shit for seven years. What did your grades look like in high school and college?"

"They were not very good."

"What the fuck does 'not very good' mean?"

"My grades really fell off in my last year of high school, from A's to D's and F's. College wasn't much better. I just couldn't stay focused."

"Do you think your drug use had anything to do with that?"

"I'm not sure, but it probably did." The patient finished his drink.

"You're not sure? You knew what you were doing at that time was destructive. Where did you go to high school and college?"

"I attended The Gordon Academy for high school and Bailey University."

"Those are two very prestigious schools. Students of those institutions usually do very well, and they are very expensive. Whose money did you fuck up, Charles?"

"My parents' money. My father is Senator Charles Kirkland and his wife is an attorney as well."

"His wife, you mean your mother?'

"My mother died when I was a baby. I've always felt he held that against me too. Anyway, I can't stand that bitch."

"They must have been pissed with you."

"They were, and my dad kicked me out the fucking mansion when I dropped out of Bailey during my second year—the fucking senator's son, out on the streets."

"I bet getting kicked out of the house must have fucked your head up."

"Yeah it did, big time. I tried to explain to him that college wasn't for me. I wanted something different for my life. His bitch of a wife, whom I can't stand, took his side like she always has."

"Do you work? How do you pay your bills?"

"I'm covered under their health plan for now. They let me keep what was left of my trust fund. I have to find a job soon though, because the money is running thin."

The doctor looked at him with disgust. "What the fuck is your problem? You're a grown-ass man, Charles. Should your father support you your whole life? According to what you've told me and what the record shows, you've been given opportunities that many kids would die for, and you fucked it all up."

"Now you sound just like my father. I tried to talk to him, but he wouldn't listen. I never wanted to go into politics or study the same shit he did. I know he thinks I'm a failure and a big disappointment, but I'm still his kid. He owes me."

"They don't owe you shit. You're a grown fucking man and you're wasting my motherfuckin' time with this crap. If you can't see that your failings are of your own making and you can't or won't accept responsibility for your fuck ups, no amount of therapy or talking in the world is going to fix it."

"I never said I'm not taking responsibility for my life, but I need help."

"If that's the case, why did you come in here talking about wanting to die? You were born with a silver spoon up your ass and you've managed to fuck that up."

"Because that's how I feel doc. I've had these thoughts for a long time now. I'm tired of feeling this way."

"Have you seen any other therapist for this shit before?"

"No, I thought things would just get better."

"Have you tried to talk to someone close to you about how you feel?"

"I don't have anyone to talk to that would understand what I'm going through."

"How do you know if you haven't tried? Do you have a woman in your life now?"

"I did a while back."

"Where is she now?"

"That's a long story."

"Give me the short version."

"When I was in college, I met a girl named Kim. She was born in South Korea. Her parents came here when she was five. We were good together during my first year of college—that's where we met. We even took classes together. When I took her to meet my parents, that's when it all fell apart."

"What happened?"

"My father's fucking wife didn't approve of me being with an Asian woman—or any woman that wasn't white. She wasn't good enough for the son of a fucking U.S. senator or his wife, who is also a successful corporate lawyer, and she let Kim know it."

"What did she do?"

"We had a dinner party at the house a while back, and that bitch told me not to bring Kim. I told her if that was the case, I wouldn't be there either. She insisted that I be at the party. This was a big fucking affair for my father, and it was important that the family be together to support him. After the party started and all the guests had arrived, I came in with Kim. No one took notice of her, except for that bitch and a few of her arrogant fucking guests. If looks could kill, Kim would have been dead.

"The bitch made sure we sat across from my father and her at our table. As dinner was served, she started asking Kim questions about her family background and crap like that. She made a big deal about her lack of a family business, about Kim's parents' working class status, and about their life in Korea before they came to the States. She made Kim feel like she was trailer trash.

"Kim tried her best to be cordial, but that bitch made her feel like shit. I tried my best to defend Kim, but no matter what I said, she wouldn't let up. I saw her talking to Kim alone after we ate. I went to get us a drink, and when I returned I saw Kim heading to the front of the house to leave. When I caught up to her, she was crying and she said she never wanted to come there again. She said that bitch told her that she didn't have a chance in Hell of being a part of our family. She told Kim she didn't need any slant-eyed, half breed, yellow babies in our family.

"I left with Kim, and I don't even speak to that fucking cunt anymore—especially after what happened between us. She didn't give a damn that I loved Kim or that, soon after that fucking party, we broke up." The patient looked away from the doctor and wiped tears from his eyes.

"Hey, don't start that crying shit in here," the doctor said. "The sight of a man crying is disgusting. Besides, it shows weakness."

"Sorry. It's just that I miss Kim."

"What happened between you and your father's wife after this incident?"

"I don't want to talk about that."

"What the fuck did I say to you earlier? You answer my questions or you get the fuck out my office. I can't help you if you don't tell me what I need to know."

"Yes, sir. You're right."

"We'll come back to that. If you miss Kim so much, why'd you allow that dumb shit she said to her to come between you two? Why didn't you man up and explain things to your woman?"

"I tried to fix things between us, but she wouldn't talk to me. After a while, I let her go."

"Then you fucked up again. Perhaps you didn't try hard enough. I can fully imagine how hurt she must have been."

"I know. I just miss her so much." His intense heartache over Kim's loss was apparent.

"Did your drug use escalate after you and Kim broke it off?"

"Yeah, it did. I didn't know how to cope with my problems. I found myself in some real bad shit, and I did some really ugly things."

"What do you mean by that?"

"I really don't want to talk about that now."

"Then why the fuck did you bring it up? If you're not gonna get this shit off your chest, then you're wasting my motherfuckin' time and I'm of no use to you."

"What I have done is something that I'm trying really hard to forget."

"Those are the memories you need to come to terms with. Suppressing painful memories, no matter how bad they are, will come back to fuck you over later in life. Charles, get another drink and let's talk about this shit."

Charles poured himself a drink and they continued.

"Talk to me about what it is that's got your head so fucked up you can't deal with it," the doctor said.

"About a year ago, I went to a bar after having gotten into an argument with the bitch on the phone. I can't talk to that bitch without arguing with her. She makes me feel like I'm nothing. Our relationship has been bad for as long as I can remem—"

The doctor interrupted the patient. "Are you aware that whenever you bring her up in conversation, you use foul language to describe her?"

Charles did not look at the doctor or respond.

"We will come back to that," the doctor said. "Continue your story."

"Like I said, I went to a bar and got pretty wasted. I wanted to go out to meet women and have a good time. As the night went on, I got pretty wasted and the ladies weren't biting, so I decided to go home. I went to the men's room to take a piss, and this guy was in there. After I was done, I went to the sink to wash my hands and he started talking to me. I didn't pay him much mind and went back to the bar. He sat next to me and asked if I knew another place that he could check out. I told him how to get to another more popular bar, and then he invited me to come along with him. I said no at first, and then decided, 'What the Hell. Maybe I'll get lucky someplace else.' Since I didn't live within walking distance from the bar we were going to, I rode with him.

"We got into his car and talked more about nothing. We smoked a joint, and then this guy told me how handsome I was and that he'd like to suck my dick. That fucked me up. At first, I thought I'd misunderstood what he said. Then he put his hand on my leg. I moved it off and laughed, thinking he couldn't be serious. I told him I wasn't gay and that I needed a woman to suck my dick.

"He kept insisting that I let him do it. He said he wanted to give me pleasure. He pulled off on the side of the road and asked if he could feel my dick. He touched me, and I got hard. It was probably the booze and the weed. I mean, I wanted some action that night, but not with another guy.

"The next thing I knew, he had my dick in his hand and was stroking me until I got hard."

Charles was extremely uneasy as he told this story, the doctor noted; Charles's hands were trembling. The doctor lit a cigarette and studied his patient as he spoke.

"This guy goes down on me," Charles continued, "and I'm ashamed to admit it, but it felt good. He sucked my dick for about twenty minutes, until I came in his mouth. Then he put my hand on him and asked me if I would like to try doing the same to him.

"I was nervous and high, but I did it. I went down on another man. I sucked another man's dick. I even liked the taste of his cum. I would've thought that I'd be disgusted by that, but I'm ashamed to say I wasn't. Then, to make matters worse, just before we were finished, a cop pulled up behind us.

"I have no idea how long he'd been behind us. He ordered us out of the car, and we were arrested for lude and lascivious acts in a public place. I had to call our family lawyer to bail me out of jail.

"I don't know if my father found out, but his bitch did, because she had to authorize the money to get me out of jail. She was beyond furious, from what our lawyer told me. Shit has gone straight downhill from that point on. I feel as if my whole life is fucked up."

"So, answer me this, Charles. Do you think you're gay?"

"No, I know I'm not gay."

"You suck another man's dick and you're not gay?" A slight smile formed on the doctor's face.

"I was wasted on booze and drugs. That's the only explanation that makes sense to me. I can't think of another explanation."

"If you need me to help you find an explanation for why you did what you did, I can't. The drugs and alcohol simply broke down your inhibitions. You are gay, and if that's unpalatable to you, there's nothing I can do. You sucked that dick and you said you liked it. So, come to terms with what you've done and who you are."

"Even if I've never been with another man since, I'm still considered gay?" Charles started to become angry with the doctor.

"You can consider yourself whatever the fuck you want. I'm telling you, you're a fucking fag. Men who don't have it in them would not do what you did."

Charles stared into nothingness. The look on his face was one of sadness and confusion. "I don't know what to say, doctor. I don't want to be gay. I don't know how to fix things."

"The first step in coming to terms with the things you've done is to acknowledge them and accept responsibility for your choices."

"It's hard, sometimes. I've done things I can't take back. Some of the choices I've made have put my life in serious jeopardy."

"Please explain what you mean by that."

Reluctantly he faced the doctor. "I found out that I'm HIV positive just over six months ago. The cost for the medications and tests is draining my trust fund like water through a faucet. When the money runs out, I'll have to figure some other way to pay for my drug regimen."

"Given the fact that your life is in danger, you don't think your father would be willing to help you?"

"I seriously doubt I can count on him for help."

"Charles, are you currently having sex with anyone, man or woman?"

"No. I honestly find myself not wanting to have sex anymore. I don't want to give this shit to anyone else. I probably jerk off ten times a day."

"Well, at least you're decent enough to not want to give that shit to others."

"But, doctor, I honestly thought about it. That fucking bastard who gave me this shit knew he was HIV positive."

"But you haven't acted on that impulse, and that's a good thing. The alternative would have been a tragedy. Your life is a little fucked up now, but with today's treatments, it doesn't have to be an immediate death sentence."

"I know I will eventually die from this shit. Sometimes I do think, 'Why not take as many motherfuckers with me as I can?'"

"Because the innocent people you would hurt haven't done shit to you, and who would your victims be? Teenage girls and boys? Unsuspecting women you meet in bars? All these people have lives and families that care about them. Why would you want to harm people who haven't done a damn thing to you?"

"When I think like that, it's because I can't get to that piece of shit who gave me this fucking disease."

"That's a goddamn chance you take when you have unprotected sex—straight or otherwise."

"Doctor, I understood what you said earlier, but I don't consider myself gay. What happened occurred because I was fucked up, and yes, I know I can't take it back. But I'm not gay."

"Denial is a dangerous thing, but we'll address that again later. You said earlier that you didn't have friends you could talk to. Why is that?"

"They don't know about the encounter I had. If I told any of my friends, I'd lose them for good. All my friends hate gays, and I don't think I could convince them I wasn't."

"Are you now acknowledging you're gay?"

"I had one fucking gay encounter. I do not consider myself gay, goddamnit!"

The doctor's expression changed to one of anger. "Motherfucker, I suggest you lower your goddamn voice. The anger inside you needs a release, but I'll be goddamned if it's me. Do you fucking understand me?"

"Yes. I'm sorry. I didn't mean to yell at you."

"Pour yourself another drink, and we'll continue."

He did and the doctor lit a cigarette.

"How is your relationship with your father?" the doctor asked.

"I don't have one anymore. I'm an embarrassment to him. I've been told my whole life that everything I do reflects on him, that my actions could have very negative consequences for his career. I had to be the perfect son, the perfect student, the perfect child. I got tired of my father's shit, and since I'm out of their lives, I don't have to worry about my shit affecting them."

"That's not necessarily true. You are still his son. What if the media ever got a hold of your HIV status, for example, or how you contracted the disease sucking a stranger's dick on the side of the highway? I can see that hurting your father's bid for re-election and continuing in office. When you're a senator's son, the shit you get caught doing does reflect on that office."

"Well, I didn't ask to be a fucking senator's son. I just wanted to be a normal kid."

"That's a very childish and self-defeating attitude."

"That's the story of my life, doctor. I could never do anything good enough for either of them."

"How is your relationship with his wife now?"

"You really don't want to know."

"If I didn't want to know, I wouldn't have asked the fucking question."

"It's beyond horrible between us, and as far as I'm concerned, it can stay that way."

"Why? Please explain."

"When I was growing up, she wasn't the most affectionate woman in the world. I never really felt the love for her that a son should feel. Primarily, our goddamn housekeepers raised me, which is why I could speak fluent Spanish by the time I was in sixth grade. Hell, that bitch never even noticed I spoke another language while I was growing up. She was always too fucking busy studying, going to class, or doing whatever it was she needed to do to advance her fucking career. I got to a point where I didn't really care whether she was around or not. I didn't see her a lot, and I always had the sense that she wished I wasn't around, so my attitude was like 'To hell with her.'"

"Was your relationship with her always so cold and distant?"

"As far back as I can remember, it's always been that way."

"Do you have any feelings for her?"

"Honestly, I'd have to say no."

"In my experience, there have been few men who have told me that and meant it. Did you ever try talking to your father about your relationship with his wife?"

"No. He wasn't much better than she was when it came to raising me and spending time with me. Like I said, the housekeepers were my parents when I was growing up."

"When you were growing up, do you remember doing things, good or bad, to get your parents' attention, like all children do?"

"The rule in my house was 'Do nothing to get noticed.' My parents are busy, important people who do not have time for the foolishness of a child. The housekeepers made sure that was drilled into my head."

"How would you describe your childhood?"

"Other than them not being in my life much when I was growing up, I'd say it was ok. I had all the shit I needed, except for parents that cared about me."

"Talk to me about these feelings you've been having concerning death. I need to understand where this is coming from."

"I feel like my life is just not worth living anymore. I've made one major fuck-up after another, and I just don't know how much longer I can go on like this."

"So you say, 'The hell with it,' and quit? Do you see yourself as that miserable a failure?"

"Yes, all the time—especially after what happened between that bitch and me."

"What happened between you two? I don't give a fuck whether you want to talk about it or not. What the fuck happened?"

He stared into space when the doctor asked that question, as if he was searching for a way to bring the information to the surface of his thoughts. "Something really awful happened between us," he finally said.

"Take your fucking time and tell me in detail what happened between you two."

Charles's eyes became glossy as he faced the doctor.

"I told you goddamnit," the doctor shouted. "Don't start that crying shit in here. Take a deep damn breath, calm the fuck down, and tell me what happened between you and your father's wife."

"I went by the house a few months ago. I had called my father at his office and asked if he and I could talk. He told me to come by the house on a Wednesday morning at 10:00 a.m. I had shown up on time and, as usual, he'd forgotten I was coming by. When I got there, he'd already left for his office. She was home, so I figured maybe I'd visit with her. The housekeeper let me in, and I asked her to let that bitch know I was there. The first thing she said when she saw me should have been a clue for me to walk away.

"'I hope you're not here to borrow any more money.'

"I told her I just wanted to see dad.

"The rest of the conversation went to shit from there, doctor. She could barely stand to look at me. She poured herself a cup of coffee and asked me again what I wanted. I told her that I was there to see Dad, but since he was gone, then maybe we could talk. I'll never forget her words to me.

"You know what she told me, doc?

"She said, 'I don't even want to look at you, Charles. So why should we talk about anything?'

"I asked her, 'Sarah, why do things have to be this way between us? Can't we sit down and talk for just a few minutes without arguing? All I want to do is just talk. I'll leave afterward.'

"She walked away from me with a disgusted look on her face. She sent the housekeeper to the grocery store and returned to the kitchen. She said, 'All right, Charles. What would you like to discuss? I know! How about your little boyfriend you were arrested with? Would you like to discuss that with me?'

"I felt so ashamed when she said that.

"She poured it on. 'What, did you think I wouldn't find out you were arrested for having sex with another fucking man? You had to stoop that low? What happened to your little slant-eyed girlfriend? Goddamnit, at least she's a woman.'

"I sat there, doctor, not knowing what to say. I wish I had just gotten up and walked out of her life for good. I tried to talk with her. I felt, at that time, that I just wanted someone close to me to show me some compassion. I wanted her to show me some kind of love. I truly wished that I had my real mother.

"I told her, 'mom, it wasn't like that. What happened was a mistake.' What she said next hurt even more.

"'Don't call me mom, I'm not your fucking mother and never wanted to be. You disgust me. It seems the only thing you know how to do right is making fucking mistakes.'

"I told her I never wanted any of that to happen. 'I know it was my fault, but I was high and didn't intend for any of that to happen.'

"Her response to me was cold and brutal. 'Do you think anyone would have cared what your excuse was for getting caught in a car with another fucking man doing what you were doing? Whatever the hell that was, and I sure as hell don't want to know.'

"She asked me another question I couldn't answer. 'Do you have any idea of the scandal your disgusting little escapade would have caused us? Your father is a goddamn U.S. senator, for Christ's sake. Do you know what that kind of scandal would do to his career? The only reason I bailed your sorry ass out of jail and called in favors was to keep that shit quiet, so your father wouldn't have to find out!'

"I knew she was angry. My response didn't help the situation. 'Sarah please listen to me. I am not gay, and what happened occurred because I was drunk and high and I made a very stupid mistake. I know I've caused you and dad a lot of trouble. I understand how disappointed you both are in me. I'm just here to say I'm sorry and to tell you that you don't have to worry anymore. I'm going to get help for my problems.'"

The doctor shifted in his seat and thought, *He's speaking with a child-like sincerity.*

"Then she let me have it. 'Believe me, Charles, I'm not worried about you. I don't give a fuck about you. Charles, you do whatever you think you have to, but we are through paying your goddamn bills. When your little trust runs out, you're on your own. You were given every fucking opportunity in the world we could give you. How did you repay us? With goddamn failure after failure! We are through wasting time and money on you. You are nothing more than a goddamn loser and a junky. It hurts me as a mother to say this, but I wish you'd never been born, and I don't care if I never see you again. Now, please, get the Hell out of my house! I don't ever want you back here again.'

"Doctor, you have no idea how hearing her say that made me feel. I felt great anger build in me after hearing her speak to me that way. I mean, this was supposed to be someone who cared about me. She was supposed to love me, no matter what. Her words hurt me so bad I wanted to die. Then, I realized I wanted to hurt her too.

"What I said next I've always wanted to say to her. 'As a mother? Is that what you just said? When were you ever a mother to me? I don't recall you ever being a mother to me. You were never around, goddamnit. I considered Rosie, our goddamn housekeeper, to be my mother. At least she cared about me. All you ever fucking cared about was your goddamn career and fucking everyone over to get ahead. Who knows how many people you fucked to get to the top?'

"At that point, she slapped me so hard I saw stars and my face went numb. That's when I lost it. I slapped her back, as hard as I could. She fell to the floor, a trail of blood flowing from the corner of her mouth. She got up holding her face. She tried to say something to me, but before she could, I slapped her again on the other side of her face. It felt good to hit that bitch. I know that's wrong, but it felt good to pay that bitch back for all she'd done to me all my life. I moved toward her, and I picked her up off the floor by her shoulders. The look in her eyes was so hate filled I couldn't stand it. I threw her ass against the kitchen wall, and she fell to the floor. She got to her knees. Her forehead was bleeding, and she was gasping.

"The next words out of her mouth, doctor, sent me into a blind rage. 'So this is the faggot son my housekeeper raised. Boy, she did one hell of a job.' Then she started laughing at me.

"I went over to her, but I didn't see a woman. I saw someone I hated. She tried to get up, but I used my foot and pushed down on her back. She tried to crawl away, but I grabbed her around her waist from behind and pulled her toward me. Looking down on her, something snapped inside me. I thought, 'I'll show this bitch who's a goddamn faggot.'

"I threw her bathrobe over her back and ripped her panties off. She fought like a wild animal, kicking at me and screaming, calling me names. I came down hard on her back with my fist, and she stopped fighting. Holding her from behind with my arm under her, I pulled her toward me and straddled her legs with mine. I took my dick out, stroked it until I got hard, and shoved it as hard as I could into her ass. I wanted to hurt that bitch, and this was the most brutal thing I could think of at the time.

"I had never had a woman that way before, and she screamed and cursed me every time I pushed my dick into her ass. It was music to my ears to hear that bitch scream. To pay her back for all those years she'd hurt me. I don't remember how long I fucked her, but I did until I came in her ass. I wanted to share something with her, and I couldn't think of a better person to share my HIV with than her.

"I looked down on her from behind after I came. My dick was still in her ass, draining, and I felt nothing for her. She was gasping for air, as if she had enjoyed it, her arms straight out on the floor. Her face was wet from crying. She turned her head to the side and spoke in a voice that sounded evil.

"She said something to me that I will never forget. 'You want some pussy, too, you fucking failure? You feel better now, you miserable, lowlife piece of shit?'

"I remember pulling my dick out of her ass, and I left that bitch on the floor. I remember running out of her damn house. I went home and sat there for two days, waiting for the police to come. I even thought that maybe my father would come to blow me away. Either way, I knew I wasn't gonna go out easy.

"A short while after that, I wanted to die. I was going to force someone to kill me. It was at that moment that I knew I wanted to die."

The doctor sat at his desk in stunned disbelief.

Charles sat in the chair, almost as if he was in a trance, until he heard the doctor's voice.

"You have got to be bullshitin' me," the doctor said. "Did you just sit here and tell me you beat and raped your father's wife? You brutally fucked your own father's wife in the ass?"

"Yes."

"I didn't think anything anybody could say to me could ever shock me. This is some next level shit here. I need a goddamn drink." The doctor got up from his desk and walked to his office bar. He poured himself a cognac and looked at Charles with a murderous gaze. He returned to his desk and lit a cigarette.

His staring made Charles increasingly uncomfortable. "I told you what I did was ugly."

"How did raping her make you feel?"

"I felt, at the time, that I just wanted to hurt her. After I left and had time to think about what I'd done, I was so ashamed I wanted to kill myself."

"Why didn't you? What stopped you? You had the courage to fuck your father's wife, but couldn't find the courage to take your own life?"

"I don't know. Maybe I thought I could find a reason to keep going. You know: something to live for. Maybe I'm afraid to die. I don't know."

"What the fuck could you possibly have to live for after what you did to her?" The doctor's tone was hostile.

"I'm so confused, doc. At this point, I don't know."

"Why do you think Sarah didn't call the police on your sorry ass?"

"I don't know. I guess I'll never know."

"Yes you do, motherfucker—" He shook his head as soon as the word left his mouth. "That term fits you better than any I could imagine. You did actually fuck someone who was supposed to be your mother. She didn't report what you'd done to her, for the same reason she covered up your shit when you got arrested. She was avoiding the goddamn scandal and media circus that no doubt would have followed, had her rape at the hands of her husband's son come out."

"It sure as hell wasn't to protect me."

"In not reporting her rape to the police, that's exactly what she's done to avoid the shame and disgrace that would have befallen her and her husband's career. She believes she's protecting herself and her husband, and your sorry ass benefits from her silence, as well."

"I don't care anymore. They can do what they want."

"Then it's a safe bet she doesn't know your HIV status."

"I didn't tell her, and I don't plan on telling her. I hope it kills her, slowly and painfully."

"Do you really believe she deserved what you did to her?"

"At the time, I did."

"What about now?"

"I hate that bitch, so I don't really care."

"You showed remorse when you were telling me that shit. Your punk ass was almost in tears. You know what you did is probably the worst thing you can do to a woman. The fact that it was your father's wife would make people want to rip your fucking head off."

"My only regret is that I don't know if she's HIV positive yet."

"Why is that a regret?"

"Because I'll probably be dead soon and I wanted to see her suffer and live with what I did to her."

"You are a sorry, twisted excuse for a human being."

"I know that. That's why I need help."

"What about your father? Does he deserve a slow painful death as well?"

"Fuck him, too."

"That's bold talk coming from someone as cowardly as you."

"I'm no goddamn coward," Charles replied, with an angry tone.

"No? What would you call someone who runs away from his problems, someone who drowns his sorrows in booze and drugs, someone who can't stand the pressures of being the son of successful parents, someone who blames others for his failures, someone who willingly sucks another man's dick and brutally fucks his father's wife?"

"I would say that sounds like someone who needs help."

"Wrong! That description fits someone who deserves death or, at the very least, an extremely long prison sentence."

"That's not where I'm going. I can't do prison," he stated defiantly.

"You're right. Someone like you wouldn't last a day in prison, especially after the other inmates learn what you did."

Charles became increasingly nervous. "If she didn't tell anyone after all this time, I don't have to worry about going to prison."

"That's where you may be mistaken, Charles."

"What are you talking about?"

"The story you just shared with me involved you committing a very serious felony offense—an offense that I'm obligated by law to share with the police. It's the rape of a woman. In your case, you brutally fucked your father's wife."

"Doctor, you can't tell anyone what we talked about!"

"Don't tell me what the fuck I can and can't do. I know what my legal responsibilities are."

"Are you saying you have to report certain crimes patients tell you they committed?"

"Yes, but if I think I can help them through psychiatric counseling and drug therapy, so that they're no longer threats, then I don't have to report their crimes to the authorities."

"Do you think I can be helped?" Charles asked nervously.

"You're a suicidal rapist with HIV. That makes you a danger to anyone you come in contact with."

"Yes, but do you think I can be helped the way you just talked about?"

"There is sometimes that possibility. In your case, however, I'd have to say no."

"Why?"

"Because anyone who could do what you did, no matter how bad a mother he perceives her to be, is capable of committing other heinous crimes. The fact that Sarah called in favors to cover up your gay encounter and subsequent arrest to avoid a scandal says to me that you know you can fuck up and not worry about it. Then, you get away with the rape of your father's wife because she is trying to protect her husband's career. Stupid, but true. That says to you that you can get away with doing whatever you want, without fear of consequences. Charles, that's not the way shit works." A slight smile formed on the doctor's face. "Do you think you should be punished for what you did?"

"Probably, I guess so."

"You guess so? What would you demand be done to a man who raped your girl Kim?"

"I'd want him dead."

"Would you care how the fucker died?"

"Hell, no. I wouldn't."

"Then why the fuck shouldn't you be punished for doing what you did to Sarah? What is it about you that makes you exempt from the consequences of your own actions?"

Charles became angry when he thought about Sarah. Then he voiced that anger. "That bitch deserved to be fucked. She does it to everybody else."

"I've been in practice for over twenty years now," the doctor said. "I've heard people say shit that would make the average person lose all hope in humanity. However, due to my training and experience, the dumb shit people say and do does not bother me. In your case, however, it's taking everything in me not to jump across this desk and throw your punk ass out the window behind me. How the fuck can you say Sarah actually deserved to be fucked in the ass by you?"

"Because, doc, that's how I felt about her then, and how I feel now."

"Acting solely on feelings can get people in a lot of trouble. You are gonna be extremely popular where you're headed."

"Where exactly would that be, doctor?"

"The only answer I can give you is this one: Prison, motherfucker!"

Charles started to get agitated and nervous, his heart was beating faster, and he trembled at the thought of going to prison.

The doctor lit a cigarette.

"I can't go to prison," Charles said. "I won't go to anyone's prison."

"Then, tell me: How you should be punished for what you did to Sarah?"

"I don't know. Why should I be punished? She's the one who should be punished. She never loved me. I had to grow up with that."

"You've gotten away with shit your whole life—fucking up in school, doing drugs, being arrested, assaulting Sarah in the worst way imaginable, possibly giving her HIV, and yet, Charles, you sit here and act as if you don't know right from wrong. You can't possibly expect any sane person to believe that you don't understand that bad actions carry consequences."

Charles looked down at the floor he said nothing.

"Do you have any idea what happens to people like you in prison?" the doctor asked.

"My father won't allow me to go to prison. He's a U.S. senator. He'll protect me from that."

"I don't think you'll be able to count on that, when he finds out what you did to his wife."

"If you say anything about my session here to anyone, you'll put your practice on the line," Charles stated defiantly, "and my father has influence."

"Believe me, motherfucker. I'm not worried about my practice or your daddy's fuckin' influence. However, I do see how you regard your father when he can come to your sorry-ass rescue. He's a piece of shit until your ass needs to be bailed out of some shit, or the power of his office works in your favor. Well, those days are soon to be over for your ass.

"I asked you how you should be punished. You didn't have an answer. You asked me could you be helped, I told you no. You have no regret or remorse for what you did to Sarah. You hate her. That's fine if that's how you feel, but to escalate your hate to the point of raping her is beyond atrocious. You don't see yourself as the bad guy. Every bad thing that has ever happened to you is someone else's fault, never your own. You are caught sucking another man's dick, but it's not your fault. Sarah bails you out of jail and gets the shit buried. Are you grateful? No. You still hate her. You easily detach yourself from the shit you do. That is probably due to your privileged upbringing. That's why therapy won't work for someone like you, but prison will do nicely."

Charles said nothing. He sat in his chair, staring into nothingness, and listened to the doctor.

"I'll clue you in on what goes on in prison," the doctor explained, "so you'll have an idea what to look forward to. I did an internship with one of the best criminal psychiatrists in the country many years ago, in one of the most notorious prisons in the country. First, you have to understand the guards are not your friends. They don't give a fuck about you. The prisoners run the prisons. The guards are just there to get a paycheck and get the fuck out of there alive each day. Understand this: the most hardened prisoners in any institution are motherfuckers who have committed multiple murders, serial killers, sadistic rapists, hardened gang members, armed robbers, arsonists, and general psychopaths of all varieties. They make it a point to torture other types of inmates—people like you. Their victims include your run-of-the-mill white-collar criminals, armed robbers, drug addicts, small time criminals, rapists, and then there are the ever popular child molesters."

The doctor smiled as he continued. "You see, even prisoners have their own code of criminal conduct regarding what is acceptable and what won't be tolerated. Two types they don't tolerate are child molesters and rapists. They have children and female family members on the outside. The rape of a woman or child on the outside is the vilest conduct imaginable to inmates. They horribly punish people like you. Before they eventually kill you, they make you suffer the torment rapists like you inflict on their victims.

"Remember how you said you wanted to hurt Sarah, and the vilest thing you could think to do was to go up her ass? Well, you'll get plenty of that, and daddy won't be able to do a damn thing to help you.

"It's not entirely clear how the types of crime one committed on the outside get around the prison. I suspect they have their own system of communication and information sharing when it comes to that. Nevertheless, rest assured that, by your first night, everyone will know why you're there. You'll be the bleeding fish in the water, and real soon, you'll be surrounded by hungry sharks.

"No one will want anything to do with you, even the most hardened inmates. Everyone you meet will simply wait for an opportunity to pounce on your ass, and when it comes, it will come in force. It could happen walking to and from your cell. It could happen in the exercise yard or in the shower. Even the food you get at chow will have human semen, piss, and shit mixed into it.

"You might request solitary confinement for your own protection. Unfortunately, it won't be granted, because the guards will lose the request, knowing what you did, and you'll be put in general population. The guards will know why you're there, and they'll feed you to the prisoners. You see, the guards love their mothers and the criminals do also. It is a fact that—no matter what those motherfuckers have done—Mom sticks by them."

Tears started to fall from Charles eyes.

The doctor continued his tale of prison life. "They'll learn what you did to Sarah, and they'll feed your handsome, tight, white ass to a prisoner known for raping his cellmates. Chances are, he'll be a skinhead or a black man two times your size, or more. Sarah would appreciate that irony.

He'll probably be a murderer sentenced to multiple life sentences. He'll be infected with all manner of diseases—a motherfucker who doesn't have a damn thing to lose and has fucked so many men he's forgotten what pussy feels like.

"When they put you in his cell, he'll welcome you into his house, and, at first, he'll pretend to be your friend. He'll instruct you on what his rules are; what you can and can't do. You will have gotten to prison in the morning and they'll process you in during the whole afternoon. You'll be hungry, but the guards don't give a fuck if you haven't eaten. When you meet your cellmate, he'll smell the fear that'll permeate the cell from every pore of your body. You see, lifers develop a sense for another man's fear and weaknesses. In addition, they are masters at exploiting those weaknesses.

"You'll be hungry as hell when you get to your cell, but your cellmate will tell you not to leave the cell for evening chow. He'll explain the guys know why you're there and it's not safe. So he'll offer to bring you your chow back to the cell. You'll do exactly what you're told.

"When he eventually returns to the cell, he's not gonna have anything for you to eat. He'll be angry as hell for no apparent reason. Remember: you're hungry as hell, but you won't say anything. You'll be intimidated by his size and apparent strength. You'll know in your heart that you're no match for him, and it wouldn't do you any good to start a fight you won't win.

"Then, the first night, the lights go out. That first night after lights out, your cellmate will make you take the bottom bunk. He'll get off his bunk and fumble with his zipper. He'll stand over you and keep watch while he pulls his dick out and makes you suck it. He'll tell you he will let you eat breakfast and lunch, but his dick is your dinner for the next few nights. He'll make you suck his dick until he's satisfied, and he'll dare you to bite his dick or spit out his cum, so you'll swallow every drop.

"He'll tell you the next morning that you are his new bitch and you belong to him. If you keep your mouth shut, he'll protect you. Then, on the second night, the process will repeat, with you sucking his dick, only this time, while you're sucking it, he'll stop you. Then, he'll get in bed with you.

"He'll make you take off your clothes and he'll fuck you for what seems to you like hours. He'll tear your asshole to shreds. You'll try to scream for help as he fucks you, but it'll do you no good. He'll have your head buried in a pillow and a powerful forearm at the back of your neck as he takes his time fucking you. You'll feel him cum in your ass multiple times and he'll still keep going. You need to understand that even if he doesn't smother your screams, no one will come to help you. You can't count on the guards and you certainly can't seek help from other inmates.

"He'll whisper a question in your ear as he buries his dick deeper in your ass the first time he fucks you, 'Was it fun fucking her, you rotten, filthy piece of shit? I'm gonna torture your ass every night. You'll be sucking my dick whenever I want you. I'm gonna make a lot of money pimping you to other inmates. We love fuckin' pieces of shit like you.'

"After he finishes fucking you, he'll make you wash his dick and clean his body using the sink in the cell. Then, he'll beat you for bleeding all over his sheets. The only thing you'll be able to do is lie there and let him fuck you, night after torturous night, and cry like a baby. You'll wish like Hell you had killed yourself when you had the chance. Prison is a bitch, and people like you don't last very long."

The doctor lit a cigarette and smiled as he observed his patient.

Charles sat trembling in his seat as the doctor finished his tale of prison life. He actually pictured himself in prison with the inmate as the doctor told the tale. He made a fateful decision that would spare him that fate. He tried to fight back the tears that were now falling down his face, but he found he didn't care what the doctor thought. *I will die before I go prison. I will die first.*

"I'll make an exception about you crying in here, goddamnit," the doctor said, "but could you please wipe your damn face before we continue?"

Charles wiped the tears from his face using his hands. "I'll die before I go to prison. No way in hell will I let what you just described happen to me."

"Do you really want to die, goddamnit?"

"Yeah, I do. My life is totally fucked up."

"Is dying easier than facing what you've done and straightening out your fucked up existence?"

"I don't want to face anything. I just don't want to be here anymore. I'm tired, and I want to die."

"All right. Fuck it. You want to die for reasons of your own. Who am I to stop you? Living or dying is certainly your call to make. I understand this shit is real to you. I'm not going to try to talk you out of your decision. However, here is some shit you might want to consider, to help you focus your reasoning.

"One second after you kill yourself, thinking your death is going to change anything, the world will continue. No one will give a damn that you're dead, unless you make them give a damn. In addition, you will have died never having faced your problems or making reparations for the shit you've done. You obviously no longer want to be here, and that is your right. I submit to you that you stop thinking about it and do it. Stop fucking whining about how fucked up your life is and how you have nothing to live for and all that other bullshit. Do us all a favor, and do it. As I said earlier, any man who could do what you did to his own mother is living on borrowed time anyway. Once that story gets out, you're a dead man.

"You're a weak motherfucker the world can do without anyway, so go ahead and fucking kill yourself. Just don't be one of those attention-seeking losers. Because if you fuck it up and are rescued or some shit, they'll have a straightjacket and a white padded room waiting for you. You were always fucked up to begin with, and people will talk about your ass forever if you don't succeed. They'll say shit like: 'The dumbass couldn't even kill himself. How do you fuck that up?'

"Unsuccessful suicides happen quite often. Since you're already a loser at everything else, don't fuck this up. This is your one chance to show everybody you could do one thing right for a change. Fuck leaving a suicide note behind. I've studied hundreds of these notes left behind by people, and honestly, no one wants to read that shit. It looks good on TV and in the movies, but the reality is: No one gives a fuck. Everyone close to you already knows you're fucked up and they wish they didn't have to deal with your ass anymore. So you wouldn't be telling them anything they didn't already know. Hell, they want to be rid of you too.

"Kill yourself because it's what you want to do. The world won't give a fuck about you dying—trust me. Look at how fucked up your life is now, and no one cares about you as it is now. School was fucked up, and your parents didn't give a fuck about you. You have no friends and no job. Booze and weed had you sucking dick and getting arrested. Then, you took your frustrations out on your mother's ass.

"When you're dead, time won't stand still. The earth will continue its journey around the sun and people will go on with their daily activities. No one will even notice you're gone, Charles, because you don't matter. No one cares about you. You're totally alone, and, to be honest with you, humanity is better off with you dead.

"Is that the statement you want your life to have made, Charles? You at least need to make people remember you after you die. If you want to die, go for it, but your death won't mean shit unless you give people a reason to remember you. Stop giving your death needless thought. It's no longer required. You've made up your mind, so don't be a pussy and back out. The only thing left to decide now is how you want to go out. Do you go out quietly, like a pussy? Or do you go out strong?

"I say if you have to go, go out strong. Pills and guns are not always successful and those are among the pussy choices. It's your call to make, Charles. I suggest that you do a little research first, but be creative. For example, if you're into pain, fire is a good choice. If you do it right, you'll go out in a beautiful blaze of glory and even if you fuck it up, you'll still die, in excruciating pain.

"Another tried and true method is to jump the fuck off the tallest building you can find. It'll be exciting and your mind will play back your entire life in a fraction of a second. It's painless, and you won't even know you're dead. Your life and all sensations will simply stop. It's a quick and painless death. If you took that route, for example, don't wait for a crowd to gather. Don't give those fuckers a show. People are nothing but voyeuristic, pleasure-seeking scum who enjoy seeing others suffer to make themselves feel alive. The people watching below would cheer you on to jump and then laugh at you. If you take the jump route, just go to the top of that motherfucker and walk the fuck off the roof. I guarantee you'll succeed, and no one will call you a loser ever again.

"Along those same lines, a high bridge would do as well, especially falling into traffic. If you're gonna kill yourself, what do you care if you fuck somebody else's day up? They don't give a fuck about you. Bottom line: do the right thing by you. You already know what the alternative is."

The doctor observed Charles for a few seconds after he finished gauging his reaction.

Charles sat in his seat, no longer trembling. The thought of his being in prison and living the nightmare described to him had his whole body in a paralyzed state. He knew he could not allow that to happen.

"Do we have anything further to discuss Charles?"

The question brought Charles back to reality. "I have one question, doctor. Are you really going to report what I did to Sarah to the police?" The sadness in Charles's eyes was apparent.

"You can count on it. Now, please get your sorry ass out of my office."

Charles said nothing in response. The look on his face was one of total confusion. He had never experienced the feelings that came to him now. He knew what needed to be done. He got up, his head hanging low, and left the doctor's office.

The time was 9:00 p.m. It had been a few hours since Charles had left the doctor's office. He had wandered aimlessly on foot, with no destination in mind. He thought only of his death now. Charles convinced himself everyone would be happier when he was gone.

Thinking about his life and all his failures saddened him. He passed a dumpster, threw his cell phone and all his ID inside, and continued his walk. I'm *not ever returning home or talking to anyone ever again.* The session with the doctor had had a devastating effect on Charles's psyche. *Everything the doctor said to me was true. How the fuck have I been able to live with myself after the things I've done? I won't let the world label me a monster, when most of that shit wasn't my fault.*

Charles knew that his life was not worth living and that he would not let himself go to prison. Before he killed himself, he decided he might as well enjoy a few more drinks: one of the few things in life that he really enjoyed anymore.

He found a bar and went inside. He ordered his favorite drink, a double Grey Goose on the rocks. *Fuck it. I'll drink as much as I can, and then I'll do what has to be done.* As he drank, he tried hard to think of someone who would miss him after he was dead. He searched his thoughts and could only come up with one name: Kim. *She was the only person that ever really loved me my whole life, and I was too stupid to hold on to her.* He wondered what his life would have been like if they were still together.

He cursed himself again for letting his mother's words come between them. That also reinforced his hate for his mother. Charles couldn't help but wonder if he'd had his mother's love, would that have changed the course his life took? Ultimately, he decided it really didn't matter. He'd not been strong enough to hold onto Kim. He was not strong enough to be his own man. He'd never been strong enough to chart his own course in life successfully. Moreover, he was not strong enough to conquer his own fears.

He asked his bartender to direct him to the closest bridge in the area. He was directed to the Wilson Bridge, which had just re-opened. The bridge was only a short two miles away from the bar. Charles pictured the bridge's location in his mind. He finished his last drink, left the bar, and walked to the bridge.

I'm walking to a bridge to end my own life, and I'm not afraid—not of dying, of pain, or of anything else.

He felt content and at peace with what he was about to do. He took in the beauty of the stars in the heavens as the bridge came into view, admiring its elegance. The air was calm and warm, and Charles felt tranquil and content.

This is a perfect night to die. The bridge really is beautiful; its construction is simple yet elegant. The bridge's lights are a nice touch as well. Why couldn't I have been the one to design and build shit like this?

Again, he was comfortable with his failures. He convinced himself that it was ok that he was not the builder of bridges—as such tasks were always for men greater than himself. A feeling of peace came over him.

I may not have built this beautiful bridge, but my death on it will be something people will remember for as long as it exists. I'll always be remembered.

That thought made him smile. He approached the bridge from the southbound lanes that crossed into Virginia. He saw his goal. The tower on the south side. He only needed to climb to the top of the tower.

The drivers that passed him as he walked to his destination paid him no attention. Everyone was too busy trying to get where they were going. Charles figured it should take him less than ten minutes to reach his goal.

As he got closer, he saw the rungs on the tower that would take him to its top and to his destiny.

Destiny. That word made all the sense in the world to him now. This is what he was meant to do. This was why he existed: to make the world notice him. This is what he was meant to do.

Charles began climbing the tower. He found that his hands were not shaking as they usually did in the past, when he was nervous or afraid. There was no trembling in him, as the warm summer air caressed his face and body and he ascended to the top of the tower and his destiny. He reached the top of the tower in less than ten minutes. He figured he was about seventy-five feet in the air, and the view was breathtaking.

The cars look so small. I can barely hear the sounds they make as they pass below me. All those people are on their way to or from somewhere. These little maggots don't have a clue what's about to happen. They may not care about me now, but soon, very soon, the whole world will know who I am.

The warm air felt good, blowing against his face. To Charles, its effect was like the caress of a lover. He closed his eyes and enjoyed the sensation as he sat atop his tower.

He opened his eyes and decided it was time: time to meet his fate, time to go to a glorious death with no fear in his heart. He would face his death with courage and honor. He stood and prepared to throw himself into the traffic below.

He looked to his left at the traffic coming toward him and then across the bridge to his right at the cars going away from him. He decided to play one last game before he died. He decided that he was going to try to pick a specific vehicle to destroy with his body. He hoped it would be filled with people—men, women, or children, it didn't matter. He was beyond caring about anyone else his actions would hurt or kill.

Like the doctor said, 'Fuck everybody and do what you need to do. I'm gonna die so I might as well fuck someone else's day up too.'

That thought made perfect sense now. Besides, Charles felt that those little insects scurrying below were now beneath his capacity to care about. He now felt he had the power to grant life or take it away, like a god. This night, his power would be used to end the lives of others, as well as his own.

It will be glorious, he told himself.

He focused on the vehicles to his right. He made test runs in his mind on exactly when to jump so that he would impact at exactly the moment he wished. He let at least thirty vehicles pass before he had the timing down in his head.

I'm ready.

He saw his target. He prepared himself to step off the edge at exactly the right moment. He could not wait to see his life played back in his mind when he stepped off the tower. He concentrated on his target, a red minivan. He focused his resolve and stepped off the tower.

The instant he stepped off the tower, he realized he'd made a critical error. He had been concentrating on the outbound lanes, on the traffic that was moving in the opposite direction. He screamed in horror. What he saw was not his life playing back, like a movie he could enjoy. He saw his last seconds of life in slow motion as he fell to the ground. His eyes opened so wide they felt as if they were going to explode out of his skull. The air was ice cold on his skin, as he plummeted to his death. He could hear his heart beating as the noise of the traffic below him got louder. He perceived everything racing toward him more and more slowly, adding to his torment.

His heart pounded so hard he felt a horrible pain in his chest, like something was exploding. He realized that his life was not playing back in his mind and what he was seeing now was his death. He felt the terror of a horrific death coming to meet him and he screamed. He felt the shock of what he had committed himself to, and he screamed again. He continued to scream as he plummeted, perceiving every horror a human could experience.

As he fell, his intended target intersected with his location, just as he had planned. He screamed until his body made contact with the top of the moving vehicle with such force that the entire right side of his body was torn open. His blood splattered to the wind on impact. He crashed through the top of the vehicle and felt the pain of his body smashing into, and through, hard objects. He felt agonizing pain as his ribs, back, and legs broke on impact as they made contact with the vehicle's cargo containers.

His fall came to a stop, and Charles realized he was still barley alive. He could not move and the only sensation he felt was agonizing pain. He was semi-conscious, but he realized somehow that he was not alone.

He could scarcely perceive a foul odor in the vehicle. He heard sounds he could not make out. Something moved under him, something he'd fallen on. He felt his own warm blood spilling from his paralyzed body, but he was helpless to stop it. There was almost no light, so he could not see what was going on inside the vehicle.

Something pulled at his legs. He couldn't feel anything, but he knew something was pulling on him because he could feel his paralyzed body shifting. Whatever it was that was under him now started to move violently, but he could not move away. His barely conscious mind and paralyzed body could do nothing except lie where it fell.

Out of the darkness, something pulled on one of his arms and then at his legs again. Something attacked his face. He saw a mouth full of teeth coming toward him. The creature bit into his face, and he smelled the creature's foul breath as its teeth tore chunks of flesh from his head. Charles realized that a pack of some kind of animals was attacking him. He didn't know what they were, and he couldn't call out for help. The creatures were not just pulling on his arms and legs: they were devouring him alive, tearing huge chunks of flesh from his body.

He felt many of the creatures now at his stomach, eating and pulling his intestines out of his abdomen and drinking his blood. He could barely feel the pain, but what he saw with his one working eye drove him insane for the few seconds he had left to live. He watched, horrified, as he was being eaten alive.

The truck Charles fell into continued its journey down the highway. The lettering on the side of the truck read "U.S. Military Animal Research Center." Charles would be one of the thousands who go missing each year. His ultimate fate would never be known, with his body digested in the stomachs of creatures the world would never see.

Earlier that same evening, after the last patient had left his office, the doctor informed his assistant it was time to close for the day. He called her over the intercom.

"Ok, Baby, get that fine ass in here. It's time to get the hell out of here."

"Coming, doctor."

She came into his office and walked to him with her arms opened to hug him. They embraced and kissed passionately.

"Baby, did you listen in on that last crazy motherfucker?"

"Yes! That bastard is truly fucked up. I almost fell out of my damn seat when he described what he did to his mother. I wish I could have seen his face when you told him that you were going to report to the police what he'd done to his mother and that his punk ass was going to prison."

"He was in here crying like a little bitch. We can talk about his crazy ass later, Baby. We still have a little work to do. All right, Baby. We have to get this office cleaned up. Get that liquor out of the cabinet and wipe down everything. Replace all his certificates and photos. I'll take care of the furniture, trashcans, and this nasty-ass ashtray. I hated smoking those damn cigarettes, but it fucked with all those looney motherfuckers. I already re-set his computers, erased all my history, and put his files back where he had them."

"You got it, Baby. I also confirmed our reservations on the redeye back to Vegas. Our flight leaves National Airport at 11:00 p. m." She proceeded to clean out the cabinet and replace the liquor with bottled water.

"Good. That'll give us plenty of time to get out of town. Tee, are all the letters ready to go?"

"Yeah. We can mail them on our way out of town. I had everything else delivered that you'd prepared and wanted sent by courier. I confirmed that all the packages and letters were received this afternoon. I also made all the phone calls you wanted. Those special calls concerning that dirty-ass cop's bullshit got to some very interested brothers in the 'hood. I'm sure that dirty bastard is six feet under by now."

"Either that or floating in the river," he replied, laughing.

"We did it, Jeff Baby! We burned his ass good," Tee said, with excitement.

"I've waited for this moment for a long time, Baby. Because of this no-good, pompous, sanctimonious asshole, I spent eight years of my life in jail.

My own fucking big brother wouldn't testify at my trial or help me with my defense, and it cost me eight years of my life. I'm going to enjoy every minute of his downfall. His practice will be ruined when those letters get out. I'm going to relish watching the great Dr. Anthony Nichols try to get his ass out of this mess. By the time he's done answering inquiries from the police, and the American Psychiatric Association, and paying out lawsuits, he'll be disgraced, broke, and stripped of his license to practice medicine. If it all goes right, he'll spend the rest of his fuckin' life in prison."

"Jeff, you were always as smart as him. You used your time wisely. You earned two advanced degrees in prison—in Psychology and Computer Science—and you've done very well for years. So, fuck him," Tee responded to her man.

Tee held up a picture of the real doctor. She was amazed at the resemblance to Jeff. "You two could be twins, Baby, even though you're five years apart. It would be hard as hell to tell you two apart in person."

"We don't have to worry about that, Baby. After we leave here, we're never coming back. So, unfortunately, you will never meet that asshole in person, unless you want to go see him in jail." Jeff laughed.

"What I'd love to see is him explain to his tight-ass wife how he was in Europe for two weeks with his white girlfriend when he was supposed to be at a medical conference in New York," Tee said and laughed. "Baby, when all this shit kicks off, he's gonna be beyond fucked up."

"When his wife gets copies of the contents of his office computer and copies of all the letters he wrote to his little playmate, she might kill his ass herself."

"Jeff, have you ever met your brother's wife?"

"No. I haven't seen or spoken to my brother in years. Our mother died while I was in prison. After my release, I changed my name so I wouldn't be reminded I'm related to his ass. So, I've never met his wife or any of their children. I've been able to keep track of his ass via the internet, his cell phones, and his own computers. You know, Baby, computers are a wonderful thing. It's amazing what you can accomplish with them if you know what the fuck you're doing."

They both laughed as they left the office, closed the door behind them, and wiped the doorknob clear of fingerprints.

At 8:00 p.m. that same evening, Channel 13 News aired a breaking news story.

"This is Virginia Summers, Channel 13 News, coming to you live tonight with two exclusive stories. Our first report concerns corruption and police misconduct of an extremely brutal nature within the Prince Georges County Police Department. Our second report concerns mysterious patient deaths at Mercy General Hospital. We have confirmed reports that Tamara Williams, a nurse at Mercy General Hospital, is suspected of having caused the deaths of at least four patients. We will show you hidden camera video of the nurse injecting unknown substances into a patient's IV bag and other disturbing footage. We would like to caution viewers that this footage may not be suitable for younger viewers."

The report continued.

That night, at the home of Jimmy and Tamara, all was not well. Jimmy sat in front of his TV in stunned silence. He could not believe what he was seeing or hearing. He did not want to believe the report, but since Tamara would not talk to him about what was going on at the hospital, he didn't know what to think. He wanted to talk to her, but he could not tear himself away from the TV.

Even as his phone rang, he sat in front of his TV like a man possessed and watched the report. The news was over at 10: 00 p.m. Jimmy decided he had to hear from Tamara herself that she was not involved in this; that they had the wrong person. He needed to hear from her that she was not involved in this insanity; that the person on the video might not be her.

He tried to convince himself. He decided that, no matter what, he was going to stand by his woman. There was no way the woman he loved could have played a role in murdering patients.

Jimmy went upstairs to the bedroom. *This has got to be a mistake. I will believe whatever she tells me. I love her, so it does not matter what they say.*

He opened the door to their bedroom, and he saw that she was asleep He decided not to bother her. *She looks so beautiful when she is sleeping, like an angel, my beautiful angel.*

He crossed the room to go to his side of the bed and sat down next to her sleeping body. He touched her face, and his love for her was confirmed in his heart. He looked on his nightstand and saw an envelope simply addressed, "To My Baby."

He picked it up and smiled as he opened the envelope. As he read the letter, his smile and the happiness he felt intensified. He continued to the second page, but his happiness quickly faded, replaced by blind panic and horror.

He threw the letter to the floor and reached for his woman, screaming at her to wake up. He held her in his arms, crying. Her body was still warm, but she would not wake up.

He screamed her name many times, as he cried, "Tamara, Baby, wake up! Goddamnit, Baby! Don't do this, Baby! We can work this out! Please God, don't do this!"

He reached for the phone and dialed 911 as he held her. He cried loudly and furiously as he held his woman in his arms, trying to wake her. His tears flowed down his face and onto hers as he called her name and held her to his chest tightly. She would not move. She would not respond to his voice.

She was pronounced dead shortly after the paramedics arrived. Jimmy refused to let her body go with the medics, and the police were called.

At 10:30 p.m., Jeff and Tee boarded their flight to Las Vegas. Two weeks later, at the Mirage Hotel on the Las Vegas Strip, they were relaxing by the pool on a sunny hot Las Vegas morning. A copy of the day's Washington Post was brought to their table. The front-page stories of the metro section caught Jeff's attention.

He read: "A nurse at Mercy General Hospital, who was suspected of killing patients, committed suicide. Her autopsy revealed that she was six weeks pregnant."

He scanned the page, spotting: "Republican Senator Charles Kirkland of Maryland is being questioned about the whereabouts of his son. The story is still under investigation, but apparently, it involves some type of sexual assault against his wife." The article went on to say more information would be forth coming as the investigation proceeded.

Then Jeff saw the story he had been waiting for. He read: "Noted Washington D.C. area psychiatrist Dr. Anthony Nichols is scheduled to go before the American Medical Association and the American Psychiatric Association on several charges of physician misconduct and ethics violations in the coming weeks. Speaking through his attorney, the only statement the doctor would release as he came out of the District Court House—where he has been charged with manslaughter and negligent homicide—was that he simply had no comment at this time and that he needed to spend time with his family as these matters were being investigated."

Jeff smiled as he put the paper in his gym bag and lay next to his sleeping beauty.

I got you, motherfucker. I finally got your sorry ass. Now it's your turn to experience life behind bars.

He laughed aloud before he faded into sleep.

We all know family fucks you first because . . . well, maybe they are not evil. However, your friends are, and they lie in wait.

COMPELLED BY EVIL

The girls met at this particular restaurant almost every Friday after work. Afterward, they took off to dance the night away at one of the many clubs they frequented on the weekends. This meeting was not like most, however. One of the group was pregnant and hadn't been able to drink or party with her friends for some time. Unfortunately, her pregnancy was not her only issue.

Lois was the first of the four to enter the restaurant. She was greeted by the host and shown to their usual table, where she waited for her friends to arrive. It would be some time before the others arrived; Lois was early and the others would not arrive before 4:00 p.m. Lois ordered a glass of sweet iced tea and sat alone with her thoughts.

My girls have been so supportive, standing by me all these months during my pregnancy. I just wish my baby's father could be equally supportive.

She rubbed her abdomen and silently told her baby everything would be ok. She had tried again last night to talk to Vic on the phone about the baby. For the one hundredth time, it had seemed to her. Their conversation went as it had in the past: not well at all. Both of them had said mean things to the other.

She replayed the past night's events back in her mind.

She had arrived home the previous night, had settled in for the evening, and had decided to call Vic for the third time that day. Her hope was that she could convince him to come over to her place so that they could talk face to face. She had picked up the phone and dialed Vic's number. It had rung five times before he answered.

"Hello, Vic," she had said, "Can we talk for a minute?"

"Hey, Lois, can I call you back?" he had replied. "I'm kind of busy right now."

"Vic, you always say that, and then you never call back. I just want to talk."

There had been a long pause.

"All right, Lois," he had finally said. "Hold on for a few seconds. I'm gonna change phones." A few minutes later, Vic had returned to the phone. "Ok, what's up, Lois?"

"How are you doing, Vic?"

"I'm fine. No major complaints."

"Vic, do you think we can get together soon, so we can discuss the baby?"

"What is there to discuss, Lois? I told you when you first came to me and told me you were pregnant that I didn't want to have a child—not now, not ever. I offered to pay for an abortion. You said no, so what do you want to talk about that's new?"

"Vic, I told you then that I don't believe in abortions. I can't just kill our baby. I want the baby, and I just want to know if you'll be a part of our child's life."

"Lois, please don't take this the wrong way. I'm trying my hardest to be nice, but I told you months ago how I felt. I told you when we got together that I had someone. You told me you didn't care. You said that the one night we had sex was about us. No strings. You even said you were on birth control and insisted that I didn't have to wear a condom. Do you remember that? So you lied to me?"

"I remember we were both twisted and wanted each other that night. I didn't plan to get pregnant, Vic."

"Well, that's the way it looks to me. Why do you want to ruin my life? I don't want kids in my life. You're forcing this shit on me."

"Vic, I do want a child, but getting pregnant now was an accident. It wasn't on purpose, but since I am pregnant, why can't you be in our lives?"

"Lois, I don't want you in my life or a baby. Look, you're a very attractive woman. Any man would be proud to have you as his woman.

Why do you want to be with someone who doesn't want to be with you? That's what I can't understand."

"Vic, I'm not trying to trap you, if that's what you're trying to say. I just don't want to do this alone. I didn't get pregnant alone."

"You didn't have to be pregnant at all. I'm not gonna change my lifestyle for you, Lois. I have open relationships and I told you that. You're twenty-seven, I'm thirty; neither of us is married. I don't want to be tied down with a damn family. I have someone in my life that I want to be with. You and me? We were just about fun. That's it."

"Well, Vic, you didn't have to fuck me. You made that choice, and now you can't face up to your responsibility!" Lois had started to get angry.

"How many times can I say I don't want to be with you or have any responsibility for you? I've never tried to mislead you or run game on you. Hell, Lois, we haven't been together since that first time! That should tell you something. It was fun, but that's all it was."

"Like I said, Vic. You could have said no."

"You practically dragged me to that damn suite in the hotel where you work. You had that shit set up in advance to take someone there. It just happened to be me that night. You were slingin' pussy. So, yeah. I took the opportunity." The agitation in his voice had become obvious.

"I don't remember forcing you to do a damn thing you didn't want to do," Lois had remarked.

"Like you didn't want to get fucked? Don't lay all this shit on me. Yeah, I know it's partly my fault, but you came on to me."

"Vic, you don't have to be with me. If you are just willing to be a part of the baby's life, that's all I'm asking."

"When the baby's born, I want a DNA test. If it shows I'm the father then we'll see, ok?"

"No, that's not ok. Why do you doubt it's yours now? I told you I hadn't been with anyone for months prior to you. I haven't been with anyone since you. Then, I found out I was pregnant, and I sure as hell haven't been fucking anyone since."

"How am I supposed to know that? I barely know anything about you. How am I supposed to know what you and your freak-ass girls do? Have you forgotten how you all were acting the night we met? You need to check your girl Monique. She told me some crazy shit about all you bitches."

"What about her? What did she say to you?" There had been tension in her voice.

"That bitch is as easy as you are. Talk to your girl."

"Oh, so now I'm a whore who just goes around fucking everybody."

"I didn't say that. You did. Look, I don't know what else to say to you. When the kid is born, we can get the DNA test. I'm not gonna let you stick me with someone else's problem."

"I'm not trying to stick you with anything. I'm carrying your baby."

"Whether I want a baby or not? You're gonna make that decision for me? How is that fair to me? I could see it, if I felt the same as you."

"Why can't you give this a chance? I'm not asking for a lot. Why can't you give us a chance, Vic? I could make you happy." Lois had felt profoundly hurt. "Do you know how many months I am? Do you want to know what the baby's sex is?"

"I don't care about none of that bullshit."

"Nigga, I'm seven-and-a-half months, and it's a girl. I'm carrying your daughter!"

"Lois, you just don't get it. Over the last few months, you've made me miserable—ever since you told me you could be pregnant with my kid. You don't care that I don't want kids, and you say you're not forcing this shit on me? What the hell would you call it?"

"I love you, Vic. Is that wrong?"

"How the fuck can you love me? You don't know anything about me. This really bothers me, Lois. For all I know, you could be a damn psycho. You've sounded like one for months. That's why I don't want to talk to you about this shit. You don't love me, and I sure as hell don't love you, so please stop saying that."

"I don't understand how you can be so cold to me. Why won't you even give me a chance? I'm all alone and pregnant, and I'm scared, Vic." Her voice had begun to tremble.

"Look, you should have thought about all that shit before you decided you wanted to have a baby. I have someone! I'm not leaving her for you. What goddamn parts of that don't you understand?"

"I understand you have a baby on the way and you're the father."

"Why me? Of all the men out there, why latch onto me? I'm not trying to hurt you. Why can't you leave me the fuck alone?"

"Because, nigga, I'm pregnant by you. Do you remember all that shit you said to me when you were in this pussy? How good it was, and all that other shit you were talking. You weren't thinking about that other bitch when you had your face buried in my pussy, were you, muthafucka!"

"This is what I'm talking about. You sound like a fuckin' street ho now. I'm tired of you kirkin' the fuck out on me."

"I wouldn't have to, if you would man the fuck up and handle your business, nigga."

"Bitch, you can go straight to hell. You and your damn baby!"

"Nigga, fuck you!"

"Ok, that's it. I don't have anything else to say to your desperate ass. Don't call me anymore. I guess I'll see you in court bitch, bye!"

Vic had hung up the phone.

Lois had put her receiver in the cradle and had lain down on her bed. She had wanted to cry, but she knew prolonged stress was not good for her baby. The tears had come anyway, as she had drifted off to sleep holding her unborn baby.

Baby, daddy didn't mean those ugly things he said. I really do love Vic.

She couldn't help wondering what Vic had meant when he had said she should talk to Monique.

The arrival of Terri and Bernice snapped Lois's attention to the present. They greeted each other and the two arriving friends took seats at the table.

"Terri, where's Monique?" Lois asked.

"I don't know" Terri responded. "She called me earlier at work and said she'd be here."

"Girl, you know Monique's ass is never on time," Bernice added. "She'll be here. We're not going anywhere for a while."

"That's true," Lois said. "I keep forgetting we're talking about Late Ass." She laughed out loud.

"Lois, have you been able to reach Vic?" Bernice asked. "Is that nigga still trippin'?"

"Yeah, I talked to him last night, finally. It didn't go well. He's still insisting that he isn't the father and he doesn't want a baby. The only thing talking to him accomplished was getting me upset."

"That sorry bastard!" Bernice said. "Girl, what you need to do is take him to court when the baby is born. I told you I can hook you up. I am a paralegal, and I know a lot of good lawyers. Lois, you have to make him at least pay child support. As much as you might think you want this guy, you can't make him be with you. If he insists he doesn't want the same thing, let his sorry ass go. Girl, as pretty as you are, finding a man won't be a problem. Vic's ass can go to Hell."

"That's right, Lois," Terri added. "The baby will have three loving aunts. You don't need that sorry-ass nigga. We'll be with you and the baby. What fuckin' man doesn't want to know the sex of his baby? What that muthafucka needs is his ass kicked. We should get some guys to fuck him up."

All the women laughed.

"That sounds good, but I don't think it would accomplish anything," Lois said.

"It might not, but he needs to know he can't just walk away from this," Terri said. "I wonder if that bitch he's seeing knows he has a baby on the way?"

"I doubt it," Lois replied. "I don't think he would have told her."

"Well, maybe we need to find this bitch and clue her in on what her man has been doing," Terri said. "Bernice, you can track that bitch down for us. You have that kind of access."

"Terri, your little ass is so damn violent," Bernice replied. "What good would that do Lois? If we did do that, Terri, would it make him accept Lois and his baby? I kind of doubt it."

"It'll let him know he can't go around fuckin' people over. Especially our girl," Terri said. "I bet he wasn't complaining when he was making that baby."

"No, he damn sure wasn't," replied Lois.

"Well, we want to make things better for Lois, not worse," Bernice said. "Maybe he'll have a change of heart when he sees the baby. This nigga might be just talkin' shit, like most men do. You seen those bullshit shows on TV where niggas and their mamas want to deny they're the daddy? The damn test is read. When the dude says, 'When it comes to this baby, Vic, you are the father,' after talkin' all that shit they get soft as a muthafucka!" They all laughed.

One hour later, at 5: 30 p.m., Monique came in and went right to her friends' table. "Hey y'all," she said. "Sorry I'm late. I had to stay a little later at work finishing some memos for my boss. Then I got caught up in damn traffic. How is everybody doing?"

The friends brought Monique up to speed on the conversation of the last hour. They ordered drinks and dinner and talked about their plans for the rest of the evening.

"Terri, what are your plans for tonight?" Lois asked.

"I'm going to a movie with Kenny about 9:00 p.m., and then probably back to his place and fuck like rabbits."

All the women laughed.

"Damn girl, that was a little too much info," Bernice replied, still laughing.

"You know I say what's up," Terri replied. "Why bullshit with it? Since when have we been shy with each other?"

"True that," Bernice replied.

"What about the rest of you?" asked Terri.

"I can't hang tonight," Bernice responded. "I have some damn legal briefs I have to finish by Monday. I'll be tied up with that shit all weekend."

"What about you, Monique?" Terri asked.

"I don't really have any plans after we leave here," Monique said. "Phil is out of town. I don't feel like being bothered right now with any strange dick. I'm not gonna lie though, I could use some head."

All the women laughed again.

"Well, in my condition, I'm not going to be doing anything but going home and sleeping," Lois told her friends.

"No! Fuck that, girl!" Monique said. "How about you and me go to a movie? But not the same theater Terri's going to. We wouldn't want to inhibit her."

"Inhibit me?" Terri laughed. "I don't think that's possible. If I want to suck that nigga's dick in the theater or driving down the highway, it's gonna happen. If I get my pussy ate the same way, it's gonna happen. So you're both welcome to join us."

The four friends laughed until their eyes watered.

"Girl, you're a mess," Monique replied.

"Aren't we all?" Terri responded.

"Yeah, I guess so," Monique admitted.

"Lois, do you want to go see a movie?" Monique asked again. "It's better than sitting at home alone all night."

"Yeah, Monique," Lois said. "That'll work, but you have to follow me home so I can drop off my car, because you're driving."

"No problem. That'll give us time to talk," Monique agreed.

The four friends said their goodbyes after dinner and took off for their evening activities.

Twenty minutes after leaving the restaurant, Lois and Monique arrived at Lois's townhouse and went inside.

"Monique, do you want something to drink?" Lois offered.

"Do you have any white wine?"

"Yeah, give me a minute."

Monique settled into the living room and turned on the TV.

Lois went into the kitchen and came back with a glass of wine for her friend.

"Lois, you look a bit tired," Monique said. "You sure you're up for a movie? We can just sit here and talk if you like. The movies will be there another time."

"I am feeling a little beat," Lois admitted. "If you don't mind, we can just stay here and talk. I'd like that. Monique, I'm just so confused right now. I'm seven-and-a-half months pregnant, and I had to pick a nigga like Vic. I mean, he talks as if I'm trying to trap him and shit. I didn't get pregnant on purpose, but he swears that's what I did."

"Lois, I know that wasn't the case. It's a damn shame he's treating you like this. If he won't even talk about the pregnancy with you, the only thing you can make his sorry ass do is pay child support after the baby is born."

"But Monique, that's not even the issue," Lois said. "I don't need his money. I've tried to tell him that. He's a physical therapist and he makes good money, I guess, for that kind of work. I make damn near six figures a year. I know I make more money than he does. I don't need his fuckin' money."

"That may be true, Lois, but it's like Bernice said—making that fucker pay child support is not about you. It's about the baby. He helped to make the baby, and if he's not going to emotionally support her, then that bastard should be made to pay support."

"Monique, I just don't know what to do. I have feelings for Vic and he won't even acknowledge me. I'm not trying to ruin his damn life. That one night we were together was good, though. That nigga has some good dick, but for me it's more than that. He told me he loved me. I know he said it when we were fuckin', but he made me believe that he could love me. We only had sex one time, but we did spend time together after that and we'd talk on the phone a lot—until I told him I was pregnant."

"Lois, you know when a man is in some good pussy and he's a little twisted, you can make his ass quack like a duck. You could make him say anything you want his ass to say. Baby, that's probably all it was. We both know men lie, especially when their dick is hard and they want to fuck. I'm not saying that your feelings for him are misplaced. I believe you do love him, and he's an asshole for treating you this way, but Lois, you can't make him love you."

Lois put her hands to her face and started to cry. "Why did I have to fall in love with a man who won't love me back?"

Monique held her friend until she calmed down. "Lois, baby, don't cry. We can't help who we fall in love with. Your love for him is real, but he wants to be an ass. I know he told you he has someone, but look at what he did behind her back. He'd do the same shit to you, too. He's not worth your tears, and he's not worthy of you. Terri was right. You have us. To hell with him."

Lois stopped crying and composed herself. "Monique, last night when I was talking to Vic on the phone, he said a lot of things to me that hurt.

Vic said something about you, too. I have to ask you something concerning some of the shit he said last night."

"Sure, Lois, anything."

"Vic said to me that you were easy, and that you told him shit about us—about Terri, Bernice, you, and me. When I asked him what he was talking about he said, 'Talk to your girl Monique.' He wouldn't say what he meant."

Monique's face went blank. Her eyes started to water, and her hands started to tremble as she began to speak. "Lois, I don't know how to explain this to you. There is something I need to tell you, and I really don't know where to begin."

As Monique spoke, her mind drifted back to events she wished had never happened. "In February, I went to the new Gaylord Hotel Complex after work. I wanted to have a drink at one of the new bars before going home, and I wanted to check the place out. I didn't plan to stay long. I was sitting at the bar and saw one of the guys who was with Vic the night we all met for the first time. Vic wasn't with him. About an hour later, Vic came up to where I was sitting and sat next to me. He didn't remember my name, but he remembered meeting me. We sat there for a while, talking about our jobs and the hotel. The whole time I was there, he was buying us drinks.

"During the course of the evening, he got a brochure from the bar that showed the hotel's room rates. I was shocked when Vic asked me would I like to check out one of the rooms with him? I told him 'Hell no' and asked him wasn't he with you? He went on to tell me that you and him were not a couple, and that he had no ties with you."

Monique continued to tremble as she told her good friend what had happened between her and Vic. "I reminded him that you were pregnant with his baby, and that I don't fuck around with my friends' men: exes or otherwise.

"By about 8:00 p.m., Lois, I knew I was past twisted and needed to go home. I got my purse and jacket to leave, but Vic insisted that I was too intoxicated to drive. By that time, I was fucked up and he persuaded me to go to a room with him. Lois, I kept telling myself that I wasn't gonna let him fuck me. I was just gonna chill until I sobered up a little. You have to believe me. He led me out of the bar and into a room he had booked."

Monique told Lois what had happened that night, holding her head in her hands and crying, but she continued the story. Monique remembered going to the room with Vic and being excited. However, she did not reveal that to Lois. She also remembered the exact thought that had crossed her mind the minute she walked through the door.

Fuck it, I'm here now and twisted too. I may as well get my freak on.

She told Lois what had happened between her and Vic, but she did not describe what they had done in detail. The memories of that night's event played back in Monique's mind as she spoke.

I took my clothes off and got in the shower. Vic joined me. The water was hot and so was his body, as he pressed against my back and cupped my breasts in his hands. He took the soap and washed my body. I turned to face him in the shower and kissed him passionately, as his hands found their way between my legs. His hands felt so good as they worked my pussy. I stroked his dick. He was long and hard. I sucked his dick in the shower, and then turned around so he could fuck me from behind.

We went to the bedroom next. I sat on the bed facing him as he came to me, his long hard dick leading the way. I held his dick in my hand and took as much of it as I could in my mouth. I sucked his dick until he came. I let him spray cum all over my breasts and in my face. I wiped his cum off my face and breasts with a towel.

I turned around on my hands and knees on the bed, and let him fuck me again, doggy style. I felt his long dick make its way deep into my pussy. I moaned loudly with pleasure as it filled my pussy completely. I begged him to stroke my pussy harder and faster. He did and was thrusting his long dick into me with all his might. I moaned louder and louder, almost screaming with every stroke of his dick. I begged him not to stop, as he pushed faster and faster. I pushed onto the dick as I came so hard my whole body spammed with pleasure. Dripping with sweat and holding me tight against his dick, I screamed when Vic came in my pussy.

When Vic was done, I turned to see that another man had entered the bedroom, carrying a bottle of liquor. I smiled and said, "Bring it on." All three of us fucked like animals, drank, and talked shit.

Monique finished telling Lois what happened between her and Vic, but her tears would not stop flowing. "Lois, I'm so sorry. I never meant for any of that to happen. I don't know what else to say, except I'm sorry. I think Vic and his boy set me up from the minute they saw me at the bar. I think they may have put something in my drink."

Lois looked at Monique through bloodshot eyes and honestly did not know what to say to her.

The only thing in your damn drink was alcohol, bitch, she thought. *How could my girlfriend of over six years have done some shit like this to me? Try to stay calm, Lois. The shit happened and it's done. There is nothing that can be done about it now. Fuck that!*

"Monique," Lois said, "I have to know: how the fuck could you do that to me, after all the shit we've been through? I know how freaky you get when you're fucked up. But, knowing I love him, how could you do that type of shit to me?" Lois tried to control her anger.

When Monique spoke, her voice trembled. "Lois, I'm sorry. I got fucked up and it happened. I didn't fuck him to hurt you. I would never intentionally hurt you, Lois. I love you. I'm sorry it happened. I only ask that you please try to find a way to forgive me."

Lois was more confused than ever. She didn't know who she could trust anymore. Her emotional state was in turmoil, and she felt extreme anger toward Monique for what she just told her concerning Vic.

This bitch, my friend, could betray me like that? What's more fucked up is what else she told Vic that night.

"Monique, what else did you tell Vic? He mentioned something about all of us, goddamnit! What did you say to him? What does he know, Monique?"

Monique started crying again as she wrapped her arms around herself. "Lois, I think I told him."

"Goddamn, Monique! Please, God, tell me you didn't. You say you 'think?' What the fuck does that mean? Did you tell him or not?"

"Yes, Lois, I told him." Monique trembled so badly her whole body visibly shook.

"How the fuck could you do that, Monique? We all swore never to talk about that night again. If you did run your fuckin' mouth to Vic, who the fuck else knows? Monique, what the fuck are you gonna say to Bernice? And you know how crazy Terri can get."

Monique sat down in the chair and cried, as she faced one of her best friends. The magnitude of what she had done hit her hard. *What have I done? Oh, God, what have I done?* She knew saying "I'm sorry" wouldn't help the situation, but at this point she had no idea what to say. She looked up at Lois with tears falling from her face. "Lois, what are you gonna say to Bernice and Terri?"

"What the fuck do you think I should say, Monique? You betrayed us all, not just me. I could almost forgive you for fucking Vic. Goddamnit, I'm pregnant by that nigga and in love with his sorry ass. On top of all that shit, you told him our secret. Monique, I'm not feelin' you right now. Please leave," Lois demanded, trying hard to control the rage she felt.

Monique begged Lois not to tell the others what she had done. She apologized to Lois again and then left her home.

Confused, hurt, and betrayed did not come close to describing how Lois felt at that moment. As if being alone and pregnant were not enough for her to have to deal with. Now she had to cope with the knowledge that other people besides those involved knew their secret. She couldn't guess at the ramifications that this might have for her life now, but they would not be good.

This has been a horrible day.

Lois knew the only way she could keep from stressing out further was to go to sleep. *How can I sleep after what Monique just told me? I need to rest especially now.*

Lois lay in bed on her side, with her nightlight on. She felt profoundly sad. She knew the emotional turmoil she was experiencing couldn't be good for her body or her baby, but she couldn't help herself. Her mind couldn't focus on anything except her conversation with Monique, and it hurt. The impact that the revelation was going to have on their friendships could be disastrous. Lois let her mind drift back to that day two years ago, when she and her friends all had sworn to keep their secret forever.

She recalled the events that had occurred on that day that had made their oath necessary.

The four friends had agreed to meet at Monique's home one particular Friday evening after work. The women had planned a long weekend of partying, to include possibly going to Atlantic City the following Saturday morning. Everyone would be staying together at Monique's house. The rule for the weekend was "leave the boyfriends at home." None of the women were married or had children, so that was not a problem. The girls had planned a weekend just for them, and they did not want their men around to add complications.

Monique had taken Friday off so that she could be free to prepare her home for her friends. She had a three bedroom, two-and-a-half bathroom house, so there was plenty of room for everybody. Terri and Bernice arrived at Monique's about 5:30 p.m., suitcases in hand. After they settled in, they all went into the living room, had a glass of white wine, and waited for Lois to arrive. Lois got to Monique's about 6:00 p.m.

After they greeted each other and had more wine, it was time to decide where they would go for dinner, and which dance club they would grace with their presence. They gathered around the dining room table, each with a glass of wine. The friends talked and had a good time discussing what their plan should be for the evening.

"Ok, ladies. What are we gonna do tonight?" Monique asked the group.

"Let's decide where we're gonna have dinner first," Bernice replied.

"How about that Italian place, Carrabas?" Lois responded. "I hear the food is good and we all like Italian."

"That's fine with me," Terri stated.

"Ok, is that place good for dinner with everybody?" Lois asked the group.

They all agreed on Italian for dinner.

"Monique, what time should we leave for dinner then?" Bernice asked.

"We need to be at the club before 10:30 p.m. or our asses are gonna be standing up all night," said Terri.

"How about we take quick showers, change up, and be out of here by 8:00 p.m.?" Monique suggested. "It's seven now, so that should give us plenty of time. The club is not that far from the restaurant."

They all agreed and prepared to get themselves ready.

"Hey, Monique, make some of those kick-ass strawberry daiquiris right quick," Terri requested.

"I can read your mind, Terri. That's already done."

Monique went into the kitchen and returned with a tray of four tall glasses filled with the requested drink. They each took one.

"Ok, ladies," Bernice said, as they drank. "We said leave the men home. This weekend is all about us, right?"

"Yeah, but what if I get that itch and I need some dick?" replied Monique.

"Have dude scratch that ass Sunday night," Lois said, laughing.

"Or go out to the parking lot and get your freak on in somebody's car," Terri offered.

They all laughed.

"No, seriously," Bernice insisted. "No phone calls, no texting, and none of that 'I miss so-and-so' shit, right?"

"No guys, Bernice," Terri said. "It's about us this weekend, but we can think about fuckin' can't we?" She laughed.

"Yeah, you can think about it, Terri," Bernice replied. "I'm gonna hold my shit till Sunday and wear Carl's ass out when we get back."

"But what if you meet a fine nigga in Atlantic City and you wanna ride that dick?" asked Monique. "You gonna walk away?"

"I'll cross that bridge when I come to it, Monique."

"Oh, bitch, stop lying," Terri said to Bernice. "Your ass will be the first one on some dick and you know it. Remember the cruise?"

"Yeah, well, what's a girl to do when she sees a fine brotha and his dick is bulging in his swimming trunks? I couldn't resist it. But how was I to know he liked the feel of his own hand?" Bernice laughed.

"Yeah, wasn't that the muthafucka who came as soon as he took his dick out of his trunks, Bernice?" Lois asked.

They all laughed.

"Yeah, that's his sorry ass. I'm in his cabin on the bed, pussy good and wet. I open my legs. This nigga takes his shit out and nuts everywhere. He never touched the pussy. Then he couldn't get it back up. Then he pissed me off by askin' me dumb shit. 'Hey, baby, can you suck it for a minute? It'll get hard again.'"

"Nigga, please," I told him. "You already came. I don't give head to little boys. I only suck dicks that are hard and ready to go. I walked out of his cabin and slammed the door. You talk about a bitch being frustrated. I wanted to grab the first dick I saw walking down the hall. I had to go take a cold-ass shower after that shit."

The women all laughed again.

"Then the next day, that muthafucka had the nerve to keep bringing his ass around me," Bernice complained. "That is, until I told his limp-dick ass to come back with some damn Viagra."

"After that, we didn't see his sorry ass again," Terri said.

They all laughed so hard that Lois and Monique almost spilled their drinks.

"Hey y'all, we need to get our happy asses in the shower so we can roll," Monique reminded her friends. "It's a quarter past seven now."

As the women get ready to leave the table, a loud clap of thunder startled them all.

"What the fuck was that?" Terri asked. "Please don't tell me it's getting ready to fuckin' thunderstorm out here now."

The women all went to the patio door and onto the deck. They looked up to see ominous black clouds moving toward them in the sky. The rain started slowly at first, and then, after a few seconds, a heavier pour began. A bolt of lightning sent the four friends running into the house. Monique went to the TV and turned on the news.

The friends gathered in the living room in time to hear the weatherman report that the entire viewing area was under a severe thunderstorm warning until 11:30 p.m. He also warned that people should drive with extreme caution or stay off the roads due to storm-force winds.

"Get the fuck outta here!" Lois moaned. "This shit would have to happen now."

"Well, at least the shit kicked off before we left," Terri replied.

A loud clap of thunder startled the women again, as they decided on a new course of action.

"Well, I know I don't want to drive in this shit," Bernice said.

"I'm not either," Monique replied.

"Well, ladies. Our asses are stuck in the house tonight," Terri announced.

"Well, seeing as how that might turn out to be the case, why don't we just fix dinner here and get fucked up?" Monique suggested to her friends. "I went to the store today, so I have plenty of food and drink."

"That works for me," Terri said. "We can watch videos, talk shit, and drink till we pass the fuck out, and then get up in the morning early and head to Atlantic City."

The women all agreed on the change of plans.

"Hey, Bernice, since you and Lois are the cooks in the group, why don't you two fix dinner?" Monique suggested. "I'll take care of the drinks and Terri, you call Caesar's in Atlantic City and confirm our reservations for tomorrow. Since you two are cooking, Terri and I will take care of the cleanup."

The women all agreed and got busy on their assignments.

At 9:30 p.m., the women sat down to a dinner of steak, mashed potatoes, string beans, and Caesar salad. They ate dinner and enjoyed more conversation and laughter.

After dinner, Monique and Terri cleaned up the kitchen and dining room, while Bernice and Lois went to take showers. When they were done, Monique had more daiquiris waiting for them, and she and Terri showered. They went into the living room to settle down and have more drinks, while Monique searched for a movie for the group to watch.

"This is really fucked up," Terri said. "We're supposed to be at the damn club getting our party on."

"We can do that tomorrow, Terri," Monique said. "It's just fucked up it had to rain on our asses today. The clubs are better in Atlantic City anyway."

"What are you gonna have us watching, Monique?" Bernice asked. "Please, no scary shit."

"Girl, chill out," Monique reassured her. "You're the only one in the group that doesn't like a good scary movie."

"It's not that I don't like them. I need my man next to me while I watch that shit."

"Well, we can't call his ass over here now, so you're stuck with us," Terri said. "Your rules, remember? No known dick around this weekend to spoil shit." Terri laughed.

"How about we drink something a little stronger? Bartender, we need four strong Long Island Iced Teas," Lois requested for the group.

"Coming right up," responded Monique.

"After two of those, you won't give a damn what we watch," Lois said and laughed.

The four friends settled down with their iced teas and watched the first movie. They agreed on a comedy. A Tyler Perry movie first, and then they would watch a scary movie and drink more.

"Hey, y'all. Since the movie is almost over, I need to go smoke one. I'll be right back," Terri told the group. She went to the balcony to smoke and the others finished the movie. When Terri returned, the credits were rolling and everybody was standing, stretching their arms and legs.

"Does anyone want another drink?" asked Monique.

"Sure. Why not? It's barely midnight," Bernice replied.

"Yeah, it's still early. Let's go for it," said Terri.

"Lois, put another movie in while I fix the drinks," Monique requested.

The others followed Monique into the kitchen, while Lois looked through the collection of movies in the horror stack. She selected a DVD titled *Dark Secrets*. She put the DVD into the machine and went to the kitchen with the others. When the women returned to the living room, the DVD had started to play.

"What the fuck is this, Lois? Look what you put on!" Terri laughed.

"Oh, damn! I didn't know it was a porno flick!"

"That bitch got her face all in that other ho's pussy," Terri stated.

They all gathered around the flat screen.

"I don't mind watching a porno if I have to, but that shit makes me horny as hell. I don't see any dick in the room," Bernice said, and started laughing.

"Your rules, damnit. We coulda been gettin' our freak on, too," Lois said, laughing too.

"Damn, that white bitch is eatin' the shit out that sister's pussy," Terri said.

"Those bitches get paid big money for that shit," Monique replied.

The women watched the movie and laughed with an almost disgusted fascination.

"I wonder if those bitches are gay?" Terri asked, to no one in particular.

"Probably swing both ways. They get paid to fuck whoever's in front of them. They probably treat it as just another job," Bernice stated.

"Well, looking at the way those bitches are eatin' each other out, I figure them for straight dykes," Terri replied.

"Shit, I wish nigga's would take time to work a pussy like that," Monique replied.

"Yeah, they want to give just enough head to make you wet so they can shove the dick in," Lois said, laughing.

"But the muthafuckas want us to suck their dicks for hours at a time," Monique responded.

"I tried that one time," Terri confessed. "I said, 'I'm gonna suck the skin off this nigga's dick. I'm gonna make him cry like a bitch.' The nigga came twice and whined like a little girl. Talkin' bout I sucked it too good, cause he couldn't get it back up. I was like, 'Fine then, you can eat this pussy for a while.' Cause, girl, my jaws were hurtin' like shit." Terri laughed when she finished her story.

"Maybe if you mean bitches taught your man how to eat the pussy, you'd be a little less frustrated," Bernice slurred.

"Niggas think they know how to eat pussy and get all fucked up when you try to show their ass something," Lois stated.

"Oh, I guess you taught Carl how to eat you out?" Terri asked.

"I damn sure did." Bernice laughed. "Practice makes perfect, goddamnit."

The women watched the video until it was almost over.

"See, after all that, I'd need some dick, a dildo, or something. Head is good, but I need something long and hard in my pussy besides fingers and a tongue," Monique said, as she watched the two women on the video pleasure each other.

"Since Lois has us watchin' this shit, I have a question," Monique stated.

"Hey, I thought this was a scary movie," Lois protested. "It's your video collection."

"I forgot it was there. Mike brought that shit over here," Monique replied.

"Yeah, yeah, tell us anything." Terri said, as she nudged Bernice. They both laughed.

"Is there something you want to tell us Monique?" Bernice asked, still laughing.

"Hell no, ain't no dyke bitch here. I like dicks of all shapes and sizes," Monique responded and laughed with them.

"I need another damn drink," Terri said.

"Seriously, though," Monique said. "I want to ask you ho's a question. Have any of you ever been eaten by another women?"

Lois and Bernice looked at Monique and replied, almost in unison, "Hell no!"

"But you know dyke bitches are always hittin' on straight women, asking can they do that shit to you. I get that shit at least once a month. I had to tell one bitch that wouldn't take 'No' for an answer that I would let her eat me after my man came in my pussy. That dyke bitch hauled ass away from me."

All the women were laughing when Terri stumbled into the living room with another drink.

"What did I miss?"

"Monique asked have we ever let a bitch eat our pussy. I told her that I had to tell one dyke that she could after my man came in me."

They all laughed again.

"Damn girl, you nasty, and y'all talk about me. Bernice's ass can get raw too," Terri said and laughed. "But you know what? I'd let a bitch eat my pussy. As much as I love head, a bitch could eat my pussy all day. I know I'm not a fuckin' dyke. I'd give that ho a stomach full of pussy juice." Terri laughed so hard she spilled her drink.

"But by letting a woman eat you, wouldn't that make you gay too?" Lois asked.

"No, because we can do that type shit," Terri replied. "For women, it's called experimentation. If a man did that shit, his ass is gay." She added,

"Which one of you horny ass bitches brought that shit up anyway? That freak-ass movie got you ho pussies tingling."

"Blame Lois for putting that shit on without dicks in the room," said Bernice.

Terri laughed.

"Monique, what about you?" Lois asked, as she finished her drink. "Have you ever got head from a woman?"

"I did one time in high school. I was taking a shower after gym and changing my clothes. I noticed this girl kept looking at me on the sly. I asked her what she was looking at, and she said I was pretty. I thanked her and didn't think anything of it. Then she came over to me and asked could she kiss my stomach. I knew what she wanted, and I was curious so I dropped my towel, stood in front of that bitch, and she went to work right there.

"We damn near got caught by the gym teacher, because when I came, I made a little too much noise. We heard the door open to the locker room, and she got off my pussy just in time. That was the only time I ever let a woman touch me like that. I never saw her again after that, but the bitch gave good head."

"See, like I said, I'd let a bitch eat me," Terri said again.

"Don't you hos get tired of not having your pussies eaten the way it should be? Tell the truth: how many times have we complained that our men don't eat us right?" Monique asked her friends.

"All the time, but that doesn't mean I'd necessarily let a women do it," said Lois. "Even though I have been curious about what it would feel like."

"Why not?" said Terri. "Head is head and the shit feels good. Especially when your fucked up and horny like all our asses are now."

"What are you saying, Terri? We should experiment with dykes to see how it feels to be eaten by a woman? I know I couldn't do that," Bernice said.

"No, fuck that. I wouldn't let one of those nasty bitches touch me either. But now that you ho's brought this shit up, I have been curious about it," Terri stated.

"Ok, so we're curious about what it feels like to get head from a woman. The only one of us that has experience with that shit is Monique. So, should we let Monique give us all some head?" Lois said and laughed.

"I'm not eatin' all you bitches, and remember, I was on the receiving end. I didn't give shit." Monique laughed and continued talking. "So, let's give each other some head and kill the fuckin' curiosity. Who the fuck is gonna find out? What the fuck? My pussy is wet, and now I'm horny as hell."

The words left her mouth before she had time to think about what she said. Her words caught the other women totally off guard. No one said a word for a few seconds.

"Are you serious, Monique? Did you just hear what your drunk ass said? We should give each other head? Girl, we're all best friends. How the hell can we eat each other?" Lois asked, stunned.

"Because, Lois, we're all horny as hell after watching that freak-ass video you put on, drunk as hell, and no men to fuck," Terri replied.

"You bitches have had a little too much to drink. I'm curious, but how do we do that? Like Lois said, we are best friends and we're gonna eat each other?" Bernice didn't laugh.

"We'd all agree to do this one time to see what it's like, and then carry our horny asses to sleep," Monique responded.

"Are you serious, Monique?" asked Lois.

"Yeah, why the fuck not?" Monique replied. "We are all friends, and we care about each other. We can make each other feel good, and it'll be our secret for life. We never have to do the shit again if everyone agrees."

"What, we partner up, go to a bedroom and eat each other?" Bernice asked.

"If we're gonna do this shit, I say no hiding behind closed doors. We can get our freak on in front of each other and get it over with," Terri replied.

"Ok, you bitches figure the shit out," Lois responded. "I need another drink."

"Hold the fuck up," Bernice protested. "I didn't agree to do no shit like this!"

"Oh bitch, come on. What, you gonna watch?" Monique slurred her words.

"I can do that," Bernice responded. "Maybe that and another drink will loosen me up. I don't know about this crazy shit . . ."

Lois returned with another drink and joined the conversation. "Look, I'm getting tired and I'm fucked up. This is some crazy shit we're talking about doing, but if we are gonna do this, y'all better make up your minds because I'm horny and getting sleepy."

"I know! We can do a Link," Monique said.

"What the hell is a Link, Monique?" asked Bernice.

"We can do this at the same time, all at once," Monique told her friends.

"How?" asked Terri.

"There are four of us. We line up. Two lie down on our backs and two on our knees. It's called a Link," Monique explained.

"But it's not all at once. The last person will be left out if it's done that way, unless somebody is flexible as Hell," Lois said.

"If that's the case, then somebody has to switch, because the first person lying down won't have a pussy to eat," Terri laughed.

"Ok, the last person will get eaten by the first person. How's that?" replied Monique.

"You bitches are crazy," Bernice said. "We're sitting here talking about how we're gonna eat each other out. This is some crazy, off-the-wall shit. Are we really that drunk and horny?"

"You gonna back out now? Three of us want to try it. What the fuck, Bernice? Be a little adventurous," Terri said.

"Oh, bitch, your little ass is always horny. What the hell? Why can't I just watch you three get off?" Bernice asked.

"Because, we all do this shit together or forget the whole thing and go masturbate our asses to sleep," Monique replied.

After a few seconds and looking at her friends, Bernice decided to go along with the group. "All right, you horny bitches. Come on, before the alcohol wears off. I can always claim I was fucked up and didn't know what I was doing." Bernice laughed.

"By the fuckin' way, Monique, how the hell do you know about this Link shit?" Lois asked.

"Watchin' those freak-ass porno movies with Mike."

"Yeah, ok Monique. Tell us anything," said Terri.

"No bullshit. I never did this before, but the Link thing I just made up. It makes sense, like a chain all connected together."

"Before we do this, we need to get one damn thing straight. As long as our asses stay black, we will never tell anybody what we did here," Bernice stated to her friends, with seriousness in her drunken voice.

"Hell, yeah. If anybody lets this shit out, the rest of us will fuck that ass up," Terri added.

The women all looked at each other and agreed.

"Lois, help me bring some blankets and pillows down here so we can make a big bed on the floor," Monique asked.

"I'll move the furniture around and dim the lights," Terri said. "Give me a hand Bernice."

"I swear, I don't believe I'm getting ready to do this," Bernice said to Terri, shaking her head.

"It'll be different. What the hell, Bernice? It'll be a new experience for all of us. Now we'll see for ourselves if it's true or not that women know what women want."

Monique and Lois returned with the blankets and pillows. Everything was laid out on the floor. The furniture and tables were moved to create a space large enough on the floor for everyone.

"Ok, are there any rules? Shit we should or shouldn't do?" Lois asked.

"I don't want to do any kissing," Bernice stated.

"Is sucking tits ok with everyone?" asked Terri.

"I'm down with that, but no dildos allowed. Fingers only," said Monique.

"Ok, no kissing on the lips," said Monique.

"Which lips?" laughed Terri.

"No kissing on the mouth, smartass."

"Ok, here it is: No kissing on the mouth by anybody, fingers only, and tits can be sucked. Ready to get started y'all?" Monique asked.

The women all looked at each other and slowly began to take off their clothes. When they got to their underwear, they stopped to decide what the order would be.

"Ok, who is gonna do what to whom first?" Lois asked.

"It doesn't matter," Terri responded. "Everybody is gonna get done."

"How about this? Bernice, you lie down first, since we have to loosen your ass up. Terri will eat you. I'll get under Terri and Lois will do me while

I lie under Terri. Lois will be on her knees. When we switch, Bernice, you'll do Lois, I'll do you, and Terri does me," Monique explained.

"I have a question. Is there a time limit on this?" Bernice asked.

"No, but we do want to make each other cum. Otherwise, what's the point?" Monique responded.

"How about those eating go until they get tired or her partner cums, and then we switch?" Terri replied.

The women all agreed.

"One last thing. Does anyone want to shower up real quick? We wouldn't want our shit to be too tart, seeing what we're getting ready to do," Terri said, laughing.

"We already took showers. We didn't do anything except sit here and watch a movie. It's getting late. I suggest we get busy before our asses go to sleep, and I back out of this crazy shit," Bernice said.

The women stood in a circle and all removed their underwear, tossing the garments to the side. They were all in their twenties, and all of them had firm, curvy bodies and full round breasts. They all looked at Bernice when her underwear was removed, and though none of them said anything, they all thought the same thing. *Her body is gorgeous.*

Bernice was the oldest of the group, at twenty-nine, and the tallest, at five feet eight inches. Her skin was beautiful and flawless, the muscles of her arms and legs well toned, her breasts big and firm. She had a defined abdomen and the hair on her pussy was shaved close and tapered.

Terri felt herself getting wet as she viewed her friend's naked body. *It's no wonder that nigga on the cruise sprayed nut everywhere when he saw this bitch naked. I see why now. I wonder if her pussy tastes as good as she looks naked? I guess I'll find out in a minute.* Terri's mouth watered as these thoughts went through her mind.

Bernice lay down on her back and spread her legs. Terri went down on Bernice and started to eat her pussy. Slowly at first, teasing, and wetting her pussy with her tongue.

Monique got under Terri and positioned herself. She pulled Terri to her so that Terri's pussy was over her mouth. Monique opened her legs and Lois went down on her. Bernice moaned with extreme pleasure as Terri worked her pussy with her wet tongue; circling the lips of her pussy and her clit; playfully teasing her as Bernice's moans got louder. Bernice cupped and squeezed her own breasts, making her nipples hard, as Terri pleasured her pussy with her tongue, lips, and fingers. Gently working her clit, Bernice felt the warmth of her body increase as her juices freely flowed.

Terri found that the combination of eating pussy and being eaten at the same time was overwhelming her senses. She found it hard to concentrate. She moved her hands to Bernice's breasts, as Monique licked and gently sucked her clit. Terri's moans got louder and her breathing came in gasps of pleasure. Terri gently responded to Monique's tongue by pressing and sliding her pussy against it. Monique squeezed Terri's breasts as she ate her pussy.

Monique felt the wetness and pleasure of Lois's tongue working her pussy. Lois's tongue was fast and gentle as she teased Monique's clit with her tongue and lips. She felt Lois insert her fingers into her wet pussy as she ate her; it was phenomenal as she felt the double pleasure of Lois's tongue and fingers inserted into her pussy.

Lois felt like electricity was coursing through her body as she became more and more wet and tremendously excited. She used her free hand to play with her own pussy as she ate Monique. She moaned gently as she felt the warmth between her legs increase.

The women pleasured themselves and their partners for hours. No one moved from her position, as they enjoyed what they were sharing. As one, they were all happy and relaxed. The feelings and pleasure they shared was unlike anything they had ever experienced. What they found here on this night transcended what they thought they knew about sex.

Monique came first, as Lois forcefully teased her clit. Monique spasmed with pleasure as she lay under Terri, sucking her pussy. She put both her hands on Terri's hips and squeezed as she came again. As Monique came, so did Terri.

Terri gripped Bernice's wet soft breasts in her hands, almost screaming with pleasure. The next hour was more of the same awesome sex. Bernice, who didn't come the first time, admitted that she had had the strongest orgasm of her life while she gave Lois head and Monique ate her.

Lois remembered that it was almost magical; they all had an orgasm at the same time, even Terri who was on the end. She remembered they all screamed at the same time when they all came at the same instant. She had never experienced anything like that before or since, and probably never would again.

Lois remembered those events as if they had happened yesterday, as she lay in her bed trying to go to sleep. Peaceful sleep was going to be so difficult, now that she knew what Monique had done. She couldn't help crying, because the magic they'd experienced that night together had been destroyed.

The next day, Lois drove home from work, still upset about what she knew.

I can't keep what Monique told me to myself, she thought. *Bernice and Terri have a right to know.* It had been a few days now since Monique had told Lois that she had revealed their secret to Vic, after having fucked him and his friend. Lois had not spoken to Monique since she had confronted her about what Vic had said to her that night on the phone. Lois also knew that she could no longer avoid Bernice and Terri's calls.

They are just worried about me, and they know that I have been having a hard time with this whole pregnancy situation and Vic's sorry ass. I'm due to have my baby in a month, and I don't know how to get through to Vic. He probably hates me, but right now, I don't care. I've started my twelve-week maternity leave, so I don't need to worry about work for a while. I need to talk to my girls.

Lois got to her driveway, and still her thoughts turned to Vic. *This would be so much nicer if Vic would share this with me and our baby, instead of being with that other bitch.*

She parked her car and went inside. Lois put her purse on the table and sat in front of her wide screen TV. *Vic would love this TV,* she thought. *All men like watching their sports on big screens. Maybe I'll invite him over soon.*

Lois decided to take a quick nap and call her friends after she woke. She rubbed her abdomen and told her daughter that everything would be ok. *You'll be born soon and daddy will be with us.*

Tears spontaneously fell from Lois's eyes. *If Vic was here, that would feel so right, to have him in our lives. I'm gonna make it happen one way or another.*

She set her alarm for 5:00 p.m. and went to sleep. She woke up when the alarm went off, took a shower, and fixed a light dinner. As she ate her meal, she tried to decide the best way to break the news to her friends. This was not something that she wanted to do, but she had to.

Monique put herself in this situation. It wasn't bad enough that she fucked my man behind my back. She had to run her fuckin' mouth about what we did, and there's no telling who Vic may have told. He obviously believed it, or he wouldn't have said what he did to me. I really don't want to do this, but I have no choice. They have to know.

Lois called Bernice and Terri and told them that she had to talk to them about something important. She asked if they could come to her place around 8:00 p.m., and they both agreed. Bernice arrived at Lois's at 7:45 p.m. Terri got there minutes later. They all went into the living room so that they could talk.

"Lois, is everything ok? How are you and the baby doing?" asked Bernice.

"We're ok," Lois reassured her. "I took my maternity leave, so I'll be off for the next twelve weeks. The doctor says I'm right on schedule."

"Any news from Vic's sorry ass?" Terri asked.

"No, I haven't heard from him in weeks, and I don't plan on calling him either. Not until the baby is born."

"Well, whatever you decide to do, we got your back. Now, why the hell haven't you returned my calls in the last couple days? Girl, you had me worried," Terri scolded her, and Bernice agreed.

"I've had a lot on my mind the last couple of weeks, and I have been trying to work some things out," Lois replied. "That's all."

"Is everything ok at work?" Bernice asked. "I know how employers trip when a woman has to take that much leave."

"No, my supervisor is cool with my leave," Lois said. "She told me to take as much time as I need. My whole twelve weeks will be paid, so that's not an issue." She looked at her friends. "Does anyone want anything to drink?"

"Do you have any soda?" Bernice replied.

"Yeah, I'll get it," Lois responded.

"No girl, you stay there. I'll get them." Terri headed to the kitchen.

"Lois, what's bothering you?" Bernice asked. "I can look at you and tell something isn't right." The concern in her voice was obvious.

Lois felt the tears that wanted to fall start to well up in her eyes when Bernice asked that question. She fought her hardest not to cry in front of her friends. She loved them both and did not want them to worry about her.

Terri returned with drinks for them all, and she too noticed the look in Lois's eyes.

"Lois, what's wrong?" Terri demanded. "What did you say to her, Bernice?"

"I asked her what's wrong."

"Ok, you two," Lois said. "Stop. We need to talk, and what I have to say isn't easy."

"You can tell us anything," Bernice insisted. "You know that we're here for you no matter what. By the way, is Monique coming over?"

At the mention of Monique's name, Lois again felt profound sadness that made her want to cry. "I didn't call her. She's the reason I called you two."

"Lois, what's going on?" Bernice said, now clearly concerned. "Now I'm starting to get worried."

"I really don't know where to start with this shit," Lois said.

"Take your time girl, we're here," Terri told her.

Lois began her tale. "Remember when we were together at the Spot, and Monique and I were gonna go see a movie? Well, we didn't make it. We came back here to talk, because I didn't feel up to a movie. The last time I talked to Vic, he'd said something to me that really bothered me, but he wouldn't explain what he meant. It concerned Monique. When I asked her what the hell Vic was talking about, she told me."

Lois paused before going on.

"She told me she fucked Vic and one of his friends at the Gaylord Hotel in February."

Bernice and Terri were shocked and sat as rigid as statues; both their mouths dropped open and their eyes opened wide in stunned disbelief as they listened to what Lois had to tell them.

"She told me Vic got her drunk, they went to a room, and she fucked him and his boy." Lois started to cry.

"Don't cry, Lois. I'm gonna kill that bitch. How the fuck could she do some foul shit like that!" Terry replied with intense anger.

"That's not all of it," Lois continued.

"When I talked to Vic, he also said that Monique told him some freaky shit concerning all of us—"

Bernice interrupted. "Lois, don't tell me Monique ran her fuckin' mouth about us. I know she didn't tell that muthafucka what happened between us."

"Yes she did, Bernice. She said she was fucked up and she told him everything."

"Where's that bitch now?" Bernice shouted. "I'm gonna fuck her up. We swore that we would never tell anybody that shit. I don't give a fuck that she was drunk!"

"Now, we haven't talked about that night in over two years among ourselves," Terri said. "She decides that she wants to run her fuckin' mouth now to other people? On top of that, she fucked Vic too, knowing how much you care for that nigga. I'm gonna fuck that bitch up good!"

Bernice couldn't stop shaking her head, with a disgusted look on her face. "How the fuck could she have done this shit to us?" Bernice asked to no one.

"I asked her the same damn question," Lois said. "All she could say was she got fucked up and it just happened. Vic and his boy set her up and she asked if I could forgive her for what she did."

"I'll never forgive that bitch!" Terri cried. "She fucked Vic and told our goddamn secret to him and his boy. Who knows how many other fuckin' people know about us? Monique deserves a serious beat down, and I'm gonna give it to her."

"What good would kicking her ass do us now, Terri?" Lois asked. "The shit is out there now. Why do we have to make it worse by beating on her? I'm pissed too, but aren't we too old for that dumb shit?"

"I don't know, Lois," Bernice said, struggling to control her emotions. "I want to kick her ass too. We've known each other for years, and as much trash as we talk, we have remained close and loyal to each other, especially after the Link. Now Monique has fucked that up."

"Please don't do this," Lois implored. "Let's get together, and we'll all sit down and talk about it, ok?" She did not want the others to hurt Monique. She put her hand on her abdomen.

"Lois, I don't want to upset you, but hearing what you told us is fucked up," Terri said. "I would have never thought Monique, of all people, would do some shit like this to us. Everything we did that night was her goddamn idea. I'm just wondering now if that bitch set us up for something." Terri's body trembled with anger.

"She had to know we'd find out sooner or later," Bernice said. "Whoever she told would run their mouths about what they heard, sooner or later. We hang out at the same spots and know a lot of the same people."

"Look y'all," Lois said. "It's been months since she told Vic and none of us has heard anything. Why don't we just get together and talk to her? I'm pissed too, but we don't have to beat on her, do we?"

"We made a promise to each other, Lois," Terri said, "and we agreed to never even talk about what happened. We also agreed what would happen if anyone ran her mouth about it. What good would talking to Monique do? She can sit here and say she's sorry all day. It won't change shit. That bitch still betrayed us."

"How do we trust her again, Lois?" Bernice asked. "Why would you want to be around her after she fucked Vic? She knew what time it was. According to what she told you, she wasn't so fucked up that she forgot you're pregnant by that nigga. I'm so pissed I really don't know what else to say at this point. I can tell you this, though. I'm done with Monique. I never want to speak to her again."

"Well, I still want to put my foot in her ass," Terri said, "but you know what? Fuck it. I don't ever need to see her again. She is gonna know how I feel about her ass though!"

"I honestly didn't want to tell y'all what she did," Lois said, "but I had to, and it wasn't to ruin our friendship."

"Lois, you're not the one who told our secret or fucked any of our men. Monique's nasty ass did that," said Bernice.

"So, what are we gonna do? Let that bitch get away with what she did?" Terri asked.

"For now," Lois suggested, "why don't we just let it go, and say the hell with her? This is hard enough to deal with as it is. I don't want to have to deal with any violent shit, ok? The baby has lost one aunt already."

"Only because you asked me to, you saved that bitch from a serious beat down, Lois," Terri replied.

"It's getting late, Lois," Bernice said. "I need to get home. If you need anything at any time, Lois, call me. I don't care what hour."

"Yeah, I'm good and pissed," Terri said. "Let me get out of here too. Same thing goes here: if you need me, call."

The women all hugged and said goodnight.

Terri and Bernice stopped to talk when they got far enough away from Lois's front door.

"I didn't want to upset Lois anymore, Bernice, but there is no way in Hell Monique is gonna get away with what she did. No fuckin' way," Terri stated.

"I agree. Call me when you get home and we'll discuss this shit."

They got in their cars and left.

After her friends left, Lois tried to relax in front of the TV. She also tried not to worry about the conversation she'd just had with her two best friends. Feeling confident that no harm would come to Monique at the hands of Terri or Bernice, she relaxed a little and the tension she felt faded away. Watching TV was not what she really wanted to do, though. She needed to talk to Vic.

The thought that his daughter was due in four weeks and he still had not committed to be a part of her life made her angry. She decided to call him. She wanted to try again to talk some sense into him. She decided she would make him listen to her, whether he wanted to or not—not for her sake, but for their daughter's. Even if she had to go to his house, he was going to listen to what she had to say.

Lois called his number repeatedly for the next hour and a half. She left many messages for him to call her. None of her messages were demands or threats, just simple pleas for him to call her at his earliest convenience. She sat and waited for a call that might never come.

At 11:00 pm, she decided to go to bed. She told herself that Vic was not going to call, and she prepared herself for bed.

At 11:45 p.m., her phone rang. Her heart beat just a little faster and she actually felt a bit of joy thinking that it might be Vic calling her back. She let out a sigh of relief when she picked up the phone.

At least he called back, that's something at least.

Lois picked up the phone and greeted the caller. "Hey, Baby—"

An unknown female voice responded immediately. "Hi, my name is Kim. I don't know you, but why are you repeatedly calling this number?"

"I was calling for Vic. I'm sorry. Do I have the wrong number?"

"No, the number you were dialing does belong to Vic. I just want to know why you're calling him."

"Who you are again?"

"I'm his woman. Now can you please tell me who you are and why you're calling Vic?"

Lois felt her heart sink in her chest and her thoughts were in turmoil.

This is the bitch he loves, the ho that he's denying his baby for, and I have the skank on the phone.

"My name is Lois," she replied, "and I need to speak to him."

"Vic is not in right now. He left without his cell phone. You can tell me what you want him to know, and I'll be happy to pass it on."

"Kim, is that your name? Well, what I have to tell Vic is between him and me. I don't mean to be disrespectful, but it has nothing to do with you."

"Lois, when another woman calls my man and won't tell me what she wants, it becomes my business. What would you say if our positions were reversed?"

"Well, I need to talk to Vic about some very important issues." Lois became angry as she talked to the woman who stood between her and Vic.

"You're not woman enough to discuss those issues with me, Lois?"

Lois sensed Kim's mockery. "Bitch, my issue has nothing to do with you!" she replied.

"You're a very angry child, aren't you?" Kim taunted. "I didn't call you out your name, nor have I used profanity when speaking to you. You may not respect yourself, but when you talk to me, please try to act like your mother taught you better."

"Where the fuck is Vic?" Lois demanded.

"Why should I tell you that? If he wanted you to know where he was, he'd have taken one of your many calls before now."

"I don't have time to sit here playing games with you," Lois said. "I need to talk to him."

"As I said earlier, why don't you tell me what you want and I'll tell him?"

Again, Lois heard the mocking tone. "All right, you wanna know? You can tell Vic that his daughter is due next month and we need to talk." Lois felt a small sense of satisfaction telling Vic's woman she was pregnant by him.

"Are you saying you're going to have Vic's child?" Kim did not sound shocked to hear this revelation.

"Yes I am, which is why we need to talk."

"Does Vic know that you're pregnant with his baby?"

"He knows. I told him months ago, when I found out I was pregnant."

"Obviously, he doesn't believe he's the father," Kim said. "If he did, you wouldn't need to call him so close to your due date. You wouldn't have to be tracking him down. I'd have known about you, if you meant anything to Vic."

"How the hell would you know shit about me, if he's fuckin' around on the down?"

"Lois, I'm going to assume you have some bit of education. You don't need to speak like gutter trash to make your point. A real woman does not need to speak in such a manner."

"How long have you known Vic?" Lois asked.

"That. my dear, is none of your business," Kim replied. "But I'll tell you anyway. I've been with Vic for just over three years now."

"Then you and he were together when I met him?"

"Yes, we were. We have a unique relationship. I don't mind Vic having his little playmates, as long as he doesn't bring me anything he didn't leave here with. We both have that freedom, although he exercises his freedoms more than I do. Did he ever tell you that?"

"He told me he had someone and that he wasn't going to leave her." Lois felt deeply depressed after her response.

"Then why did you continue to pursue him?"

"I probably wouldn't have, if I hadn't gotten pregnant."

"Lois, you have to understand something," Kim explained. "I'm not angry with you. I know what Vic does in the street. I'm fine with that because we both have the same understanding. However, you need to know that someone like Vic will never be faithful to you or to anyone else. Did you know he doesn't like being around children? He's a physical therapist, and the sight of a pregnant woman disgusts him. I could never figure that out, considering his line of work."

Lois's heart broke when she heard that from the woman that Vic had been with for years.

"He told me he didn't want to have any kids," Lois said.

"But you do?" Kim asked.

"Yes, I want my baby."

"Lois, do you think that having his baby will somehow bring him into your life and change the person that he is?"

"I don't know. I just want him in our lives. He thinks I got pregnant on purpose. I didn't plan this, although he thinks that's what happened."

"Did you get pregnant on purpose?"

"No, I didn't. But when I found out I was pregnant, I wasn't going to have an abortion."

"Lois, are you sure he's the father?"

"Yes. I tried to explain that to him, but he won't listen. He wants to take a DNA test after my daughter is born."

"Of course he wouldn't believe you. A man like him doesn't need a child in his life, Lois. He enjoys his freedom too much, and he won't let himself be tied down with a child or a family. So, no matter what you do, he'll never be with you."

Lois started to cry on the phone.

"Lois, don't cry," Kim said. "I know this is upsetting, but that is the man you chose to have a baby with."

In a trembling voice, Lois responded to Kim's statement. "I just don't know what to do."

"Lois, honestly, there isn't a lot you can do, but I'll tell you this. I enjoy my freedoms and my lifestyle, just like Vic. However, I'm coming to a point where I need a change in my life as well. Whether or not this turns out to be Vic's baby, I don't know how much longer I want to stay with him."

"Are you saying that you and he are breaking up?" Lois started to feel hope when she heard Kim say that.

"I'm saying it's going to happen, regardless of what happens in your situation. I'll clue you in to something. Vic is not a violent man, but Vic is the kind of man who responds to extreme action. Words don't have much of an effect on him."

"Does he know you're leaving him?" Lois asked.

"It doesn't matter what he knows. I, like him, can come and go as I please. However, I will tell you this: I'll talk to him concerning your situation. I will try my best to persuade him to speak with you. I can't say that he will, but I'll try."

"Kim, can I ask you why you would do that? I mean, get him to talk to me."

"Because, if Vic is your baby's father, he needs to do right by his child. I do not want to be with a man who has the responsibility of children. I will not be second to anyone. It's time he and I go our separate ways anyway—not because of your situation, but because I am ready to move on. The fact that my father was not in my life is another reason Vic needs to step up if this is his child. I personally know how terrible not having a father around can be for a child."

"Do you love him, Kim?"

"Not in the way you think of love. I'm not married to him, and I am under no obligation to remain with him forever. Besides, I've never been with a man with children, and I'm not about to start now."

"Thank you for your help," Lois said.

"Don't thank me yet. I just want what's best for the baby. No matter what happens between you two, it is not the baby's fault. If this is what needs to happen for him to talk to you concerning your baby, then I don't have a problem with it. So, expect a call from him soon. One last thing, Lois. If you really care for Vic, you have to give him his baby in a way that will shock him into letting him know how much you care for him. Show him what you are willing to sacrifice to make this happen. You have to do something that will make him want his baby—an action that will bind you two forever. Do you understand, Lois?"

"I think I do, Kim, and thanks. Goodnight."

"Goodnight, Lois, and good luck with the baby."

Lois got into bed. *That bitch doesn't give a damn about Vic. She's gonna leave him, and he doesn't know how she really feels about his stupid ass. She's a cold-hearted bitch, because she never loved him. Not the way I love Vic. This is my opportunity to show Vic how much I really care about him. I can take him away from that ice-cold bitch he's been dealing with. I can accept that he doesn't want me, if it turns out that way, but our baby deserves to have her father in her life. I didn't have my father in my life either, and my daughter will not be put through the same shit I had to deal with growing up. I know how to make him come to his damn senses. My daughter will have her father in her life, even if I have to do something crazy. My baby deserves to have her father. That nigga will have no choice but to accept his daughter. I'm gonna make sure of that. Nothing is more important than my baby's well-being.*

That thought made her smile as she turned off her phone and drifted off to sleep.

Two days after talking to Kim, Lois still awaited Vic's call. She got up Friday morning to start her day. There was only one pressing thought on her mind.

He still hasn't called. It's been two days since I spoke with Kim and still no word from him. I guess I need to get it through my head that he'll never be with us, even after that bitch he's dealing with leaves his stupid ass.

Lois took a shower and got dressed. She had one last appointment to see her doctor before the baby was due. She grabbed her purse and her cell phone and headed out to her car. She got into her car and turned on her cell phone. She went to start the engine, but her phone buzzed, signaling a message. She picked up the phone and saw Vic's phone number on the display. Lois was so excited she called him right back.

Vic answered immediately.

"Hello, Vic," Lois said. "This is Lois. How are you doing?"

"I'm doing real fucked up right now," he yelled. "How could you call my girl and tell her the shit you told her?"

"I didn't call her. I called your cell number and she answered. She wouldn't put you on the phone. She said you had stepped out."

"I was home asleep the whole time you two talked."

"How was I to know that, Vic? I called you a few times and you never called me back. I just wanted to talk to you about the baby. I'm due in a few weeks."

"What the fuck did you two talk about?"

"I told her that I was gonna have your baby."

"Do you have any idea how you have fucked things up for me by telling my girl that shit? We don't even know the baby is mine."

"Vic, I'm sorry you're mad, but look: I'm on my way to my doctor's office. I have an appointment at 11:00 a.m. Can I call you back when I get home?"

"Yeah, we do need to talk. What you did was totally fucked up and out of line."

"I'm sorry you're angry with me, but let's do this. Why don't you come by for dinner tonight at my place, about 8:00 p.m.? We can talk things over."

"I'll be there at eight, but I don't want to have dinner with you. I just need to talk to you."

"All right, then. I'll see you at eight. Write down my address."

Lois gave Vic her address and hung up the phone. She realized his tone was hostile, but she found it did not bother her.

Maybe when he sees me again, pregnant with his baby, he will finally have a change of heart. In any event, he'll have no choice but to accept his baby after tonight.

Lois left for her doctor's office and her final check-up. After the examination, the doctor explained everything was fine with her and the baby. Although she was happy with the news, Lois found she could not think about anything but seeing Vic tonight.

We have a lot to talk about and I have a big surprise for him.

Lois briefly considered calling Terri and Bernice and having them there when Vic showed up, but she dismissed the idea. It would spoil her surprise for Vic, and she did not think Vic would hurt her. Besides, if her friends were there, then she and Vic could not really talk the way they needed to.

Lois got home at 4:00 p.m. At 5:00 p.m., she started to prepare for her evening with Vic. *Even though he said he did not want to have dinner with me, I'll make a nice meal for two. I remember he ordered Patrón when I met him, so I'll run out and get a bottle before he gets here.*

By 7:00 p.m., Lois had everything set up and ready for her baby's father. *The food will be ready by the time he gets here. The table is set for two, and I will pour him a drink while we eat dinner and talk about our child's future, and possibly our own. This is my chance to turn everything around for us, and I intend to do just that.*

Lois sat and waited patiently for Vic to arrive. It was 8:45 p.m., and he had not called or gotten to her place yet. She was keeping the dinner she prepared for them warm, but if he did not come soon, it would be ruined. *Maybe he had some last minute things to take care of, but he could at least call me.* Lois heard her doorbell ring at quarter past nine. She knew it was Vic. Her mood brightened instantly. *I can forgive him for being late.* She rushed to the door, opened it, and let Vic in.

"Hi Vic, I've been waiting for you. What kept you?"

Vic entered Lois's home, and she saw a look of disgust on his face when he looked at her bulging abdomen.

"I had some other things I had to take care of first," he said.

"It's ok. I kept dinner warm. We can eat now, if you like," she said with a smile.

"Lois, I told you I didn't want to have any dinner. I just want to talk to you and leave." The anger in his voice was clear.

"Well, Vic, you're here now. We may as well have something to eat, and everything is ready. I was just waiting for you. Why don't we go into the living room and relax there."

Vic followed her into the living room and Lois turned on the TV. "How do you like my place?" she asked.

"You have a nice spot," Vic replied, as he looked around her home.

"Vic, if you like we can sit in here and you can watch a game or something while we eat."

"Lois, I don't want any of that. Can we please just sit down and talk, without the TV on, so I can get the fuck out of here?" Vic insisted, as his patience started to run out.

Lois was devastated by his words. She agreed to just sit and talk. She sat across from Vic as he began the conversation.

"Lois, I didn't come here to upset you or hurt you in any way. I need to know why you won't stay out of my life. My damn girl is leaving me because of what you told her the other day. Was that your intent? To break us up and destroy my damn life?"

"Vic, that's not the way it was. I tried to talk to you, but you wouldn't answer my calls. I didn't tell her what's happening with me to make her leave you, I swear," Lois tried to explain as she held back tears.

"Well, what did you think would happen when you told her you might be carrying my baby? I honestly don't know if the kid is mine or not. We went through all this before. You knew exactly what you were doing. Lois, I don't hate anybody, but what I feel for you right now is damn close."

"Vic, it's not like that, I just wanted to talk to you. I wasn't trying to cause trouble in your life. I just wanted you to know what was going on with me and the baby, that's all." Lois started crying, and the emotional pain she felt overwhelmed her. She wanted to reach out to him so that he could hold her but she knew she could not.

"Look, don't do that. You don't need to be getting all upset and crying and shit. I just want to know what it will take for you to stay out of my life and leave me the fuck alone?"

She looked at him and the sadness in her eyes spoke volumes. "Vic, how is that gonna be possible? I'm having the baby in a few weeks, and all I've ever wanted is for her father to be a part of her life the way my father never was. That's all I've ever asked." Lois repeated her last sentence twice, as she felt her heart breaking again.

"Lois, you just don't understand. I know Kim told you I don't even like kids. In fact, I can't stand to be around those little muthafuckas. So how can I be a father to your daughter? I wouldn't know how and that's not what I want for myself, ever."

Lois looked at Vic and something inside Lois's mind snapped when Vic made that last statement to her. "Look Vic, I know you're probably not gonna be here much longer and you want to leave. Do you want a drink at least? We can talk for a little while longer and then you can leave. I see now that this just won't work out, knowing how you feel. Maybe it was a bad idea for you to come here. I really can raise my baby on my own. You still want that drink?"

"Sure, what do you have?" Vic felt a little relieved now that Lois was starting to see things his way.

"I saw you ordered Patrón when we met. I have that, if you want."

"That's cool."

Lois returned from the kitchen with a drink for him and one for herself. Vic took his drink and Lois sat back down where she was.

"You're not drinking alcohol are you?"

"No silly, it's water. I haven't had a drink since I found out I was pregnant," Lois replied with a fake smile on her face.

"Lois, I'm sorry if it seems like I don't care what you're going through. I've tried to make you understand I don't want kids in my life. I know Kim told you that because she told me everything you two talked about."

"Did she leave out the part about her leaving you?"

"No, she didn't and it's because of what you told her about your baby." Vic quickly finished his drink.

"Do you want another one? I bought that drink for you."

"Sure. Why not?"

Lois took his glass and returned with another double shot of Patrón for Vic.

"Lois, what do you want from me? Can you please tell me that?"

"Vic, it's like I told you. I would like for you to be in our lives. I know that's not going to happen now. I guess I just had to hear it from you in person. Can we at least be friends for the baby's sake, after we have the DNA test done? That's all I want. You don't have to worry about child support or any of that, because I can support us."

Vic quickly finished his drink, looked at Lois, and said nothing. He rose to get out of his seat, but flopped back down. He dropped his glass on the floor and passed out.

Vic woke up two hours later, lying on his back with his head propped up on pillows, and he felt cold. His vision was blurry and he had a splitting headache. He tried to move his arms and legs, but was unable to do so.

Lois sat in the room at the foot of the bed when he woke. In a voice that was barely intelligible, Vic asked what had happened to him.

"I put a little something extra in your drink, nigga." Lois replied. "I knew you wouldn't listen to reason, so I'm gonna make you listen." Lois went into the bathroom, wet a towel with cold water, and brought it to Vic. She wiped his face and forehead, then his chest and stomach.

Vic's vision became a little clearer, and he understood why he was cold and could not move. He was naked and his limbs had been tied to the bedposts. His first reaction was to panic, to try to break away from his restraints. However, he felt too weak and his head was still pounding. Upon realizing what had happened to him, his anger cleared his vision, as his eyes focused on Lois. He also found his voice, as the panic in his mind became stronger. He pulled against his restraints with what little strength he could muster.

"Bitch, what the fuck are you doing?" he demanded. "What the fuck did you do to me?" He tried to make his voice sound forceful, but he was scared.

Lois looked at her captive and moved back to the chair at the foot of the bed so she could face Vic as she spoke. "All I've ever wanted from you, since I found out I was pregnant, was for you to be with me so that our child would have a family. I would have settled with you just being a part of the baby's life, if not mine. You don't even want to be a father to your own child, but this is your daughter, Vic, no matter how much you want to deny it. Then, on top of all that, you had to fuck one of my best friends. You knew who she was when you fucked her! I loved you, nigga. My pussy wasn't good enough for you. You could have had this anytime you wanted it, but instead you want to fuck every bitch you see!"

"Bitch, let me fuckin' go!" Vic shouted with false bravado, as his fear grew by the second. "Untie me from this motherfuckin' bed. I'll kill your skank ass."

Lois smiled. "Nigga, you can't do shit. I put enough shit in your drink to keep you here for as long as I want. Unless you're Spiderman, you're not breakin' those straps either. Now, like I said, you're gonna listen to me. For fucking my friend, I should cut your dick off. You wouldn't be able to do shit about it." As she spoke, Lois pulled out a large knife.

Vic's eyes grew large at the sight of the knife in her hands and his heart pounded in his chest as Lois looked at his naked body.

Lois focused her eyes on his limp penis.

"No!" he shouted. "Untie me right now!" He could not quell his panic. "Please, Lois, don't hurt me! Don't do this. I didn't do anything to you. I didn't come here to hurt you."

"You didn't do anything to me?" she shouted.

She reached for his penis with her free hand, pulled it, and brought the knife closer to it.

He screamed with everything he had, as he watched the knife move closer. He pulled and struggled against his restraints, but to no avail.

She brought the knife ever closer until its cold edge was almost touching the skin of his dick.

"Vic, how can you say that?" she asked. "You avoid my calls. You rejected and belittled me every time I've tried to talk to you. You've called me names and disrespected me because you could. You cost me one of my best friends, because you need to fuck everything you see. You knew she was my friend when you and your boy fucked her."

Lois moved to sit on the edge of the bed, getting closer to his dick until her lips were barely touching it.

Vic was now in a blind panic. His whole body trembled, and he sweated profusely.

Lois kissed the head of his dick and let it go. "Why shouldn't I cut that off, Vic? You don't want me to have it, but you have no problem using it on every other bitch you see. You don't give a fuck that I care for you, that I love your sorry ass, do you, nigga?" Lois's face was now contorted with anger.

"Look, Lois," Vic pleaded, "Just let me go. I swear I won't tell anyone. Please let me go. I'll do anything you want me to do."

"Let you go? No baby. I'm not done with you yet." Lois raised the knife over her head.

Vic's eyes focused on the blade, as she slammed the knife down onto the bed between Vic's legs with enough force to drive it into the mattress. Vic's scream of terror continued as she left the knife stuck in the mattress.

"All I've ever wanted from you is for you to love me and our child," Lois said, "but you'd rather be with a cold-hearted bitch that you know is gonna leave your sorry ass anyway. I don't understand that shit. I could be everything to you. The bitch you're seeing doesn't even love you the way I do. Please explain that to me, Love."

Vic felt as helpless as a child, unable to free himself and terrified. The muscles of his arms and legs were now cramped so badly he thought they must be torn. He could not stop the tears that poured from his eyes.

"Don't cry now, nigga," Lois ordered. "You're a bad ass on the phone. Now answer my fuckin' question! Why can't you love us? Your goddamn family?" she shouted.

In a trembling voice, Vic responded, even as he continued crying in terror, "I don't know. I don't know what to say except give me a chance. I can change. Please God, don't hurt me."

Lois moved closer to Vic as she spoke. Her eyes held a deranged look that numbed him to the core.

"Do you understand how it feels now, muthafucka?" she asked. "To be rejected and belittled? Do you understand how it feels to beg someone for forgiveness when you've done nothing wrong? Do you see, Vic, how it feels to beg someone to love you and not hurt you? Do you fuckin' understand now how I've felt since the first time you fucked me? Nigga, you have a lot of fuckin' nerve to ask me not to hurt you! After the way you've treated me for months? And on top of all that, what you did with one of my best friends? Vic, you think you can use women any way you please. Well now, nigga, it's my turn."

She moved to the foot of the bed and removed her sweat pants and panties. She pulled the knife out from the mattress and threw it into the chair next to the bed. She climbed on top of Vic, took his dick in her hand, and rubbed it against her wet pussy.

"What's wrong, Vic?" she taunted. "Can't get it up now, nigga? You can get it up to fuck everybody else. I saw how you looked at me when you came in my house tonight. Do I disgust you because I'm pregnant? Come on nigga! Get it up for me. I need dick too," Lois pleaded. "Don't you want to give me some? I need some dick so bad. I haven't had any since I found out I was pregnant with your baby." She continued to rub his dick against her pussy.

Vic was too terrified to respond, and his body couldn't stop trembling. "Please stop this, Lois," He pleaded. "Please let me go. Please untie me. I swear, I'll never treat you bad ever again. I swear I can love you." Tears poured down his face.

"I don't believe you, Vic," she said, still rubbing her pussy against his limp dick. "If what you said was true, I'd have your big dick in my pussy right now. You can't even get it up for me, so how can you love me? You love every other bitch's pussy though, don't you? Just not mine. So, we're gonna fix that right now."

"What are you gonna do to me?" Vic screamed, as she climbed off him.

"Baby, where's your dick? It slipped out of my hand. As big as I remember it, it looks like it crawled into your stomach. I'm sorry I scare you so badly. Don't worry baby, it's almost over. Oh, another thing. You can stop screaming. No one is gonna hear you down here. There are no windows, and I have music playing just loud enough to drown out the screams."

Vic felt as if his heart was going to burst from his chest. He was so frightened, he thought he saw sound and heard color. Vic's thoughts made no sense to him at this point, except one—Death was coming.

He knew in his heart that Lois had snapped. *This crazy bitch is going to kill me.* Vic knew there was nothing he could do about it.

Lois took the knife from the chair and sat down. She held it in her right hand and rubbed her abdomen with her left as she spoke to Vic's trembling form. "I can, and I have, accepted the fact that you and I are never going to be together. I even felt the way you do about relationships until I got pregnant. Then I realized that there is more to life than partying and fucking.

"Becoming a mother and the fact that family members sexually abused me as a young girl made me realize something. I had no father to protect me, but my daughter will have her father one way or another. The lack of a father probably had a lot to do with my promiscuous attitude. I don't want that for my daughter, Vic. I'm ashamed to admit it, but if I raise her alone she'll probably turn out just like me—or worse—fucking guy after guy, looking for approval and love. I don't want that for her. She deserves better."

"What are you talking about? I won't let that happen. I promise! We can do a good job raising our kid together." Vic tried to sound convincing.

"Oh, nigga, please." Lois sneered. "I thought you didn't want kids in your life. Besides, I think you'd say just about anything right about now. Just like you said you loved me when you were fucking me."

Vic's hands and feet were so numb he couldn't feel them anymore. Through his terror, the thought came to him that he was going to die unless he could convince Lois he wanted the baby.

"Vic, all you had to do was give me a chance to make you happy," Lois said. "I know I could have."

Looking at her through bloodshot eyes, Vic tried one more time to convince Lois that he was sincere. "All I can do is try," he said. "I'm willing to give our love another try."

"Oh, you love me now, nigga? Since when did you love me? See muthafucka, I don't need you playing fuckin' games with me, and that's what you do. You know damn well you don't now and never did love me. I don't need lies. I only ever wanted to be loved by someone as much as I loved them!" Lois was now crying. She stared at his prone body from her seat. "You can't even get it up so I can fuck you, so I know you don't love me. Now I know what I need to do."

Lois stood up with the knife in her hand and came toward the bed. Vic saw the look in her eyes and panic overwhelmed him.

"Don't worry, Vic," she said. "I'm not gonna hurt you, but I'm not gonna let you walk away from our child either."

Lois dropped the large knife at the foot of the bed. Vic watched as she turned, walked over to the dresser, picked up another object, and returned to the bed. She knelt between his legs, the way she had when she had tried to have sex with him. She sat on top of his penis.

"I don't want to fuck," she said. "You ruined that. I just want you to watch."

Lois placed the object in her hand next to her, then she removed her outer top and bra and threw them onto the floor.

"You see, Vic, pregnant women really are beautiful. We glow with the life that's growing inside of us."

Vic stared at Lois, wide-eyed, not knowing what to say or do, but too scared to move.

Lois took the small object she had laid next to her on the bed in her right hand. With her left hand, she rubbed her large round abdomen, and smiled as she talked to Vic. "Vic, I made a promise to our daughter that I'd make sure her daddy was in her life. Now we can do even better, because you'll be here during her birth. Now there's no way you can deny her."

"What do you mean, baby? You said you're not ready for a few weeks," Vic responded. Her words now petrified him.

Lois held at her side the object in her hand, which looked to Vic like a scalpel. She looked at Vic and cut the bottom of her abdomen below the navel from left to right about ten inches in length, screaming in agony as she did so.

Vic screamed for her to stop as loud as he could. "What are you doing? STOP! Oh my God. What are you doing?" He screamed louder and fought against his bonds.

Lois's blood spilled onto Vic's body, all over his stomach and dick, as she continued to cut herself. She screamed in pain as she finished the incision. Bleeding more profusely now, she leaned back on her feet and screamed again. "Oh, God! It hurts, Vic! It hurts so bad, Baby!"

Lois came forward again and tried to insert her hand inside the cut, but it would not go in. Her blood was everywhere, all over Vic and the bed.

He vomited violently. He watched helplessly as Lois's blood poured out of her body. She was in agony and crying, as she realized she had not cut herself deeply enough.

She took the scalpel again, and with all the force she could muster, she stabbed it into the left side of the first incision. Screaming as she did so, she pulled the scalpel with what strength she had left across her abdomen.

Vic could do nothing except scream with all his might for her to stop. "*FUCK,* Lois! *STOP!!* Please don't do this. You're killing yourself!"

She did not hear him, as more and more of her blood poured out of her body.

Vic vomited all over his chest.

With her head hanging down and her pain beyond description, Lois leaned up and tried to insert her hands again into her open abdomen. This time, they went in, as blood and urine poured out of her, like from a faucet, onto Vic. He screamed like a man insane.

Lois continued to explore the gash until she felt something in her move. She knew it was her baby. She pushed her hands in harder, her screams of pain becoming ear shattering. She pulled on the amniotic sack until it burst.

The fluid shot out onto Vic's naked body. He continued to scream for a God he never believed in and for Lois to stop. Vic had now lost the ability to stop or control his own vomiting.

Through her pain and exhaustion, Lois managed to speak to Vic. "I feel her, Vic. I feel the baby moving." Her voice was low and weak. Impossibly, Lois managed to smile.

Vic had now stopped screaming due to his own vomiting and the spasms of his body.

Lois managed to get a hand on her baby and pull, but something was preventing the baby from coming out. Lois let out another scream of agony as she dug into her abdomen to find her baby. She pushed down on something soft and round, and more fluid shot from her body onto Vic.

Lois tried again to feel for her baby, and this time she found the small, wet body inside her. She pulled until she saw the baby's bottom. Through her pain, she pulled the baby straight out of her body. She smiled as the little body, still folded in half, tried to straighten out.

Lois brought the baby to her chest, held her with both bloody arms, and greeted her as she started to cry. "Hey, Victoria. Mommy and Daddy are right here." She looked over to Vic. "You see, Vic? She's beautiful. Doesn't she look like both of us?"

Lois spoke to him in a weak voice as she looked at the baby, and her eyes slowly closed.

Vic did not respond to her question. He had choked to death on his own vomit. Lois did not notice he had stopped moving.

"Victoria, go to Daddy now. Mommy is tired. Let Daddy hold you. Now our family will be linked forever."

Lois placed the crying, squirming newborn baby on Vic's vomit-covered chest. She fell on top of him, her arm cradling the crying baby.

Lois died holding onto both of them.

On Saturday morning, Bernice called Monique and invited her for a night out. "Hey, Monique, what's up girl?"

"Not a lot. What's going on with you?"

"Terri and I are planning on going out tonight and we need to get together to plan Lois's baby shower. You know she's due in a few weeks."

"Yeah I know," Monique replied. "That sounds good to me. Just let me know where we're gonna meet up."

"We haven't been to the club at the Gaylord yet, so we want to check that out. I hear it's real nice there."

"Ok, that's fine. What time should I get there?"

"We're gonna be there at 9:00 p.m."

"Ok, I'll see you there."

"Monique, try to be on time," Bernice said and laughed.

"I will be. See you then."

At 8:00 p.m. that evening, Bernice and Terri were at The American Sports Bar inside the Gaylord Hotel Complex having a drink and waiting on Monique to show. At 8:45 p.m., Monique walked into the bar. The friends all greeted each other, and Bernice bought Monique a drink.

"Has anybody talked to Lois today?" Terri asked.

"No. I tried to call her yesterday but I didn't get an answer," Bernice replied.

"Well, we need to go check on her," Monique responded.

"I'll drive by her place tomorrow morning. I'm sure she's fine, but we need to take care of our girl," said Bernice.

"We got her back, but tonight we're gonna get our party on and get bent," said Terri.

"Ok, but before we do all that, can we make plans for the baby shower?" Bernice asked. "It shouldn't take long."

"Yeah, party pooper. I'm not going home tonight, so we can go upstairs to my room and get that out of the way," Terri replied

"Somebody must have met a new guy," Monique said, laughing. She finished her drink.

"Yeah, and I'm gonna ride that dick all night."

"Bernice, order three more Long Islands," Terri said. "I'll pay for them. You follow us upstairs, room 620. Let's roll, Monique."

"Ok, no problem. I'll be right up," Bernice replied.

Terri and Monique laughed and talked as they got on the elevator and made their way to room 620.

They entered the room and Monique asked, "Terri, how much was this room? This is nice and the view is awesome."

"You know, I really don't know. Mark, the guy I'm staying with tonight, is paying for it. He put it on his credit card."

"I heard that this was a real classy hotel, and it's no lie."

A few minutes later, Bernice knocked on the door.

Monique opened the door and let Bernice in.

"I paid for the drinks at the bar. Room service is going to bring them up," Bernice told the women.

"Ok, let's get busy planning the shower, so we can go back down stairs," Terri said.

Terri locked the door and the women all went into the living room area of the room and took seats.

Terri started the conversation. "Ok, first things first. So, Monique, how do you like the room?" Terri asked.

"It's real nice. Like I said, I'm gonna have to stay here some time."

"Are you sure you've never been here before?" asked Terri.

"No. This is my first time at this hotel."

"What would you say if I told you I know that's a damn lie?" Bernice responded. "Don't you remember being here in this very room back in February with Vic and one of his boys, fucking them?"

Monique was shocked when she heard that. Her heart started to beat faster and she got very nervous.

She realized they knew. Lois must have told them. Monique was scared. In a trembling voice, she began to speak, "Lois told you what I did? I'm sorry for what happened. I don't know what else to say."

"Monique, how could you let Vic fuck you? Of all the goddamn guys out here, why him? You know Lois loves that nigga," Bernice demanded.

"Like I tried to explain to Lois. Y'all, I was fucked up. I think they gave me something in my drink, and it happened. I'm so sorry. Look, I feel bad enough about this as it is. I'm gonna go home."

Monique stood to leave, but Terri approached her and smacked her hard across the face. Monique cried out and held her face.

"Bitch," Terri screamed. "Do you think we're just gonna let you leave here after what you did?" Terri drew back her fist and hit Monique in the face.

Monique fell back on the couch crying.

Terri stood over her, drawing back her fist to hit Monique again, and this time the blows rained down on her. Crying, Monique did not know what to do except hold her face in her hands and plead for Terri not to hit her anymore. Monique was no fighter, and she knew even though she and Terri were about the same size, she could not beat Terri in a fistfight.

Bernice watched the beating from across the room.

"Bitch, did you think that was cute? Fuckin' that nigga when you knew Lois is in love with his sorry ass?" Terri shouted.

Monique sat up on the couch, crying. She looked over to Bernice to help her.

"Don't look over here bitch," Bernice said. "I'm not gonna help you. What you did was all the way fucked up."

Terri smacked Monique again with everything she had. Monique tried to cover her face with her hands and arms, but it did not do any good. Terri simply moved her arms out of the way and punched her in her chest. Monique cried like a baby as she took the beating.

"Terri, stop hitting her face," Bernice commented. "We don't want that part fucked up yet."

Terri moved away from Monique.

Monique wanted to run, but she knew they would get to her before she got to the door and beat her more. Monique thought she would try begging them to stop and let her go. "I thought y'all were my friends."

"We were your damn friends for years, bitch, until you did what the fuck you did!" Terri was so enraged she moved to hit Monique again.

"Terri, stop!" Bernice shouted. She approached the couch. "Monique, not only did you fuck Vic, what else did you do? Bitch, tell me what else you did. Tell us what you told that muthafucka!"

Monique cried like a baby.

"Bitch, if you don't talk to me, both of us are gonna beat the living shit out of you!" Bernice shouted again.

Bernice pulled Terri away from Monique so that she could uncover Monique's face and make her look at them standing over her while she confessed what she did.

Crying and wiping her face, Monique told them what they already knew. "Y'all, I'm so sorry. I'm so sorry. I told Vic about the Link."

Terri rushed to attack Monique again, but Bernice grabbed her just inches away from Monique's face and pulled her back.

Monique threw up her arms in a defensive posture.

"Bitch, don't you raise your fuckin' hands to me," Terri screamed. "I'll kill your sorry ass in here!"

Bernice pulled Terri away and stood in front of Monique. "Bitch, do you understand how you've betrayed us?" Bernice shouted. "The Link was a magical experience for all of us. It brought us closer than anything could have. You and your fuckin' drunk-ass mouth ruined all that. And you think we're not supposed to be fucked up with you?"

"I'm sorry, Bernice. I'm sorry, Terri. I didn't mean for any of that to happen. If I could fix what I did, I would. I didn't mean to put our business out there like that," Monique sobbed.

"Well, you did, bitch, and what we shared is all fucked up now. On top of that, you got Lois's head all fucked up, you fuckin' dirty-ass skank. You're lucky Bernice is here. That's the only reason why your ass ain't bleedin'." Terri's fury was almost out of control.

Monique was terrified and alone. She realized that the women who had been her closest friends for years had now turned on her as if they'd never known her. The only thing she could do was beg their forgiveness and hope they wouldn't hurt her anymore.

"I'm sorry," Monique pleaded through her tears. "Please don't do this to me anymore. I made a mistake. Please forgive me. I'll do anything. I said I'm sorry."

"Ho, what the fuck can you do to fix what you've done to us?" Terri shouted.

Monique looked at Terri and saw the hate in her eyes, and it terrified her. "I'll do anything I have to," she said, sobbing. "I can't beg anymore for y'all to forgive me than I am now."

Terri looked at Bernice and then Monique. "I got somethin' you can do, bitch. Take your clothes off, Monique," Terri demanded.

Monique looked at her and repeated what she heard. "Take my clothes off?"

"Yeah, bitch. Take your fuckin' clothes off now, or I will make your ass bleed in here," Terri told her.

Monique froze for a second, until Bernice also ordered her to remove her clothes.

Monique completely undressed in the living room and all three women walked to the bedroom. Monique, still crying, led the way. As they walked, Terri removed her shoes and belt. She stopped briefly to take her pants off, as they continued to the bedroom.

"Lay your ass on the bed, bitch," Bernice ordered Monique.

Crying, Monique did as she was told.

Bernice sat in a chair facing the bed.

Terri took off her panties and walked to the bed. "Open your fuckin' mouth, bitch," Terri ordered.

Terri got on the bed and positioned herself so that her pussy was over Monique's mouth.

Bernice looked on.

"Eat my pussy, bitch," Terri ordered, "and if you bite me, I'll pull your fuckin eyes out!"

Monique ate Terri's pussy, as the tears rained down her face. There was no joy in the act this time. For Terri, this was about payback. This action was about punishment and hatred.

Monique did not think anymore, she was too terrified. These women were no longer her friends, but her tormentors. Monique tried to push Terri up a little and was rebuffed.

"Bitch, don't touch me," Terri said, with a hiss. "Get your fuckin' hands off me. Just suck my pussy till I cum in your mouth. You can fuckin' cry all you want."

Terri leaned down, grabbed Monique's head, and forcefully pushed her pussy onto Monique's tongue. Terri moaned with pleasure as she took the head from Monique. "That's it, bitch! Right there. All I better feel is your lips and tongue."

Terri forced Monique to stay in that position for thirty minutes, until she came. When Terri got off Monique's face, Bernice took off her clothes and she lay on the bed. She made Monique go down on her face first.

Terri took the chair and watched as Monique ate Bernice's pussy for the next hour.

"Don't touch her, bitch," Terri warned Monique. "Keep your fuckin' hands to yourself. You lost the right to touch us when you ran your fuckin' mouth about the Link." The act of watching Monique eat Bernice made Terri come again.

When Bernice was satisfied, she pushed Monique away with her feet, got up, and put her clothes back on. Bernice sat in the room with Monique while Terri stepped out.

Monique lay on her side, facing away from Bernice, crying like a child whose mother had abandoned her. Terri came back in the room and closed the bedroom door. She looked at Bernice and gave her a nod. Terri walked over to the bed, and put a box on the dresser.

Monique was still lying on her side, no longer crying but still shaking.

"Ok, bitch," Terri said. "This is the way it is. Since you like to fuck and tell, and you want us to forgive you, we have a plan. Look at me when I'm talking to your nasty ass."

Monique turned to face Terri, shaking like a leaf in the wind.

"Like I said, since you like to fuck and tell, you see this?" Terri held up a box of ten condoms. "You said you'd do anything for us to forgive you, so you're gonna let ten dicks link with that pussy. Then we can be friends again. Now, don't start crying, bitch. Your ass wasn't crying when you fucked Vic and his boy. You should feel lucky, 'cause we won't let any of them fuck you in your ass. We're gonna watch every one of them fuck the shit out of you."

Bernice opened the door, and the first of ten men walked in.

Monique felt like a trapped rat and was terrified for her life. She cried anyway, covered her eyes, and wished she were dead, knowing now her life was ruined. She wished for someone to save her, but she knew that was not going to happen. The first of the ten unknown men put on a condom and fucked her.

Terri and Bernice watched until the last condom was used, and Monique was bloodied.

In that beautiful room, Monique learned the hard way that the cost of betrayal is devastating and life altering.

Isn't friendship a beautiful thing?